Praise for Jeffery Deaver

THE EMPTY CHAIR

'The best psychological thriller writer around'
Peter Millar, *The Times*

'Deaver is the master of the ticking bomb suspense'
People

'Dozens of twists and a couple of first class shocks'
Kirkus Reviews

'Slick, breathless stuff from a master of suspense in
full flight' Maxim Jakubowski, *Guardian*

THE DEVIL'S TEARDROP

'Another winner' *Crime Time review*

'Rapidly paced, wholly engrossing tale' *Publisher's
Weekly*

'A truly engrossing thriller' *The Times Crime
Supplement*

THE COFFIN DANCER

'Engrossing, entertaining, and fizzing with energy' Val McDermid

'Deaver is just as cunning and deceptive as his killer; don't assume he's run out of tricks until you've run out of pages' *Publishers Weekly*

'A terrific, high-paced thriller' *Wales on Sunday*

THE BONE COLLECTOR

'Sophisticated chiller . . . compulsive reading' *Guardian*

'Another genuinely compulsive chiller from the best psychological thriller writer around' *The Times*

About the author

Jeff Deaver was a lawyer before quitting work to become a full-time writer. He divides his time between Washington, DC and California.

Hell's Kitchen

Jeffery Deaver

CORONET BOOKS
Hodder & Stoughton

First published in the United States of America in 2001
by POCKET BOOKS,
A division of Simon & Schuster, Inc.
First published in Great Britain in 2002 by Hodder and Stoughton
First published in paperback in 2002 by Hodder and Stoughton
A division of Hodder Headline

A Coronet Paperback

2

British Library Cataloguing in Publication Data
A Catalogue record of this book is available from the
British Library.

ISBN 978-0-340-92326-9

Typeset by Palimpsest Book Production Limited,
Polmont, Stirlingshire
Printed and bound in Great Britain by
Clays Ltd, St Ives plc

Hodder and Stoughton
A division of Hodder Headline
338 Euston Road
London NW1 3BH

"I'm a professional. I've survived in a pretty rough business."

– Humphrey Bogart

Hell's Kitchen

1

He climbed the stairs, his boots falling heavily on burgundy floral carpet and, where it was threadbare, on the scarred oak beneath.

The stairwell was unlit; in neighborhoods like this one the bulbs were stolen from the ceiling sockets and the emergency exit signs as soon as they were replaced.

John Pellam lifted his head, tried to place a curious smell. He couldn't. Knew only that it left him feeling unsettled, edgy.

Second floor, the landing, starting up another flight.

This was maybe his tenth time to the old tenement but he was still finding details that had eluded him on prior visits. Tonight what caught his eye was a stained-glass valance depicting a hummingbird hovering over a yellow flower.

In a hundred-year-old tenement, in one of the roughest parts of New York City . . . Why beautiful stained glass? And why a hummingbird?

A shuffle of feet sounded above him and he glanced up.

He'd thought he was alone. Something fell, a soft thud. A sigh.

Like the undefinable smell, the sounds left him uneasy.

Pellam paused on the third-floor landing and looked at the stained glass above the door to apartment 3B. *This* valance – a bluebird, or jay, sitting on a branch – was as carefully done as the hummingbird downstairs. When he'd first come here, several months ago, he'd glanced at the scabby façade and expected that the interior would be decrepit. But he'd been wrong. It was a craftsman's showpiece: oak floorboards joined solid as steel, walls of plaster seamless as marble, the sculpted newel posts and banisters, arched alcoves (built into the walls to hold, presumably, Catholic icons). He—

That smell again. Stronger now. His nostrils flared. Another thud above him. A gasp. He felt urgency and, looking up, he continued along the narrow stairs, listing against the weight of the Betacam, batteries and assorted videotaping effluence in the bag. He was sweating rivers. It was ten P. M. but the month was August and New York was at its most demonic.

What *was* that smell?

The scent flirted with his memory then vanished again, obscured by the aroma of frying onions, garlic and overused oil. He remembered that Ettie kept a Folgers coffee can filled with old grease on her stove. "Saves me some money, I'll tell you."

Halfway between the third and fourth floors Pellam paused again, wiped his stinging eyes. That's what did it. He remembered:

A Studebaker.

He pictured his parents' purple car, the late 1950s, resembling a spaceship, burning slowly down to the tires. His father had accidentally dropped a cigarette on the seat, igniting the upholstery of the Buck Rogers car. Pellam, his parents and the entire block watched the spectacle in horror or shock or secret delight.

What he smelled now was the same. Smoulder, smoke. Then a cloud of hot fumes wafted around him. He glanced over the banister into the stairwell. At first he saw nothing but darkness and haze; then, with a huge explosion, the door to the basement blew inward and flames like rocket exhaust filled the stairwell and the tiny first-floor lobby.

"Fire!" Pellam shouted, as the black cloud preceding the flames boiled up at him. He was banging on the nearest door. There was no answer. He started down the stairs but the fire drove him back, the tidal wave of smoke and sparks was too thick. He began to choke and felt a shudder through his body from the grimy air he was breathing. He gagged.

Goddamn, it was moving fast! Flames, chunks of paper, flares of sparks swirled up like a cyclone through the stairwell, all the way to the sixth – the top – floor.

He heard a scream above him and looked into the stairwell.

"Ettie!"

The elderly woman's dark face looked over the railing from the fifth-floor landing, gazing in horror at the flames. She must've been the person he'd heard earlier, trudging up the stairs ahead of him. She held a plastic grocery bag in her hand. She dropped it. Three oranges rolled down the stairs past him and died in the flames, hissing and spitting blue sparks.

"John," she called, "what's . . . ?" She coughed. ". . . the building." He couldn't make out any other words.

He started toward her but the fire had ignited the carpet and a pile of trash on the fourth floor. It flared in his face, the orange tentacles reaching for him, and he stumbled back down the stairs. A shred of burning wallpaper wafted upward, encircled his head. Before it did any damage it burned to cool ash. He stumbled back onto the third-floor landing, banged on another door.

"Ettie," he shouted up into the stairwell. "Get to a fire escape! Get out!"

Down the hall a door opened cautiously and a young Hispanic boy looked out, eyes wide, a yellow Power Ranger dangling in his hand.

"Call nine-one-one!" Pellam shouted. "Call!—"

The door slammed shut. Pellam knocked hard. He thought he heard screams but he wasn't sure because the fire now sounded like a speeding truck, a deafening roar. The flames ate up the carpet and were disintegrating the banister like cardboard.

"Ettie," he shouted, choking on the smoke. He dropped to his knees.

"John! Save yourself. Get out. Run!"

The flames between them were growing. The wall, the flooring, the carpet. The valance exploded, raining hot shards of stained-glass birds on his face and shoulders.

How could it move so fast? Pellam wondered, growing faint. Sparks exploded around him, clicking and snapping like ricochets. There was no air. He couldn't breathe.

"John, help me!" Ettie screamed. "It's on that side. I can't—" The wall of fire had encircled her. She couldn't reach the window that opened onto the fire escape.

From the fourth floor down and the second floor up, the

flames advanced on him. He looked up and saw Ettie, on the fifth floor, backing away from the sheet of flame that approached her. The portion of the stairs separating them collapsed. She was trapped two stories above him.

He was retching, batting at flecks of cinders burning holes in his work shirt and jeans. The wall exploded outward. A finger of flame shot out. The tip caught Pellam on the arm and set fire to the gray shirt.

He didn't think so much about dying as he did the pain from fire. About it blinding him, burning his skin to black scar tissue, destroying his lungs.

He rolled on his arm and put the flame out, climbed to his feet. "Ettie!"

He looked up to see her turn away from the flames and fling open a window.

"Ettie," he shouted. "Try to get up to the roof. They'll get a hook and ladder . . ." He backed to the window, hesitated, then, with a crash, flung his canvas bag through the glass, the forty thousand dollars' worth of video camera rolling onto the metal stairs. A half dozen other tenants, in panic, ignored it and continued stumbling downward toward the alley.

Pellam climbed onto the fire escape and looked back.

"Get to the roof!" he cried to Ettie.

But maybe that path too was blocked; the flames were everywhere now.

Or maybe in her panic she just didn't think.

Through the boiling fire, his eyes met hers and she gave a faint smile. Then without a scream or shout that he could hear, Etta Wilkes Washington broke out a window long ago painted shut, and paused for a moment, looking down. Then she leapt into the air fifty feet above the cobblestoned alley beside the building, the alley that, Pellam recalled, contained the cobblestone on which Isaac B. Cleveland had scratched his declaration of love for teenage Ettie Wilkes fifty-five years ago. The old woman's slight frame vanished into the smoke.

A wheezing groan of timber and steel, then a crash, like a sledgehammer on metal, as something structural gave way. Pellam jumped back to the edge of the fire escape, nearly tumbling over the railing and, as the cascade of orange sparks flowed over him, staggered downstairs.

He was in as much of a hurry as the escaping tenants – though the mission on his mind now wasn't to flee the ravaging fire but, thinking of Ettie's daughter, to find the woman's body and carry it away from the building before the walls collapsed, entombing it in a fiery, disfiguring grave.

2

He opened his eyes and found the guard looking down at him.

"Sir, you a patient here?"

He sat up too fast and found that while the efforts of escaping the fire had left him sore and bruised, sleeping these past five hours in the orange fiberglass chairs of the ER's waiting room was what had really done him in. The crook in his neck was pure pain.

"I fell asleep."

"You can't sleep here."

"I *was* a patient. They treated me last night. I fell asleep."

"Yessir. You been treated, you can't stay."

His jeans were pocked with burn holes and he supposed he was filthy. The guard must've mistaken him for a bum.

"Okay," he said. "Just give me a minute."

Pellam moved his head in slow circles. Something deep in his neck popped. An ache like brain freeze from a frozen drink spread through his head. He winced, then looked around. He could understand why the hospital guard had rousted him. The room was completely filled with people awaiting treatment. Words rose and fell like surf, Spanish, English, Arabic. Everyone was frightened or resigned or irritated and to Pellam's mind the resigned ones were the most unsettling. The man next to him sat forward, forearms resting on his knees. In his right hand dangled a single child's shoe.

The guard had delivered his message and then lost interest in enforcing his edict. He wandered off toward two teenagers who were smoking a joint in the corner.

Pellam rose, stretched. He dug through his pockets and found the slip of paper he'd been given last night. He squinted and read what was written on it.

Pellam picked up the heavy video camera and started down a long corridor, following the signs toward the B wing.

The thin green line hardly moved at all.

A portly Indian doctor stood beside the bed, staring up, as if trying to decide if the Hewlett-Packard monitor was broken. He glanced down at the figure in the bed, covered with sheets and blankets, and hung the metal chart on a hook.

John Pellam stood in the doorway. His bleary eyes slid from the grim dawn landscape outside Manhattan Hospital back to the unmoving form of Ettie Washington.

"She's in a coma?" he asked.

"No," the doctor responded. "She's asleep. Sedated."

"Will she be all right?"

"She's got a broken arm, sprained ankle. No internal injuries we could find. We're going to run some scans. Brain scans. She hit on her head when she fell. You know, only family members can be in ICU."

"Oh," an exhausted Pellam responded. "I'm her son."

The doctor's eyes remained still for a moment. Then flicked toward Ettie Washington, whose skin was as dark as a mahogany banister.

"You . . . son?" The blank eyes stared up at him.

You'd think a doctor working on the rough-and-tumble West Side of Manhattan would've had a better sense of humor. "Tell you what," Pellam said. "Let me sit with her for a few minutes. I won't steal any bedpans. You can count 'em before I leave."

Still no smile. But the man said, "Five minutes."

Pellam sat down heavily and rested his chin in his hands, sending jolts of pain through his neck. He sat up and held it cocked to the side.

Two hours later a nurse pushed briskly into the room and woke him up. When she glanced at Pellam it was more to survey his bandages and torn jeans than to question his presence.

"Who'all's the patient here?" she asked in a throaty Dallas drawl. "An' who's visitin'?"

Pellam massaged his neck then nodded at the bed. "We take turns. How is she?"

"Oh, she's one tough lady."

"How come she isn't awake?"

"Doped her up good."

"The doctor was talking about some scans?"

"They always do that. Keep their butts covered. I think she'll be okay. I was talking to her before."

"You were? What'd she say?"

"I think it was, 'Somebody burned down my apartment. What kinda blankety-blank'd do that?' Only she didn't say blankety-blank."

"That's Ettie."

"Same fire?" the nurse asked, glancing at his burnt jeans and shirt.

Pellam nodded. He explained about Ettie's jumping out the window. It wasn't cobblestones she landed on, however, but two days' worth of packed garbage bags, which broke her fall. Pellam had carried her to the EMS crews and then returned to the building to help get other tenants out. Finally, the smoke had gotten to him too and he'd passed out. He'd awakened in the same hospital.

"You know," the nurse said, "you're all . . . um, sooty. You look like one of those commandoes in a Schwarzenegger movie."

Pellam wiped at his face and examined five dirty fingertips.

"Here." The nurse disappeared into the hall and returned a moment later with a wet cloth. She paused – debating, he guessed, whether or not to clean him herself – and chose to hand off to the patient. Pellam took the cloth and wiped away until the wash-cloth was black.

"You, uh, want some coffee?" she asked.

Pellam's stomach churned. He guessed he'd swallowed a pound of ash. "No, thanks. How's my face?"

"Now you just look dirty. That is to say, it's an improvement. Got pans to change. Bah now." She vanished.

Pellam stretched his long legs out in front of him and examined the holes in his Levi's. A total waste. He then spent a few minutes examining the Betacam, which some kind soul had given to the paramedics and had been admitted with him to the emergency room. He gave it his standard diagnostic check – he shook it. Nothing rattled. The Ampex recording deck was dented but it rolled fine and the tape inside – the one that contained what was apparently the last interview that would ever be conducted in 458 West Thirty-sixth Street – was unhurt.

"Now, John, what're we gonna talk about today? You want to hear more about Billy Doyle? My first husband. That old son of a bitch. See, that man was what Hell's Kitchen was all about. He was big here, but little everywhere else. He was nothing anywhere else. It was like this place, it's its own world. Hmm, I got a good story to tell you 'bout him. I think you might like this story . . .

He couldn't remember much else of what Ettie had told him at their last interview a couple of days ago. He'd set the camera up in her small apartment, filled with the mementos of a seven-decade life, a hundred pictures, baskets, knickknacks, furniture bought at Goodwill, food protected from roaches in Tupperware she could barely afford. He'd set the camera up, turned it on and just let her talk.

"See, people live in Hell's Kitchen get these ideas. They get schemes, you know. Billy, he wanted land. He had his eye on a couple of lots over near where the Javits Center is today. I tell you, he'da brought that off he'da been one rich mick. I can say 'mick' 'cause he said that 'bout himself."

Then, motion from the bed interrupted these thoughts.

The elderly woman, eyes still closed, picked at the hem of the blanket, two dark thumbs, two fingers lifting invisible pearls.

This concerned Pellam. He remembered, a month ago, the last living gestures of Otis Balm as the 102-year-old man had glanced toward the lilac bush outside the window of his West Side nursing home and began picking at his sheet. The old man had been a resident of Ettie's building for years and, though hospitalized, had been pleased to talk about his life in the Kitchen. Suddenly the man had fallen silent and started picking at his blanket – as Ettie was doing now. Then he stopped moving. Pellam called for help. The doctor confirmed the death. They always did that, he explained. At the end they pick at the bedclothes.

Pellam leaned closer to Ettie Washington. A sudden moaning filled the air. It became a voice. "Who's that?" The woman's hands grew still and she opened her eyes, but still apparently couldn't see too well. "Who's there? Where am I?"

"Ettie." Pellam spoke casually. "It's John. Pellam."

Squinting, Ettie stared at him. "I can't see too good. Where am I?"

"Hospital."

She coughed for a minute and asked for a glass of water. "I'm so glad you came. You got out okay?"

"I did, yep," he told her. Pellam poured a glass for her; Ettie emptied it without pausing.

"I kind of remember jumping. Oh, I was scared. The doctor said I was in surprisingly good shape. He said that. 'Surprisingly good.' Didn't understand him at first." She grumbled, "He's

Indian. Like, you know, an overseas Indian. Curry an' elephants. Haven't seen a single American doctor here."

"Does it hurt much?"

"I'll say." She examined her arm closely. "Don't I look the mess?" Ettie's tongue clicked, looking over the imposing bandages.

"Naw, you're a cover girl, all things considered."

"You're a mess too, John. I'm so glad you got out. My last thought as I was falling toward the alley was: 'no, John's going to die too!' What a thought that was."

"I took the easy way down. The stairs."

"What the hell happened?" she muttered.

"I don't know. One minute nothing, the next the whole place was gone. Like a matchbox."

"I was shopping. I was on my way to my apartment—"

"I heard you. You must have gotten back just before I got there. I didn't see you on the street."

She continued, "I never saw fire move like that. Was like Aurora's. That club I told you 'bout? On Forty-ninth Street. Where I sang a time or two. Burned down in forty-seven. March thirteenth. Buncha people died. You remember me telling you that story?"

Pellam didn't remember. He supposed the account could be found somewhere in the hours and hours of tapes of Ettie Washington back in his apartment.

She blew her nose and coughed for a moment. "That smoke. That's the worst. Did everybody get out?"

"Nobody was killed," Pellam answered. "Juan Torres's in critical condition. He's upstairs in the kids' ICU."

Ettie's face went still. Pellam had seen this expression on her face only once before – when she'd talked about her youngest son, who'd been killed in Times Square years before. "Juan?" she whispered. She didn't speak for a moment. "I thought he was at his grandma's for a few days. In the Bronx. He was *home*?"

She looked heartsick and Pellam was at a loss to comfort her. Ettie's eyes returned to the blanket she'd been picking at. An ashen tone flooded her face. "How 'bout I sign that cast?" Pellam asked.

"Why, of course."

Pellam took out a marking pen. "Anywhere? How 'bout here?" He signed with a round scrawl.

In the busy hall outside a placid electronic bell rang four times.

"I was thinking," Pellam said, "you want me to call your daughter?"

"No," the old woman responded. "I talked to her already. Called her this morning when I was awake. She was worried sick but I said I'm not in the great by-and-by yet. She oughta wait 'bout coming and let's see what happens with those tests. If they're gonna cut I'd rather her come then. Maybe hook her up with one of those handsome doctors. Like on *ER*. 'Lisbeth'd like a rich doctor. She has that side to her. Like I was telling you."

A knock sounded on the half-open door. Four men in business suits walked into the room. They were large, somber men and their presence suddenly made the hospital room, even with the other three empty beds, seem very small.

Pellam glanced at them, knew they were cops. So, arson was suspected. That would explain the speed of the fire.

Ettie nodded uneasily at the men.

"Mrs Washington?" the oldest of the men asked. He was in his mid-forties. Thin shoulders and a belly that could use a little shrinking. He wore jeans and a wind-breaker and Pellam noticed a very large revolver on his hip.

"I'm Fire Marshal Lomax. This is my assistant—" He nodded at a huge young man, a bodybuilder. "And these are detectives with the New York City Police Department."

One of the cops turned to Pellam and asked him to leave.

"No, no," Ettie protested, "he's my friend. It's okay."

The officer looked at Pellam, the glance repeating the request.

"It's okay," Pellam said to Ettie. "They'll want to talk to me too. I'll come back when they're through."

"You're a friend'a hers?" Lomax asked. "Yeah, we'll want to talk to you. But you aren't coming back in here. Give your name and address to the officer there and take off."

"I'm sorry?" Pellam smiled, confused.

"Name and address to him," Lomax nodded to the assistant. Then he snapped, "Then get the hell out."

"I don't think so."

The marshal put his large hands on his large hips.

We can play it this way, we can play it that way. Pellam crossed his arms, spread his feet slightly. "I'm not leaving her."

"John, no, it's okay."

Lomax: "This room's sealed off from visitors. Uh, uh, uh, don't ask why. It's none of your business."

"I don't believe my business is any of yours," Pellam replied. The line came from an unproduced movie he'd written years ago. He'd been dying for a chance to use it.

"Fuck it," said one of the detectives. "We don't have time for this. Get him out."

The assistant curled his vice-grip hands around Pellam's arm and walked him toward the door. The gesture shot a jolt of icy pain through his stiff neck. Pellam pulled away abruptly and when he did this the cop decided that Pellam might like to rest up against the wall for a few minutes. He pinned him there until his arms went numb from the lack of circulation, his boots almost off the floor.

Pellam shouted at Lomax, "Get this guy off me. What the hell is going on?"

But the fire marshal was busy.

He was concentrating hard on the little white card in his hand as he recited the Miranda warning to Ettie, then arrested her for reckless endangerment, assault and arson.

"Yo, don't forget attempted murder," one of the detectives called.

"Oh, yeah," Lomax muttered. He glanced at Ettie and added with a shrug, "Well, you heard him."

———◆·◆·◆———

3

E ttie's building, like most New York tenements built in the nineteenth century, had measured thirty-five by seventy-five feet and been constructed of limestone; the rock used for hers was ruddy, a terra cotta shade.

Before 1901 there were no codes governing the construction of these six-story residences and many builders had thrown together tenements using rotten lathe and mortar and plaster mixed with sawdust. But those structures, the shoddy ones, had long ago crumbled. Tenements like *this* one, Ettie Washington had explained to John Pellam's earnest video camera, had been built by men who cared about their craft. Alcoves for the Virgin and glass hummingbirds hovering above doorways. There was no reason why these buildings couldn't last for two hundred years.

No reason, other than gasoline and a match . . .

This morning Pellam walked toward what was left of the building.

There wasn't much. Just a black stone shell filled with a jumble of scorched mattresses, furniture, paper, appliances. The base of the building was a thick ooze of gray sludge – ash and water. Pellam froze, staring at a hand protruding from one pile of muck. He ran toward it then stopped when he noticed the seam in the vinyl at the wrist. It was a mannequin.

Practical jokes, Hell's Kitchen style.

On a hump of refuse was a huge porcelain bathtub sitting on its claw feet, perfectly level. It was filled with brackish water.

Pellam continued to circle the place, pushed closer through the crowd of gapers in front of the yellow police tape, like shoppers waiting at the door for a one-day Macy's sale. Most of them had the edgy eagerness of urban scavengers but the pickings were sparse. There were dozens of mattresses, stained and burned. The skeletons of cheap furniture and appliances, water-logged books. A rabbit-ears antenna – the building wasn't wired for cable – sat on a glob of plastic, the Samsung logo and a circuit board the only recognizable part of the former TV.

The stench was horrific.

Pellam finally spotted the man he'd been looking for. There'd been a costume change; he was now wearing jeans, a windbreaker and fireman's boots.

Ducking under the tape, Pellam walked up to the fire marshal, pasting enough authority on his face to get him all the way to the building itself without being stopped by the crime scene techs and firemen milling about.

He heard Lomax say to his huge assistant, the man who'd pinned Pellam against the wall in Ettie's room, "There, the spalling." He was pointing to chipping in the brick. "That's a hot spot. Point of origin's behind that wall. Get a photog to shoot it."

The marshal crouched and examined something on the ground. Pellam stopped a few feet away. Lomax looked up. Pellam had showered and changed clothes. The camouflage on his face was gone and it took a moment for the marshal to recognize him.

"You," Lomax said.

Pellam, thinking he'd try the friendly approach, offered, "Hey, how you doing?"

"Get lost," the marshal snapped.

"Just wanted to talk to you for a second."

Lomax's attention returned to the ground.

At the hospital they'd taken his name and checked with NYPD. Lomax, his detective friends and especially the big assistant seemed to regret that there was no reason to detain Pellam, or even to search him painfully, and so they settled for taking a brief statement and shoving him down the corridor, with the warning that if he wasn't out of the hospital in five minutes he'd be arrested for obstruction of justice.

"Just a few questions," he now asked.

Lomax, a rumpled man, reminded Pellam of a high school coach who was a lousy athlete. He rose from his crouch, looked Pellam over. Quick eyes, scanning. Not cautious, not belligerent, just trying to figure him out.

Pellam asked, "I want to know why you arrested her. It doesn't make any sense. I was there. I know she didn't set the fire."

"This is a crime scene." Lomax returned to his spalling. His words didn't exactly sound like a warning but Pellam supposed they were.

"I just want to ask you—"

"Get back behind the line."

"The line?"

"The tape."

"Will do. Just let me—"

"Arrest him," Lomax barked to the assistant, who started to.

"Not a problem. I'm going." Pellam lifted his hands and walked back behind the line.

There he crouched and took the Betacam out of the bag. He aimed it at the back of Lomax's head. He turned it on. Through the clear viewfinder he saw a uniformed cop whisper something to Lomax, who glanced back once then turned away. Behind them, the smoldering hulk of the tenement sat in a huge messy pile. It occurred to Pellam that, even though he was just doing this for Lomax's benefit, it was grade-A footage.

The fire marshal ignored Pellam for as long as he could then he turned and walked to him. Pushed the lens aside. "All right. Can the bullshit."

Pellam shut the camera off.

"She didn't start the fire," Pellam said.

"What're you? A reporter?"

"Something like that."

"She didn't start it, huh? Who did? Was it you?"

"I gave my statement to your assistant. Does he have a name, by the way?"

Lomax ignored this. "Answer my question. If you're so sure she didn't start the fire then maybe you did."

"No, I didn't start the fire." Pellam gave a frustrated sigh.

"How'd you get out? Of the building?"

"The fire escape."

"But she says she wasn't in her apartment when it started. Who buzzed you in?"

"Rhonda Sanchez. In 2D."

"You know *her*?"

"Met her. She knows I was doing a film about Ettie. So she let me in."

Lomax asked quickly, "If Ettie wasn't there then why'd you go in at all?"

"We were going to meet at ten. I figured if she was out she'd be back in a few minutes. I'd wait upstairs. Turns out she'd been shopping."

"Didn't that seem kind of strange – an old lady out on the streets of Hell's Kitchen at ten p.m.?"

"Ettie keeps her own hours."

Lomax was now in a talkative mood. "So you just happened to be beside the fire escape when the fire started. Lucky man."

"Sometimes I am," Pellam said.

"Tell me exactly what you saw."

"I gave him my statement."

Lomax snapped back, "Which didn't tell me shit. Give me some details. *Be helpful*."

Pellam thought for a moment, deciding that the more cooperative he was the better it would be for Ettie. He explained about looking into the stairwell, seeing the door blow outward. About the fire and smoke. And sparks. Lots of sparks. Lomax and his pro-wrestler assistant remained impassive and Pellam said, "I'm not much help, I suppose."

"If you're telling the truth you're tons of help."

"Why would I lie?"

"Tell me, Mr Lucky, was there more flame or more smoke?"

"More smoke, I guess."

The fire marshal nodded. "What color was the flame?"

"I don't know. Fire-colored. Orange."

"Any blue?"

"No."

Lomax recorded these facts.

Exasperated, Pellam asked, "What do you *have* on her? Evidence? Witnesses?"

Lomax's smile pled the Fifth.

"Look," Pellam snapped, "she's a seventy-year-old lady—"

"Hey, Mr Lucky, lemme tell you something. Last year, fire marshals investigated ten thousand suspicious fires in the city. More than half were arson and a third of those were set by women."

"That doesn't really seem like admissible evidence. What was your probable cause?"

Lomax turned to his assistant. "Probable cause. He knows probable cause. Learn that from *NYPD Blue*? *Murder One*? Naw, you look like an O.J.-Simpson-watcher to me. Fuck you and your probable cause. Get the hell out of here."

Back behind the police line Pellam continued to take footage and Lomax continued to ignore him.

He was filming the grimy alley behind the building – memorializing the stack of garbage bags that had saved Ettie's bacon – when he heard a thin wail, the noise smoke might make if smoke made noise.

He walked toward the construction site across the street, where a sixty-story high-rise was nearing completion. As he approached, the smoke became words. "One a them. I'ma be one a them." The woman sat in the shadow of a huge Dumpster beside two eroded stone bulldogs, which had guarded the stairs to Ettie's building for one hundred and thirty years. She was a black woman with a pretty, pocked face, her white blouse smudged and torn.

Crouching, Pellam said, "Sibbie. You all right?"

She continued to stare at the ruined tenement.

"Sibbie, remember me? It's John. I took some pictures of you. For my movie. You told me about moving down here from Harlem. You remember me."

The woman didn't seem to. He'd met her on the doorstep one day when he'd come to interview Ettie and she'd apparently heard about him because without any other greeting she'd said she would tell him about her life for twenty dollars. Some documentary filmmakers might balk on the ethical issue of paying subjects but Pellam slipped her the bill and was shooting footage before she'd decided which pocket to put it in. It was a waste of money and time, though; she was making up most of what she told him.

"You got out okay."

Distracted, Sibbie explained that she'd been at home with her children at the time of the fire, just starting a dinner of rice and beans with ketchup. They easily escaped but she and the youngsters had returned, risking the flames to save what they could. "But not the TV. We try but it too heavy. Shit."

A mother'd let her children take a risk like that? Pellam shivered at the thought.

Behind her were a girl of about four, clutching a broken toy, and a boy, nine or ten, with an unsmiling mouth but eyes that seemed irrepressibly cheerful. "Somebody burn us out," he said, immensely proud. "Man, you believe that?"

"I ask you a few questions?" Pellam began.

Sibbie said nothing.

He started the Betacam, hoping her short-term memory was better than the recollections of her youth.

"Yo, you with CNN?" the boy asked, staring at the glowing red eye of the Sony.

"Nup. I'm working on a movie. I took some pictures of your mother last month."

"Geddoutahere!" He cloaked his astonished eyes. "A movie. Wesley Snipes, Denzel, yeah! Shit."

"You have any idea how the fire started?"

"Be the crews," the boy said quickly.

"Shutcha mouth," his mother barked, abruptly slipping out of her mournful reverie.

Crews meant gangs. "Which ones?"

The woman remained silent, eyes fixed on a key that passing traffic had pressed deep into the asphalt. Beside it was the butt end of a brass pistol cartridge. She looked up at the building. "Lookit that."

Pellam said, "It was a nice building."

"Ain't shit now." Sibbie snapped her fingers with a startling pop. "Oh, I'ma be one a them."

Pellam asked, "One of who?"

"Livin' on the street. We gonna live on the *street*. I'ma get sick. I'ma get the Village curse and I gonna die."

"No, you'll be okay. The city'll take care of you."

"The city. Shit."

"You see anybody around the basement when the fire started?"

"Hells, yeah," the boy said. "What it is. Be the crews. I seen 'em. This nigger keep his eyes open. I—"

Sibbie viciously slapped her son's cheek. "He didn't see *nothing*! All y'all ain't worry about it no more!"

Pellam winced at the slap. The boy noticed his expression but the tacit sympathy didn't comfort any more than the blow'd seemed to hurt.

"Sibbie, it's not safe around here," Pellam said. "Go to that shelter. The one up the street."

"Shelter. Shit. I save me a few things." Sibbie motioned toward her shopping bag. "Be looking for my mama's lace. Can't find it, shit, it gone." She called out to a cluster of sightseers, "All y'all find any lace 'round here?"

No one paid her any attention. "Sibbie, you have any money?" Pellam asked.

"I got fi' dollar some man give me."

Pellam slipped her a twenty. He stepped into the street and flagged down a cab. Pellam held up a twenty. "Take her to the shelter, the one on Fiftieth."

He glanced at his potential fare. "Hey, man, I'm going off duty—"

Pellam silenced him with another bill.

The family piled in. From the back seat Ismail, eyes cautious now, stared at Pellam. Then the cab was gone. He hefted the Betacam, which now weighed a half ton, and lifted it to his shoulder once again.

What's this? A cowboy?

Boots, blue jeans, black shirt.

All he needs is a string tie and a horse.

Yee-haw, Sonny thought. *Everybody's tawking at me . . .*

He'd watched as the cowboy had stuffed the shriveled-up nigger lady and her little nigger kids into a cab and had returned to the charred remains of the tenement.

As he'd been doing for the past several hours Sonny studied the destroyed building with pleasure and a modicum of itchy lust. At the moment he was thinking about the *noise* of fire. The floors had fallen, he knew, with a crash but nobody would have heard. Fire is much louder than people think. Fire roars with the sound of blood in your ears when the flames reach your, say, knees.

And he was thinking of the smell. He inhaled the unique perfume of scorched wood and carbonized plastic and oxidized metal. Then, reluctantly, he surfaced from his reverie and studied the cowboy carefully. He was taping the fire marshal as he directed an exhausted fireman to hoe through some refuse with his Halligan tool, a combination axe and crowbar. Invented by Huey Halligan. An all-time, world-class firefighter, pride of the NYFD. Sonny respected his enemies.

He knew a lot about them too. For instance, he knew that there were 250 fire marshals in the City of New York. Some were good and some were bad but this one, Lomax, was excellent. Sonny watched him taking pictures of the alligatoring on a piece of charred wood. The marshal had spotted *that* right away, God bless him. The black squares on the surface were large and shiny, which meant the fire was fast and it was hot. Useful in the investigation. And the trial – as if they'd ever catch him.

The marshal picked up a six-foot hook and broke through a ground-floor window, shone his flashlight inside.

A few years ago the city created the Red Hat patrol in the fire marshal's department. They'd given marshals red baseball caps and sent them cruising through high-risk arson areas. Those were the days when Sonny was just learning his trade and it had been very helpful to flag the marshals so obviously. Now they dressed like regular plainclothes schmucks but Sonny had enough experience that he didn't need red hats to spot the enemy. Now Sonny could look in a man's eyes and know that he made fires his living.

Either starting them or putting them out.

Sonny, no longer quite so happy, feeling shakier and sweatier, glanced at the big camera in the cowboy's hand. A cable ran to a battery pack in a canvas bag. It wasn't one of those cheap videocams. This was the real thing.

Who exactly *are* you, Joe Buck? What exactly are you doing here?

Sonny began to sweat harder (which didn't bother him though he'd been sweating an awful lot lately) and his hands began to shake (which *did* bother him because that was a very bad thing in someone who assembled incendiary devices for a living).

Watching tall, thin Joe Buck take some more footage of the burnt-out tenement. Sonny decided he hated the cowboy more for his height than because he was shooting so fucking much tape of a building he'd just burned down.

Still, in some part of his heart, he hoped the tapes were good; he was proud of this little fire.

After he'd started the blaze and slipped back out through the basement door, he'd hidden in the construction site across the street and turned on his Radio Shack scanner. He heard the dispatcher put out a second-alarm assignment. It had been a 10–45, code 2 call. He was pleased about the alarm – which meant a serious fire – but disappointed about the code, which meant that there'd been only injuries, not fatalities. Code 1 meant death.

The cowboy continued to shoot for a few minutes. Then he shut the big camera off and slipped it back into his bag.

Sonny glanced again at the fire marshal and his cronies – my gosh, that's one *huge* faggot assistant. Lomax told the big boy to order a backhoe and start the vertical excavation as soon as possible. Silently Sonny told them that this was the correct procedure for investigating a fire like this.

But Sonny was getting more and more worried. Pretty soon he was all worry, the way a corridor fills with smoke; one minute it's clear, the next it's dense as cotton.

The reason, however, wasn't Lomax or his huge assistant. It was the cowboy.

I hate that man. Hate him, hate him, hate him hatehimhatehim.

Sonny tossed his long blond ponytail off his shoulder, wiped a sweating forehead with shaking hands and eased through the crowd, closer to Joe Buck. His breathing was labored and his heart slammed in his chest. He sucked smoke-laden air into his lungs and exhaled very slowly, enjoying the taste, the smell. Beneath his hands the yellow tape trembled. Stop that stop that stop that stopthatstopthat!

He glanced up at Pellam.

Not *quite* a foot taller. Maybe a lot less than that. Ten inches, if Sonny stood up straight. Or nine.

Suddenly a new spectator eased between them and Sonny

was jostled aside. The intruder was a young woman in a rich, deep-green double-breasted suit. A businesswoman. She said, "Terrible. Just awful."

"Did you see it happen?" the cowboy asked.

She nodded. "I was coming home from work. I was on an audit. You a reporter?"

"I'm doing a film about some of the tenants in the building."

"A film. Cool. A documentary? I'm Alice."

"Pellam."

Pellam, Sonny thought. Pellam. Pell-am. He pictured the name and spoke it over and over and over in his mind until, like the top of a column of smoke, it was there but was no longer visible.

"At first," she continued, looking at the cowboy's, at *Pellam*'s lean face, "it was like there was nothing wrong, then all of a sudden there were flames everywhere. I mean, totally everywhere." She carried a heavy briefcase stamped Ernst & Young in gold and with her free hand twined her short red hair nervously about her index finger. Sonny glanced at her laminated business card, hanging from the handle.

Pellam asked, "Where exactly did it start?"

She nodded. "Well, I saw the flames break through the window there." Pointed to the basement.

She didn't seem at all like an Alice to him. She looked like that somber little thing on *The X-Files*, whom Sonny, in a private joke, called "Agent Scullery."

Like Pellam, Scullery was taller than Sonny. He disliked tall men but he *venomously* hated women taller than he was and when she happened to glance down at him the way she'd glance at a squirrel his hatred turned from anger to something very calm and very hot.

"I was the one that called the fire department. From that box on the corner. Those boxes, you know, you see but you never think about."

He also hated short hair because it didn't take very long to burn away. He wiped his hands on his white slacks and listened carefully. Agent Scullery rambled on about fire trucks and ambulances and burn victims and smoke victims and jump victims.

And mud.

"There was mud all over the place. You don't think about mud at fires."

Some of us do, Sonny thought. Go on.

Agent Scullery told Joe Buck the faggot cowboy about glowing-red bolts and melting glass and a man she'd seen pulling burnt pieces of chicken from the embers and eating them while people screamed for help. "It was . . ." she paused, thinking of a concise word, "excruciating." Sonny had worked for a number of business people and he knew how they lived to summarize.

"Did you see anyone near the building when it started?"

"In the back I did. There were some people there. In the alley."

"Who?"

"I didn't pay much attention."

"You have *any* idea?" the cowboy persisted.

Sonny listened intently but Agent Scullery couldn't recall very much. "A man. A couple of men. That's all I know. I'm sorry."

"Young. Teenagers?"

"Not so young. I don't know. Sorry."

Pellam thanked her. She lingered, maybe waiting to see if he'd ask her out. But he just smiled a noncommittal smile, stepped into the street, flagged down a cab. Sonny hurried after him but the cowboy was already inside and the yellow Chevy was speeding away before Sonny even got to the curbside. He didn't hear the destination.

He was momentarily enraged that Pellam the tall Midnight Cowboy had gotten away from him so easily. But then he reflected that that was all right – this wasn't really about eliminating witnesses or punishing intruders. It was about something much, much bigger.

He held up his hands and noticed that they'd stopped shaking. A tatter of smoke, a dissolving ghost, wafted before Sonny's face and, helpless, he could only close his eyes and inhale the sweet perfume.

Remaining this way for a long moment, motionless and blind, he came back to earth slowly and dug into his shoulder bag. He found out that he only had a pint or so of juice left.

But that was plenty, he decided. *More* than enough. Sometimes you only needed a spoonful. Depending on how much time you had. And how clever you were. At the moment Sonny had all the time in the world. And, as always, he knew he was clever as a fox.

4

W indy this morning.

An August storm was approaching and the first thing Pellam noticed when he woke, hearing the wind, was that he wasn't swaying.

It'd been over three months since he'd parked the Winnebego Chieftain at Westchester Auto Storage in White Plains and temporarily forsaken his nomadic lifestyle. Three months – but he still sometimes had trouble sleeping in a bed that wasn't atop steel springs badly in need of replacement. With this much wind today he ought to be swaying like a passenger in a gale.

He also hadn't gotten used to paying fifteen hundred a month for a one-bedroom East Village shotgun flat, whose main attraction was a bathtub in the kitchen. ("It's called a bitchen," the real estate woman told him, taking his check for the broker's fee and first month's rent as if he'd owed her the money for months. "People're totally dying for them nowadays.") Fourth-floor walk-up, the linoleum floor a dirty beige and walls green as Ettie Washington's hospital room. And what, he'd been wondering, was that *smell*?

In his years doing location work Pellam had scouted in Manhattan only a few times. The local companies largely had the business locked up and, besides, because of the high cost of shooting here the Manhattan you saw in most movies was usually Toronto, Cleveland or a set. The films actually shot in the city had little appeal to him – weird little Jim Jarmusch student-quality independents and dull mainstreams. *EXT. PLAZA HOTEL – DAY, EXT. WALL STREET – NIGHT.* The scouting assignments had less to do with being the director's third eye than filling out the proper forms in the Mayor's Film Office and making sure cash went where it was supposed to go, both above and below the table.

But scouting was behind him for the immediate future. He was a month away from finishing the rough cut of his first film in years and the first documentary he'd ever made. *West of Eighth* was the title.

He showered and brushed his unruly black hair into place, thinking about the project. The schedule allowed him only another week of taping then three weeks of editing and post-pro. September 27 was the deadline for mixing and delivery to WGBH in Boston, where he'd work with the producer on the final cut. PBS airing was planned for early next spring. Simultaneously he'd have the tape transferred to film, re-edited and shipped for limited release in art theaters in the U.S. and on Channel 4 in England next summer. Then submissions to festivals in Cannes, Venice, Toronto and Berlin and to the Oscars.

Of course that *had* been the plan. But now?

The motif of *West of Eighth* had been the tenement at 458 West Thirty-sixth Street and the residents who lived there. But Ettie Washington was the centerpiece. With her arrest he wondered if he was now the proud owner of two hundred hours of fascinating interviews that would never find their way to TV or silver screen.

Outside he bought a newspaper then flagged down a cab.

The clattering vehicle wove right and left through traffic, as if the cabbie were avoiding hot pursuit, and Pellam tightly gripped the handhold as he tried to read about the fire. The story was dwindling in news value and today's paper reported only that Ettie'd been arrested and confirmed what he'd known – that the only serious injury was Juan Torres. Pellam remembered the boy clearly. He'd interviewed his mother and recalled the energetic twelve-year-old, standing in his apartment, by the window, left-hooking a package of Huggies like a punching bag and saying to Pellam insistently, "My daddy, he know Jose Canseco. No, no, no. Really. He does!"

The boy's condition was still critical.

A picture of Ettie, being led by a woman cop out of Manhattan Hospital, accompanied the article. Her hair was a mess. Light flares sparked off the chrome cuffs on her wrists, just below the cast that Pellam had signed.

Etta Washington, formerly Doyle, née Wilkes, was seventy-two years old. Born in Hell's Kitchen she'd never lived any-where else. The 458 W. Thirty-sixth Street building had been her home for the past five years. She'd resided for the prior forty in a similar tenement up the street, now demolished. All her other residences had been in the Kitchen, within five square blocks of one another.

Ettie had ventured out of New York state only three times for brief trips, two of them funerals of kin in North Carolina. Ettie had been a star student in her first two years of high school but dropped out to work and try to become a cabaret singer. She'd performed for some years, always opening for better-known talent. Mostly in Harlem or the Bronx, though occasionally she'd land a job on Swing Street – Fifty-second. Pellam had heard some old wire recordings transcribed onto tape and was impressed with her low voice. For years she'd worked odd jobs, supporting herself and sometimes lovers, while resisting the inevitable proposals of marriage that a beautiful woman living alone in Hell's Kitchen was flooded with. She finally married, late and incongruously: her husband was an Irishman named Billy Doyle.

A handsome, restless man, Doyle left her years ago, after only three years of marriage.

"He was just doing what a man does, my Billy. They got that runaway spirit. Maybe their nature but it's hard to forgive 'em for it. Wonder if you've got it too, John."

Sitting beside the camera as he'd recorded this, Pellam had nodded encouragingly and reminded himself to edit out her last sentence and her accompanying chuckle.

Her second husband was Harold Washington, who drowned, drunk, in the Hudson River.

"No love lost there. But he was dependable with the money and never cheated and never raised his voice to me. Sometimes I miss him. If I remember to think about him."

Ettie's youngest son, Frank, had been caught in a cross fire and killed by a man wearing a purple top hat in a drunken shoot-out in Times Square. Her daughter, Elizabeth, of whom

Ettie was immensely proud, was a real estate saleswoman in Miami. In a year or two, Ettie would be moving to Florida to live near her. Her oldest son, James – a handsome mulatto – was the only child she had by Doyle. He too caught the wanderlust flu and disappeared out west – California, Ettie assumed. She hadn't heard from him in twelve years.

The elderly woman had been, in her youth, sultry and beautiful if somewhat imperious (as evidenced by a hundred photos, all presently burned to gray ash) and was now a handsome woman with youthful, dark skin. She debated often about dyeing her salt-and-pepper hair back to its original black. Ettie talked like a quick, mid-Atlantic Southerner, drank bad wine and cooked delicious tripe with bacon and onions. And she could unreel stories about her own past and about her mother and grandmother like a natural actress, as if God gave her that gift to make up for others denied.

And what would happen to her now?

With a jolt the cab burst across Eighth Avenue, the Maginot Line bordering Hell's Kitchen.

Pellam glanced out the window as they passed a storefront, in whose window the word *Bakery* was painted over, replaced by: *Youth Outreach Center – Clinton Branch*.

Clinton.

This was a raw spot with longtime residents. The neighborhood to them was "Hell's Kitchen" and would never be anything but. "Clinton" was what the city officials and public relations and real estate people called the 'hood. As if a name change could convince the public this part of town wasn't a morass of tenements and gangs and smokey bodegas and hookers and pebbles of crack vials littering sidewalks but was the New

Frontier for corporate headquarters and yuppie lofts.

Remembering Ettie's voice: *"You hear the story how this place got its name? The one they tell is a policeman down here, a long time ago, he says to another cop, 'This place is hell.' And the other one goes, 'Hell's mild compared to here. This's hell's kitchen.' That's the story, but that's not how it happened. No sir. Where the name came from was it's called after this place in London. What else in New York? Even the name of the neighborhood's stolen from someplace else."*

"Look I am saying," the cabbie broke into Pellam's thoughts. "Same fucking thing fucking yesterday. And for weeks."

He was gesturing furiously at a traffic jam ahead of them. It seemed to be caused by the construction work going on across from the site of the fire – that high-rise nearing completion. Cement trucks pulled in and out through a chain link gate, holding up traffic.

"That building. I am wanting them to go fuck themselves. It has ruins fucking neighborhood. All of it." He slapped the dashboard hard, nearly knocking over his royal orb air freshener.

Pellam paid and climbed out of the cab, leaving the driver to his muttered curses. He walked toward the Hudson River.

He passed dark, woody storefronts – Vinnie's Fruits and Vegetables, Managro's Deli, Cuzin's Meats and Provisions, whose front window was filled with whole dressed animals. Booths of clothing and wooden stands filled with piles of spices and herbs packed the sidewalks. A store selling African goods advertised a sale on ukpor and ogbono. *"Buy now!"* it urged.

Pellam passed Ninth Avenue and continued on to Tenth. He

passed the shell of Ettie's building, floating in a surreal grove of faint smoke, and continued on toward a scabby six-story, red-brick building on the corner.

He paused in front of the handwritten sign in the grimy window of a ground floor apartment.

Louis Bailey, Esq. Attorney at Law Abogado. Criminal, Civil, Wills, Divorces, Personal Injuries. Motorcycle Accidents. Real Estate. Notary Public. Copies Made. Send Your Fax.

Two window panes were missing. Yellow newspaper had replaced one. The other was blocked by a faded box of Post Toasties. Pellam stared at the decrepit building then checked to make sure he had the name right. He did.

Send your fax . . .

He pushed inside.

There was no waiting room, just a single large room of an apartment converted into an office. The place was jam-packed with papers, briefs, books, some bulky, antiquated office equipment – a dusty, feeble computer and a fax machine. A hundred law books, some of which were still sealed in their original, yellowing cellophane wrappers.

A sign proclaimed *NOTARY PUBLIC*.

The lawyer stood at his copier, feeding pages of legal documents through the wobbly machine. Hot sun came through the filthy windows; the room must have been a hundred degrees.

"You Bailey?"

His sweaty face turned. Nodded.

"I'm John Pellam."

"Ettie's friend. The writer."

"Filmmaker." They shook hands.

The portly man touched his coif of long gray hair, which was thinning reluctantly. He wore a white shirt and wide, emerald-colored tie. His gray suit was one size off in both directions – the pants too big, the jacket too small.

"I'd like to talk to you about her case," Pellam said.

"It's too hot in here." Bailey stacked the copied papers on the desk and wiped his forehead. "The A.C.'s misbehaving. How about we retire to my other office? I've got a branch up the street."

Another branch? Pellam thought. And said, "Lead the way."

Louis Bailey waved toward the doughy woman bartender. He said nothing to her but she waddled off to fix what must have been the lawyer's usual. In a brogue she called to Pellam, "Whatcha want?"

"Coffee."

"Irish?"

"Folgers," he replied.

"I meant with whisky?"

"I meant without."

Bailey continued. "So. The scans came back negative. The MRI or whatever. She'll be fine. They've moved her to Women's Detention Center."

"I tried to visit her yesterday. They wouldn't let me. Lomax, that fire marshal, wasn't much help."

"They usually aren't. If you're on our side of the fence."

Pellam said, "I finally found a cop who told me she'd hired you."

With an awkward squeak the door opened and two dark-suited young men entered, looked around with dismay and left.

Bailey's uptown office – the abysmal Emerald Isle Pub – was not the sort of place for a business brunch.

"Can I see her?" Pellam asked.

"Now that she's in detention we can work that out, sure. I've talked to the A.D.A."

"The . . . ?"

"Assistant District Attorney. The prosecutor. Lois Koepel's her name. She's not bad, not good. She's got an attitude. Jewish thing, I think. Or a woman's thing. Or a young thing. I don't know which is worse. I threatened her with an order to show cause, they don't take better care of Ettie – make sure she gets pain pills, change her bandages. But they couldn't care less, of course."

"Guess not."

Over Pellam's sour coffee and Bailey's martini the lawyer gave his assessment of the case. Pellam was trying to gauge the man's competence. From the man's mouth came no statutes, case citations or court rules. Pellam reached a vague conclusion that he'd have preferred someone more outraged and, if not smarter, at least chronologically closer to law school.

Bailey sipped the drink and said, "What's this film of yours about?"

"An oral history on Hell's Kitchen. Ettie's my best source."

"The woman *can* tell her stories, that's for sure."

Pellam folded his hands around the hot mug. The bar was freezing. A bitter wind shot from a sputtering air conditioner above the door. "Why'd they arrest her? Lomax wouldn't tell me anything."

"Yeah, well, I gotta tell you, they've found some stuff."

"Stuff."

"And it's not good. A witness saw her entering the basement just before the fire. It started down there, next to the boiler. She's got a key to the back door."

"Don't all the tenants?"

"Some do. But she was the one seen opening the door five minutes before the fire started."

"I met somebody at the building yesterday," Pellam said. "She told me she saw some people in the alley. Just before the fire. Three or four men. She couldn't describe them any better than that."

Bailey nodded and jotted a few sentences in a battered leather notebook embossed with initials not his own.

"She couldn't have done it," Pellam said. "I was there. She was on the stairs above me when it started."

"Oh, they don't think she actually started the fire. They think she opened the basement door and let a pyro in."

"A professional arsonist?"

"A pro, yeah. But a psycho too. A guy's been working in the city for a few years. The M.O.'s that he mixes gas with fuel oil. Just the right proportion. He knows what he's doing. See, gas alone's too unstable so he adds oil. The fire takes a little longer to get going but it burns hotter. Then – get this – he also adds dish detergent to the mix. So the stuff sticks to clothes and skin. Like napalm. Burning-for-bucks guys, I mean, pure for-hire stuff, they wouldn't do that. And they don't set fires when there're people around. They don't *want* anybody to get hurt. This guy likes it . . . The fire marshals and the cops're worried. He's getting crazier. There's pressure on 'em from above to get him."

"So Lomax thinks she hired him," Pellam mused. "What about the fact that she was almost killed too?"

"The A.D.A.'s speculating she tried to get to her apartment so she'd have an alibi. There was a fire escape outside her window. Only the timing got screwed up. They also think she planned it when you were coming over so you could confirm she was there."

Pellam scoffed. "She wouldn't hurt me."

"But you were early, weren't you?"

Pellam finally said, "A few minutes, yeah." Then: "But everybody's missing one thing. What's her motive supposed to be?"

"Ah, yes. The motive." As he'd done several times before Bailey paused and organized his thoughts. He drained his martini and ordered another. "Full jigger this time, Rosie O'Grady. Don't let those massive olives lure you into cheating. Last week Ettie bought a tenant's insurance policy for twenty-five thousand dollars."

Pellam sipped from the cup then pushed it away from him. The vile taste in his mouth was only partly the coffee. "Keep going."

"It's a declared-value policy. Ever hear of that? It means she pays a high premium but if the apartment is destroyed the insurer pays off whether she's got Chippendale furniture or orange crates inside."

"Pretty damn obvious. Buying a policy then burning the building the next month."

"Ah, but the police *love* obvious crimes, Mr Pellam. So do juries. New Yorkers don't do well with subtleties. That's why clever bad guys get away with murder." The martini arrived and Bailey hovered over the glass, like a child eyeing a present on Christmas morning. "On top of that, women are prime suspects in insurance fraud and welfare scams. See, if you're a welfare mom and your place burns down you get moved to the top of the list for a nicer place. Happens everyday. The fire marshal saw a woman, an insurance policy and a suspicious fire. Bingo, his job's done."

"Somebody's setting her up. Hell, if it was insurance, why burn the whole building? Why not just her own apartment?"

"Less suspicious. Anyway, this pyro goes for the most damage he can. She just happened to hire *him*. Probably didn't even know what he was going to do."

Pellam, a former independent filmmaker and script writer, often thought of life as a series of storylines. There seemed to be some holes in this one. "Okay, they must've sent the insurance policy to her. What did Ettie say when she saw it?"

"The agency claims she picked up the application, filled it out, mailed it back. They forwarded it to the home office. Her approved copy of the policy'd just been mailed from the headquarters the day before the fire so she never received it."

"Then the agent or clerk could testify that it wasn't Ettie," Pellam pointed out.

"The clerk identified her picture as the woman who picked up the application."

Pellam, long suspicious of conspiracy theories, felt a plot worthy of an Oliver Stone movie at work. "What about the premium check?"

"Paid in cash."

"And Ettie says?" Pellam asked.

"She denies it all, of course," Bailey said, dismissingly, as if a denial were as forensically useful as the fly walking on the bar beside them. "Now, let's talk practicalities. The arraignment is scheduled for tomorrow. The A.D.A.'s making rumblings about a postponement. You know what the arraignment is? That's where—"

"I know what it is," Pellam said. "What's the bail situation?"

"I don't think it'll be too high. I'll talk to some bailbondsmen I know. She's a good risk, not being very mobile. And it's not a homicide."

"Mr Bailey," Pellam began.

The lawyer held up a hand. "Louis, please." *Louie*. Bailey growled the name and for a moment he became the Damon Runyon character he aspired to be.

"You've done this before?" Pellam asked. "Cases like this?"

"Ah." Bailey leaned his head back, touched a flabby jowl and caught Pellam's gaze with eyes suddenly clear and focused. "I've seen you studying me. My bargain-cellar tie. My frayed cuffs. My Men's Shack suit. Notice the plaid's a bit mismatched? I wore out the original pants a year ago and got the closest I could find. And you've been gentlemanly enough not to mention my liquid brunch."

He pointed to his right hand – an otherwise dramatic gesture he managed to underplay. "This's a class ring from New York Law School. That's *not* NYU, by the way. Big difference. And I went at night while I served process during the day. And graduated somewhere to the left of the middle of my class."

"I'm sure you're a fine lawyer."

"Oh, of course I'm not," Bailey snorted a laugh. "But so what? This isn't an Upper East Side case. It's not a SoHo or Westchester case. For those, you need a good lawyer. This is a Hell's Kitchen case. Ettie's poor, she's black, the facts are against her and the jury'll've found her guilty before they're even empaneled. The law's irrelevant."

"What *is* relevant?"

"The gears," he whispered, the theatricality filling his voice like sump water.

Pellam didn't feel like playing straight man. He remained silent. A car drove past slowly. A BMW convertible. Even inside the bar you could hear the raw bass beat of a popular rap song Pellam had heard several times before on neighborhood radios.

"It's a white man's world, now don't be blind . . ."

The car cruised on.

"The gears," Bailey continued, teasing his olive. "Here's what I mean: the first thing you learn about the Kitchen is that anybody can kill you, for any reason. Or for no reason. That's a given. So what can you do to stay alive? Well, you can make it an inconvenience to kill you. You stay away from alleys when you walk down the street, you don't make eye contact, you dress down, you stay close to people on street corners, you drop the names of union bosses or cops from Midtown South in bars like this one . . . You see what I'm saying? You gum up the gears. If it's too much trouble to kill you, maybe, just maybe they'll go on to someone else."

"And Ettie?"

"Everybody – the A.D.A., the cops, the press – they take the path of least resistance. If something clogs up the gears of the case they'll go fishing for somebody else. Find themselves another jim-dandy suspect. That's the only thing we can do for Ettie. Gumming gears."

"Then let's give them another suspect. Who else'd have a motive? The owner, right? For the insurance."

"Possibly. I'll check the deed and find out what the owner's insurance situation is."

"Why else would somebody burn a building?"

"Kids do it for kicks. That's number one in the city. Number two, revenge. So and so is sleeping with somebody's wife. Squirt a little lighter fluid under his door, presto. Lot of perps set fires to cover up other crimes. Rape murders especially. Burglary. Welfare fraud, like I said. Vanity fires – the mailroom boy sets a fire in the office and then puts it out himself. He's a hero . . . Then in the Kitchen we see a lot of landmark torching – the city gives old buildings this special status 'cause they're historical. Generally if a landlord owns an old building that doesn't make money because it's too expensive to maintain he tears it down and builds a more profitable one. But landmarked buildings can't be torn down – they're protected. So what happens? Lord have mercy, there's a fire. What a coincidence! He's free to build whatever he wants. If he doesn't get caught."

"Was Ettie's building landmarked?"

"I don't know. I can find out."

The way Bailey emphasized the last sentence explained a little bit more about how gears got gummed up. Pellam slipped his wallet out of his back pocket, set it on the bar.

The lawyer's face broke into a ginny smile. "Oh, yessir, that's how it works in Hell's Kitchen. Everybody's a sellout. Maybe even me." The smile faded. "Or maybe I just have a high price. That's ethics around here – when it takes a lot to buy you."

A police car shot past the window with its lights going but its siren off. For some reason the silent passage made its mission seem particularly harrowing and urgent.

Then Bailey grew very somber, so suddenly that Pellam guessed the second – or was it third? – Beefeater had kicked in with a stab of melancholy. He touched Pellam's arm in a fatherly way and you could see reluctant shrewdness through the haze in his eyes. "There's something I want to say."

Pellam nodded.

"You're sure you want to get involved in this? Wait. Before you answer, let me ask you something. You've talked to a lot of people around here? For your movie?"

"Ettie mostly. But also a couple dozen others."

Bailey nodded, examining Pellam's face up close, scanning it. "Well, people in the Kitchen're easy to approach. They'll pass you a quart of malt liquor and never wipe the bottle when you hand it back. They'll sit on doorsteps with you for hours. Sometimes you can't shut 'em up."

"That's what I've found. True."

"That puts you right at ease, right?"

"Does. Yep."

"But it's just talk," Bailey said. "It doesn't mean they accept you. Or trust you. And don't ever think you'll hear anybody's real secrets. They won't tell 'em to somebody like you."

"And what are *you* telling me?" Pellam asked.

The lawyer's shrewdness became caution. There was a pause. "I'm telling you it's dangerous here. Very dangerous. And getting more dangerous. There've been a lot of fires lately, more than normal. Gangs . . . shootings."

The *Times* Metro section was full of shooting stories. Kids smuggling guns into grade school. Innocent people were gunned down in cross fires or by crazed snipers. Pellam had stopped reading the papers his second week in town.

"This is a rough time in the Kitchen."

As opposed to when? Pellam wondered.

Bailey asked him, "Are you really sure you want to get involved?" As Pellam started to speak the lawyer held up a hand. "Are you sure you want to go where this might take you?"

Pellam answered the question with one of his own. "How much?" He tapped his wallet.

Bailey dipped again back into his alcohol haze. "For everything?" Shrugged. "I'll have to find a cop to sneak me the arson report, the name of the insurance agent, anything else they have on her. The landlord and deed're public records but it takes weeks if you don't, you know—"

"Grease the gears," Pellam muttered.

"I'd say a thousand."

Pellam wondered what the real object of the bargaining was: abstract morality or his own gullibility.

"Five hundred."

Bailey hesitated. "I don't know if I can do it for that."

"She's innocent, Louis," Pellam said. "That means we have God on our side. Doesn't that buy us a discount?"

"In Hell's Kitchen?" Bailey roared with laughter. "This is the neighborhood that God forgot. Give me six and I'll do the best I can."

5

He had the map spread out on the beautiful butcher-block table.

Smoothing the paper under his long, thin fingers, Sonny took pleasure in paper, knew it was the reincarnated skin of trees. He liked the sound of paper when it moved, he liked the feel. He knew that it burned best of anything.

Sonny looked up and surveyed the cavernous loft.

Back to the map. It was of Manhattan and he traced his finger along the colored lines of streets to find the building in which he now sat. With an expensive ballpoint pen he marked an X on that spot. He sipped ginger ale from a wine glass.

He heard a shuffle and a sound like a cat mewing. He glanced to his right – at the witness who'd been flirting with Joe Buck. Poor redheaded Agent Scullery from Ernst & Young; must have been paid a shitload of money at work because this was a very nice loft indeed. He looked her up and down, deciding again that she would look a lot better if she had long hair like his.

She lay on her side, feet and hands bound with duct tape. She was gagged too.

Matter-of-factly he said to her, "Your show? On TV? I don't really believe the FBI does all that stuff. Do you think federal agents give a shit if there are really aliens up there?" He spoke in a soothing voice, though absently. He touched the colorful squares of the map – they reminded him of blocks his mother'd bought him as a child.

Here.

He marked another building.

Here.

Another.

He touched several others and marked them with X's. It'd be a lot of work. But one thing that Sonny didn't mind was work. Virtue is its own reward.

Agent Scullery peeked over the gray metallic tape and drummed a loud, panicked dance with her feet.

"Dear, dear, dear." Folding the map carefully, he replaced it in his back pocket. The pen went in his breast pocket, diligently retracted. He hated ink on his clothing. Then he walked in a circle around Agent Scullery, who kicked and rolled and mewed.

In the kitchen he examined the gas oven and stove. It was a top-of-the-line model but Sonny knew about appliances only from his profession. He used *his* own stove just to heat water for herbal tea. He ate only vegetables and never cooked them; he found the whole idea of heating food abhorrent. He dropped to the immaculate tile floor and pulled open the stove. He had the bimetal gas cutoff valve disabled in five seconds and the gooseneck hose off in ten. The sour scent of the natural gas odorant (the gas itself has no scent) poured into the room. Sweet and bitter and curiously appealing – like tonic water.

He walked to the front door of the loft and flicked the light switch on then off to see which bulb went on – an overhead one not far away. Sonny climbed onto a chair, reaching up, stretching, cracking the bulb with his wrench and sending the sleet of glass down on his hair and shoulders. The ceilings were high and it was quite a stretch. As he'd struggled to reach the bulb he was sure that tall Agent Scullery was laughing at him.

But laughter's in the eye of the beholder, Sonny thought, glaring at her as he returned to his bag, took out the jar of juice and poured it over her blouse and skirt. She writhed away from him.

He asked, "Who's laughing now? Hmm?"

Sonny walked throughout the loft, shutting off the lights, and closing all the drapes. He walked to the front door and stepped into the corridor, leaving the door slightly ajar. In the lobby he jotted down the names of six of the residents in the building.

A half hour later he was standing in a phone kiosk a block away, a half-eaten mango in one hand, the phone crooked under his chin, punching in phone numbers.

On his fifth try someone answered. "Hello?"

"Say, is the Roberts residence?"

"It's Sally Roberts, yes."

"Oh, hi, you don't know me. I'm Alice Gibson's brother? In your building."

"Alice, sure. Four-D."

"That's right. She'd mentioned you live there and I just got your number from directory assistance. You know, I'm a little concerned about her."

"Really?" The woman's voice was concerned too.

"We were talking on the phone a little while ago and she said she was feeling real sick. Food poisoning, she was thinking. She hung up and I tried to call back and there was no answer. I hate to ask but do you think you could go check on her? I'm worried that she passed out."

"Of course. You want to give me your number?"

"I'll just hold on if you don't mind," said Sonny the polite sibling. "You're too kind."

He leaned his head against the aluminum of the kiosk. It left sweat stains. Why all this sweat? He thought again. But it's hot out. *Everybody's* sweating. Not everybody's hands are shaking though. He pushed that thought away. Think about something else. How 'bout dinner? Okay. What would he have for dinner tonight? he wondered. A ripe tomato. A good Jersey one. They were hard to find. Salt and a little—

This was weird. The sound of the massive explosion reached him through the phone before he heard it live. Then the line went dead as the kiosk shook hard under the wave of the blast. Typical of natural gas explosions there was a blue-white flare and very little smoke as the windows imploded from the inrush of oxygen then immediately exploded outward from the force of the combustion.

Fire draws more than it expands.

Sonny watched for a moment as the flames spread to the top floor of the late Agent Scullery's apartment. The tarred roof ignited and the smoke turned from white to gray to black.

He wiped his hands on a napkin. Then he opened the map and carefully drew a check through the circle that had marked the loft. He pitched the mango out and started back to his apartment, walking quickly, in the opposite direction from all the spectators, noting their excitement and wishing they knew they had him to thank.

"How you feeling, Mother?"

"How she feeling?" a voice called across the cold cement floor. "How she doing?"

Ettie Washington lay on the cot, legs tucked up under her. She opened her eyes. Her first thought: the memory that her clothes had been a problem. Always concerned that she looked nice, always ironing her dresses and blouses and skirts. But here, in the Women's Detention Center in downtown Manhattan, where they let you wear street clothes – minus belts and laces, of course – Ettie Washington had had no clothes.

When they'd brought her from the hospital all she had on was her pale blue robe with dots on it, open up the back. No buttons, just ties. She was dreadfully embarrassed. Finally one of the guards had found her a simple dress, a prison shift. Blue. Washed a million times. She hated it.

"Hey, Mother, you hear me? You feeling okay?"

A large black form hovered over her. A hand stroked her forehead. "She feel hot. Mebbe got a fever."

"God gonna watch over that woman," came another voice from the far side of the detention center.

"She be okay. You be okay, Mother." The large woman, in her forties, shrank down on her knees next to Ettie, who squinted until she could see the woman clearly.

"How's yo arm?"

"It hurts," Ettie responded. "I broke it."

"That quite a cast." The brown eyes took in John Pellam's signature.

"What's your name?" Ettie asked her, struggling to sit up.

"No, no, Mother, you stay lying down. I'm Hatake Imaham, mother."

"I'm Ettie Washington."

"We know."

Ettie tried again to sit. She felt helpless, weaker than she already was, on her back.

"No, no, no, Mother, you stay there. Don't get up. They brung you in like a sacka flour. Them white fuckers. Dropped you down."

There were two dozen cots, bolted to the floor. The mattresses were an inch thick and hard as dirt. She might as well have been lying on the floor.

Ettie had a vague memory of the cops moving her here from the hospital room. She'd been exhausted and doped up. They used a paddy wagon. There was nothing to hold onto and it seemed to her that the driver had taken turns fast – on purpose. Twice she'd fallen off the slick plastic bench and often she banged her broken arm so badly it brought tears to her eyes.

"I'm tired," she said to Hatake and looked past the huge woman to the other occupants of the cell. The detention center was a single large room, barred and painted beige. Like many Hell's Kitchen residents Ettie Washington knew something about holding cells. She knew that most of these women would be in here for pissy crimes, who-cares crimes. Shoplifting, prostitution, assault, fraud. (Shoplifting was okay because it helped you feed your family. If you were a prostitute – Ettie hated the term "ho" – it was because you couldn't get a job doing decent work for decent pay (besides at least you were *working* and not on the dole). Assault – well, whaling on your husband's girlfriend? What's wrong with that? Ettie'd done it herself once or twice. And as for ripping off the welfare system – oh, please. Trees ripe for the picking . . .)

Ettie had a taste for some wine. Wanted some badly. She'd snuck a hundred dollars into her cast but it didn't look like anybody here was connected enough to get her a bottle. Why, these're just girls, here, most of 'em babies.

Hatake Imaham stroked Ettie's head once more.

"You lie right there, Mother. You be still and don't you worry 'bout nothing. I'ma look out for you. I'ma get you what you need."

Hatake was a huge woman with cornrows and dangling, beaded African hair – exactly the way Elizabeth had worn it the day she left New York City. Ettie noticed that the holes in Hatake's ear lobes were huge and she wondered about the size of the earrings that had stretched the skin so much. She wondered if Elizabeth wore jewelry like that. Probably. The girl had an ostentatious side to her.

"I've gotta make a phone call," Ettie said.

"They let you but not now." The woman touched her good arm, squeezed it gently.

"Some son of a bitch took away my pills," Ettie complained. "One of the guards. I need 'em back."

Hatake laughed. "Honey, them pills, they ain't even in this building no more. They sold an' gone. Mebbe we see what we can find, us girls. Something help you. Bet it hurts like the devil's own dick."

Ettie almost said that she had some money and could pay.

But she knew instinctively to keep the money secret for the time being. She said, "Thank you."

"You lie back. Get some rest. We look out for you."

Ettie closed her eyes and thought of Elizabeth. Then she thought of her husband Billy Doyle and she thought of, finally, John Pellam. But he was in her thoughts for no more than five seconds before she fell asleep.

"Well?"

Hatake Imaham returned to the cluster of women on the far end of the cell.

"That bitch, she the one done it. She guilty as death." Hatake didn't claim to be a real mambo but it was well known in the Kitchen that she did possess an extra sense. And while she hadn't had much success laying on hands to cure illness everyone knew that she could touch someone and find out their deepest secrets. She could tell that the hot vibrations radiating off Ettie Washington's brow were feelings of guilt.

"Shit," one woman spat out. "She burn that boy up, she burn up that little boy."

"The boy?" another asked in an incredulous whisper. "She set that fire in the *basement*, girl – didn't you read that? On Thirty-sixth Street. She coulda killed the whole everybody in that building."

"That bitch call herself a mother," a skinny woman with deep-set eyes growled. "Fuck that bitch. I say—"

"Shhhh," Hatake waved a hand.

"Do her now! Do the bitch now."

Hatake's face tightened into a glare. "Quiet! Damballah! We gonna do this th'way I say. You hear me, girl? I ain't kill her. Damballah don't ask more than what she done."

"Okay, sister," the girl said, her voice hushed and frightened. "Okay. That's cool. Whatcha saying we do?"

"Shhhhh," Hatake hissed again and glanced out the bars, where a lethargic guard lounged out of earshot. "Who gonna see the man today?"

A couple of the girls lifted their arms. The prostitutes. Criminal Term batched those arraignments and disposed of them early, Hatake knew. It was like the city wanted them back on the street with a minimum of lost time. Hatake looked at the oldest one. "You Dannette, right?"

The woman nodded, her pocked face remained peaceful.

"I'ma ask you do something for me. How 'bout that, girl?"

"Whatchu want me to do?"

"You talk to yo man when you get into the courtroom."

"Yeah, yeah, sister."

"Tell him we make it worth his while. After you get out, I wan' you to come back."

Dannette frowned. "You want . . . You want what?"

"Listen to me. I want you to get back in here. Tomorrow."

Dannette had never stopped nodding but she didn't understand this. Hatake continued, "I want you to get something, bring it in here to me. You know how, right? You know where you hide it? In the back hole, not the front. In a Baggie."

"Sure." Dannette nodded as if she hid things there every day.

She looked around at the other women. Whatever she was being asked to do was being seconded by everybody.

"I'll pay you for this, for coming back again."

"You get me rock?" the girl asked eagerly.

Hatake scowled. It was well-known that she hated drugs, dealers and users. "You a cluckhead, girl?"

The pocked face went still. "You get me rock?"

"I give you money," the huge woman spat out. "You buy whatever you want with it, girl. Fuck up your life, you want. That your business."

Dannette said, "What it is you want me to bring you back?"

"Shhh," whispered Hatake Imaham. A guard was wandering past the door.

6

"Hell of a visiting room."

"Oh, John, am I in the soup?"

Pellam told Ettie, "Not exactly. But you're walking around the edge of the bowl, looks like."

"It's good to see you." They sat across from each other in the fluorescent-lit room. A roach meandered slowly up the wall, past the corpses of his kin crushed to dry specks. Beneath a sign that read *NO PHYSICAL CONTACT* John Pellam took the bandaged hand of Ettie Washington. The squat uniformed matron nearby looked coldly at this disregard of regulations but didn't say anything. Pellam said, "Louis Bailey's going to get you out on bail."

Ettie looked bad. She seemed too calm, considering everything that had happened to her. He knew she had a temper. He'd seen it when she talked about her husband – Billy Doyle's leaving her. And about the time she was fired from her last job. After years working for a jobber in the Fashion District she'd been let go without a single day's severance. He expected to see her fury at whoever had set the blaze, at the police, at the jailors. He found only resignation. That was a lot more troubling to him than anger.

She picked at a worn spot on her shift. "The guards're all saying it'll go easier if I tell 'em I did it and tell 'em who I hired. I don't know what they're talking about."

Pellam debated for a moment then decided to ask. "Tell me about the insurance policy."

"Hell, I didn't buy any insurance, John. They think I'm a stupid old lady, doing something like that?" She pressed the palm of her good hand against her stiff gray-and-black hair as if fighting off a migraine. "Where I'm gonna get money to buy insurance?" She winced in pain, continued. "I can barely pay my bills, as is. I can't even do *that* half the time. Where'm I gonna get money to buy insurance?"

"You've never been in any insurance agencies in the last month?"

"No. I swear." Her face was drawn up, as she eyed the guard suspiciously.

"Ettie, I've got to ask you these questions. Somebody recognized you taking out the policy."

"That's *their* problem," she said, tight-lipped. "It wasn't me."

"Somebody else saw you at the back door of the building that night. Just before the fire."

"I go in the back door usually. A lot of times I do that – if I've been to the A&P. It's a shortcut. Saves me some steps."

"Do all the tenants have keys to the back?"

"I don't know. I suppose so."

"You locked it behind you?"

"It locks by itself. I think I heard it close."

Ettie was often digressive. One thought brought up ten others. One question could lead via a colorful stream of consciousness to a different time and place. Pellam noted that today, though, her responses were succinct, cautious.

The guard had tolerated Pellam's hand upon Ettie's arm long enough. "No contact," she snapped. Pellam sat back. The guard's nose was pierced three times with gold studs and each ear sprouted ten or twelve small rings. Her belligerence suggested that she was waiting for someone to ridicule the jewelry.

"Louis Bailey," Pellam asked Ettie. "You think he's a good lawyer?"

"Oh, he's good. He's done stuff for me before. I hired him six, eight months ago, for this social security problem I had. He did an okay job . . . That guard over there keeps looking at us with an evil eye, John. She's too jaunty for my taste. Sticking pins in her nose."

Pellam laughed. "This witness told me she saw some men in the alley just before the fire. Did you see them when you got home from the store?"

"Sure."

"Who was it?"

"Nobody I recognized. Some boys from the neighborhood. They're always there. You know, it's an *alley*. Where kids always hang out. Did fifty years ago. Do now. Some things never change."

Pellam remembered what Sibbie's son had told her – what earned him the slap in the face. He asked Ettie, "Were they from the gangs?"

"Could be. I don't know much about them. They leave us alone pretty much . . . And maybe there were some of those workers too. From that big building they're putting up across the street: You know, with those telescopes they have. For surveying. Yeah, I'm sure I saw some of them in the alley. I remember 'cause they wear those plastic helmets. Some of them were those men who came around with the petition we signed."

Pellam remembered Ettie telling him about the high-rise, how the locals had greeted the huge project with such excitement. Roger McKennah, as famous as Donald Trump, was building a glitzy skyscraper in Hell's Kitchen! His company had sent representatives out into the 'hood, asking residents in the blocks around the high-rise to sign waivers so that the building could go five stories higher than the zoning laws allowed. In exchange for their approval of the variance he pledged that the building would feature new grocery stores and a Spanish restaurant and a twenty-four-hour laundry. Ettie had signed, along with most of the other residents.

And then they'd found that the grocery store was part of a gourmet chain that charged $2.39 for a can of black beans, the laundry charged three dollars to wash a blouse, and as for the restaurant, it had a dress code and the limos parked out in front created a terrible traffic jam.

Pellam now made a mental note about the workers, wondered why they were surveying in the alley *across* the street. He wondered too why they'd been working at ten o'clock at night.

"I think we should call your daughter," Pellam said.

"I already did," Ettie said and looked at her cast in surprise – as if it had just materialized on her arm. "I had a long talk with her this morning. She's sending money to Louis for his bill. She wanted to come tomorrow but I was thinking I'll need her more 'round the trial."

"I'm voting that there won't even be a trial."

The bejeweled guard examined her watch. "Okay. Come on, Washington."

"I just got here," Pellam said coolly.

"An' now you just be leavin'."

"A few minutes," he said.

"Time's up. Move it! And you, Washington, *hustle*."

Pellam lowered his eyes to the guard's. "She's got a sprained ankle. You want to tell me how the hell's she supposed to hustle?"

"Don't want lip from you, mister. Less go."

The door swung open, revealing the dim hallway, in which a sign was partially visible. *PRISONERS SHALL NO*

"Ettie," Pellam said, grinning. "You owe me something. Don't forget."

"What's that?"

"The end of the story about Billy Doyle."

Pellam watched the woman tuck away her despair beneath a smile. "You'll like that story, John. That'll be a good one in your film." To the matron she said, "I'm coming, I'm coming. Give an old lady a break."

━━◆◆◆◆━━

7

Inside Bailey's office a gaunt man hunched over the desk, listening to instructions the lawyer was firing at him over a paper cup filled with jug Chablis.

Bailey saw Pellam enter and nodded him over. "This is Cleg."

The thin man shook Pellam's hand as if they were good friends. Cleg wore a green polyester jacket and black slacks. A steel penny gleamed in his left loafer and he smelled of Brylcreem.

The lawyer was looking through an impacted Rolodex. "Let me see . . ."

Cleg said to Pellam, "You play the horses."

It wasn't a question.

"No," Pellam admitted.

The slim man was dismayed. "Well. I got a lock for you, you interested."

"What's a lock?"

"Bet," Cleg responded.

"A bet?"

"That you can't lose."

"Thanks anyway."

He stared at Pellam for a moment then nodded as if he suddenly understood everything there was to know about him. He searched his pockets until he found a pack of cigarettes.

"Here we go," Bailey said. He jotted a name on a yellow Post-it that had been reused several times. He took two bottles of liquor from his desk, slipped them into large interoffice envelopes along with smaller packages that contained, presumably, Pellam's former cash.

He handed Cleg one envelope. "This's for the Recorder of Deeds, the clerk. He's the fat man on the third floor. Sneely. Then this one goes to Landmark Preservation. Pretty Ms. Grunwald with the cat. A receptionist. She gets the Irish Cream. As you probably guessed."

Greasing gears.

Or maybe clogging them.

The man nestled the bottles among his sporting papers and left the office. Pellam saw him pause outside to light a cigarette then continue toward the subway.

Bailey said, "The A.D.A., Ms Koepel, asked for a postponement of Ettie's arraignment. I agreed."

Pellam shook his head. "But she'll have to stay in jail longer."

"True. But I think it's worth it to keep the bitch happy." His head dropped toward the chipped mug he held. "Koepel's a madwoman. But then there's a lot of pressure to catch the firebug. Things're getting worse. Did you hear?"

"Hear what?" Pellam asked.

"There was another fire this morning."

"Another one?"

"A loft. It wasn't too far from here, matter of fact. Destroyed two floors. Three dead. Looked like it was a gas explosion but they found traces of our boy's special brew – gas, fuel oil and soap. And one of the victims was bound and gagged." Bailey shoved a limp *Post* toward Pellam. He glanced at the picture of a burnt-out building.

"Jesus." Pellam had scouted for a lot of action adventure films. Most of the spectacular explosions on screen, supposedly C4 or TNT or dynamite, were actually containers of gasoline-soaked sawdust, carefully assembled by the arms master on the set. Everybody kept far back when he rigged the charges. And stuntmen who thought nothing about free-fall gags from twenty stories up were damn cautious around fire.

Bailey looked over his notes. "Now, what've I found, what've I found? . . . God*damn* air conditioner! Jiggle that switch. It's the compressor. Jiggle it. Did it go on?"

Pellam jiggled. No response from the dusty old unit. Bailey grumbled something inaudible over the throbbing motor. He pulled a fax off his desk. "The prelim arson report about Ettie's building. Getting it cost most of your money. I made a copy for you. Read it and weep."

> *Privileged and Confidential*
> *MEMORANDUM*
> *From: Supervising Fire Marshal Henry Lomax*
> *To: Lois Koepel, Esq., Assistant District Attorney*

Re: Preliminary findings, Fire of Suspicious Origin, 458 W. Three-six street

At 9:58 p.m. on August tenth, a call was received from box 598 on Tenth Avenue regarding a fire at the 458 W. Three-six street. A 911 was received at 10:02 p.m., regarding same. Ladder company Three Eight responded to the first alarm assignment and the captain at the scene concluded that because of the gravity of the fire and the presence of injuries a second alarm assignment was needed. This assignment went out at 10:17 p.m.

Present at the blaze were Two Six Truck, Three Three Truck, Four Eight engine, One Six Engine, and One Seven Ladder. Lines were run immediately, and water was laid down on the three top floors. Access to the premises was gained by entry through the third floor and the building was successfully evacuated.

The captain on the scene concluded that the flames had so weakened the top floors that access through the bulkhead on the roof was inadvisable, and pulled the firefighters back. Shortly thereafter the roof and top two floors collapsed.

The fire was finally knocked down at 11:02 p.m. and all units took up at 12:30 a.m.

The captain requested a fire marshal because certain observations about the fire suggested it was of suspicious origins.

I arrived at 1 a.m. and began my investigation.

I concluded that the point of origin was the basement of the building. Spalling on the brick and melted aluminum confirmed this. I observed that the basement windows had been broken outward not due to heat fracturing but due to being struck with an object of some sort, possibly to provide better oxygen supply to feed the fire. This is consistent with witnesses' observations that the flames did not have a bluish tint (which would indicate a high level of carbon monoxide and might be expected with a fire in a closed space) but orange, indicating a plentiful oxygen source.

I observed fragments of melted and shattered glass consistent with a large (possibly half-gallon or gallon) bottle at the apparent site of origin and burn marks on the floor indicating that a liquid accelerant might have been used.

Subsequent spectrographic analysis indicated that there was such a substance, hydrocarbon-based (See NYFD laboratory Report 337490). The substance was approximately 60 percent 89-octane, unleaded gasoline, thirty percent diesel fuel, and ten percent dish detergent, determined by subsequent photospectrometric analysis to be Dawn brand.

This is consistent with witnesses' observations that the fire appeared to burn orange in color with a large amount of smoke, indicating a hydrocarbon-based accelerant.

A gasoline can found on the premises contained residue of 89-octane, unleaded gasoline. But a comparison of the dyes added to both the gasoline contained in the accelerant, and those in the gasoline can indicated that they came from different sources.

Photospectrometric analysis was able to differentiate the fuel oil in the tank at the premises from the composition *of the fuel oil found at the point of origin. An attempt was made to ascertain the supplier of the gasoline and fuel oil used in the accelerant but they were found to be blends, and so a source could not be determined.*

In addition, it should be noted that thirteen semiautomatic pistols (four 9mm Glock, three 9mm Taurus and six .380 Browning) were found secreted behind the oil tank in the premises. The weapons were unloaded and there was no ammunition present. They were shipped to NYPD forensic lab for latent fingerprint testing. AFIS search came back with no match. BATF and NYPD Major Crimes was notified.

Witnesses reported they had seen a tenant (E. Washington) enter the building through the back door, ten feet from the point of origin, shortly before the blaze.

On the basis of this I instituted a search of the National Insurance Underwriters Fraud Prevention Service which revealed that on July 14 of this year, Suspect Washington applied for and received an insurance policy from New England Mutual Casualty and Indemnity, Policy No. 7833-B-2332. $25,000 declared value policy. Proceeds payable into her checking account (East Side Bank Trust, Acct. No. 223–11003).

Fingerprints taken from several of the glass bottle shards located near the point of origin were compared with fingerprints taken from three Knows found in the remains of the premises and known to be Subject Washington's. Two partials matched.

This provided the basis for probable cause and Suspect Washington was arrested at New York Hospital, where she was recuperating from injuries sustained in the fire.

Subject Washington was read her rights and refused to say anything, and was given the opportunity to seek legal representation.

The investigation is ongoing, and I am continuing to search for evidence to assist the District Attorney's Office in prosecuting this offense.

Note: The vast majority of for-profit arsons involve a suspicious fire on the top floor and to the rear of the premises. This serves two purposes. It destroys the roof which in most cases is the most expensive portion of a building to repair. A destroyed roof will usually result in an insurance company declaring the building a total loss. Second it causes severe water damage throughout the rest of the premises, and thus causes significant additional damage, with minimal loss of life.

This particular fire was set in the basement – that is, without any concern whatsoever for human life. If the perpetrator is the individual who has set similar fires over the past several years, as the M.O. and nature of accelerant indicate, we have reason to believe that this individual is a particular threat to others.

We recommend that all pressure possible be brought to bear on Suspect Washington to have her reveal the identity of this perpetrator who, in my opinion, she hired for the purposes of perpetrating insurance fraud.

Insurance.

And fingerprints . . .

And damn if the color of the fire and the amount of smoke, all that technical stuff, hadn't come right from his own mouth when he'd confronted Lomax at the scene, Pellam thought.

"The A.D.A.'s having a document examiner go over the insurance application to see if the handwriting matches hers. But there *is* a tentative match." Bailey nodded his head in the direction Cleg, his green-jacketed emissary, had just disappeared. "I'm getting a copy of the report at the same time it's sent to Ms Koepel. If she hadn't denied having the policy it probably wouldn't have looked so bad for her."

Pellam said, "Maybe she denied it because she didn't take out the policy." Bailey didn't respond to that. Pellam returned to examining the report again. "The insurance is payable directly into her account. Is that unusual?"

"No, it's pretty common. If a house or apartment burns, the company pays the proceeds directly into the bank. So the check wouldn't be mailed to a place that no longer existed."

"So whoever took out the policy would have to know her account number."

"That's right." Bailey's yellow pad was sun-faded around the edges. It looked like it was ten years old.

"Guns," Pellam said, eyes on the report. "What do you think that means?"

Bailey laughed. "That the apartment's in Hell's Kitchen. That's *all* it means. There're more guns here than on L.A. freeways."

Which Pellam doubted very much. He asked, "Did you find out who the landlord is? And if the building was landmarked."

"That's why Cleg is delivering my thank-you presents." Bailey rummaged in a file and dropped a photocopy on the desk. It bore the seal of the state attorney general. Bailey seemed to think this was a significant piece of paper but to Pellam it was legal gibberish. He shrugged, looked up.

The lawyer explained, "Yes, the building was landmarked but that's irrelevant."

"Why?"

"The owner's a nonprofit foundation." Bailey flipped through several pages and tapped an entry. Pellam read: *The St Augustus Foundation. 500 W. Thirty-ninth Street.*

Everybody in the Kitchen knew about St Augustus. It was a large church, rectory and Catholic school complex in the heart of the neighborhood and had been here forever. To the extent Hell's Kitchen had a soul, St Aug was it. In an interview Ettie had told him that Francis P. Duffy, the chaplain of the Kitchen's famous World War I regiment, the Fighting 69th, had celebrated masses at St Augustus before becoming pastor of Holy Cross Church.

Pellam asked skeptically, "You think they're innocent just because it's a church?"

"It's the *nonprofit* part," Bailey explained, "not the theological part. Any money that a not-for-profit makes has to stay in the organization. It can't be distributed to its stockholders. Even when it's dissolved. And the Attorney General and the IRS are *always* checking upon the books of nonprofits. Besides, the foundation had it insured for its book value – that was only a hundred thousand. Oh, sure, I've known a lot of priests who ought to go to jail for one thing or another but nobody's going to risk sailing up to Sing Sing for that kind of small change."

Pellam nodded at the papers. "Who's this Father James Daly? He's the director?"

"I called him an hour ago – he was out finding emergency housing for the tenants of the building. I'll let you know when he calls back." Pellam then asked, "Can you get the name of the insurance agent Ettie talked to."

"Sure, I can."

Can. It was turning into the most expensive verb in the English language.

Pellam slid another two hundred, in stiff twenties, toward the lawyer. He sometimes thought ATMs should flash a message that read, "Are you going to spend this money wisely?"

He nodded out the window toward the high-rise. Bailey's office was only two doors from Ettie's burnt tenement and a haze of lingering smoke still obscured his view of the glitzy place. "Roger McKennah," he said slowly. "Ettie said some of his workers from across the street were in the alley behind her building the night of the fire. Why'd they be there?"

But Bailey was nodding as if he wasn't surprised at this news. "They're doing some work here."

"Here? In your building?"

"Right. He's part-owner of this place. That's the work going on outside. That you hear." He nodded toward the sound of hammering in a hallway upstairs. "The new Donald Trump himself – renovating my building."

"Why?"

"That's a source of some speculation but we think, we *think* he's fixing up a hideaway for his mistress on the second floor. But you know rumors. You don't suspect him, do you?"

"Why shouldn't I?"

Bailey glanced toward his wine bottle but forewent another glass. "I can't believe he'd do anything illegal. Developers like

McKennah steer clear of shenanigans. Why bother with small potatoes like burning an old tenement? He's got hotels and offices all over the northeast. That new casino of his on the Boardwalk in Atlantic City just opened last month . . . You don't look convinced."

"A rule in Hollywood thriller scriptwriting is that if you don't want to spend a lot of time developing your villain's character just make him a real estate developer or oil company executive."

Bailey shook his head. "McKennah's too top-drawer to do anything illegal."

"Let me make a call." Pellam took the phone.

The lawyer apparently changed his mind about the wine and graciously poured himself another. Pellam declined with a shake of his head as he punched in a long series of numbers. "Alan Lefkowitz, please." After several clicks and long moments on hold, a cheerful voice came on the phone.

"Pellam? *The* John Pellam? Shit. Where you be?"

Hating himself for it, Pellam slipped into producer-speak. "Big Apple. What's cooking, Lefty?"

"Doing that thing with Polygram. You know. The Costner one. On the way to the set right now."

Pellam couldn't recall whether he owed multimillion-dollar producer Lefkowitz anything at the moment or whether Lefkowitz owed *him*. But Pellam took on a the creditor's attitude when he said, "I need some help here, Lefty."

"You bet, Johnny. Talk to me."

"You know all the big boys out here on the Right Coast."

"Some."

"Roger McKennah."

"We rub elbows. He's on the film board at Columbia. A trustee. Or NYU. I don't remember."

"I want to get in to see him. Or let's say I want to look *at* him. Socially. His crib. Not the battlefields."

Silence from the other coast. Then: "So . . . Why'd you be interested in that?"

"Research."

"Ha. Research. Poking around. Gimme a minute." Lefty remained on the line but grunted, somewhat breathlessly – as if he was making love though Pellam knew he was leaning across a massive desk and flipping through his address book. "Well, how's this?"

"How's what, Lefty?"

"You wanta go to a party. You live to party, right?"

The last party Pellam could recall attending had been two or three years ago. He said, "I'm a party animal, Lefty."

"McKennah pokes the social beast all the time. Drop my name and you'll get in. I'll make some calls. Find out where and when. I'll call Spielberg." (Spielberg's assistant, he meant. And the call would finally end up with an assistant's assistant located in an entirely different town than the chief raider of the lost ark was in.)

"My undying gratitude, Lefty. I mean it."

"So," the producer said coyly, "research, huh, John?"

"Research."

Silence while the signals of ambition bounced off a satellite somewhere in cold space and shot back down to earth. "I've been hearing things, John."

"What? That Oakland's losing and the Cardinals're winning?"

"Somebody in some post-pro house out here was telling somebody I know you've booked editing time."

"That's a lot of somebodies," Pellam observed.

"And that's not the only thing I've heard."

"Isn't it?"

"A couple studios've tried to get you to scout for them but the word is you're out of the scouting business."

Somebody told somebody about something.

The Word in Hollywood was as quick as the Word on the streets of Hell's Kitchen.

"Naw, naw, I'm just on vacation."

"Oh. Sure. Got it. And you need a good editor to clean up that footage you took of Mickey and Goofy when you were at Epcot. Sure."

"Something like that."

"Come on, John. I always had faith in you."

A safe way of saying that whatever had gone down, however bad it looked for Pellam (and it'd looked pretty bad at one time), Lefkowitz hadn't abandoned him. Which was, with some creative recasting, slightly true.

"It's always warmed my heart knowing that."

"So? You're trying to get something on, aren't you?"

"It's a little thing, Lefty. A small project. You wouldn't be interested. All I need at this point is domestic distribution."

"You got *financing*? And I didn't hear about it?" He whispered this.

"It's a *very* small project."

"Your Palm D'or and your L.A. Film Critics award were for small projects too, you'll recall."

"Distribution, I was saying."

Producers love distribution-only deals because if the film bombs they don't lose millions. It's a percentage arrangement. The execs don't get the Academy awards and they don't get as rich but they don't get as poor either and hence don't get fired as soon.

"My ears're turned your way, Pellam. Talk to me."

"I'm in a meeting now—"

"Yeah, with who?"

"A lawyer. Can't really go into it." Pellam winked at Bailey.

"Wall Street? Which firm?"

"Hush, hush," Pellam whispered.

"What's going on, John? This could be big. A new Pellam feature."

If Lefkowitz found out he was slavering over a documentary he'd hang up the phone in an instant and the Pellam he had always been behind one hundred per cent would cease to exist. Distribution for the art-house circuit meant selling the film to a total of about one hundred screens around the country, like the Film Forum in New York and the Biograph in Chicago. Feature films went to thousands of multiplexes.

Pellam, deciding he didn't feel guilty, said, "You get me in to see McKennah and I'll have my lawyer here give you a call." There was a pause that screenwriters call a beat. "I may have to burn some bridges but I'd do it. For you."

"Love you, Johnny. I mean that. Sincerely. Oh, about McKennah, you know he's unchained shit, don't you?"

"I just want to crash his party, Lefty. I don't want to sleep with him."

"You have that lawyer call me."

They hung up.

"Was that," Bailey asked, "a Hollywood person?"

"To the core."

"Do you really want me to call him?"

"I wouldn't do that to you, Louis. But I do have a legal question."

Bailey tipped the jug of wine into his cup once more.

Pellam asked, "What's the sentence for carrying an unlicensed pistol in New York City?"

There were probably some questions that gave the lawyer pause and some that surprised him. This wasn't in either of those categories. He answered as if Pellam had asked him about the weather. "Not good here. It's technically a mandatory sentence but the judge has some discretion. Unless of course you're a felon. Then it's a year mandatory. Riker's Island. And the sentence comes with several large boyfriends, whether you want them or not. You're not talking about yourself, are you?"

"I'm just asking theoretically."

The lawyer's eyes narrowed. "Is there something about you I should know?"

"No. There's nothing you should know."

Bailey nodded to the window. "What do you need a gun for anyway? Look outside, young man. You see tumbleweeds? You see cowpokes? Indians? This isn't the streets of Laredo."

"I don't think that's a lock, Louis."

———◆◆◆———

8

From somewhere in his apartment building Pellam heard that song again, strident and loud. It must've been number one on the rap charts.

"*. . . now don't be blind . . . Open your eyes and whatta you find?*"

A large stack of videocassettes sat at his feet, representing several months' worth of taping. They weren't edited yet or even organized beyond subject and date written in his sloppy handwriting on first-aid tape stuck to each cassette. He found one and slipped it into a cheap VCR that rested precariously on a cheaper TV.

Through the wall came the steady bass thud of the song.

"*It's a white man's world. It's a white man's world.*"

The screen of the cheap Motorola flickered reluctantly to life, showing this:

Ettie Wilkes Washington sat comfortably in front of the camera. She'd wanted to be filmed in her favorite rocker, an oak relic her husband Billy Doyle had bought for her. But even the slight rocking motion had been a distraction and he'd moved her to a straight-backed chair. (As a young assistant Pellam had worked on *Jaws* and remembered Spielberg telling the director of photography to bolt the camera to the deck of Robert Shaw's boat during the location shots. The seasoned DP wisely suggested that they better shoot handheld – or else risk sending sea-sick audiences racing for rest-rooms around the country.)

So Pellam had moved her to an overstuffed armchair. He'd wanted her in front of a window, with the construction work going on outside. You could also see, in the frame, another antique – an old rolltop desk, filled with papers and letters. On the wall behind it hung a dozen pictures of family.

"You asking 'bout Billy Doyle, my husband? I'll tell you, he was a funny man. Nobody like him I ever met. I'll tell you what he looked like first of all. He was handsome, yessir. Tall and, well, you know, very white. We'd walk down the street together. He always made me take his arm. Didn't matter whether we were uptown near San Juan Hill, where the blacks were mostly, and they didn't like mixed couples, or in Hell's Kitchen, where it was white. The Irish and Italian boys there didn't like mixed couples either. We got glares from everybody. But he always had me on his arm. Day or night.

"And he'd always go to clubs with me when I sang. He'd sit at a table with a whisky in front of him – the man loved his whisky – sit there, th'only white man in the whole place and he kept getting looks. But after a while

*nobody'd pay any attention to him. I'd look down from the
stage and there he'd be, eating chitlins and talking with a
couple, three men, smiling up at me, knocking them on the
shoulders and saying I was his gal. Then I'd look down
and see him arguing. I knew he was talking 'bout Billie
Holliday and Bessie Smith.*

*"But the thing about him was he never found himself.
And that was hard for a man. Hardest thing there is,
a man who doesn't come into his own. Sometimes he
doesn't really have to find it. Sometimes he just ends
up someplace and digs his heels in and some years go
by and that's who he is and he's all right with that. But
Billy was always looking. What he wanted most was land.
To own something. That's the funny thing – it's why we
never really had a home, because he wasted all his time on
these schemes to get a building, get some land. He wanted
it bad and that was why he served that time in jail."*

Documentary filmmakers should never intrude. But off camera
a surprised Pellam asked, "He did time?"

But just then Ettie shifted in her chair and looked up, turned
her head. Pellam remembered that Florence Besserman, Ettie's
friend from the third floor, had come to the door unexpectedly.
The tape went blank. She'd never finished the story about Billy
Doyle's criminal history and Pellam had agreed to come back
– on the night of the fire, as it had turned out – to record
the details. Pellam now rewound the tape to the beginning
and found what he'd been looking for. Not Ettie but some
footage of pretty, pudgy Anita Lopez, apartment 2A, who
spoke in her machine gun voice, her fire-engine-red nails

flying everywhere, despite Pellam's reminders to keep her hands still.

". . . *Sí, sí*, we got gangs. Just like what you see in the movies. They got guns, they get into trouble, they drink, they got cars. Boom-boom, these big speakers. *Ai!* So loud. Used to be the Westies. They gone now. What we got is we got the *Cubano* Lords, they is the big gang now. They got a apartment and they don't mind if everybody know where. I tell you. On Thirty-ninth, between Ninth and Tenth. Oh, they scare me. Don't say nothing to nobody I told you. Please."

Pellam shut the VCR off. He dropped to his knees and inventoried the canvas bag, which contained everything an astute documentarian ought to have: the Betacam, the Ampex deck, the Nicad battery pack, two extra cassettes, a cardioid mike with sponge wind guard, steno notebook, pens. And a Colt Peacemaker single-action pistol. Five of the six chambers loaded with .45-caliber shells. The rosewood grip was battered and sweat-stained.

He was thinking of what his mother had told him just before he'd left the placid town of Simmons, N.Y., en route to Manhattan last May. "That's a crazy city down there, New York is. You keep an eye out, Johnny. You just never know."

Pellam had lived long enough to understand that, no, you never did.

He walked west along the sweltering concrete of Thirty-ninth Street. On a doorstep sat a heavy woman, holding a long, dark cigarette and rocking a dilapidated baby carriage. She read *el diario*.

"*Buenos días*," Pellam said.

"*Buenas tardes*." The woman's eyes swept over Pellam, examining the jeans, the black jacket and white T-shirt.

"I wonder if you could help me."

She looked up, exhaled as if she were smoking.

"I'm making a movie about Hell's Kitchen." He held up the camera bag. "About the gangs here."

"*No* gangs *aquí*."

"Well, some of the young people. Teenagers. I didn't mean to say 'gang.'"

"*Faltan* gangs. No gangs."

"Somebody told me about the *Cubano* Lords."

"*Es un* club."

"Club. They have a clubhouse here, right? *Un apartmento?* I heard it was on this street."

"*Buenos muchachos*. No shit happen 'round here. They make sure of that."

"I'd like to talk to them."

"Nobody come here, nobody bother us. They good *hombres*."

"That's why I want to talk to them."

"And look at *las calles*." She waved her hand up and down the street. "They clean, or what?"

"Could you give me the name of who's in charge? Of the club?"

"I don't know none of them. You no hot in that jacket?"

"Yeah, I am. I heard they hang out around here."

She laughed and returned to the paper.

Pellam left her and crisscrossed the neighborhood – over to the river and back again, skirting the squat, black Javits Convention Center. He didn't find what he was looking for (which is what? he wondered. A half-dozen young men standing around like George Chakiris and the Sharks in *West Side Story*?).

A young Latino family walked toward him – the couple in tank tops and shorts, a teen girl in a short tight dress. They lugged a cooler and blankets and toys and lawn chairs. Dad's day off, they were headed for Central Park, Pellam guessed. He was watching the family vanish toward the subway when he saw the man on top of the building.

He was about Pellam's age, a few years younger maybe. Latino. He wore close-fitting jeans and a T-shirt, brilliantly white. He stood on the roof of a tenement, looking down, with dark eyes that even from this distance seemed to beam displeasure.

The man leapt from one building to another and was directly above him. Pellam could see only a silhouette. He was making his way east, along the roofs of the tenements.

Pellam turned and headed in the same direction. He paused at the corner, lost sight of the young man. Then, a sudden flash of white disappeared into a crowd of workers along Tenth Avenue. Crossing the street fast, Pellam tried to follow but the man had vanished. How the hell had he done that? He asked the workers if they'd seen anyone but they claimed they hadn't seen anybody and the alley they stood in front of – the only place the man could have escaped – was blind. Barred windows. No doors. No exit.

Pellam gave up and returned to Thirty-sixth Street, wandering toward the charred remains of Ettie's building.

It wasn't the noise that warned him but its absence; some raucous hammering from the construction site across the street suddenly dulled, the sound absorbed by the young man's body and clothing. Without even looking sideways at the running footsteps Pellam set the bag down and reached inside. He hadn't yet found the Colt when a piece of metal – a pistol barrel, he guessed – touched the back of his neck.

"The alley," the voice said in a melodic, Spanish accent. "Lessgo."

9

H is thick brows were knitted together and beneath them his lids dipped slightly as if he was nursing a deep grudge.

They stood in the alley behind Louis Bailey's building, on greasy cobblestones. The smell of rotten vegetables and rancid oil filled the heavy air. Pellam stood, crossed his arms, glancing down at the tiny black automatic pistol.

Then he studied his captor again. A pink, leathery scar traversed the man's forearm. It was recent. On his hand, in the *Y* between his thumb and forefinger, was a blurred tattoo in the form of a dagger. Pellam lived in L.A.; he recognized a crew insignia when he saw one.

Pellam asked, "*Habla inglés?*"

The man looked down into the bag. Keeping the automatic trained on Pellam's chest he bent down and lifted the Betacam partially out.

"Appreciate your leaving that alone. It's—"

"Shut up."

The man didn't find the Colt. He lowered the camera, stood up.

"You're a *Cubano* Lord," Pellam said.

He was as tall as Pellam. Most Latinos he knew were shorter. "I've been looking for you," Pellam said.

"Me?"

"One of you."

"Why?"

"To have a talk."

His eyebrows twitched in surprise. "You talking now."

"I'm doing a film on Hell's Kitchen. I want to talk to some of the people in gangs. Or is it a club?"

"The other day, what you doing?"

"The other day?"

"What you looking for? Talking to people? On the street here. You taking pictures. What you do that for?"

Pellam remained silent.

The young man let a disgusted sigh case from his lungs. "You gonna say we did it? You gonna say we torch that building?"

"I'm making a film. I—"

The terse young man's brows nestled closer. "There a TV news show here. In the city. Latino station. You never hear of it, I know. They slogan is '*Primero con la verdad.*' You believe in that? Is *la verdad siempre primero* with you? The truth?" Arms crossed again, he lifted a hand to his chin and with a callous thumb rubbed a short, deep scar below his mouth. "You some kind of *reporter?* You some kind of Geraldo?"

Pellam nodded toward the cobblestoned alley. "This where you play basketball? Have bake sales? Pony rides for the kids? All those things a club does?"

"What're you asking me, man?"

"I heard some of your boys were hanging out here just before the fire."

"You *heard* . . . So that make it true? A *white* man say *los Cubanos* burn down a building, so it true. A *black* man say it, so it true." Pellam didn't answer and he continued, "You no think this old nigger lady do it. You think *I* do it. Why? 'Cause you like niggers more'n you like spics."

Pellam didn't think more anger could be inside the young man but more anger now flooded his face. He shifted his weight on expensive running shoes and Pellam wondered if he was going to shoot. He glanced sideways for a place to roll. Wondered if he could get to his Colt in time. Decided he couldn't.

Make the call – apologize or get tough?

Pellam frowned, leaned forward. He spat back, "I'm here to do a job. You don't want to answer my questions, that's your damn business. But I'm not interested in any fucking lectures."

The dark eyes narrowed suddenly.

I'm gonna get shot. Hell. Should've kissed ass. Knew it.

But the man didn't pull the trigger. And he didn't pistol-whip him either – the second option, Pellam'd figured.

He put the gun away and walked around the front of Ettie's building, gesturing Pellam after him. He ducked under the police line and walked up the stairs to what was left of the tiny entryway. Pellam dug the Colt out of the bag and slipped it into the back waistband of his jeans. He lifted the bag and walked out to the sidewalk.

With a booted foot the young Latino was kicking in the shattered front door of Ettie's building. He shouldered his way inside, filthying his T-shirt on the charred wood. Pellam heard breaking glass and loud crashes. The man returned a minute later with a rectangle of metal. He tossed it to Pellam, who caught the heavy frame. It was the building directory. With a long finger the *Cubano* Lord tapped a name. *C. Ramirez.* "She my aunt. Okay? She live there with two *niños*. My mother's sister! Okay? You figure it out? I'm not gonna burn down no building my family living in.

"And you wanna know something else? That lady, my aunt Carmella, she see one of Jimmy Corcoran's micks drop the hammer on some guy last month and she testify against him. He up in Attica now and Jimmy, he no so happy about what she say. How you like *that* story, my friend? You like the truth now? The truth about a white mick? Now, get outta here. Get outta the Kitchen."

"Who's that? Corcoran? Jimmy Corcoran?"

The man wiped the sweat off his forehead. "You go back to you news station, you go back and tell them the *Cubano* Lords, they no do this kind of shit!"

"I'm not a reporter."

"So now you no have to *talk* to me. You know *la verdad.*"

Pellam asked, "Your name's Ramirez? What's your first name?"

The man paused and held a muscular finger to his lips, silencing him, then pointed it at Pellam's face. "You tell them." His eyes sank down to Pellam's boots then rose again as if he were memorizing him. Then he walked slowly out of the shadow of the ruined building into the crisp hot sunlight.

But Jimmy Corcoran was a ghost.

No one had heard of him, no one knew *any* Corcorans.

Pellam had wandered around the neighborhood, stopping in Puerto Rican bodegas, Korean vegetable stands, Italian pork stores. Nobody knew Corcoran but everybody had a funny lilt in their voices when they said they didn't – their denials seemed desperate.

He tried a bodega. "He hangs out around here someplace," Pellam encouraged.

The ancient Mexican clerk, with an immensely wrinkled face, stared at his fly-blown tray of lardy pastry, smoked his cigarette and nodded silently. He offered nothing.

Pellam bought a coconut drink and stepped outside. He ambled up to a cluster of T-shirted men lounging around a Y-stand sprinkler hookup and asked them. Two of them quickly said they'd never heard of Jimmy Corcoran. The other three forgot whatever English they knew.

He decided to try further west, closer to the river. He was walking past the parochial school on Eleventh when he heard, "Yo."

"Yo yourself," Pellam said.

The boy stood in a tall, battered Dumpster and looked down, hands on scrawny hips. He wore baggy jeans and, despite the heat, a red, green and yellow windbreaker. Pellam thought the mosaic haircut was pretty well done. The razor notch mimicked the grin that was etched deep into his dark face.

"Whassup?"

"Tell you what . . . Come on down here."

"Why?"

"I want to talk to you. Don't jump, climb around the back. No—"

He jumped. The boy landed on the ground, unhurt. "You don't 'member me."

"Sure I do. Your mother's Sibbie."

"Straight up! You be CNN. The man with the camera."

On the playground behind him four baseball diamonds stood empty. Two basketball courts too. The gates were chained. Easily a hundred cans of paint had been sacrificed to decorate the yard.

"Where's your mother and sister?"

"Be at the shelter."

"Why aren't you in school?"

"Ain't no school, be summer."

Pellam had forgotten. Despite heat or snow, cities are virtually seasonless. He had trouble imagining what summer vacation in Hell's Kitchen might be like. Pellam's Augusts had been filled with sneaking into movies and trading comics and occasional softball games. He remembered many summer mornings bicycling like a demon, zipping over smooth concrete marked by the slick paths of confused snails and slugs.

"What's your name?"

"Ismail. Yo, what's yours?"

"I'm John Pellam."

"Yo, homes, I ain't like John. Slob nigger I know called John. He ain't down to do nothing, you know what I'm saying? I'ma call you Pellam."

Wasn't *Mr* an option?

"How's the shelter?"

His smile faded. "This nigger don't like the peoples there. Slanging all the time. Cluckheads all over the place."

Drugs, the boy was saying. A cluckhead was a crack addict.

Pellam had worked on several films in South Central L.A. He knew some gangspeak.

"It's only for a little while," Pellam said. But the reassurance sounded leaden; he had no idea how the boy took it.

Ismail's eyes suddenly flashed happily. "Yo, you like basketball? I like Patrick Ewing. He the best, you know what I'm saying? I like Michael Jordan too. Yo, ever see the Bulls play?"

"I live in L.A."

"Lakers! Yeah! Magic, he be fine. I like Mr B. The Barkley. He the man to have at yo' back ina fight." He sparred against an unseen adversary. "Yo, yo, you like basketball, cuz?"

Pellam had been to a few Lakers games though he gave that up when he found that a good percentage of the spectators were in the Industry and bought season passes just to see or be seen. As Jack Nicholson does, so shall you do. "Not really," he confessed.

"And Shaq too. Man be ten feet tall. I wanna be that nigger."

Ismail danced around on the sidewalk and performed a mini slam dunk.

Pellam glanced at the boy's tattered high-tops and dropped to his knees to retie a dangling lace. This made the boy uncomfortable; he stepped back and clumsily tied it himself. Pellam rose slowly. "You started to tell me something the other day. About the gangs burning down your building. Your mother hit you when you started to tell me something. I won't say anything to her."

He looked surprised, as if he'd forgotten the slap.

"I heard Corcoran's gang might've had something to do with it. You know 'bout his crew?"

"How you know Corcoran?"

"I don't. I'm trying to find him."

"Man, that fucked-up, you doin' that. His set, they some bad O.G.s."

Original gangstas. Senior members of the crew, who'd earned the status by killing someone.

The young face grew agitated. "Nigger, spic – anybody – dis him, don't matter who, Corcoran wax him. He see peoples he don't like, bang, they ass be *gone*, you know what I'm saying?" Ismail closed his eyes and leaned his head against the fence, looking at the school. "Why you axing me all this shit?"

Pellam asked, "Where's his kickback? Corcoran's?"

Impressed that Pellam talked the talk, Ismail said, "I ain't know were they hang, man." He kept his eye on Pellam and did a few layup shots. "Yo. You got a daddy?"

Pellam laughed. "A father? Sure."

The grin was gone. "I don't got one."

Pellam reflected that a large percentage of black households were missing an adult male. Then felt ashamed this news bite was his immediate reaction to the boy's comment.

The boy continued, matter of factly, "Got hisself shot."

"Hey, I'm sorry, Ismail."

"There these cluckheads outside on the street, okay? Selling rock. My daddy go out and they just smoke him right there. I seen 'em do it. He didn't do nothing. They just smoke him."

Pellam exhaled in shock, shook his head. "They find who did it?"

"Who, the jakes?"

"Jakes?"

"You know, jakes. Joey. The man. The *Man*. The poe-leece?"

Ismail laughed with a frighteningly adult sound. "Jakes do shit, you know what I'm saying? My daddy gone. And my mama, she sleep a lot. She do copious shit. Where she be, the shelter I'm saying, there shit all over the place if you got the green. Rock mostly. She do lotsa rock. Men come by eyeballing her all the time. I don't think I go back there. Where yo' crib, Pellam?"

A Winnebago, currently stored. A two-bedroom bungalow in L.A., currently sublet. A four-flight walk-up under short-term lease.

"I don't really have one," he told the boy.

"Check it out, you just like me! *Damn!*"

Pellam laughed at this then decided the parallels were unsettlingly accurate.

John Pellam, single, former independent film director and itinerant location scout, sometimes missed family life. But then he'd laugh and try to picture himself attending a suburban grade school PTA parent-teacher night.

"Where're you going to go?" he asked the boy.

"Dunno, cuz. Maybe get my own crew together. Ain't no nigger crews 'round here. Get a kickback on Thirty-sixth. I'ma call it the Trey Six Ghosts. How that sound? 'I from the Trey Sixes.' Shit, that'll fuck 'em up. Fuck up their minds good."

Pellam asked, "You have lunch?"

"No. And I ain't have breakfast neither," Ismail said proudly. "You sit at the shelter, men come up and they, you know, be dissing you and touching you. They ax you come into the back with them. You know what I'm saying?"

Pellam shook his head, gripped the strap of the camera bag. "Come on, I'm hungry. I saw this place up the street. Cuban. Let's eat, you want to?"

"Rice and beans. Yeah! An' a Red Stripe!"

"No beer," Pellam said.

The boy grabbed the bag from Pellam's hand and slung it over his shoulder. He listed against what was probably half of his own weight.

"I'll get that," Pellam said. "It's heavy."

"Shit. Don't weigh nothing."

"Yo, over there."

"There?"

"No, more back. Yeah. Yo. *Back* is what I'm saying. *Back!*"

Ismail was pointing out to Pellam where he thought the fire had started. "I smell smoke then see all these flames, cuz. Right here. An' a big pop. Yeah."

"Pop."

"And I run inside th'apartment and I go, 'Yo, all y'all gotta get out! There this fire!' And my mama, she start to scream."

"You see anybody by the window before the fire?"

"This old lady is all. She live upstairs, on the top floor."

"Anybody else?"

"I dunno. People hanging. I dunno."

Pellam looked at what was left of the back door. It was metal and had two large locks on it. Would've been a tough job to break through. He leaned down and peered through the window. He'd wondered if the pyro could have thrown the bomb through the bars. But they were too close together for anything but a beer bottle; the wine jug never would have fit. Somebody would have to've let him in.

"The back door was locked right?"

"Yeah, they try an' keep it locked. But, shit, there a lotta traffic, you know what I'm saying? In that back place there, see it, Pellam? This fag doing business, you know? Givin' head and all. He a cluckhead too."

A male prostitute . . . "So people'd come through the back door? His customers?"

"Yeah, we'd sit outside, some of us, what it is, and these guys'd come out the back door and we'd say, 'Fag, fag . . .' And they'd run away. Shit, that was fun!"

"You seen that guy around lately?"

"Naw, cuz. He gone."

Pellam picked up the building directory, lying where he'd let it fall after Ramirez had tossed it to him the other day. "You know this Ramirez?"

"Shit, Hector Ramirez? His crew be the *Cubano* Lords. They bad motherfuckers too but they don't give this nigger no shit. Not like Corcoran. He's sprung, cuz, Corcoran is. Man be a hatter. But Ramirez, see, he'd wax you but only if he *had* to."

Even this ten-year-old was better patched in to the Word on the street than Pellam. He glanced at the name *E. Washington* on the directory and tossed it to the ground.

A police car cruised slowly past the building and paused. The officer in the driver's seat was looking his way. He gestured Pellam out of the police tape.

"Ismail—"

The boy was gone.

"Ismail?"

The squad car drove on.

He searched for several minutes but Ismail had vanished. A brittle sound of falling brick and hollow metal filled the night. A soft grunt followed.

"Ismail?" Pellam stepped into the alley behind the building and saw a boy, about eighteen, blond, in faded blue jeans and a dirty white shirt. He crouched beside a pile of trash. He was digging something out, occasionally dislodging a small avalanche, leaping back like a spooked raccoon then digging again. He had fine, baby hair, self-cut, ear length. The obligatory Generation X goatee was anemic and untrimmed.

He glanced at Pellam, squinted then returned to his task.

"Gotta get some *stuff*, man. Some stuff."

"You lived here?"

The boy said gravely, "In the back." He nodded toward where the rear basement apartment had been. "Me and Ray, he was like my manager."

Me and Ray, he was like his pimp.

This was the one Ismail was talking about. The male prostitute. He seemed so young for a life on the street. Pellam asked, "Where's Ray now?"

"Dunno."

"Can I ask you some questions about the fire?"

With a grunt of exertion he pulled what he'd been looking for from beneath the pile and wiped at the cover of the book. *Kurt Cobain – the Final Year*. He gazed at it lovingly for a moment then he looked up. "That's what I was going to talk to *you* about, man. The fire. You Pellam, right?" He flipped through the book.

Pellam blinked in surprise.

"So, here's the deal. I can tell you who started the fire and who hired them. If you're, like, interested."

———◆◆◆———

10

"How'd you know about me?"

"Just did." The boy caressed the glossy cover of the book with a filthy hand.

"How?" Pellam persisted, as curious as he was suspicious.

"You know. Like, you hear things."

"Tell me what you know. I'm not a cop."

His laugh said he already knew this about him.

The Word. On the street.

The boy's attention returned to his book, like a child's Golden Book, just a photo laminated on a cardboard cover. The type was large and the words sparse. The photos were terrible.

Pellam prompted, "So who set the fire? Who hired him?"

In a very young face, the very old eyes narrowed. Then the boy broke out into a laugh.

Gear-greasing is expensive work.

Pellam mentally totaled his two savings accounts and an anemic IRA, penalty for early withdrawal, and some remaining advance money from WGBH. The figure eighty-five hundred floated into his mind. There was a little equity left in the house on Beverly Glen. The battered Winnebago had to be worth something. But that was it. Pellam's lifestyle was often liquid but his resources largely were not.

The boy wiped his nose. "A hundred thousand."

He thought a grunge-stud like this would have more modest aspirations. Pellam didn't even bother to negotiate. He asked, "How'd you find out about the fire?"

"The guy who did it, I sorta know him. He's a hatter. Crazy dude, you know. He gets off burning things."

The pyro Bailey had told him about – the one A.D.A. Lois Koepel, whom Pellam already detested, was so eager to track down.

"He told you who hired him?"

"Like, not exactly but you can figure it out. From what he told me."

"What's your name?"

"You, like, don't need to know it."

You, like, know mine.

"I could give you one," the boy continued. "But so what? It wouldn't be real."

"Well, I don't have a hundred thousand bucks. Nowhere near."

"Bullshit. You're, like, this famous director or something. You're from Hollywood. Of *course* you got money."

In front of them the police cruiser eased down the street again. Pellam thought about tackling the skinny kid and calling the cops over.

But all it took was one look into Pellam's eyes.

"Oh, nice *try*, you asshole," the boy shouted. Clutching the precious book under his arm, he burst down the alley.

Pellam waved futilely at the police car. The two cops inside didn't see him. Or they ignored the gestures. Then he was racing through the alley, boots pounding grittily on the cobblestones, after the kid. They streaked through two vacant lots behind Ettie's building and emerged onto Ninth Avenue. Pellam saw the boy turn right, north, and keep sprinting.

When the kid got to Thirty-ninth Street Pellam lost him. He paused, hands on hips, gasping. He examined the parking lots, the approaches to the Lincoln Tunnel, the rococo tenements, bodegas and a sawdust-strewn butcher shop. Pellam tried a deli but no one in there had seen him. When he stepped out into the street Pellam noticed, a half block away, a door swinging open. The boy sprinted out, lugging a knapsack, and vanished in a mass of people. Pellam didn't even bother to pursue. In the crowded streets the boy simply turned invisible.

The doorway the kid had come out of was a store-front, windows painted over, black. He remembered seeing it earlier. The Youth Outreach Center. Inside he saw a dingy fluorescent-lit room sparsely furnished with mismatched desks and chairs. Two women stood talking in the center of the room, arms crossed, somber.

Pellam entered just as the thinner of the two women lifted her arms helplessly and pushed through a doorway that led to the back of the facility.

The other woman's pale, round face was glossy with faint makeup, barely hiding a spray of freckles. She wore her red hair shoulder-length. He guessed she was in her mid thirties. She wore an old sweatshirt and a pair of old jeans, which didn't disguise her voluptuous figure. The long-sleeved top, maroon, bore the Harvard crest. *Veritas*.

Pellam had a fast memory of the *Cubano* Lord. *Verdad*, he recalled.

Primero con la verdad.

She glanced up at him with some curiosity as he stepped inside. She glanced at his camera bag. He introduced himself and the woman said, "I'm Carol Wyandotte. The director here. Can I help you?" She adjusted a pair of thick tortoiseshell glasses, a break in the frame fixed with white adhesive tape – shoving the loose glasses back up her nose. Pellam thought she was pretty the way a peasant or farm girl would be. Absurdly, she wore a choker of pearls.

"A kid left here a minute ago. Blond, grungy."

"Alex? We were just talking about him. He ran inside, grabbed his backpack and left. We were wondering what was going on."

"I was talking to him down the street. He just ran off."

"*Talking* to him?"

Pellam didn't want to say that the boy knew about the arson. For the youngster's sake. The Word on the Street traveled far too fast. He remembered the gun in Ramirez's hand and how the whole world seemed terrified of Jimmy Corcoran.

"You can," Carol said dryly, "tell me the truth." Shoved her glasses onto her nose.

Pellam cocked an eyebrow.

"Happens all the time. One of our kids cops a wallet or something. Then somebody comes in, blushing, and says, 'I think one of your boys "found" my wallet.'"

Pellam decided she was a smart, rich girl turned social

worker. Which was probably a very tough category of person to deal with.

"Well, he might be a great thief but he didn't steal anything from me. I'm making a film and—"

"A reporter?" Carol's face went ice cold – much angrier than if he'd accused Alex of "finding" his wallet. He thought: her eyes are remarkable. Pale, pale blue. Almost blending into the surrounding white.

"Not exactly." He explained that *West of Eighth* was an oral history.

"I don't like reporters." A bit of brogue slipped into Carol's voice and he had a clue to the feistiness inside her – a grit that the director of a place like this undoubtedly needed. A temper too. "All those damn stories on preteen addicts and gang rapes and child prostitutes. Makes it hard as hell to get money when the boards of foundations turn on *Live at Five* and see that the little girl you're trying to rehabilitate is an illiterate hooker with HIV. But, of course, it's exactly kids like that who're the ones you *need* to rehabilitate."

"Hey, ma'am," Pellam held up his hand. "I'm just a lowly oral historian here."

The hardness in Carol's round face melted. "Sorry, sorry. My friends say I can't pass a soapbox without climbing on top. You were saying, about Alex? You were interviewing him?"

"I've been talking to people in the building that burned down. He lived there."

"Off and on," Carol corrected. "With his chicken hawk."
Me and Ray.

She continued, "You know Juan Torres?"

Pellam nodded. "He's in critical condition."

The son of the man who met Jose Canseco.

Carol shook her head. "It just kills me to see something like that happen to the good ones. It's such a damn waste."

"You don't have any idea where Alex took off to?"

"Ran in, ran out. Don't have a clue."

"Where's home?"

"He claimed he was from Wisconsin somewhere. Probably is . . . I'm sorry, I've forgotten your name."

"Pellam."

"First?"

"John Pellam. Go by the last usually."

"You don't like John?"

"Let's say I don't lead a very Biblical life. Any chance he'll come back?"

"Impossible to say. The working boys – you know what I mean by 'working' – only stay here when they're sick or between hawks. If he's scared about something he'll go to ground and it could be six months before we see him again. If ever. You live in the city?"

"I'm from the Coast. I'm renting in the East Village."

"The Village? Shit, Hell's Kitchen sleaze beats *their* sleaze hands down. So, give me your number. And if our wandering waif comes home I'll let you know."

Pellam wished he hadn't thought of her as a peasant. He couldn't dislodge the thought. Peasants were earthy, peasants were lusty. Especially red-haired peasants with freckles. He found himself calculating that the last time he'd slept with a woman they'd wakened in the middle of the night to the sound of winds pelting the side of his Winnebago with wet snow. Today the temperature had reached 99.

He pushed those thoughts aside though they didn't go as far away as he wanted them to.

There was a dense pause. Pellam asked impulsively, "Listen, you want to get some coffee?"

She reached for her nose, to adjust the glasses, then changed her mind and took them off. She gave an embarrassed laugh and readjusted the glasses again. Then she gave a tug at the hem of her sweatshirt. Pellam had seen the gesture before and sensed that a handful of insecurities – probably about her weight and clothes – was flooding into her thoughts.

Something in him warned against saying, "You look fine," and he chose something more innocuous. "Gotta warn you, though. I don't do espresso."

She brushed her hair into place with thick fingers. Laughed.

He continued, "None of that Starbucks, Yuppie, French-roast crap. It's American or nothing."

"Isn't it Colombian?"

"Well, *Latin* American."

Carol joked, "You probably like it in unrecyclable Styrofoam too."

"I'd spray it out of an aerosol can if they made it that way."

"There's a place up the street," she said. "A little deli I go to."

"Let's do it."

Carol called, "Be back in fifteen."

A response in Spanish, which Pellam couldn't make out, came from the back room.

He opened the door for her. She brushed against him on the way out. Had she done so on purpose?

Eight months, Pellam found himself thinking. Then told himself to step.

They sat on the curb near Ettie's building. At their feet were two blue coffee cartons depicting dancing Greeks. Carol wiped her forehead with the souvenir Cambridge cotton and asked, "Who's he?" Pellam turned and looked where Carol was pointing.

Ismail and his tricolor windbreaker had mysteriously returned. He now played in the cab of the bulldozer that had been leveling the lot beside Ettie's building. "Yo, my man, careful up there," Pellam called. He explained to Carol about Ismail, his mother and sister.

"The shelter in the school? It's one of the better ones," Carol said. "They'll probably get them into an SRO in a month or so. Single room occupancy – a residence hotel. At least if they're lucky."

"So, you know the neighborhood pretty well?" he asked.

"Cut my social work teeth here."

"You'd know the good stuff then. The stuff that we *touristas* never find out."

"Try me." Carol glanced at the tooling on Pellam's battered black Nokona cowboy boots.

"The gangs," he said.

"The crews? Sure, I *know* about them. But I don't deal much with them. See, if a kid's in a set he's gonna get all the support he needs. Believe it or not, they're better adjusted than the lone wolves."

"Yo," Ismail called to Carol. "I going back to L.A. with my homie there," he said, pointing at Pellam.

"I don't recall that being on the agenda, young man." He raised his eyebrows to Carol.

"No, no, it's cool, cuz. I come with you. Hook up with a Blood or Crip crew. I get myself jumped in with them. Be cool. You know what I'm saying." He vanished down the alley.

"Give me a lesson," Pellam said. "Gangs 101 in Hell's Kitchen."

Carol's glasses had reappeared and he wanted to tell her she looked better without them. He knew better than that.

"Gangs, huh? Where do I start? All the way back to the Gophers?" Carol smiled coyly. Then she laughed in surprise when Pellam said, "I heard One-Lung Curran's outa business now."

"You know more than you're letting on."

Pellam remembered an interview with Ettie Washington.

"... *Battle Row, Thirty-ninth Street, the turn of the century. Grandma Ledbetter told me what a dreadful place it was. That's where One-Lung Curran and his gang, the Gophers, hung out – in Mallet Murphy's tavern. Grandma'd go to dig in bins for scraps of gabardine, or maybe look for knuckle bones and she had to be careful 'cause the gang was always shooting it out with the police. That's where it got the name. They had real battles. Sometimes it was the Gophers that won, believe it or not, and the cops wouldn't come back for weeks, until things'd settled down.*"

He now said to Carol, "How 'bout the gangs now?"

She thought for a moment. "The Westies used to be *the* gang here and there're still some around but the Justice Department and the cops broke their back a few years ago. Jimmy Corcoran's gang's pretty much replaced them – they're the dregs of the old Irish. The *Cubano* Lords're the biggest now. Mostly Cuban but some Puerto Rican and Dominican. No black gangs to speak of. They're in Harlem and Brooklyn. The Jamaicans and Koreans are in Queens. The tongs in Chinatown. The Russians in Brighton Beach."

The director within Pellam stirred momentarily at the thought of a story about the gangs. Then he thought, Been done. Two words that are pure strychnine in Tinseltown.

Carol stretched and her breast brushed Pellam's shoulder. Accidentally or otherwise.

It had been a remarkable evening, that night eight months ago. The snow hitting the side of the camper, the wind rocking it, the blonde assistant director gripping Pellam's earlobe between very sharp teeth.

Eight months is an incredibly long time. It's three quarters of a year. Practically gestation.

"Where's Corcoran's kickback?" he asked.

"His headquarters?" Carol asked, shaking her head. "Those boys're a step away from caves. They hang out in an old bar north of here."

"Which one?"

Carol shrugged. "I don't know exactly."

She was lying.

He glanced at her pale eyes. He was letting her know she'd been nabbed.

She continued, unapologetically. "Look, you gotta understand about Corcoran . . . it's not like the gangs on TV. He's psycho.

One of his boys killed this guy'd tried to extort them. Jimmy and some of his buddies cut up the body with a hacksaw. Then they sunk the parts in Spuyten Duyvil. But Jimmy kept one of the hands as a souvenir and tossed it into a toll basket on the Jersey pike. *That's* the kind of crew you're dealing with here."

"I'll take my chances."

"You think he'll just grin and tell you his life story on camera?"

Pellam shrugged, nonchalant – though an image of hacksaws had neatly replaced the image of making love in a snow-swept Winnebago.

Carol shook her head. "Pellam, the Kitchen isn't Bed-Sty. It isn't the South Bronx or East New York . . . There, everybody *knows* it's dangerous. You just stay away. Or you know you're going to get dissed and you can see trouble coming. Here, it's all turned 'round. You got yuppie lofts, you got nice restaurants, you got murderers, whores, corporate execs, psychos, priests, gay hookers, actors . . . You're walking past a little garden at noon in front of a tenement, thinking, Hey, those're pretty flowers, and the next thing you know you're on the ground and there's a bullet in your leg or an ice pick in your back. Or maybe you're singing Irish songs in a bar and the guy next to you, somebody walks up and shoots his brains out. You never know who did it and you never know why."

"Oh, hell," Pellam said, "I *know* that Jimmy Corcoran spits poison and walks through walls. That's not news."

Carol laughed and lowered her head to Pellam's arm. He felt another sizzle from the contact, hot enough to melt January snow. She said, "Okay, sorry about the preachin'. It's in my job description. Don't say I didn't warn you. You want Jimmy, I'll give you Jimmy. The Four Eighty-eight. It's a bar on the corner of Tenth and Forty-fifth. You can probably find him there three or four days a week. But if you go, go during the day. And –" She laid a firm grip upon Pellam's arm. "– I'd recommend you take a friend."

"Yo!" Ismail jumped onto the stairs next to them. "I be his friend."

"I'm sure that'll have Corcoran quaking in his shoes."

"Fuck, yeah!"

Ismail ran off to find more earth-moving equipment. Carol kept her eyes on Pellam for a long moment. Pellam looked away first and Carol stood up. "Back to the salt mines," she said. Laughing, taking the glasses off.

As they walked back to the Youth Outreach Center she said, "You know, you're not the first creative sort I've run across. One of our Youth Outreach graduates was an author."

"Really?"

"Wrote a best-seller – about a murderer. The bad news is it was an autobiography. Call me sometime, Pellam. Here's my card."

Dannette Johnson was standing on Tenth Avenue.

This was a broad street. The buildings lining it were low and it seemed even wider because of that. The sun, sinking over New Jersey, was still very bright and hot. She stood in one of the few shaded places for blocks around, under the awning of an abandoned late night club, a relic from the eighties.

She thought: Nosir, not that one. Examining drivers who slowed and looked at her in a particular way.

Nope. Not that asshole.

Nope, not him neither.

She stood in the shade not because of the heat – she was wearing no more than eight ounces of clothing on her extravagant body – but because teenage acne had dimpled her face and she believed she was ugly.

Another car drove past, slowed almost to stopping. Like most of them here it had New Jersey plates; this was an approach to the Lincoln Tunnel, a main route for commuters who lived in the Garden State.

It was also a very easy place for a girl to make five, six hundred a night.

But not from this fellow, not today. She looked away and he drove on.

Dannette had been working the street for eight years, since she'd turned nineteen. To her, the profession was absolutely no different from any other job. Most of the johns were decent guys, who had a job they didn't really care for, bosses who didn't particularly like them, wives or girlfriends who'd stopped giving them head after the first baby.

She provided a necessary service. Like the stenographer her mother had dreamt she'd be.

A red Iroc-Z turned onto Tenth and cruised slowly toward her, the exhaust bubbling sexily. Behind the wheel was a pudgy Italian boy in an expensive, monogrammed white shirt. His moustache was trimmed carefully and he wore a gold Rolex on his left wrist. He looked like a salesman at one of the car dealerships on the West Side. "Wanna fuck?"

She smiled, leaned forward, said in a sexy voice, "Kiss my black ass. Git outa here."

As Dannette retreated to the shade again the car vanished.

A few minutes later a Toyota cruised by. Inside was a thin white man wearing a baseball cap. He looked around nervously. "Hi," he said. "How you doing today? Hot, isn't it? Sure is hot."

She looked around and then walked to the car, her high heels tapping on the concrete with loud pops.

"Yeah, hot."

"I go home this way from work," he said. "I've seen you out here."

"Yeah? Where you work?"

"A place. Up the street."

"Yeah, what kinda place?" she asked.

"Office. It's boring. I seen you a couple times. Here, I mean. On the street." He nervously cleared his throat.

This boy was *too* much.

"Yeah, I hang here some," she said.

"You're a pretty lady."

She smiled again, wondering, as she did a hundred times a day, if a plastic surgeon could smooth out her cheeks.

"So," he said.

Dannette eyed him again. Echoed, "So." After a moment she added, "Well, honey, you innerested in a date?"

"Maybe. You sure got nice boobs. You don't mind I tell you that, do you?"

"Everbody like mah tits, sugar."

"So whatta you do?" The boy wiped his face. He was sweating. He started to take his cap off but changed his mind.

"What I do?" she asked, frowning.

"Like if we were to have a date, you and me, what'd we do to have fun?"

"Oh, I tell you. I do everthing. I suck and I fuck and you can put it up my ass, you want. S'okay with me. You gonna be wearing a rubber anyways. And I got me some K-Y."

"Wow." He seemed embarrassed but she definitely had his attention. "I like it, you talking that way. Dirty talk."

"Then I'll talk t'you that way on our date."

"Man, you are one hot woman."

"Shit, honey, that ain't news," Dannette said, straight-faced.

"What's your name?"

"Dannette. What's yours?"

"Joe." There was a warehouse across the street. Joe Septimo's Hauling and Storage, painted in letters twenty feet high. Half the guys who stopped here were named "Joe."

"Well, Joe, how's that date sounding?" she leaned forward, letting him get a good look at the tits he seemed to like and letting him see they were real and that she wasn't a transvestite.

"Sounding pretty good."

He whispered something she couldn't hear. She leaned forward on the car, her hands inside now. He looked at her nine rings.

"What's that you said, honey?"

"I said, how much we talking? For our date, I mean?"

"Fo' a nice boy like you? What it is is I go down on you for fifty. You can fuck my pussy for a hundred. You can fuck my ass for two. And we can do it right in your backseat. There this alley I know 'bout. Now, whatchu—" She gasped in shock as the boy's eyes hardened and he reached into his pocket, grabbing the handcuffs in one hand and her wrists in the other. He was skinny but surprisingly strong.

"What're you doing?" she screamed.

With a click the cuffs ratcheted onto her narrow wrists.

"Well, I'll tell you what I'm doing, Dannette. I'm arresting you for soliciting sexual services in violation of the New York State Penal code. I want you to stand over there, with that lady who's coming up right behind you." The boy pulled her purse off her shoulder.

"What?" Dannette turned around, eyes wide.

The policewoman appeared behind the car and walked up to Dannette, led her to the shaded part of the sidewalk.

"Oh, shit," she said, astonishment in her voice. "You don't mean you a cop."

"Fooled you pretty good. I do that."

"Oh, shit, man. I don't believe it. I just got outa detention! Shit. I coulda swore you was just another asshole from Jersey."

Pleased with this review of his performance, the vice officer nodded to the policewoman, said, "Get her in the wagon. Take 'em downtown."

The stocky woman cop gripped Dannette by the arm and led her around the corner where a Dodge Caravan waited – an unmarked paddy wagon – and helped her up inside the vehicle, where two other prostitutes sat, bored and sweating.

"Man, they on a fucking fishin' trip," Dannette blurted. "Don't they got nothin' better to do w'their time. I mean, shit. Don't you got nothing better to do?"

"We'll get you downtown in ten, fifteen minutes," the woman said. "I'll tell 'em to turn on the air conditioning when we start moving. You, what's so funny?"

But Dannette was laughing too hard to answer.

*   *   *

More sweat. And look how these poor hands shake.

Ah, momma, can this really be the end?

Sonny walked through the construction site across from the burned-out building on Thirty-sixth Street, which, he'd decided, was rapidly becoming one of his favorite jobs of his whole career. A trophy job. Despite Pellam, the faggot Joe Buck midnight cowboy hee-haw. Or maybe *because* of him.

To be stuck inside of Mobile with the Memphis blues again . . .

Sonny paused, looking for Pellam. No sign of him. He kept hearing the music in his head, thinking of his mother, dead five years now. Thinking of her walking around the house, listening to Dylan on that thing, that *turntable*. All those records she had! LPs. Funny things, scratchy and jumpy and when you burned them they melted into weird shapes. His mother played Dylan, Dylan, Dylan all night long, month after month after month.

For a moment now he actually heard the music, thought his mother was back. He spun around. No, she wasn't there. He saw only workers, yellow hard hats, stacks of Sheetrock.

Tanks of diesel oil and gasoline and propane. Nice . . .

He continued east until he came to a grating over the subway tunnel at Eighth Avenue. He crouched behind a series of small Dumpsters, wiped the sweat from his face with his trembling hands.

Can this really be the end? . . .

Not yet, no, but soon. The end was looming. The moment of his death was approaching and Sonny knew it. While most people are consumed by a vision of what their lives might be – as egotistical as those visions were, as wrong as they'd ultimately prove – Sonny was possessed by the vision of his *death*.

This made him, he felt, Christlike. Our Savior, born to die. Our Flesh, our Blood, counting down the minutes to Calvary. Indeed, he resembled Jesus, at least the Vatican-approved, souvenir shop, Cecil-B.-DeMille version: lean, narrow of face, wispy goatee, long blonde hair, hypnotic blue eyes. Skinny.

Whoa, we're getting pretty dramatic here, Sonny thought. But when you're in love with fire, your thinking can easily become apocalyptic.

The image of his death was a complicated one and had been forming since he was a young boy. Unable to sleep he would lie in his mother's silent, still house (sometimes in her silent arms, sometimes her restless arms) and picture it, embellish, edit. He'd be in a large room, surrounded by thousands of people writhing in agony as gallons of marvelous juice, his sticky concoction, flowed over them. He'd be in the middle of the chaos, listening to their screams, smelling their burnt flesh, watching their agony as the substanceless yet undeniable fire caressed their hair and groins and breasts and fingertips. And he'd be grappling with his enemy – the Antichrist, the creature that had arrived on earth to take Sonny away. Quiet, tall, dressed in black.

Just like Pellam.

He pictured the two of them chained together as the flowing, fiery liquid surrounded them. Strong, sweating bodies entwined as the flames removed their clothes then their skin, their blood mixing. The two of them, and ten thousand others, a packed Broadway theater, a coliseum, a school auditorium.

Sonny was filled with energy and purpose. He *had* to tell the world about the coming conflagration.

And so he did. In his special way.

As the subway rumbled into the station and screeched to a stop beneath him he glanced around and poured the two gallon canister of juice through the ventilation grate. He lit and dropped in after it a novelty birthday candle – the kind that can't be blown out – stuck in a wad of modeling clay.

With a subdued *whooosh*, the flaming liquid flowed into the vents of the subway cars and inside.

"Happy birthday to you," he sang. Then regretted his flippancy, recalling that he was engaged in important work. He stood and left slowly, reluctantly, sorry that he couldn't stay longer and listen to the screams rising through the black smoke, the screams from those dying underground, beneath his feet.

Momma, can this really be the end . . .

The sirens seemed to come from all around him. They were raw, urgent, hopeless. But Sonny thought all the fuss was silly. He was just getting started; the city hadn't seen anything yet.

———◆◆◆———

11

H atake Imaham was holding court in the Women's Detention Center.

"Now listen here," she told the young women gathered around her. "Don't buy that crap. High John Conqueror root? Black-bat oil, lodestones, Bichon's two-hearts drawing candle? That be bullshit, all that crap people be trying to sell you. Just to take yo' money. Y'oughta know better."

Ettie Washington, across the cell, listened with half her attention. She hurt more today than she had right after the fire. Her arm throbbed, sending waves of pain into her jaw. Her ankle too. And her headache was blinding. She'd tried again to get some painkillers and the guards had merely stared at her the way they sometimes stared at the mice scurrying around on the floors here.

"But I know it work," one skinny woman said. "One time mah man was cheatin' and what it was—"

"Listen to me. If you got the sight you don't need them oils and candles and roots. If you ain't got the sight then there's nothing gonna do it. You come to make a sacrifice at my honfour, you leave a few pennies for Damballah. That's all you gotta do. But mosta the mambos and houngnans in New York're just out fo' money." Her voice lifted, "What about you, Mrs Washington? You believe in Damballah?"

"In?—"

"The serpent god? Santeria, hoodoo?"

"Not really, no, I don't," Ettie said. She didn't feel like explaining that Grandma Ledbetter, bless her heart, had squeezed every shred of religion out of Ettie by her fierce lectures that mixed Catholicism and fiery Baptist dogma. Which, come to think of it, didn't seem to Ettie very different from the crazy stuff Hatake was talking about. Incense and holy water instead of High John Conqueror root.

Hatake tugged at her naked, punctured earlobe and continued to expound on the silliness of man-fetching spells and law stay-away oil. What was in your *heart* was what was important, Hatake said. Ettie's mind wandered and she thought again about John Pellam. Wondered when he'd come to visit her again. *If* he'd come. That man *ought* to be a hundred miles away by now. What the hell was he helping her for? She thought with horror how he'd almost been trapped by the fire. Thought about little Juan Torres too. She said a nonbeliever's prayer for the boy.

Then a noise from the front of the cell. The clank of metal on metal. Some of the women shouted hello to a new prisoner.

"Yo, girl. Weren't out but one day? You got yo' ass busted that quick?"

"Shit, Dannette, yo' bad luck. I staying away from you, girl."

Ettie watched the young woman with the pocked face and the beautiful figure walk uncertainly into the large cell. She was one of the prostitutes who'd been released just yesterday. Back so soon? Ettie smiled at her but the woman didn't respond.

Dannette walked up to the circle of women sitting around Hatake Imaham, who nodded to the woman. "Hey, girl. Good to see you."

Which sounded a little odd. Sort of like Hatake had been expecting her.

And the woman continued her lecture on hoodoo, talking now about Damballah, the highest in the voodoo order. Ettie knew this because her sister had dabbled in that craziness some years ago. Then the huge woman's voice faded and the women began talking among themselves, very quietly. One or two of them glanced at Ettie but they didn't include her in the conversation. That was all right. She was thankful for the quiet and for a few minutes' peace. She had many things to think about and, as the good Lord, or Damballah, she laughed to herself, knew, there were few enough moments of peace in here.

One of those feelings. Somebody watching him.

Pellam stood on the curb in front of Ettie's building, wasting his time asking amnesia-struck construction workers if they'd been in the alley when the fire started or if they know who had.

He turned suddenly. Yep, there it was. About fifty feet away a glistening black stretch limo was parked in the construction site, under the large billboard on which an artist had rendered a dramatic painting of the finished building. Pellam had seen a number of billboards like this one on the West Side; whoever painted them managed to make the high-rises look as appealing, and as completely phoney, as the drawings of women modeling lingerie in the Saks and Lord & Taylor newspaper ads.

Pellam focused on the limo. The windows were tinted but he could see that someone in the backseat – a man, it seemed – was gazing at him.

Pellam suddenly lifted the camera to his shoulder and aimed at the limo. There was a pause and then some motion in the backseat. The driver punched the accelerator and the long vehicle bounded out of the drive. It vanished in traffic toward the fish-gray strip of the Hudson River.

He stepped off the curb, still aiming the camera, and so he never saw the second car, the one that nearly broadsided him.

When he heard the brakes he spun around and stumbled back over the curb out of the way, falling. He lost some skin on his elbows rescuing the Betacam – which was worth more than he was at the moment.

A man was all over him in an instant, a huge man. Vice-grip hands grabbed Pellam's arms, jerking him to his feet, lifting the camera away. Not even time to blurt a protest before he was flung into the backseat of the sedan. At first he thought Jimmy Corcoran had found out he was looking for his crew and sent some boys to find him.

Hacksaws . . . The image just *wouldn't* leave him alone.

But he realized these men weren't gangies. They were in their thirties and forties. And they wore suits. Then he remembered where he'd seen the one who grabbed him, the one with the smooth, baby skin and muscles upon muscles. And so wasn't surprised to see who was in the front passenger seat.

"Officer Lomax," Pellam said.

The huge assistant climbed into the front seat and started to drive.

"I'm not an officer," Lomax said.

"No?"

"Uh-uh."

"Then what do I call you? Inspector? Fire marshal? Kidnapper?"

"Ha. Maybe I should call you Mr Funny. Instead of Mr Lucky. Ain't he a kick?" Lomax asked his assistant. The wrestler didn't respond.

Neither did the the man beside Pellam, a scrawny cop or marshal, tiny as a rooster. He didn't seem even to notice Pellam and just stared at the scenery as they drove past.

"How you doing?" Lomax asked. Around the man's neck was a badge on a chain. It was gold and had a mean-looking eagle perched on top of a crest.

"So-so."

To his assistant the marshal said, "Take him where we just were." Then added: "Only where nobody can see us."

"The alley?"

"Yeah, the alley'd be good."

This seemed rehearsed. But Pellam wasn't going to play the intimidation game. He rolled his eyes. Three cops – or whatever fire marshals were – weren't going to shoot him in an alley.

"We want to know one thing," Lomax said, looking out the window at a recently burned store. "Only one thing. Where can we find that shit the old lady hired? That's it. Just that. Tell us and you won't believe the kind of deal we'll cut for her."

"She didn't hire anybody. She didn't torch the building. Every minute you spend thinking she did is another minute the real perp is free."

This was another line from one of his movies. It sounded better on paper than it did when spoken aloud. But that may have been the circumstances.

Lomax said nothing for a few minutes. Then he asked, "You wanta know a difference between women and men? Women break down easy. A man'll hard-ass you for days. But you stand in front of a woman and scream and they start crying, they say, yeah, yeah, I did it, don't hurt me, don't hurt me. I didn't mean to or I didn't know anybody'd get hurt or my boyfriend made me do it. But they break down."

"I'll share that with Gloria Steinem next time I see her."

"More of the humor. Glad you can laugh at times like this. But you maybe better listen to what I'm saying. I intend to break that woman one way or another. I don't care how I do it. Tommy, am I saying this?"

The marshal's huge assistant recited, "I don't hear you saying anything."

Beside Pellam, the skinny cop, the silent one, examined some kids opening a hydrant. He didn't seem to hear anything either.

Lomax said, "I am gonna stop this fucking psycho and you're in a position to make it easier on Washington and save a lot of innocent people in the process. You can talk to her, you can – Ah, ah, ah, don't say a word, Mr Lucky. Tell him what happened this morning, Tony."

"Fire on the Eighth Avenue Subway."

Lomax was looking at Pellam again. "How many injured, Tony?"

The assistant recited, "Sixteen."

"How bad?"

"Real bad, boss. Four critical. One's not expected to live."

Lomax looked at the sidewalk, said to the driver, "Go the back way. I don't wanna be seen."

They were all very grim, these men – two of them outweighing Pellam by fifty pounds at least. And it was starting to occur to Pellam that while they might not shoot him they *could* beat the crap out of him. They'd probably even enjoy it. And break the forty-thousand-dollar camera that wasn't his.

"You know what we call an easy case? One with witnesses and solid evidence?" Lomax asked.

"A grounder," offered Tony.

Lomax continued, leaning close to Pellam, "You know what we call a case we can't figure out?"

"A balk?" Pellam tried.

"We call it a mystery, Mr Lucky. Well, that's what we got here. A big fucking mystery. We know the lady hired this guy but we can't find any fucking leads. And I just don't know what to do about it. So I don't have any choice. All I can think of is to start hitting that old lady hard. Am I saying this, Tony?"

"You're not saying anything."

"And if that doesn't work, Mr Lucky, then I'm going to start hitting *you* hard."

"Me."

"You. You were at the building around the time of the fire – like you were supposed to be an alibi for the old lady. Now you're walking around, talking to witnesses, with that big dick of a camera you got. You're a man's been around cops, I can smell that. I think you've seen more of 'em than you'd like, you ask me. So before I start whaling on her and on you, I want a straight answer: What's your interest in all this?"

"Simple. You arrested the wrong person. Getting that to register in your mind – that's my interest."

"By destroying evidence? Intimidating witnesses? Fucking up the investigation?"

Pellam glanced at the man beside him. A nebbishy guy. The sort you'd cast for an accountant or, if he had to be a cop, one from Internal Affairs.

Pellam said, "Let me ask you a few questions." The marshal grimaced but Pellam continued. "Why'd Ettie burn down a whole building if she's just got a policy on her apartment?"

"Because she hired a fucking psycho would couldn't control himself."

"Well, why'd she need to hire somebody at all? Why couldn't she fake a grease fire?"

"Too suspicious."

"But it was suspicious anyway."

"Less suspicious than just burning her place. Besides, she didn't know about the insurance fraud database."

"She lost everything in the fire."

"What everything? A thousand bucks worth of old furniture and crap?"

Pellam said, "And her fingerprints? What about *them*? You think she's going to hire somebody then give the pyro a bottle with *her* fingerprints on them? And isn't it kind of funny that the parts of the bottle with her prints on them don't get melted into bubble gum?"

"What should I ask this fellow now, Tony?" Lomax asked his belabored assistant, who thought for a moment before answering. Then said, "I'd wonder how he *knew* we got her prints on the bottle."

"Well?" Lomax raised an eyebrow.

"Lucky guess," Pellam responded. "True to my name."

"Turn here," Lomax said to the driver. The car skidded around a curve. And stopped. "Tony," the marshal gave the cue.

The assistant turned and Pellam suddenly found a very large pistol resting on his temple.

"Jesus . . ."

"I got more trivia for you, Pellam. Us fire marshals aren't cops. We don't have to worry about P.D. regs. We can carry whatever kind of weapons we want. What kind of gun is that you're holding, Tony?"

"This is a .38 Magnum. I load it with Plus P rounds."

"So you can fuck around with innocent people more efficiently?" Pellam asked. "Is that the idea?"

The cop holding the gun drew it back. Pellam laughed again, shaking his head. He knew he wasn't going to get hit. Physical evidence of a beating was the last thing these boys wanted. Tony looked at Lomax, who shrugged.

The gun disappeared into the big man's pocket. He and Lomax climbed out of the front seat, looked away.

Pellam was thinking, Called their bluff, when the skinny man slammed his bony fist, wrapped around a roll of quarters or nickels, into Pellam's head just behind the ear. An explosion of pain shot through him.

"Man . . . Christ."

Another blow. Pellam's face bounced off the window. Outside Lomax and Tony were examining a pile of trash in the alley, nodding.

Before he could lift his hands the skinny man delivered another fierce blow. There was a burst of yellow light and more astonishing pain. It occurred to him that the bruise and the welt would be virtually impossible to see through his hair.

So much for evidence.

The man dropped the roll of coins into his pocket and sat back. Pellam wiped pain tears from his eyes and turned to the man. Before he could say anything – or haul off and break the man's jaw – the door opened and Lomax and Tony pulled him out, dropped him in the alley.

Pellam touched his scalp. No blood. "I'm not going to forget that, Lomax."

"Forget what?"

Tony dragged Pellam up the deserted alley.

No witnesses was all Pellam could think.

Lomax escorted them halfway for about thirty feet. Motioned to Tony, who pinned Pellam to the wall, just like he'd done in Ettie's hospital room the other day.

Pellam flinched. Lomax shoved his hands into his pocket. He said in a low voice, "I've been a supervising fire marshal for ten years. I've seen a lot of pyros before but I've never seen anybody like this guy. This is your ground-zero asshole. He's out of control and it's gonna get worse before we get him. Now, are you going to help us?"

"She didn't hire him."

"Okay. If that's the way you want it."

Pellam balled his fists. He wasn't going down without a fight. They'd arrest him for assault probably but they were going to arrest him anyway, it looked like. Go for Tony first, try to break his nose.

Then Lomax nodded to Tony, who released Pellam. The big guy walked back to the car, where the skinny man with the coins was reading the *Post*.

Lomax turned to Pellam, who shifted his weight, ready to start slugging it out.

But the marshal only gestured toward an unmarked gray door. "Go through there and up to the third floor. Room three-thirteen. Got it?"

"What're you talking about?"

"In there." He nodded toward the door. "Room three-thirteen. Just do it. Now, get out of my sight. You make me sick."

Stepping into the elevator and pressing the disk of oily plastic that said 3.

The building was a hospital, the same one where he'd been treated and where Ettie Washington had been arrested.

Pellam followed the corridors and found the small room that Lomax had directed him to.

Pausing in the doorway, he didn't pay any attention to the couple who stood inside. He didn't notice the fancy medical equipment. He didn't acknowledge the white-uniformed nurse, who looked at him briefly. No, all John Pellam saw was the pile of bandages that was a twelve-year-old boy. Young Juan Torres, the most serious injury in the fire at 458 W. Thirty-sixth Street.

The son of the man who knew Jose Canseco.

Pellam looked around the room, trying to figure out why Lomax had sent him here. He couldn't figure it out.

In Pellam's heart was a balanced pity – equal parts for the child and for Ettie Washington. (But, he wondered, were these

sorrows exclusive? He debated for a difficult moment. If Ettie
Washington was guilty, then yes they were.)

Forget it, he told himself. She's innocent. I know she is.

Wondering again why Lomax had directed him here.

"*La iglesia*," the woman said evenly. "*El cura.*"

Another nurse walked brusquely into the room, jostling
Pellam, and continued on without apology. She offered the
mother a small white cup. Maybe the woman was sick too.
At first Pellam supposed she'd been hurt in the fire. But he
remembered helping her out the doorway herself, behind the
fireman who carried her son. She'd been fine then though
now her hands trembled and the two tiny yellow pills spilled
from the wax cup and tapped on the floor. He realized that
something about this room differed from the others he'd just
walked past.

What is it?

Something odd was going on here.

Yes, that's it . . .

The monitor above the bed was silent. The tubes had been
disconnected from the boy's arm. The chart had been removed
from a hook welded to the bedframe.

Cura. Pellam had a Southern Californian's grasp of Spanish.
He remembered that the word meant priest.

The child had died.

This was what Lomax wanted him to see.

The boy's mother ignored the dropped pills and leaned
against her companion. He turned his head, covered with tight
short-shorn curls and looked at Pellam.

"*My daddy, he knows Jose Canseco. No, no, no. Really*
He does!"

The nurse again walked past Pellam, this time uttering an soft "Excuse me."

Then the room was silent or almost so. The only sound was white noise, an indistinct hiss, like the soundtrack on the tape of Otis Balm in his death pose or the tape of Ettie's empty armchair after she rose to answer the door in the last scenes he shot of her. Pellam remained frozen in the center of the room, unable to offers words of condolence, unable to observe or to analyze.

It was some moments later that he finally realized the other implications of this silent event – that the charge against Ettie Washington would now be murder.

———◆◆◆———

12

B usiness was brisk at New York State Supreme Court, Criminal Term.

John Pellam sat in the back of the grubby, crowded courtroom beside Nick Flanagan, the bail bondsman Louis Bailey had hired, a round, world-weary man with grime under his nails and a rapid-fire mind that could figure various percentages of bail faster than Pellam could use a calculator.

After the boy's death Bailey had revised his estimate of the bail upward – to a hundred thousand dollars. According to the usual bond arrangements, Ettie would have to come up with cash or securities worth ten percent of that. Flanagan agreed to post on five and a half percent. He did this grudgingly, revealing either his nature or – more likely – some vast, resented debt owed to Bailey that this was in small part repaying.

Ettie Washington would contribute her savings to the cash deposit – nine hundred dollars. Bailey had arranged through one of his faceless Street Contacts to borrow the rest. Ettie wouldn't let Pellam put up one penny, not that he had much to contribute.

Pellam was impressed with the dealings Bailey had orchestrated but he wondered if the lawyer's skills in a courtroom would be equal to his sleight of hand in bars, clerk's offices and filing departments.

Bailey had also received the handwriting report and the news wasn't good. Ettie's bouts of bursitis and arthritis made her handwriting very inconsistent. The signature on the insurance application was, according to the report, "more probably than not that of subject Washington."

Pellam examined the assistant district attorney, Lois Koepel, a young woman with a sharp jaw, small mouth and a tangle of very unlawyerly hair. She seemed self-assured, brittle and far too young to be handling a murder case.

The clerk muttered, "People of the State of New York versus Etta Wilkes Washington."

Bailey and, at his urging, Ettie, stood. His eyes were up, hers downcast. The elderly judge reclined along the bench in boredom, his fingertips supporting his temple, which was disfigured by a prominent vein, visible even from the back of the courtroom.

The A.D.A. said, "We've amended, Your Honor."

The judge glanced down at the young woman. "The boy died?"

"Correct, Your Honor." Not a single *S* in the sentence and she still managed to sound extremely shrill.

The judge scanned papers. "Ms Washington," he droned, "you're charged with murder in the second degree, manslaughter in the first degree, criminally negligent homicide, arson in the first degree, arson in the second degree, assault in the first degree, criminal mischief in the first degree and criminal mischief in the second degree. Do you understand these charges?"

Startling the first several rows of spectators, Ettie Washington called out firmly, "I didn't kill anybody. I didn't do it!"

The A.D.A.'s ground-glass voice snapped, "Your Honor."

The judge waved her silent. "Mrs Washington, you've had the charges explained to you, have you not?"

"Yessir."

"How do you plead to each of these charges?"

Without prompting, she said, "Not guilty, Your Honor."

"All right. What is the state seeking for bail?"

"Your Honor, the People request Ms Washington be held without bail in this case."

Bailey grumbled, "Your Honor, my client is a seventy-two-year-old woman with no resources, no passport and severe injuries. She isn't going anywhere."

The A.D.A. droned, "She is charged with murder and arson—"

"I wouldn't kill that boy!" Ettie shouted. "Never, never!"

"Counsel will instruct his client . . ." The judge roused himself from his boredom long enough to deliver this lethargic command.

The A.D.A. continued, "We have here a woman accused of a very elaborate scheme to defraud an insurance company, involving premeditation and the hiring of a professional arsonist."

"Do you have *that* suspect in custody?"

"We do not, Your Honor. This is the man we believe to be responsible for a series of other fires around the city, resulting in a number of deaths and serious injuries. It seems he's on some kind of rampage. I'm sure Your Honor's read about it in the paper."

"*Those* fires?"

"Yes, sir."

"Your Honor," Bailey said, sounding appalled.

"Quiet, counselor." The judge's brow furrowed, the most emotion he'd displayed so far.

"We've had three fires in two days. The most recent was a subway, and I just heard a report before coming to Your Honor's courtroom that there was another one."

Bailey turned slowly and glanced at Pellam. *Another* fire?

Koepel continued. "At a department store on Eighth Avenue."

"What happened?" the judge asked.

The A.D.A. continued, "That homemade napalm again, Your Honor. In a women's clothing department. A clerk just happened to be standing by a fire extinguisher station in the store when it started. She put it out before it did much damage. But it could've been a real tragedy." The A.D.A. fell out of character. She sounded exasperated as she said, "Judge, the police just don't know what to do. They can't find this perp. There are no witnesses. These fires just keep appearing. And frankly it's got everybody on the West Side scared as hell."

"Your Honor," Bailey said in the voice of a melodramatic stage actor, "this is the most rampant form of speculation. Why, the month is August. It's been hot, people's tempers are flaring—"

"Thank you for the weather report, Mr Bailey. What's your point?"

"Copycat crimes."

"Counselor?" The judge raised an eyebrow at the A.D.A.

"Unlikely. The mixture he uses in his bombs is unusual. It's like a fingerprint of this particular arsonist. And the press has cooperated in not mentioning the exact substances. We're sure the same perpetrator is behind them. The defendant's been completely uncooperative in identifying him and—"

"She's uncooperative," Bailey said, echoing Pellam's thought, "because she doesn't know who he is."

"This is, as I was saying, a very elaborate scheme to perpetrate a vicious crime, resulting in a child's death. And in light of her prior fraud conviction, we—"

"What?" the lawyer asked.

"Are you objecting, Mr Bailey?"

"No, Your Honor, I'm not objecting."

"Because if you're objecting, it's misplaced. There's no jury here. There are no evidentiary issues."

"I'm not objecting. What prior conviction?" He glanced at a mute Ettie, whose eyes were downcast.

Pellam was sitting forward.

"Well, Ms Washington's felony conviction for fraud and extortion six years ago. Arson was threatened in that case too, Your Honor."

She has a *record*? An arson threat? Pellam's memory fast-forwarded through his many conversations with Ettie. This had never come up on the tapes. Not even a hint. His thumb and forefinger rubbed together heatedly.

Bailey's head turned to Ettie but her eyes remained downcast. "This is the first I've heard of it, Your Honor." He whispered something to Ettie, who shook her head and said nothing.

"Well," the A.D.A. said, "that's not the state's problem."

"True, Mr Bailey," the judge said. The vein on his flushed temple seemed to change course. He wanted to move on to the other cases on his calendar. "Your knowledge of your client's history is hardly relevant. Can we wrap this up?"

"On the motion," Koepel hissed, "the people request the suspect be held without bail."

The judge reclined in his tall black chair. "Bail denied." He banged the gavel with a sound like gunshot.

"We got outflanked."

Louis Bailey stood beside Pellam on the sidewalk beside the Criminal Courts Building. An odd smell – sour – filled the hot August air.

The lawyer gazed down absently at his feet. His navy blue sock sported a hole but the green one looked almost new. "I should've seen it coming. The A.D.A. pulled a fast one. She kept requesting a delay in the arraignment. She hinted that if I agreed she'd be more likely to go along with a bail reduction."

Pellam was nodding. "A technical legal strategy called lying."

"Ah, that's old news. But the sick thing is that she was just delaying until the boy died. Put her in a better spot to ask for a no-bail order."

Our public servants, Pellam thought. God bless 'em. He asked, "You didn't know about her conviction?"

"No. She never mentioned it."

"News to me too. How bad is it?"

"Well, they can't use it in her trial. Unless she takes the stand and I won't let her do that. But it's just . . ."

"Troubling," Pellam muttered.

Bailey sought a better word but settled for echoing, "Troubling."

They each looked at the black-and-gray County Court building across the street. Their gazes took in a somber discussion between a keen-faced, dark-suited lawyer and his dumpling of a gloomy client. As it happened, Pellam's eyes were fixed on the lawyer; Bailey's, the man he represented. Two bailiffs sat down near them and began eating cold noodles with sesame paste. The courthouse was three blocks from Chinatown. *That* was the smell, Pellam understood: overused vegetable oil.

"I'm worried about her, Louis. Can you get her into protective custody?"

"Nobody's doing me any favors. Not until the pyro's caught."

Pellam tapped his wallet.

"I've got no connection with the Department of Corrections. If I can do anything, it'll have to be the old-fashioned way. A noticed motion. Order to show cause."

"Can you do that?"

"I don't think they'll buy it but I can try." His eyes watched a huge cluster of pigeons in a frenzy over a scrap of hotdog bun a businessman had thrown onto the ground.

"Level with me," Bailey said.

Pellam cocked an eyebrow.

"The bail situation threw you, didn't it? You were pretty upset."

"I don't want her to spend any more time in jail," Pellam said.

"I don't either but it's not the end of the world." After a moment he asked, "What exactly is this all about?"

"What?—"

Bailey said, "I'm asking what're you doing here, Pellam."

"She's an innocent woman in jail."

Bailey said, "So're, say, twenty percent of the people in there." He nodded toward the detention center. "That's old news too. Why're you playing detective, what's your stake in this whole thing?"

Pellam looked out over busy Centre Street. Courthouses, government buildings . . . Justice at work. He thought of an ant farm. Finally he said, "If she goes to jail, my film's worthless. Three months of work down the tubes. And I'll end up probably thirty, forty thousand in hock."

The lawyer nodded. Pellam supposed that this commercial motive wouldn't sit too well with Bailey, who may have been a worldly gear-greaser but was also a friend of Ettie's. But that was all Pellam was willing to say to the lawyer on the subject.

Bailey said, "I'll get started on the protective custody order. You want to come back to the office?"

"Can't. I've got to meet somebody about the case."

"Who?"

"The worst man in the city of New York."

Seven men stared silently at him.

T-shirts dusty with cigarette ash. Long hair, dark from dirt and sweat. Black crescents under fingernails in need of a trim. Pellam thought of a word from his adolescence, a word that'd been used to describe the black-leather-jacket element at Walt Whitman High in Simmons, New York: Greasers.

A young woman sat on one man's lap. He had a long, bony face and gangly arms. He swatted the girl on her taut butt and she scooted off with a resentful scowl. But she snagged her purse and left quickly.

Pellam glanced at each of the seven. They all stared back though only one – slightly built, curly-haired, resembling a monkey – returned his gaze with anything that resembled a flicker of sobriety and intelligence.

Pellam had already decided not to go through the pretense of ordering anything at the bar. He knew there was only one way to handle this and he asked the long-faced man, "You're Jimmy Corcoran?"

Of all the things the man might've said he offered none of them and surprised Pellam by asking, "You're Irish?"

He was, as a matter of fact, on his father's side. But how could Corcoran tell? He believed his other side was more prominent – a hybrid traceable, so the family legend went, to Wild Bill Hickok, the gunfighter turned federal marshal. It included Dutch and English and Arapahoe or Sioux.

"Some," Pellam told him.

"Yeah, yeah. Thought I could see it."

"I'd like to talk to you."

On the table he saw seven shot glasses and a forest of tall-necked beer bottles, too many to count.

Corcoran nodded, gestured at an empty table in the corner of the bar.

Pellam glanced at the bartender, a man who had that rare talent of being able to look over an entire room and not see a single person in it.

"You're not a cop," Corcoran said, sitting down. This wasn't a question. "I can tell. It's like a sixth sense for me."

"No. I'm not."

Corcoran called out, "Bushy."

A moment later a bottle of Bushmills and two glasses appeared. In the far corner of the bar six large hands groped for beers and six voices resumed a heated conversation of which Pellam could hear nothing. Corcoran poured two glasses. The men tapped them together, a dull sound, and they tossed back the liquor.

"So, you're the man from Hollywood. The moviemaker."

The Word, of course, had gotten around.

Corcoran grinned and tossed back another drink. He thumped the tabletop with his monstrously large hands, little finger and thumb extended, as if playing a bodhran drum, keeping excellent rhythm. "So where are you from?" he asked.

"The East Village. I—"

"Where in *Ireland* you from?" he said.

"I was born here," Pellam told him. "My father was from Dublin."

Corcoran halted the percussion. He gave an exaggerated frown. "I'm from Londonderry. You know what that makes us, you and me?"

"Mortal enemies. So if you know who I am then you know what I want."

"Mortal enemies? You're quick, ain't you? Well, I don't know *exactly* what you want. All's I know is you're making a movie here."

"The word is," Pellam said, "you know everything about the Kitchen."

A heavy, dull-looking man gazed at Pellam belligerently from the corner table. A black plastic pistol grip protruded from his belt and he kneaded it with fat fingers.

Pellam said, "I know you run a gang."

Laughter from the table.

"A gang," Corcoran repeated.

"Or is it a club?"

"No, it's a gang. We don't mind saying it. Do we, boys?"

"Yo, Jimmy," was the only response.

Corcoran busied himself with a metal tin then extracted a wad of Copenhagen and shoved it into his mouth, further altering the eerie, almost deformed shape of his equine face. "Tell me – what do you think of the Kitchen?" he asked Pellam.

In all his months here no one – of the thirty or so people he'd interviewed – had ever asked Pellam his opinion of the neighborhood. He thought for a moment and said, "It's the only 'hood I've ever seen that's getting better, safer, cleaner, and the old-timers here don't want any goddamn part of that."

Corcoran nodded with approval, smiling. "That's fucking good." The table got another spanking and he poured two more shots. "Have some more poteen." He looked out the window and his bony face grew wistful. "That's good, man. The Kitchen *ain't* what it used to be, that's for certain. My father, he come over the water, was in the forties. 'Coming over the water,' that's what they called it. Had a hell of a time getting work. The docks was *the* place to work then. Now it's just a fucking tourist thing but back then the big ships'd come in, cargo and passengers. Only to get a job you had to pay the bosses. I mean, payoff. Big. My pa, he couldn't get it up to get a job in the union. So he worked day labor. He was always talking about the Troubles, about Belfast and Londonderry. Into all that stuff, the politics, you know. That don't interest me. Your pa, was he a Sinn Feiner, Republican? Or was he a Loyalist?"

"I have no idea."

"How do you feel about independence?"

"I'm all for it. I stay away from nine-to-five jobs."

Corcoran laughed. "I went to Kilmainham jail one time. You know where that is?"

"Where they hanged the rebels of the Easter Rebellion."

"It was, you know, weird being there. Walking on the same stones they walked on. I cried. I don't mind admitting it neither." Corcoran smiled wanly, shook his head. He sipped his liquor then scooted back slightly in the chair.

It was pure instinct that saved Pellam's wrists.

Corcoran leapt to his feet, grabbed a chair and brought it down on the tabletop in a hissing arc, just as Pellam shoved himself back into the wall.

"You fucker!" he screamed. "Cock-sucking fucker!" He slammed the chair into the table again. The legs met the oak tabletop and cracked with a noise loud as twin gunshots. Fragments of glass and a mist of smoky whiskey showered through the air.

"You come here to *my* home, to spy on *me* . . ." His words were lost in a stew of rage. "You want my fucking secrets, you fucking tinker . . ."

Pellam crossed his arms. Didn't move. Gazed calmly back into Corcoran's eyes.

"Aw, Jimmy, come on," a voice from the corner called. It was the man Pellam had noticed when he walked in, the smallest of the crew. Monkey Man.

"Jimmy . . ."

"It's the liquor talking," the man offered.

"Look, mister, maybe you better—" another started to say.

But Corcoran didn't even notice them. "You come into *my* fucking home, into my neighborhood and ask questions about me. I heard what you was doing. I know. I know everything. You think I don't? What kind of stupid asshole are you? It's fuckers like you that've ruined this place. *You* took the Kitchen away. We was here first, all you fuckers come with your cameras and look at us like fucking insects."

Pellam stood up, dusted glass off his shirt.

Corcoran broke the remaining legs on the chair with another fierce blow. He leaned forward and screamed, "What gives *you* the right!"

"He didn't mean nothing, Jimmy," Monkey Man said calmly. "I'm sure he didn't. He's just asking a few questions's all he's doing."

"*What gives him the right?*" Corcoran shrieked. He tossed another chair across the room. The bartender found more glasses that desperately needed polishing.

"Have a drink, Jimmy," someone said. "Just be cool."

"Don't any of you cock-sucking tinkers say a fucking word!" The gun appeared in Corcoran's hand like a black snake striking.

The table fell silent. No one moved. It was as if their bodies were somehow wired to the trigger.

"Hey, Jimmy, come on," Monkey Man whispered. "Sit yourself down now. Let's not do nothing stupid."

Corcoran found a glass on the floor, walked to the bar and snagged a new bottle. He slammed it down in front of Pellam, poured it to the brim with Bushmills. Enraged, he snarled, "He's going to take a drink with me and he's going to apologize. If he does that I'll let him go."

Pellam lifted his hands, smiled pleasantly. To the bartender. "Okay. But make it a soda."

Just like in *Shane*. Alan Ladd orders a soda pop for Joey. Pellam had *loved* that movie. He'd seen it twenty times. In school his friends wanted to be Mickey Mantle; Pellam dreamed of being the director, George Stevens.

"Soda?" Corcoran whispered.

"Pepsi. No, make it a Diet Pepsi."

The bartender stepped toward his refrigerator. Corcoran spun, lifting the gun toward the terrified man. "Don't you fucking dare. This faggot's drinking whiskey and he's—"

All a blur, leather spun through the air and suddenly Corcoran was on the ground, face down, his right arm extended straight up, wrist and pistol twisted in Pellam's hands.

Damn, not bad. Pellam hadn't been sure he could remember the move. But it came back to him just fine. From his stuntman days, when he was doing battle gags on the set of some Indochina flick fifteen years ago. He'd learned a few martial arts tricks from the fight choreographer.

Pellam lifted the gun from the Irishman's grip and pointed it toward each of the six frozen thugs. He didn't let go of Corcoran's wrist.

No one moved.

"Fucker," Corcoran wheezed. Pellam twisted harder. "Oh, shit. You're dead, man, you're . . ."

A little harder.

"All right, fucker. All right!"

Pellam released the wrist and pressed the muzzle of the gun against Corcoran's forehead.

Pellam said, "What a mouth you got on you. King of the

Kitchen, huh? You know everything? Then you know I was gonna offer you five hundred bucks to find out who torched that building on Thirty-sixth Street. *That's* what I was doing here. And what do I get? A pissing contest with a teenager who needs a bath." He pointed the gun at Monkey Man, who raised his hands. Pellam asked him, "Would you please get me that Pepsi now?"

The man hesitated then walked to the bar. The bartender had materialized again and his corporeal form looked on the verge of death. He stared at red-faced Corcoran, who raged, "Get him the fucking drink, you asshole."

In a quavering voice the bartender said, "I, uhm . . . The thing is, we don't have . . ."

"A Coke'll be fine," Pellam said, pointing the Smith & Wesson at the fat man at the table. "Just toss that piece on the floor, would you?"

"Do it," Corcoran grumbled.

The gun hit the floor. Pellam kicked it into the corner.

The bartender asked in a trembling voice, "Was that Diet you wanted, sir?"

"Whatever."

"Yessir." The bartender opened the can, nearly dropped it. With steady hands Monkey Man poured the soda into a glass and carried it to Pellam.

"Thank you." He drank it down and set the empty glass on the table, backed toward the door, wiped his face with a napkin the man had provided as well.

Corcoran rose to his feet and, turning his back to Pellam, returned to the table. The lanky Irishman sat down again, snagged a Bud and began talking a mile a minute, cheerful as could be. He banged the beer bottle to punctuate for emphasis, lecturing colorfully about the Easter Rebellion and the Black 'n' Tans and the hunger strike of '81 – as if, in his mind, Pellam was already gone.

Pellam unloaded the gun, tossed the bullets into the ice tray under the bar and the gun into the corner with the other one, then stepped outside into a truly blistering heat.

Thinking: August in New York City. Man.

———◆◆◆◆———

13

S tanding in the ugly, concrete park across the street from the Javits Center.

Wondering if the man would show or not?

Or more to the point, Pellam reflected, if he does show, will he shoot me?

He studied this part of Hell's Kitchen, where even the blaring sun couldn't mute the bleakness. Here, in the valley between the Javits Center and the towering gray aircraft carrier – the *Intrepid*, converted into a floating war museum – the blocks were stubbly lots and one-story buildings long abandoned or burnt-out, a graveyard of chopped cars, razor-wire-topped fences, weeds, old boilers and factory machinery melting into rust.

After ten minutes of hypnotically studying the boat and barge river traffic on the Hudson he heard a cheerful voice call out, "Hey, you crazy fuck."

Well, the man *had* showed.

And no gunshots. So far.

The man was walking toward him through heat ripples rising from the concrete. Despite the temperature he still wore the long black leather jacket. And he still looked like a monkey.

He slipped the cigarette he held into his mouth and muttered, "Jacko Drugh."

"John Pellam."

They shook hands. "You got some balls, Pellam, giving me the high sign right under Jimmy C's nose." He said this with the boisterousness of a born loser.

Drugh was exactly the sort of fish he'd gone trolling for at the 488 Bar and Grill. His point in going there wasn't to get information *from* Jimmy Corcoran, who was exactly the petty little weasel he'd expected, if somewhat more psychotic. No, he'd been after a snitch. "You looked like somebody I could trust."

Read: *buy.*

"Ah, sure. Jacko's somebody you can trust. To a point, my man. Up to a point."

Pellam offered a slight smile. And slipped him the five hundred, the amount they'd agreed to when Pellam announced it in the bar and Drugh had handed him a soggy napkin with the name of this park on it when he'd brought Pellam the soft drink.

Drugh didn't look at the money. He shoved the wad into his pocket with the air of someone who's rarely, if ever, cheated.

"So, your boss? Is he going to try to kill me?" Pellam asked.

"Don't know, do I? Any other time, you'd already be swimming in Hell Gate in four different GLAD bags. But lately, the old J.C.'s playing stuff close to his chest. He don't do mucha the wild stuff no more. Which I don't know why. Thought it was a woman at first but Jimmy don't usually go nuts over pussy. Least not a rump-bunny like that Katie you seen him with. So, I dunno. Maybe he'll forget about you. Hope so. For your sake. If he wants you dead you'll be dead and there's nothing you can do 'bout it. I mean, you could leave the state. But that's all."

They sat on a bench. The heat made his back itch fiercely. Pellam sat forward. Drugh finished his cigarette and lit another.

Pellam stroked, "So, you're the one really in charge, right?"

Drugh shrugged. "Some of the time."

"You're a lot cooler than he is."

The downward glance and smile bespoke considerable mutiny in the ranks. Pellam guessed that either Drugh or Corcoran would be dead within six months. Pellam decided the smart money was on Corcoran as survivor.

"We don't got things like capos and shit, you know. But I'm number two, yeah. And I stand in for Jimmy a lot. 'Specially when he loses his head. His brother's a lightweight. The elevator don't stop at every floor." Reflecting, Drugh added, "But I'm careful. I know the line. See, Jimmy's a crazy fuck a lot of the time. But when he's not, he looks out for his people. And he's got a fuck of a lot of friends." Drugh looked him over. "You don't got an accent. You didn't come over."

"No, I was born here."

"You know the Emerald Underground?"

"No."

"See, somebody comes over from Ireland and there's this, you know, network of people look out for 'em till they get on their feet. Jimmy, he does a lot for 'em. He's got 'em a job lined up and an apartment 'fore they're outa customs at JFK. Men in construction, girls in bars or restaurants. Making good money too. He arranges marriages for the card, loans people money."

"Keeping some for himself."

"Oh, Jimmy's a businessman, isn't he?"

Drugh was gazing at the black Javits Center, functional and boxy – as if it were still in a packing crate. He laughed. It became a cough and as if this reminded him it was time for another cigarette he lit one. "You really making a movie?"

"Yep."

"I never knowed anybody done that before. I like movies. You see *State of Grace*?"

"Sean Penn and Gary Oldman. Ed Harris. Good movie."

"It was about *us*," he said proudly.

"Which one played you?" Pellam asked. Joking. The movie had been about a gang in Hell's Kitchen but it was fictional.

"A guy I'd never heard of," Drugh responded, dead serious.

There was silence for a moment. Then both men knew the social pleasantries were over. Time for business. Pellam lowered his voice. "Okay, the arson on Thirty-sixth Street. There're some rumors that Jimmy was behind it." He was recalling what Hector Ramirez had told him.

"Jimmy?" Drugh asked. "Where'd you hear that shit? Naw. He don't burn the old buildings."

"What I heard was there was a witness living there, this woman. Jimmy wanted to get even with her for testifying."

Drugh nodded but it was a gesture of dismissal. "Oh that? You mean when Spear Driscoe dropped a cap on Bobby Frink. That whosie whatsis spic lady saw it. Carmella Ramirez? Well, sure she *was* a witness and sure she testified. But Driscoe was so wasted on the old Black Jack that he waxed Bobby in the front of a corner deli on Saturday night. There was like *ten* witnesses. Even if the spic lady hadn't talked, there was no way Spear wasn't gonna go play with the jiggaboos in Attica for ten to fifteen."

Pellam vamped. "But I've heard that Corcoran's burned buildings before."

"Sure. But not the old places. The *new* ones. We all do that. Fuck, it's like they take our homes away, whatta they expect? The *Cubano* Lords and us, we bombed that new place, that office building on Fiftieth Street."

"Ramirez did that?"

"Sure. 'Bout the only thing we agree on. And me too, my man. Oh, Jacko throws a good cocktail, he does. But see, it's *okay*." Drugh said this earnestly. "We used to have the whole west side. From Twenty-third up to Fifty-seventh. It was *ours*. Man, we don't got nothing left now. We're defending our homes is all we're doing. From spics and niggers and real estate assholes. People who're from east of Eighth." Drugh pulled long on his cigarette. "Naw, naw, Jimmy didn't burn that place. I *know*."

"Why're you so sure?"

"Jacko knows. See, J.C.'s got something going."

"Something?"

Drugh explained that Jimmy Corcoran and his brother had bought some property and were involved in a big business deal. "Something gonna make him a million bucks or so he says. The last thing Jimmy's gonna do is draw attention to the Kitchen by burning buildings. J.C.'d definitely ice anybody torching places in the neighborhood. He and Tom, that's his brother, don't want no, you know, uhn . . ." His thoughts failed him.

Pellam supplied a word.

"Exactly. They don't want no disruptions."

Pellam tended to believe Drugh. He said, "Let's say it isn't Jimmy. Who might it've been?"

"Oh, didn't you hear? Where you been? They collared this old nigger lady."

"Forget about her for a minute. Any other rumors?"

"Well, yeah, you hear things. Jacko hangs out, Jacko hears things."

"Such as?"

"'Bout this weird kid. You pay him money, he'll torch anything – a church or school, it don't mean nothing to him. Kids, ladies, he don't care, does he? Was hanging out on Thirty-sixth the past few weeks."

Pellam shook his head. "I've heard about him. You know who he is?"

"Nope."

Discouraged, Pellam asked, "There's also a boy I'm looking for. Blond. Seventeen, eighteen. A hooker. Calls himself Alex but it's not his real name. Sound familiar?"

"That narrows it down to, maybe, a thousand." Drugh squinted young-old eyes and stared at the flat plain of the Jersey horizon. "You listen to Jacko. It's Ramirez did it. Hector el spic-o. Guarantee it."

"But his aunt lived there."

"Aw, she was probably gonna move. Or get evicted, more likely. Spics never pay their rent. That's a true fact, it is. I'll bet he's already got her a better place."

He was right, Pellam recalled. Ramirez had.

"I know it's him. See, Ramirez rousted Johnny O'Neil."

"Who's that?"

"Guy we sometimes do business with. Johnny rents apartments around town and stores things there." Drugh's voice dropped. "You know what I'm saying?"

"Well, up to and including the part about renting apartments around town."

"Shhh, my man. Not a word. Jacko's putting you on your honor."

"Fair enough."

"O'Neil trades in guns, doesn't he? He had a apartment in that building." He gestured toward Ettie's tenement. "Oh, yeah, my man. A safe house." He said this as if every New Yorker ought to have one.

Pellam remembered the burnt guns that the fire investigators had found in the basement.

"The other day Ramirez jacked one of O'Neil's trucks and had him sucking on a Glock. Told him to keep the armament out of that part of the Kitchen."

"What'd O'Neil say?"

"What'd he say? He said, 'Yessir, Mr Spic. I'll stop.' What'd *you* say you got your pearlies 'round a nine millimeter? So my money's Ramirez heard about the guns from his auntie, shit a brick and hired that spooky guy to nuke the place."

Pellam shook his head. So Ramirez had told him some but not all of the story. "Do me a favor? Put the word out about Alex? I need to find him."

"Oh, Jacko'll keep his eyes peeled for you. I'll ask around. People talk to me. If there's a little something in it for me Jacko gets the right answers."

Pellam reached for his wallet again.

But Drugh shook his head. The young man seemed to grow

embarrassed. "Naw, naw, I don't mean that. You paid me already. What I'm saying, when you make that movie of yours, you keep me in mind, you do that? You give Jacko a call. They made that movie, that *State of Grace*, they shoulda called me. I mean, there oughta be laws about them using your life and not asking you 'bout it. I mean, fuck, I didn't wanta be the star or nothing. I just wanted to be in the fucking movie. I'd be good. I know I would."

Pellam made sure not to smile as he said, "If we ever get to casting, I'll call you, Jacko. You bet."

Ettie Washington stared out the window of the Women's Detention Center.

It was high above her head and the glass was so filthy you couldn't see through it. But the light was comforting. She was thinking back to Billy Doyle, remembering how much the two of them liked to be outside, walking around the neighborhood. Saying hi to their neighbors. Her second husband, Harold Washington, didn't like being indoors either though he was a *sitting* kind of man. The two of *them*, when he was home and more or less sober, would sit on the steps and share a bottle. But living by herself Ettie had discovered the pleasure of a good rocking chair and a window. A joy that now seemed to be gone forever.

Mistakes, she was thinking of mistakes she'd made throughout her life. And secrets and lies . . . Some serious and some not so. How slightly bad things you did grew into very bad things. How the good things you tried to do faded away like smoke.

And she was thinking of Pellam's face when that bitch in court told everybody about her conviction. Would he ever come to visit her again? she wondered. She guessed not. Why should he? Oh, this thought cut her deeply. But what she felt was pain, not surprise. She'd known all along that he'd be vanishing from her life. He was a man, and men left. Didn't matter if they were fathers or brothers or husbands. Men left.

Footsteps sounded behind her.

"Mother," Hatake Imaham cooed, "how you feeling? You feeling good?"

Ettie turned around.

Several of the prisoners were standing behind the large woman. They all approached slowly. Six others stood at the far end of the cell, looking out into the corridor. Ettie couldn't figure out why they were in a line like that. Then she realized they were blocking the guard's view of the cell.

A cold feeling pierced her. It was just like the feeling that sliced through her when the two policemen showed up at her door and asked, grim-faced, if her son was Frank Washington. Could they come inside? There was something they had to tell her.

Hatake continued in a calm voice, "You feeling good?"

"I'm okay," Ettie said, looking uneasily from one woman to another.

"Bet you feeling better than that boy, Mother."

"What boy?"

"That little boy you killed. Juan Torres."

"I didn't do it," Ettie whispered. She drew back, against the wall. "No, I didn't do it."

She looked again toward the door but she was completely hidden by the line of women.

"I *know* you done it, bitch. You kill that little boy."

"I didn't!"

"An eye for an eye." The large woman stepped closer. She had a cigarette lighter in her hand. The woman next to her, Dannette, had one too. Where had they gotten those? Then she understood. Dannette had purposely gotten arrested again and smuggled in the lighters.

Hatake stepped close.

Ettie shrank away then suddenly lunged forward, swinging her cast into Hatake's face. It connected with her nose, a loud thud. The woman screeched and fell back. The other women gasped. No one moved for a moment.

Then Ettie took a deep breath to scream for help and found herself tasting sour cloth. Someone had come up behind her and flipped the gag over her face. Hatake was on her feet, wiping blood from her nose, smiling cruelly.

"Okay, mother, okay." She nodded to Dannette, who lit a cigarette and tossed it onto Ettie's shift. She tried to kick it off but two other women held her down. She couldn't move. The ember began to burn through the dress.

Hatake said, "You shouldn't be smokin' in here. 'Gainst the rules, Mother. An' accidents happen. Them lighters, they spill sometimes. Get that stuff inside, that gas, all over you. Burn up yo hair, burn up you face. Sometime it kill you, sometime it don't."

Hatake stepped closer and Ettie felt the icy spray of the butane on her scalp and cheek. She closed her eyes, trying to twist away from the women who held her.

"Lemme," Hatake snapped, snatching the lighter out of Dannette's hands. She muttered something else but Ettie couldn't hear it over her own squealing and muttered pleas. There was a snap and a hiss and the huge woman walked closer and closer, holding the lighter like a beacon.

14

A star can make a movie open.

Open.

The classic, revered Hollywood verb defined as: "to make enough people plunk down their hard-earned bucks on opening weekend so film company execs don't have to spend all Monday thinking up excuses for their wives, mistresses, bosses and *Daily Variety* reporters to explain why they've just spent millions of other people's dollars to make a flop."

Bankable stars can make a movie open.

So can a drop-dead story line.

Nowadays even special effects can do it, particularly if they involve explosions.

But nothing in the universe can make a documentary open. Documentaries might be enlightening or touching or inspiring. They can represent the highest form of movie-making art. But they don't do what people go to feature films for.

To escape from their lives, to enjoy themselves for a few hours.

Walking through downtown Manhattan, toward the sooty carnival of the courts and prisons, Pellam was reflecting: He had directed four independent films, all of them cult classics, two of them award winners. He had degrees in film making from NYU and UCLA. He'd written dozens of articles for *Cineaste* and *Independent Film Monthly* and he could recite the dialog from most of Hitchcock's films. His credentials were impeccable.

Of the eighteen studios and production companies he'd approached with the idea for this documentary all had rejected him.

Oh, everyone had been full of praise and enthusiasm for *West of Eighth: An Oral History of Hell's Kitchen.* But not a single dollar from a big studio was forthcoming to back it.

As he'd pitched the idea he explained that the neighborhood offered a wonderful mix of crime, heroism, corruption, beauty.

"Those are all capitalized words, Pellam," a friend, a VP for development at Warner Brothers, had told him. "Capitalized words do not good movies make."

Only Alan Lefkowitz had expressed any interest and he didn't have the foggiest notion what the film was about.

Still, Pellam had great hopes for the flick and believed it had a shot at an Oscar – confidence founded largely on an encounter that had occurred on West Thirty-sixth Street last June.

"Excuse me," he'd asked, "you live in this building?"

"Yes, I do, young man," the elderly black woman had answered, eyes confident, amused. Not wary.

He'd looked up and down the street. "This is the last tenement on this block."

"Used to be nothing but tenements. Place I lived in for forty years was right there, see that vacant lot? There? I lived here for, lessee, five years or so. How about that? Almost half a century on the same block. God*damn*, that's a scary thought."

"Your family lived in the neighborhood all your life?"

The woman had set down the thin plastic grocery bag, containing two cans, two oranges and a half gallon jug of wine.

"You bet I have. My Grandpa Ledbetter came up from Raleigh in 1862. His train, it came in at ten at night and he walked out of the station and saw these boys, dozens of 'em, in an alley and said, 'Lord, why ain't you home?' and they said, 'What're you talking? This *is* our home. Go on with you, old man.' He felt so bad for those boys. Sleeping outside was called 'carrying the banner,' and thousands of children had to do it. They had no home otherwise."

She'd spoken without a trace of accent, a deep, melodious voice – a singer's voice as he would later learn.

"Was it a nice building?" Pellam had asked, gazing at the vacant lot, overgrown with weeds, where apparently the woman's old tenement had once stood.

"Where I lived? That old thing?" She'd laughed. "Falling down ug-*ly!* You know something interesting though. *I* thought it was interesting, anyway. When they tore it down there was a big crowd of people came to complain. You know, protestor sorts. 'Don't take our homes,' they were yelling. 'Don't take our homes.' Course I didn't recognize most of 'em from the neighborhood. I think they were students come down from Morningside Heights or the Village 'cause they smelled a good protest. Get the picture? *Those* sorts.

"Anyway, who'd I meet but a woman I knew a long, long time

ago. Many years. She was close to ninety then, been married to a man much older run a livery stable and sold horses to the army. Hell's Kitchen used to be the stable of New York. Still have the hansom cab stables here. Anyway, this woman, she'd been born in that very building they were tearing down. Ineeda Jones. Not Anita, like you're thinking. Ineeda. Like *I need a*. That was a southern name, a Carolina name. She was up in Harlem for years then she came back to the Kitchen and was poor as me. Cradle to grave, cradle to grave. Say, mister, I don't take any offense but what exactly're you smiling at?"

"Can I ask your name?"

"I'm Ettie Washington."

"Well, Ms Washington, my name's John Pellam. How'd you like to be in a movie?"

"A movie? Hell. Say, why don't you come on upstairs? Have some wine."

The interviews had begun the next week. Pellam would climb the six flights to her apartment and turn on the recorder and let Ettie Washington talk.

And talk she did. About her family, her childhood, her life.

Age six, sitting on a scrap of purloined Sears Roebuck carpet beside a window, listening to her mother and grandmother swap stories about turn-of-the-century Hell's Kitchen, Owney Madden, the Gophers – the most notorious gang in the city.

". . . My Grandpa Ledbetter, he used a lot of slang he heard on the street when he was a young man. He'd say 'booly dog' for a policeman. A 'flat' was a man you could fool, like at a card game. 'Blue ruin' was gin. And 'chips' was money. My brother Ben'd laugh and say, 'Grandpa, don't nobody use those words no more.' But he was wrong. Grandpa always said 'crib' for where you live, your home, you know? And people're saying that again nowadays."

Ettie at age ten, working her first job, sweeping sawdust and wrapping meat in a butcher store.

Age twelve, in school, numbers easy and words hard, but getting mostly As. Stealing scraps from restaurant bins for lunch. Classmates vanishing as the need for money edged out the need for learning.

Age fourteen, her beloved and feared Grandma Ledbetter dying as she sat on the couch at Ettie's side one hot Sunday afternoon a week before her 99th birthday.

Age fifteen, Ettie herself finally leaving school, working for twenty cents an hour, sharpening knives and chisels in a paperboard factory, stropping blades on long, speeding bands of leather. Some of the men gave her extra pennies because she worked hard. Some would call her back into the stock room and touch her chest and say don't tell. One touched her between her legs and before he could say don't tell he received his own knife deep in his thigh. He was bandaged up and given the day off with pay. Ettie was fired.

Age seventeen, sneaking into clubs to hear Bessie Smith on Fifty-second Street.

". . . Wasn't much in the way of entertainment in the Kitchen. But if Mama and Papa had an extra dollar or two, they'd go down to the Bowery on the East Side, where they had what they called 'museums,' which weren't what you think. They were arcades – freak shows and varieties and dancers. Vaudeville. For a really good time Mama and Papa'd go to Marshall's on Fifty-third. You never heard of that but it was a hotel and nightclub for blacks. That was the big time, none better. Ada Overton Walker sung there. Will Dixon too."

Age thirty-eight, a decade of cabaret jobs behind her, the singing work drying up. Ettie, falling for a handsome Irishman. Billy Doyle, a charmer, a man with, apparently, a criminal record (Pellam was still waiting to hear the end of that story).

Age forty-two, the marriage not working. She was restless, still wanting to sing. Billy was restless too. Wanting to succeed, looking for his own niche. Finally he told her he was going off to find a better job and would send for her. Of course he never returned and that broke her heart. All she ever heard from him was a short note that accompanied the Nevada divorce decree.

At forty-four, marrying Harold Washington, who died drunk in the Hudson River some years later. A good man in many ways, a hard worker, he still left more debt than seemed fair for a man who never played the horses.

Tape after tape of these stories. Five hours, ten, twenty.

"You *can't* really be interested in all of this, can you?" Ettie had asked Pellam.

"Keep going, Ettie. You're on a roll." Pellam had told himself to get outside and interview other residents of the infamous neighborhood. And he had – some of them. But Ettie Washington remained the heart of *West of Eighth*. Billy Doyle, the Ledbetters, the Wilkeses, the Washingtons, Prohibition, the unions, gangs, epidemics, the Depression, World War Two, the stockyards, the ocean liners, apartments, landlords.

Ettie *was* on a roll. And the roll never stopped.

Until her arrest for murder and arson.

Now, a blistering afternoon, a uniformed guard handed John Pellam a pass and ushered him through the dank halls, where the scent of Lysol ran neck and neck with that of urine. He passed through the metal detector then stepped into the visiting room to wait.

The Detention Center was chaotic today. Shouts in the distance. A wailing voice or two.

"Me duele la garganta!"

"Yo, bitch—"

"Estoy enfermo!"

"Yo, bitch, I'ma come over there and shut you up fo' good."

Five minutes later the green metal door opened, with a two-note creak. A guard came in, glanced at him. "You here for Washington? She's not here."

Pellam asked where she was.

"You better go to the second floor."

"Is she all right?"

"Second floor."

"You didn't answer me."

But the guard was gone.

He walked through the bleak corridors until he came to the dark alcove where he'd been directed. It was no less dirty but it was cooler and quieter. A guard glanced at his pass and let him through another door. He pushed inside and was surprised to see Ettie sitting at a table, hands clasped together. There was a bandage on her face.

"Ettie, what happened? Why're you up here?"

"Isolation," she whispered. "They were going to kill me."

"Who?"

"Some girls. In the cell downstairs. They heard about the Torres boy dying. They fooled me pretty good. I thought they were my friends but they were planning all along to kill me. Louis got some court order or another to move me. The guards came just as those girls were about to burn me. They sprayed stuff on me and were gonna burn my face, John. The stuff, it hurt my skin."

"How're you feeling now?"

She didn't answer. She said, "Oh, I never thought that boy'd die. That gave me a turn. Oh, the poor thing. He was such a sweet little one. If he'd been at his grandmother's like he was supposed to be he'd still be alive . . . I prayed for him. I did! And you know me – I don't waste *any* time on religion."

Pellam put his hand on Ettie's good arm. He thought about saying, 'He wasn't in any pain,' or 'He went quickly,' but of course he had no idea how much pain the boy had experienced or how quickly he'd died.

Finally she glanced at his unsmiling face. "I saw you in court. When you heard 'bout that time I got myself arrested . . . You want to know about that, I'll bet."

"What happened?"

"Remember the time Priscilla Cabot and me were working at that factory? The clothing place?"

"They fired you. A few years ago."

"It was a desperate time for me, John. My sister'd been sick. And I didn't have *any* money at all. I was beside myself. Anyway, this man Priscilla and I worked with, we all got laid off together and he had this idea to scare the company so they'd pay us money. We figured we were owed it, you know. Hell, I went along with 'em. Shouldn't've. Didn't really want to. But the long and short of it was they called up the owner and said his trucks were going to get wrecked if he didn't pay us. We weren't really going to do anything. At least, *I* wasn't. And I didn't know they threatened to *burn* them. I didn't call; *they* did, Priscilla and this man.

"Anyway, the boss, he agreed but he called the police and we all got arrested and the other two said it was my idea. Well, the police didn't believe I was the ringleader but I did get arrested and I spent some time in jail. I'm not proud of it. I'm pretty ashamed . . . I'm sorry, John. I didn't tell you the truth 'bout that. I should've."

"There's no reason for you to tell me everything about yourself."

"No, John. We were friends too. I shouldn'ta lied. Shoulda told Louis too. Didn't help in court any."

Near them someone laughed hysterically, the sound rising higher and higher until it became a faint scream. Then silence.

"You've got your secrets; I do too," Pellam said. "I've kept some things from you."

She looked at him closely. City life gives you a quick eye. "What is it, John?"

He was debating.

"Something you want to tell me, isn't there?" she asked.

Finally he said, "Manslaughter."

"What?"

"I did time for manslaughter."

Her eyes grew still. It was a story that he had no interest to tell, no desire to relieve. But he thought it was important to share it with her. And tell it he did – the story about the star of Pellam's last feature film – the one never completed (the four canisters of film were sitting at the moment in his attic back in California). *Central Standard Time*. Tommy Bernstein, lovable, crazy, out of control. Only six setups left to shoot, four second-unit stunt gags. A week. Only a week. "*Just give me a little, John. Just to get me through wrap.*"

But Pellam hadn't given him a little. Pellam had given him a lot and the man had stayed up in his coke-induced frenzy for two days straight. Railing, laughing, drinking, puking. He died of a heart attack on the set. And the City of Angels' District Attorney chose to go after Pellam in a big way for supplying the cocaine that caused it. He was the guilty party, the D.A. claimed, and the jury agreed, bestowing on Pellam a conviction and some time in San Quentin.

"I am sorry, John." She laughed, "Isn't that a stitch? You, me and Billy Doyle. We're all three of us jailbirds." She squinted again. "You know who you remind me of? My son James."

Pellam had seen pictures of the young man. Ettie's oldest son, her only child by Doyle. Photographed in his early twenties, he was light-skinned – Doyle had been very pale – and handsome. Lean. James had dropped out of school several years ago and gone out west to make money. The last word from him was a card saying the young man was going to work in the "environmental field."

That had been over a decade ago.

The guard glanced at her watch and Pellam whispered, "We don't have much time. I've got to ask you a few questions. Now, that insurance policy they claim you bought had your checking account number on it and your signature on it. How'd somebody get them?"

"My checking account? Well, I don't know. Nobody's got my account number that I know 'bout."

"Have you lost any checks lately?"

"No."

"Who do you write checks to?"

"I don't know . . . I pay my bills like everybody. Mama put that in me. Never let 'em get the edge on you, she always said. Pay on time. If you've got the money."

"You written any checks to somebody you wouldn't ordinarily?"

"No, not that I can think. Oh, wait. I had to pay some money to the government few months ago. They gave me too much social security by mistake. One check had three hundred more'n I ought to get. I knew about it but I kept it anyway. They found out and wanted it back. That's what I hired Louis for. He handled it for me. All I had to pay was half what they wanted. I gave him a check and he sent it to 'em with this form. See, the government, maybe they're out to get me, John. Maybe the social security people and the police're working together."

This manic talk of conspiracies unsettled him. But Pellam cut her some slack. Under the circumstances she was entitled to be a little paranoid.

"How 'bout samples of your handwriting? How could somebody get them?"

"I don't know."

"Have you written any letters lately to somebody you don't normally write?"

"Letters? I can't think of any. I write to Elizabeth and send cards sometimes to my sister's daughter in Fresno. Send 'em a few dollars on their birthdays. That's about it."

"Anybody broken into your apartment?"

"No. I always lock my windows and door. I'm good about that. In the Kitchen you got to be careful. That's the first thing you learn." She played with her cast, traced Pellam's signature. The answers made sense but they weren't compelling. To a jury they might be true, might be fishy. As with so much else about Hell's Kitchen he wasn't sure what to believe.

Pellam slipped his notebook into his pocket and said, "Will you do something for me?"

"Anything, John."

"Tell me the end of the Billy Doyle story."

"Which story? About his doing time?"

"That one, yeah."

"Okay. My poor Billy. Here's what happened. I told you all along that his goal in life was to own land. For a man with wanderlust he couldn't go past a lot or a building with a for-sale sign on it without looking it over and calling up the owner and asking questions about it."

Ettie's eyes glowed. This was where she belonged, Pellam thought, weighing memories and using them to spin her stories. He knew the seductive lure of story-telling too; he was after all a film director. Except that her stories were true and she expected nothing in return for them. No critical acclaim. No percentage of gross.

"You remember I told you about my brother, Ben. He was about Billy's age, a year or two younger. Ben came to Billy and said he had this idea how to get some money for a down payment for some land, only he needed a partner to help him. Well, it wasn't an idea at all. It was just a scam. Ben knew some people at a union headquarters and he did some fake contracts and got them slipped in when the bosses weren't there. Ben listened too much to Grandpa Ledbetter's stories about the Gophers and the gangs. He wanted to be in one real bad – even though there weren't any black gangs in the Kitchen, then or now. But he was real proud of this scam of his.

"But Ben didn't tell my Billy about the scam part. He thought they were just real contracts for hauling and stuff, they were taking a broker's fee on. He lived on the edge, Billy did, but he wasn't stupid. There might've been people he'd scam but the union wasn't one of them. Then Lemmy Collins, the longshoremen's vice-president, found out there was money missing. He thought Ben'd done it. He knew Billy was tight with Ben but he knew an Irishman wouldn't steal from his own but a black man'd steal from Irish without thinking twice. So Lemmy came to see my brother with two other men from the union and a baseball bat.

"Just as they were about to beat him to death they got a call from union headquarters. The police had called. It seemed that my Billy'd confessed to the whole thing. It was all his idea. Since the police were involved then Lemmy couldn't kill Ben even thought he wanted to. The union got the money back and Billy did a year in jail. See, he knew being Irish and white he could get away with his life. If Ben had gone down he would've died. If not in the Kitchen then in Sing Sing."

"He took a rap for somebody," Pellam said.

"For my own brother," Ettie said.

Pellam added softly, "He did that for you, you know."

"I know he did." Ettie was wistful. "But I think that year changed him. I got my brother saved but I think I might've lost my husband because of it. It was a year after he got out that I came home one night and found the note."

"Excuse me, sir," the guard said pleasantly. "I'm afraid time's up."

Pellam nodded to the guard. "Just one more thing. Hey, Mrs Washington, look up."

There was a snap and the soft buzz of a small motor.

She blinked at the flash as Pellam took the Polaroid.

"What're you doing there, John? You don't want to remember me this way. Lemme fix my hair, at least."

"It's not for me, Ettie. And don't you worry. Your hair looks just fine."

15

L efty came through.

Pellam was in his bitchen, boots off, listening to messages, as he sat on the plywood sheet turning the bathtub into a table. There was one hang-up, then another. Finally Alan Lefkowitz's mile-a-minute voice was telling him about a party Roger McKennah had planned and that Pellam had only to drop Lefty's name and he'd be admitted into the "inner sanctum of New York business," a line the producer actually recited without noticeable irony. Pellam, however, rolled his eyes as he listened to it, kicking his foot against the wall to scare off a wise-ass pigeon that alighted on his window sill.

The lengthy message continued with relevant details, including the orders to dress for the event.

An hour later, Pellam, suitably "dressed" (new black jeans and polished Nokona cowboy boots) strolled out into the suffocating heat and took a subway to the Citicorp building.

From there he walked to an address on Fifth Avenue and ducked into the revolving door. Once inside nobody knew that he, unlike most of the other guests, hadn't arrived via Bentley, Rolls-Royce, or – for the impoverished – the stately yacht of a Lincoln Continental.

"Look, it's another one."

The woman spoke breathlessly and the crowd on the top floor of the triplex murmured less in horror than appreciation.

"Oh, man. Look at that. You can see the flames."

"Where?"

"There. See?"

"Ronnie, go see if someone's got a camera. Joan, look!"

Pellam eased closer to the window, six hundred feet above the sidewalk on which Cartier, Tiffany and Henri Bendel hawked their wares. He gazed west. Another fire, he noticed with disgust. A building somewhere in Hell's Kitchen, north of Louis Bailey's block. Occasionally you'd see a lick of flame shooting through a massive cloud of smoke. Rising a thousand feet into the milky sky, it blossomed like the mushroom of an atomic bomb.

"Oh, God," a woman whispered. "It's the hospital! Manhattan Hospital."

Where he and Ettie had been treated, he realized. Where Juan Torres had died.

"You think it's him? Where *is* that camera? I want to get a snap. You know who I mean? That crazy man I read about in the *Times* this morning?"

"Is that the fifth one he's set? Or the sixth?"

The flames had grown and were now clearly visible.

No cameras materialized and after five minutes the fire became just another part of the scenery. Alone or in groups of two or three the guests turned back to the party.

Pellam continued to watch for a few moments. The silent ballet of the flames, the cloud of gray smoke rising high above Manhattan.

"Hey, how you doing?" The man's voice was close by, riddled with Long Island lockjaw. "You're dressed like an artiste. Are you an artiste?"

Pellam turned, found himself standing in front of a drunk, beefy young man in a tuxedo.

"Nope."

"Ah. Quite a place, isn't it?" He gestured his groggy head around the two-story living room in the Fifth Avenue penthouse triplex. "Roger's little abode in the sky."

"Not too shabby."

At that moment Pellam caught sight of his quarry across the room. Roger McKennah. Then the real estate developer was lost in the crowd again.

"You know the story?" Pellam's new friend began laughing drunkenly. Sipped more of his martini.

"The story?" Pellam responded.

The young man nodded enthusiastically but said nothing more.

Pellam prompted, "The one about the priest, the rabbi and the nun?"

The man frowned, shook his head then continued drunkenly and began explaining how the triplex here was latticed with rabbit warrens of rooms McKennah described as *dens* and *parlors* and *music rooms* and *entertainment spaces*.

"Uh-huh," Pellam said uncertainly, looking over the crowd for McKennah once more.

"They're really just bedrooms, see?" the young man told Pellam, spilling vodka on his patent leather shoes. "But there're fifteen of them and the thing is, Roger McKennah doesn't have a single friend – I mean, *forget* fifteen – who'd be willing to endure him long enough to stay overnight."

The young man shivered with laughter and drank some more of the alcohol that the butt of his mean joke was providing. A blonde in a low-cut red dress cruised past. She caught the eyes of both Pellam and the young man and suddenly the young man vanished as if he were the tail and she, the dog.

Pellam gazed out the window again, at the huge plume of smoke.

In the hour he'd been here he'd learned a few things about McKennah, much of it like the sniping he'd just heard, none of it particularly helpful. The developer was forty-four. Stocky but fit. His face was a younger, puffier Robert Redford's. His net worth was rumored to be two billion. Pellam had observed that the developer had a kaleidoscope of expressions; McKennah's visage flipped from boyish to greedy to demonic to pure ice in a fraction of a second.

In fact the most telling thing that Pellam had learned was that no one really knew much about Roger McKennah at all. His only conclusion was that the developer had some inexpressible quality that drove guests like these – attractive or powerful or obsessed with the attractive or powerful – to pray for invitations to his parties, where they would drink his liquor and think of clever ways to insult him behind his back.

He eased closer to McKennah, who had moved on and was cruising slowly through the crowded room.

A young couple double-teamed the developer by the beluga table.

"Nice, Roger," the husband said, looking around. "Very nice. Know what this room reminds me of? That place in Cap d'Antibes. On the Point? L'Hermitage. That's where Beth and I always stay."

"You know it?" the woman, presumably Beth, asked McKennah. "It's *so* wonderful."

The developer demurred with a faint pout. "'Fraid I don't," he said, to their delight. Then he added, "When I'm over there I usually stay with the prince in Monaco. It's just easier. You know."

"I hear you," the husband said, hearing nothing really. The couple pasted glazed smiles on their faces, evidence of how snugly their hearts had been nailed by the chubby Roger McKennah.

The substantial crowd milled and hovered over the tables filled with caviar like black snowdrifts and sushi like white jewels, while a tuxedoed pianist played Fats Waller.

"But he didn't *go* to Choate," Pellam overheard someone whisper. "Read it carefully. He gives them money, he lectures there, but he didn't *go* there. He went to some parochial school on the West Side. In his old neighborhood."

"Hell's Kitchen?" Pellam asked, breaking into the circle.

"That's it, yes," responded the woman, whose face-lift was remarkably good.

So, McKennah was a Kitchen pup himself. It must've taken years to polish off the rough edges.

Then suddenly Pellam himself became the prey. The crowd had momentarily parted like the Red Sea and McKennah was staring directly at him, fifty feet away. A memory came back to Pellam – the limousine in front of Ettie's building. It had probably been McKennah's.

But the developer gave no greeting. And as the crowd swept back together McKennah turned and stepped into a cluster of guests and turned his attention on them like klieg lights on a movie set. Then the developer was moving again, on stage, always questioning, poking, probing.

Ambition's a bitch, ain't it?

He was about to follow when, from behind him, a woman's voice said in a very Northeastern accent, "Howdy, partner."

Pellam turned to see an attractive blonde woman in her forties, holding a champagne flute. Her eyes were faded, but not from drinking, merely from exhaustion. With a sequined shoe she tapped Pellam's boot, explaining the greeting.

"Hi," he said.

Her eyes flitted to McKennah. Pellam followed her gaze. She said, "Which one?"

"I'm sorry?" Pellam asked.

"You a betting man?"

He said, "To paraphrase Mark Twain, there are only two times a man shouldn't gamble. One, when he can't afford to lose money. And two, when he can."

"That didn't answer my question."

"Yep, I'm a gambling man," Pellam said.

"You see those two women. The brunette and the redhead?"

Pellam spotted them easily. They stood by the sweeping

staircase, chatting with McKennah. Both in their late twenties, good figures, attractive. The redhead was by far the sexier and more voluptuous. The brunette had a colder face and she seemed distracted, almost bored.

"In about five minutes, Roger'll disappear upstairs. That's where the bedrooms are. Five minutes after that, one of those women will follow. Which one do you think it'll be?"

"Does he know either of them?"

"Probably not. You on?"

Pellam studied the redhead: The extreme *V* of her neckline, revealing the upper slope of white breasts. Hair tumbling around her shoulders. A seductive smile. And freckles. Pellam loved freckles.

"The redhead," he said, thinking: Eight months, eight months. Eight goddamn months.

The woman laughed. "You're wrong."

"What're we betting?"

"A glass of our host's champagne. As Mark Twain also said, it's always better to gamble with somebody else's money than your own."

They tapped glasses.

Her name was Jolie and it seemed that she was unaccompanied. He followed her to the window in the corner of the room, where it was quieter.

"You're John Pellam."

He gave a perplexed smile.

"I heard somebody mention your name."

Who? he wondered. It didn't seem likely that the Word on the streets of Hell's Kitchen would rise all the way into this stratosphere.

"I saw one of your films," she said. "About an alchemist. It was very good. I can't say I completely understood it. But that's a compliment."

"Is it?" he asked, looking at her steady, green eyes.

She continued. "Think about Kubrick's *2001*. It's not a very good movie. So why did it endure? The Blue Danube with the space ship? Anybody could've thought of that. The monkeys beating each other up? No. Special effects? Of course not. It was the *ending*. Nobody knew what the hell it was about. We forget the obvious. We remember the uncertain."

He laughed. "I do love my ambiguity," Pellam said, eyes on McKennah. "So, okay, I'll consider it a compliment."

"Are you making a film here?"

"Yes," he answered.

Across the room McKennah glanced around, trying to look casual, then trotted up the stairs.

Maybe he was just going to take a pee, Pellam thought. They hadn't considered the contingency of a draw. Pellam didn't care; he was enjoying her company. Jolie had a *V*-shaped neckline that held its own with the redhead's very admirably. Pellam even thought he saw a few freckles where the white flesh disappeared beneath black sequins.

"What's it about?" Jolie asked. "Your new film?"

"It's not a feature. It's a documentary. About Hell's Kitchen."

"That fire's an interesting metaphor, isn't it?" She nodded out the window. There was a faint smile on her face. "It'd be a good motif for your film." She added cryptically, "Whatever it's *really* about."

"How do you know McKennah?" he asked. Then the words registered: *Really about* . . .

Across the room the sullen brunette stubbed out a cigarette and, lifting her slinky skirt a few inches, looked around discreetly. She climbed the stairs in the tracks of the developer.

"Good guess," Pellam said.

"Wasn't a guess," Jolie responded. "I know my husband pretty well. Now get me the champagne you owe me. Get one for yourself too. Then let's go in there and drink it." She nodded toward a small den off the main room. And smiled as the piano player launched into *Stormy Weather*.

"You know, one of our cleaning ladies sells what she finds in our trash cans to the government. IRS, SEC. Competitors, too, I'm sure. Roger has fun putting phoney info in the trash along with Tampax wrappers and condoms."

"The IRS pays for that?" Pellam asked.

"Yep."

"So that'd be *my* tax dollars at work?" Pellam asked.

"You don't really pay tax, do you?" she seemed surprised. "If you do I'll give you the name of my accountant."

They sat in the teak-paneled den, the sounds of the party and the music filtering through the walls. Pellam picked up a picture of McKennah with his arm around a large Mickey Mouse.

"A few years ago," Jolie said, entranced by the frantic bubbles in her champagne, "he was really into Euro Disney. He took a bad hit there. I told him it was a bad idea. I just couldn't see French people wearing big black ears."

"Why are you so cool about what just happened? With your husband?"

"You're from Hollywood, I assume you know the difference between being cool and acting cool."

"Touché. How'd you figure the brunette?"

"She was the tougher one. More of a challenge. Roger never takes the easy way. His office is on the seventieth floor of this building. He walks up every one of those flights in the morning."

"Quite a view," Pellam said, walking to the floor-to-ceiling windows. He gazed out over dusky Manhattan. Jolie pointed out several buildings that bore McKennah's name and several more, older ones, that she explained were owned or operated by his companies.

Pellam lifted his hands and pressed the cold glass with his fingers. Because of the faint light in the den his reflection appeared to be an angel floating outside, touching Pellam's fingertips with its own.

"Your film, it's about Roger, isn't it?"

"No. It's about the old West Side."

"Then why are you spying on him?"

He said nothing.

Jolie said, "We're getting divorced, Roger and I."

Pellam continued to stare at the lights of the city. Was this a setup? Was *she* spying on him? Hollywood made you paranoid for your job; Hell's Kitchen, your life.

But he had a vague sense that he should trust her. He recalled the look in her eyes when she saw the brunette lift her skirt and start up the stairs. Pellam had worked with many actresses, some of them excellent, but very few had enough command of the Method to summon up that kind of pain.

"There's talk about you," Jolie McKennah said.

In the distance the fire on the West Side had been mostly extinguished. Still, you could see a hundred lights from the emergency vehicles, flashing like lasers in a tawdry disco.

"Did he say anything?" Pellam didn't know whether nodding at the ceiling, where McKennah was bedding the tough brunette, was appropriate.

"No, but he knows about you. He's been watching you."

"So, why are we here? Talk to me."

She sipped then smiled mournfully. "We never had any secrets, Roger and I. None. It got to the point where I even knew his girlfriends' bra sizes. But then something happened."

"Attrition?"

"That's good, Pellam. Yes, exactly. Little by little things got worn down. We haven't been in love for a long time. Oh, ages. But we were close and we were friends. But then that went away. That friendship part. He began lying to me. That broke the rules. We decided to get divorced."

He decided to get divorced, she meant.

"And you feel betrayed."

She considered refuting this. But she said, "Yes, I felt betrayed."

He was gazing out the window, past his reflection. "The arson on Thirty-sixth street? Some of the men who work for his company were nearby that building just before the fire."

This got her attention.

"So, you're a crusader, are you?"

"Not hardly. I just want to know who was behind it."

"I don't think Roger would ever do anything like that."

" 'Think.' "

He could see she wasn't sure. She held the champagne

beneath her nose and inhaled. "You find me attractive?"

"Yes." It was true and had nothing to do with the glacial eight months.

"You want to make love to me?"

"Another time, another place, yes, I would."

This satisfied her. How fragile is our vanity and how recklessly we wear it for all to crush.

"Tell me what you're really after and maybe I can help you."

And maybe she can cut me off at the knees.

"Ah, you're hesitating," she continued. "Think I'll report back to him. Think I'm a spy?"

"Maybe."

"I thought you were a gambling man."

"The stakes're high."

"How much? One billion? Two?"

"Ten years of an old woman's life."

She hesitated. "I don't have any power over him anymore. Not like I did." She nodded toward the party but the gesture was aimed like a sniper rifle at all the brunettes and redheads and blondes in the room. "And I'll never get that back. He's won, hands down, in that arena – the bedroom, our home. So I have to hurt him the only way I still can. In his business."

He said, "That woman I mentioned. She was a tenant in the building that burned down. She's been arrested for the arson and she didn't do it."

"Washington's her name," Jolie said. "I read about that. An insurance scam or something."

Pellam nodded. "Did your husband burn the place down?"

Jolie thought for a long moment, staring again at the needlepoint bubbles. "Not the old Roger. No, he wouldn't. The new Roger . . . all I can say is he's become a stranger. He doesn't talk to me anymore. He's just not the same man I married. I *will* tell you he's been going out a couple times a week. At night. He's never done that before – I mean, not without telling me. And he's never lied to me about it. He'll get a phone call then leave."

"You know who's calling?"

"I did that star 69 thing on the phone. To dial back the call that just came in? It was a law firm. Not one that I've ever heard of before."

"What was the name?"

"Pillsbury, Millbank & Hogue," she said. Pellam heard an edge in the woman's otherwise controlled voice. It quavered. She continued. "The chauffeur drops him off on Ninth Avenue and Fiftieth. He meets someone, some man. The meetings are secret."

"The chauffeur," Pellam asked delicately, "could he be more informative?"

"He'd be willing to," she said. "But Roger makes sure he leaves after he drops him off."

Pellam jotted down the name of the firm and the address.

She said, "You know, he has good qualities. He gives money to charities."

So presumably do some serial killers. At least those who need write-offs.

Jolie took his glass from the table and sipped it. Hers was empty. Pellam said, "What you just told me could cost him a lot. And it could cost you a lot too."

"Me?"

"The divorce? Isn't he going to be paying you a settlement, alimony?"

Laughter. "You dear man, why you really *do* pay taxes, don't you? Let's just say, I've looked out for myself. Whatever happens to Roger won't affect me in any fiscal way."

Pellam glanced down at her taut, tanned skin. Eight months. A hell of a long time.

"To another time, another place," she said, lifting the glass.

He remained at the window for a moment, gazing at the radiant buildings of Manhattan, then stepped toward the door, while outside, reflected in the window, Pellam's angel also turned, lowered his ghostly arms and faded into the night above the city.

Fire points up not down.

Fire climbs, it doesn't fall.

Sonny gazed at the map.

The hospital had been a good fire, not a great fire. Too many good citizens were vigilant. Too many cops, too many fire marshals. Looking and poking. Everybody ready to dial nine-one-one. Everybody ready to shoot carbon dioxide from extinguishers.

They all took this so fucking seriously.

He was distracted too – by thoughts of the Antichrist cowboy, Pellam. Sonny thought he saw him everywhere. In shadows, in alleys. He's after me . . .

He's the reason I'm sweating. *He's* the reason my hands shake.

Sweat poured from Sonny's brow and soaked his hair. Usually the shade of pale citrus, the strands today were dark with moisture. His breath came fast and occasionally his tongue would protrude like a pink eel and dampen a parched lip.

A movie theater was next on his list. He'd debated about whether to burn a faggot porno theater or a regular theater. He decided on a regular one.

First, though, he needed some more supplies. Arsonist are lucky because, unlike bombers or snipers, the tools of their trade are completely legal. Still, they have to be careful and Sonny alternated the places where he bought his ingredients, never showing up at the same gas station more frequently than once a month or so. But Manhattan had surprisingly few gas stations – they were mostly in Jersey or on Long Island – and, because he had no car, he could only shop at those stations within walking distance of his apartment.

He was now on his way to the East Village, to a station he hadn't been to for more than a year. It was a long walk and would be an even longer walk back with the five gallons of gas. But he was afraid to tempt fate by making a purchase any closer to home.

He thought about how many jars of his juice he'd need for a movie theater.

Just one probably.

Sometimes Sonny would crouch for hours outside a building and try to decide how he could burn it down most efficiently. He was very thin, excruciatingly thin, and when he squatted outside Grand Central Station, say, playing the how-many-jars game, people would drop coins at his feet, thinking he was homeless and had *AIDS* or just thinking *That man is so damn thin* and all the time he'd have a thousand dollars in his pocket, be fit as a fiddle and was merely squatting on the curb enjoying his fantasy about razing the baroque station with as few fires as possible.

Grand Central would require seven fires, he'd decided.

Rockefeller Center, sixteen. The Empire State Building, merely four. The World Trade towers, five each (those crazy Arabs got it all wrong).

Sonny now walked past the gas station, nonchalant, looking carefully for police or fire marshals. He'd seen more squad cars patrolling the streets around stations in the last day. But here he saw none and returned to the station, walking up to the pump furthest from the attendant's office. He uncapped the can and began to pump.

The sweet smell brought back many wonderful memories.

Sonny had known from the first hour of his first visit to the city eight years ago that he would live and die here. New York! How could he live anywhere else? The asphalt streets were hot, steam flowed like smoke from a thousand manholes, buildings burned daily and no one seemed to pay that fact much mind. This was the only city in the world where somebody would ignite trashcans and cars and abandoned buildings, and passersby would glance at the fire and continue on their way as if flames were just a part of the natural landscape.

He'd come to the city after his release from Juvenile Detention. For a time Sonny worked office jobs – messenger, mail boy, Xerox operator. But for every hour in offices or in his probation counselor's office Sonny spent two honing his craft, working for landlords and real estate developers and even the Mafia occasionally. Gasoline, natural gas, nitrates, naphtha, acetone. And his precious juice, created by Sonny himself, virtually patented, adored by him the way Bach loved the keyboard.

Juice. Fire that kisses human skin and won't let go.

In his first years living in the city, on the West Side, he wasn't as solitary as he was now. He'd meet people on the job and he even dated some. But he'd soon grown bored with people. Dates became awkward early in the evening and after several hours the only thing they had in common was a persistent desire to be rid of each other's company. In restaurants he tended to stare at the candles more than his companion's eyes.

In the end Sonny proved to be his own best friend. He lived alone in small, neat apartments. He ironed his clothing perfectly, balanced his checkbook, attended art films and lectures on nineteenth-century New York, watched *This Old House* and educational specials and sitcoms.

And he lived to watch things burn into exquisite, still ash.

As the gasoline can filled with tender, rosy liquid he found himself thinking again about Pellam. The tall, black-clad angel of death. The Antichrist. The moth frying itself to death against the bulb that so attracts him.

Ah, Pellam . . . Isn't it astonishing how our lives have become so entwined? Like the strands of a wick. Isn't it odd how fate works that way? You're looking for me and I'm looking for you . . . Will you be my mate forever? We'll lie together in a bed of fire, we'll turn into pure light, we'll be immortal . . .

Three gallons. As he glanced at the pump gauge he happened to look past it and he focused on the attendant, who was stepping quickly back inside the tiny cashier stand.

188 • *Jeffery Deaver*

Three and a third gallons . . .

Sonny left the nozzle in the can, stepped toward the attendant's stand, saw the man on the phone. He returned to the pump. *Hmm.* Problem here. Problem.

What do we do?

As the three squad cars rolled silently into the station the police officers found Sonny standing motionless, looking uncertainly toward the attendant station, the pump nozzle in his hand.

Problem . . .

"Excuse me, sir," a cop's voice called. "I wonder if you could hang that pump up and come over here?"

The police climbed out of the cars.

Five of the six cops had their hands on their pistol grips.

"What's the problem, officer?"

"Just hang that up, that nozzle. Okay? Do it now."

"Sure, officer. Sure."

He shoved the high-test nozzle back into the pump.

"You have some ID on you, sir?"

"I didn't do anything. I don't even have a car. What do you want to give me a ticket for?" He fished into his pocket.

"Just step over here, sir. And if we could see some ID."

"Okay, sure. Did I do something wrong?" Sonny didn't move.

"Now, sir. Step over here now."

"Yessir. I'd be happy to."

"Oh, Christ, no!" a heavily accented voice shouted from behind him. Sonny was surprised it had taken the station attendant so long to notice. "The gas! The *other* line's the one turned on."

Sonny smiled. When he'd seen the police cars in the reflection of the pump he'd dropped the open gas hose on the ground and grabbed the high-test hose – the one he'd dutifully hung up, as ordered. At least twenty gallons of gas had poured out onto the apron and was flowing toward the cops and their car, invisible on the black asphalt.

In an split second, before a single officer could draw his gun, Sonny had his lighter out. He flicked it. A small flame burned on the end. He crouched down.

"Okay, mister," one cop said, holding up his hands. "Just put that down. Nobody's going to hurt you."

For a moment no one moved. But then, in a snap, they all knew it was coming. Maybe Sonny's eyes, maybe his smile . . . maybe something else gave it away. The six cops turned, fleeing from the deadly pool.

Sonny was on a dry patch of asphalt, though when he touched the flame to the flowing river of gasoline he leapt back fast, like a roach. The fireball was huge. He grabbed the container and fled.

A huge whoosh as the flames swept under the police cars, igniting them. The fiery river continued past them, flowing down Houston Street, roaring, sending a black cloud rolling into the sky. Screams, horns, collisions, as cars stopped and backed away from the flames.

Sonny got a half-block away and couldn't help himself. He paused and turned to watch the chaos. He was at first disappointed that the main tank didn't go up but then he grew philosophical and simply enjoyed the fire for what it was.

Thinking:

Fire is not energy but a creature that lives and grows

and reproduces; it's born and it dies. It can out-think any-one.

Fire is the messenger of change.

The sun is fire and the sun is not even particularly hot.

Fire eats the dirt of men. Fire is the most blind justice.

Fire points toward God.

———◆◦◆◦◆———

16

"Hey, mister, you got yourself a famous lawyer working for you. He sued the Port Authority and won. You ever hear of anybody suing the city and winning?"

The man sitting at Louis Bailey's desk rose the instant Pellam entered the room. It was the green-jacket handicapper from yesterday. The man with a lock.

"Cleg, please," Bailey said, self-effacing.

"And tell him about the time you sued Rockefeller."

"Cleg."

The skinny guy seemed to have forgiven Pellam for not taking his tip about the horses. He said, "Rockefeller stole this guy's invention and Louis took him to court. *He* caved too. Louis scared the bejeebers out of him. Hey, sir, you look like a cowboy. Anybody ever tell you that? You ever ride broncos? What is that exactly, a bronco? I just know about the O.J. one. The white truck, I mean."

"It's an untamed horse," Pellam said.

"Well, how 'bout that," Cleg said, astonished – a handicapper who'd just discovered a different kind of horse. He took more gear-greasing envelopes from Bailey and left the office.

"He's quite a fellow," was all that Pellam could offer.

"You don't know the half of it," Bailey said ambiguously. Then he opened that morning's paper. Slapped it. "Look at this." The front page story was about a fire at a gas station in the Village. "That's our boy."

"The pyro?" Pellam asked.

"They're pretty sure. Almost got him but he got away. Seriously injured two cops and three pedestrians. Almost a million dollars in damage."

Pellam examined the picture of the devastation.

Bailey swallowed a mouthful of wine. "This is turning into a nightmare. There's a public uproar. The Police Department and the Attorney General are under incredible pressure to get this guy. They think that he's gone nuts. Like Ettie switched him on and he won't shut off now. It's become a citywide crusade to stop him."

Pellam bent wearily over the paper. There was a sidebar that included a map of Hell's Kitchen. Tiny drawings of flames marked the spots of the fires. They were in a pattern, it seemed – a semicircular shape north of Ettie's building.

Bailey found a slip of paper, handed it to Pellam. "That's the insurance agency where Ettie got the policy. The woman who sold it is a Florence Epstein."

"What'd she say?"

Bailey looked at Pellam with a significance that escaped him completely.

"I'm sorry?" Pellam tried.

"I can't talk to her. I'm Ettie's attorney of record."

"Oh, I get it. But I can."

Bailey sighed. "Well, yes, but . . ."

"But what?"

"You know, sometimes . . . well, with that black outfit of yours, you look a little intimidating. And you don't smile a lot."

"I'll be charm itself," Pellam said. "As long as she's not lying."

"If there's any hint of intimidation . . ."

"Do I look like the sort who intimidates?"

Bailey was suddenly very uncomfortable and he changed the subject. "Here. I went to the library." He set some clippings down in front of Pellam.

"You went yourself? You didn't bribe some librarian to bring them to you?"

"Ha." Bailey was too busy wrestling the seal off a new wine bottle to smile. "Some back-grounders about Roger McKennah."

Pellam shuffled through the clippings.

Business Week offered:

> *The best part of the prior decade for McKennah was the late eighties – when the market cindered, the boom went bust and careers 'Chappaquidicked' (a popular McKennahism) throughout Wall Street. Yet that was when he had shone the brightest.*

New York magazine:

> *. . . Roger McKennah, the self-confessed megalomaniac,*

*marched into third-world sections of the New York metro
area and strewed them with affordable (and profitable)
housing projects. He is also credited with revitalizing real
estate investment trusts and with prying a good portion
of midtown out of foreign hands and returning it to local
developers. Notable for his wit as well as his lifestyle and
business acumen, it was McKennah who coined the term
"vulturing" – spotting deals going bad and grabbing them
out from under receivers and trustees.*

From baroquely metaphorical *People*:

*Anyone – a Trump, a Zeckendorf, a Helmsley – could
ride the crest of prosperity. But only a genius like Roger
McKennah dared answer the call of "surf's up" when the
only place to hang ten was in the tunnel of the wave.*

Pellam put the articles aside.

"Makes him greedy and smart but hardly an arsonist," Bailey
commented.

"Then I better tell you about my date last night."

"The party at his place?"

"The caviar was a bit too warm. But I had champagne with
his wife."

Bailey was delighted. Fraternizing with the enemy was probably an important technique for gear-cloggers. "And?"

"She wants to sink him like the *Titanic*."

Pellam told the lawyer about McKennah's clandestine meetings and the calls to and from the law firm.

"Pillsbury, Millbank?" Bailey asked.

"I'm pretty sure that's what she said."

Bailey pulled a huge volume of Martindale Hubbell Lawyers Directory off his shelf and flipped it open. He found a listing of the firm. He read carefully, nodding. "I think I can get to somebody there."

Can get.

Pellam was reaching for his wallet.

"Not this time. I've got another idea. Oh, and I've got more good news. Something I forgot to tell you. A friend of mine has a friend who plays cards with a senior fire marshal. There's a poker game tonight and my buddy's going to get his buddy to lose big and pour a bottle of Macallan scotch very freely. We'll get some inside dope on the case."

"How old?"

"How old what?" Bailey asked.

"Is the Macallan?"

"I don't know. Twelve years probably. Maybe older."

"I'm thinking, Louis," Pellam said. "Maybe I'll do a documentary about you. I'll call it *Greasing Gears*. Say, did you really sue Rockefeller?"

"Oh, well, yes, I did," Bailey gazed modestly down at his desk. Then he shrugged. "But it wasn't one of *the* Rockefellers."

The footsteps were close behind him and moving in closer.

Pellam spun around, his hand slipping into the small of his back, where the Colt rested, heavy and hot, against his spine.

He looked down.

"Yo, cuz. Where you been?" Ismail was grinning, hands on his scrawny hips. Sweating furious but still in his beloved African National Congress windbreaker.

"Around, and you?"

"Yo, you got a gun. You carryin'."

"No I'm not."

"Yo. You be! You was reaching for yo' piece. Lemme see it, Pellam. Whatchu got? You got a Glock, you got a Brownin'? A trey five-seven? Man, I want a Desert Eagle. Blow yo' ass to kingdom come. Fucker be fifty caliber."

"I was reaching for my wallet. I figured you were a mugger."

"I ain't jack you, cuz." Ismail looked genuinely hurt.

"Where've you been?" Pellam asked him.

"Flaggin' and saggin'. You know."

Pellam laughed. "Your jeans aren't hanging down to your knees, my man. And I'll give you ten bucks you flash me some real crew signs."

But the boy knew them and gestured broadly. Pellam had no idea what the signs meant but they looked authentic. In an L.A. crew Ismail'd be considered a perfect T.G., a tiny gangster. He slipped him the ten dollars, hoping it would go for food.

"Thanks, cuz."

"How's your mother?"

"Dunno. She gone. My sister too."

"Gone? What do you mean?"

He shrugged. "Gone. Ain't 'round the shelter no more."

"Where're you hanging?"

"Don't got no place. Hey, whatchu looking, Pellam? You giving me the eye like that."

"Come on. There's somebody I want you to meet."

"Yeah? Who?"

"This woman."

"She a fox?"

"*I* think so. I don't know how you'll feel."

"Why you wanna introduce me to yo' bitch, Pellam?"

"Watch the language."

"No way."

"Ismail."

"No motherfuckin' way," he grumbled.

Pellam clamped his hand down hard on the boy's arm and dragged him into the Youth Outreach Center.

"Ismail, stop the swearing."

"Yo, cuz, I know what that bitch want. Man, she try to run a drag on me . . ."

"What's his name?" Carol Wyandotte asked, unfazed by the little ball of angry child in front of her.

"Ismail."

"Hello, Ismail. I'm Carol. I run this place."

"Yo, you a slob bitch and I ain't staying here—"

"That's it, young man," Pellam barked.

He responded, surly, "You keep that white bitch away from me."

Pellam thought he'd try the soft approach. He said calmly, "Ismail, look, some people don't think that's a very nice word to use."

"Okay, okay." The boy looked contrite. "I ain't say 'white' no more."

"Very funny."

"Oh, he doesn't mean 'bitch' that way," Carol said matter-of-factly, rocking back and studying him. "It's just verbal window dressing."

"Don't be telling me what I mean, bitch."

Pellam snapped, "You want to be my friend or not? Watch your mouth."

The boy crossed his arms and dropped sullenly onto the windowsill.

"His mother and sister've vanished," Pellam told her.

"Vanished?"

"From the shelter," Pellam explained.

"Ismail, what happened?"

"Dunno. I come back and they gone. Dunno where."

The boy had spotted a stack of comic books in the corner. He began flipping through an old issue of *X-Men*.

"Anything you can do for him?" Pellam asked.

Carol shrugged. "We could call SSC, Special Services for Children. They'll place him in an emergency home in twenty-four hours. He'll run away in twenty-five. I think we should keep him here for a few days, see if his mother shows up . . . Ismail?"

The boy looked up.

"You have a grandmother?"

"Hey, you don' know shit. The whole everbody got a grandmother."

"I mean, who you know."

He shrugged.

"Where's yours live?"

"Dunno."

"Either of them? How about aunts? Anybody else?"

"Dunno."

It hit Pellam hard that the boy didn't know any of his relatives. But Carol calmly said, "You like those books? We've got a lot of them."

He snorted, said defiantly, "Shit. I could 'jack myself a thousand motherfuckin' comics, I wanted to."

Pellam walked over to the boy, crouched down. "You and me, we're friends, right?"

"I guess. I dunno."

"Will you stay here for a while? And not make any waves."

Carol said to him, "We'll help you find your mother."

"I don't *want* her. She a cluckhead bitch. Doing rock all the time. She put the rush on all these guys, make some money. Mother*fuckers*, you know what I'm saying?"

Pellam offered, "Just stay for a little while. For me?"

He put down the book. "Okay, fo' you, Pellam, I do that." He eyed Carol. "But listen up, bitch—"

"Ismail!" Pellam shouted. "Once more, and I'm cutting you loose."

The boy blinked in surprise at this outburst. He nodded uncertainly.

Carol said to the boy, "We'd like you to stay. There are some kids you can hang with. Go on in the back. Ask for Miss Sanchez. She'll find you a bed in the boys' dormitory."

He looked at Pellam. "I come see you?"

"It's not a prison," Carol told him. "You come and go as you like."

Ignoring Carol, he said to Pellam, "We hang in the 'hood together, cuz?"

"I'd like that."

Ismail's dark, contracted eyes appraised the dim office. "Okay," he muttered, "but nobody better be dissing me, you know what I'm saying?"

"Nobody'll dis you here," Carol said.

He looked at Pellam with eerily adult eyes and said, "Later, cuz."

"Later."

He disappeared into the back, pushing through the door like a wild west gunfighter.

Carol laughed. "So what're you doing out on these mean streets? Aside from playing social worker." She glanced down at her Harvard sweatshirt, brushed some dust off with her pudgy fingers. The gesture made her seem both strong and vulnerable at the same time.

"Just walking around. Looking for camera angles. Looking for people to talk to. You hear anything from Alex?"

"Nothing, sorry. He hasn't been back, nobody's seen him. I asked around."

Neither of them said anything for a minute. A teenage girl, very pregnant, walked through the lobby, cradling a stuffed Barney dinosaur toy in her arms.

Carol poked her glasses up on her nose and exchanged a few words with the girl. When she was gone, Pellam asked the social worker, "You interested in another cup of politically incorrect coffee?"

A brief hesitation. Pellam thought she was pleasantly surprised. But it might have been something else.

"Well, sure."

"If you're busy . . ."

"No. Just let me change. Give me two minutes? I was schlepping boxes around all day," she added apologetically, shaking dust off her sleeves again.

"No problem."

She vanished into the backroom. A young Latino woman appeared, nodded to Pellam and took over desk duty.

Carol appeared a few moments later; a loose green blouse had replaced her sweatshirt and black stretch pants, the jeans. She wore short black boots, instead of the Nikes. The woman at the desk glanced at the outfit with surprise and muttered an indiscernible response when Carol said she'd be back later.

Outside she asked, "You mind if we stop by my apartment? It's only four blocks. I forgot to feed Homer this morning."

"Cat, boa constrictor or boyfriend?"

"Siamese. I named him Homer Simpson. No, not the one you're thinking of."

"I was thinking of the character in *Day of the Locust*," Pellam responded.

"Well," Carol said, surprised. "You know it?"

Pellam nodded.

"I had my cat first. *Then* they came up with that cartoon show on TV and I wished I'd called him something else."

Pellam felt one of those little bursts in the gut when you find someone who's moved by the same obscure work of art as you are. Pellam had seen *Day of the Locust* twelve times and could see it another twelve. So, Carol was a kindred soul. "Donald Sutherland's role. Great film. Waldo Salt wrote the script."

"Oh," Carol said. "It was a movie? I just read the book."

Pellam had never gotten around to the book. Well, they were *distant* kindred. But that was all right too.

They turned south, the rush-hour traffic jammed the street, the yellow cabs interspersed between the battered trucks and cars. Horns honked constantly. The heat had unleashed tempers like geysers and occasionally one driver turned on another with rageful gestures. No one seemed to have the energy, though, for any physical damage.

Despite the prickly heat the sky was clear, and crisp shadows stretched across the street before them. Two blocks away McKennah Tower caught the last of the light and glowed like oiled ebony. The sparks fell from the welders' flames as if the sunlight was being sheared off by the slabs of black glass.

"Did you ever find Corcoran?" she asked.

"We had a chin-wag, like my mother used to say."

"And you lived to tell about it."

"He's a sensitive person deep down. He's just misunder-stood."

Carol laughed.

"I don't think he did it," Pellam said. "The arson."

"You really think that old woman's innocent?"

"I do."

"Unfortunately, one thing I've learned is that innocence isn't always a defense. Not in the Kitchen."

"So I'm finding."

They continued slowly along bustling Ninth Avenue, dodging the hordes of workers from the main post office and discount stores and fashion district warehouses and greasy-spoon restaurants. In L.A. the streets were impassable at rush hour; here, it was the sidewalks.

"He seemed smart, Ismail," Carol said after a moment. "Had spirit. It's a crying shame it's too late for him."

"Too late?" Pellam laughed. "He's only ten."

"Way, way, *way* too late."

"Isn't there a program or something you can get him into."

Carol apparently thought he was kidding and burst out

laughing. "A program? Nope, Pellam. No program, no nothin'."
They stopped in front of a store selling exotic gypsy dresses.
Carol, in her fat-hiding clothes, looked wistfully at the outfits on
the anorexic mannequins. They walked on. "His father's dead or
gone, right?"

"Dead."

"His mother? He called her a cluckhead. That means she's
a crack addict. No other relatives. You showed some interest.
That's why he attached himself to you. But you can't give him
what he needs. Nobody can. Not now. Impossible. He's making
gang contacts now. He'll be jumped in in three years. Five years
from now he'll be a street dealer. In ten he'll be in Attica."

Pellam was angered by her cynicism. "I don't think it's
that bleak."

"I know how you feel. You wanted to let him stay with
you, right?"

He nodded.

"I used to be optimistic too. But you can't take 'em all in.
Don't even try. It'll only drive you crazy. Save the ones you
can save – the three-, four-year-olds. Write off the rest. It's
sad but there's nothing you can do about it. Forces beyond our
control. Race'll be the death of this city."

"I don't know," Pellam said. "Making this film, I see a
lot of anger. But not angry blacks or whites. Angry *people*.
People who can't pay their bills or get good jobs. *That's* why
they're mad."

Carol shook her head emphatically. "No, you're wrong. The
Irish, Italian, Poles, West Indians, Latinos . . . they were all
despised minorities too at one time. But there's one insur-
mountable difference – it may have been in steerage but their

ancestors *booked* passage to the New World. They didn't come on slave ships."

Pellam wasn't convinced. But he let it go. This was her world, not his.

I be his friend . . .

He was surprised at how bad he felt about the boy.

"I hear so much rhetoric," Carol continued angrily.

"'Ghettocentric.' 'Fragmented family units.' What incredible *bullshit* you hear. We don't need buzzwords. We need somebody to get the fuck into these neighborhoods and *be* with the kids. And that means getting to them in the nursery. By the time they're Ismail's age, they're set in concrete."

She looked at him and her eyes, which had grown icy, softened. "Sorry, sorry . . . You poor guy. Another lecture. The thing is, you're an outsider. You're entitled to a certain amount of optimism."

"Bet you've got a little left, though. To stay here, I mean. Do what you're doing."

"I really don't think I'm doing very much."

"Oh, that's not what your neighbors say."

"What?" Carol laughed.

Pellam tried to remember. The name came to him. "Jose Garcia-Alvarez?"

Carol shook her head.

"I taped him for my film. Just last week. He spends every afternoon in Clinton Park. Shares his Wonder bread with a thousand pigeons. He said something about you."

"That I'm a fiesty bitch probably."

"That he's forever grateful. You saved his son."

"Me?"

He told the story. Carol had found the sixteen-year-old boy, strung out and unconscious, in a tenement that was just about to be torn down to make way for McKennah Tower. If she hadn't called the police and medics the teenager might've been crushed to death by the bulldozers.

"Oh, him? Sure, I remember that. I wouldn't exactly call it heroic." She seemed embarrassed. Yet part of her was pleased, he could see. She suddenly grabbed Pellam's arm to stop at a shoe store. It was an upscale place, doing no business whatsoever. Joan and David Shoes, Kenneth Cole. A single pair probably cost a week's paycheck for most of people walking past. The owner was praying for gentrification and couldn't hold out much longer.

"In my next life," Carol said, though whether she was talking about being able to afford the svelte rhinestone-studded black heels she looked at or fit into a dress that would go with them, Pellam couldn't guess.

Halfway down the street Carol asked, "You married?"

"Divorced."

"Kids?"

"Nope."

"Going with anybody?" she asked.

"Haven't been for a while."

Eight months to be precise.

If you could call a lusty night in a snowbound Winnebago "going with."

"You?" He didn't know if he should ask. Didn't know if he wanted to.

"Divorced too."

They dodged around a hawker in front of a discount cosmetics store. "Yo, bee-utiful lady, we make you mo' bee-utiful than you already be."

Carol laughed, blushing, and continued quickly past him.

A block farther she nodded at a shabby tenement, similar to Pellam's.

"Home sweet home," she said.

Carol gave a quarter to a panhandler she greeted as Ernie. They stopped at the deli, exhanged a few words with the counterman and walked to the back of the store. She held up a can of coffee and a six pack of beer. "Which one," she mouthed.

He pointed to the beer and he could see that that was her choice too.

Not *too* distant kindred souls . . .

Her apartment was next door, a decrepit walk-up with beige and brown paint slapped over dozens of generations of other layers. They walked up the stairs. He smelled old wood, hot wallpaper, grease and garlic. Another firetrap, Pellam thought in passing.

On the landing she abruptly halted, stopping him on the step below. A pause. She was debating. Then she turned. Their faces were at the same height. She kissed him hard. His hands slid down her shoulders into the small of her back and he felt the ignition inside him. Pulled her even closer.

"*Turiam pog*," she whispered, kissing him hard.

He laughed and cocked an eyebrow.

"Gaelic. Guess what it means."

"I better not."

"'Kiss me,'" she said.

"Okay." And did. "Now, what does it mean?"

"No, no." She laughed. "That *is* what it means." She giggled like a girl and stepped to the door closest to the stairs. They kissed again. She dug for her keys.

Pellam found himself looking at her. And as she bent forward, glassesless, squinting her bad eyes to open the lock, he saw an image of a Carol Wyandotte very different from the stony, hustling Times Square social worker. He saw the sad pearls, the sweatshirts, an elastic-shot cotton bra, the fat at her throat that Fiber-Trim would never melt away. Whose nights were filled with the tube, in a room peppered with *Atlantic Monthlys* and Diet Pepsi empties, a dresser filled with more cotton socks than black pantyhose. The Archway cookies packages she'd automatically tucked out of sight when guests walked into the kitchen, a fat person's instinct.

Don't do this for pity, Pellam thought to himself.

And in the end he didn't. Not at all.

Eight months is, after all, eight months.

He kissed her hard and, when the last deadbolt clicked, he pushed the door eagerly open with his booted foot.

17

O n the west side of Manhattan near the river was a forlorn
 triangle of a tiny city block that contained seven or eight
old buildings.

To the west, where the sun was now setting, were vacant,
weedy lots, the highway and, beyond, the brown Hudson River.
To the east, across a cobblestoned street, was a low row of
apartments, a gay bar and a bodega in whose window was a
display of filthy pastry, sliced pork and custard. This was the
Chelsea district of New York, the bland, harmless cousin of
Hell's Kitchen, which was just to the north.

The tricorner building at the northern-most end of the block
ended in a sharp prow. It was a shabby place to call home
but the residents had few complaints about their apartments
and they didn't know that there was really only one major
problem here, a building code violation: Gallons of gasoline, fuel oil, naphtha, and acetone were stored in the basement. The explosive force of these liquids was sufficient to

level the building and to do so in a particularly unpleasant way.

This particular apartment was a spartan place and contained minimal furnishings – a chair, cot, two tables and a battered desk covered with tools and rags. There was neither an air conditioner nor a fan. The TV, however, was a thirty-two-inch Trinitron and it sported a remote control that was ten inches long. On this screen at the moment was an MTV music video, the sound off.

Sitting immediately in front of the flickering screen, which he paid little attention to, Sonny was slowly braiding his long blond hair. Without the benefit of a mirror, the task was taking him longer than he wanted. No damn mirror, he thought angrily. Though the problem really was his shaking hands. Damn *sweaty*, shaking hands.

At one point he looked up – toward but not really at the TV screen – and paused. He leaned toward a fifty-five gallon drum filled with acetone and knocked several times, listening to the sonar echo of the thump. It calmed him somewhat.

But not enough.

No one was cooperating!

The incident at the gas station had scared him and fear was a feeling he wasn't used to. Arson is the safest crime there is for the perp. It's anonymous, it's secretive, and most of the evidence is disposed of by God's own accomplice – the laws of physics. But now people knew what he looked like. And on top of *that*, he'd heard that that little chicken fag from the building – Alex – had seen him and had tried to deal him to the cops.

And there were still three more fires to go until the big one.

He removed the map, now tattered, from his back pocket. He stared at it absently.

Yeah, the gas station was bad. But the most troubling was the fire at the hospital. Because it had given him no pleasure. Fire had always calmed him down. But that one hadn't. Not a bit. As he'd listened to the screams, cocked his head and heard them mix with the rustling roar of the flames, his hands had kept trembling, his high forehead continued to sweat. Why? he wondered. Why? Maybe because it was a small fire. Maybe because there was only one fire he truly cared about, the one that would star him and the faggot Joe Pellam Buck. Maybe because everybody was after him.

But he had a feeling there was more to the sweat and agitation than that.

His heart stuttered a bit more when he thought that he now had to spend even more time stopping his pursuers – when he could be planning the big fire. Rockin' and rollin' with the Antichrist.

Knock, ping. Knock, ping. Like sonar in a submarine movie.

Sonny's head of half-braided hair leaned against the big drum. He thumped it again with a knuckle. *Knock, ping.*

A bit calmer now? He thought so. Maybe. Yes.

Sonny finished braiding his hair and spent a half-hour mixing soap and gas and oil. The fumes were very strong – as dangerous as the fire the juice produced – and he could only work in small batches or else he'd pass out. When he was finished he took several incandescent light bulbs and put them on the table. With a diamond-bladed saw he carefully cut through the metal collar where the glass bulb met the screw base. He heard the hiss of air filling the vacuum. He sawed a wedge out – just big enough to let him pour in his magic juice. Not too full. That was the mistake a lot of amateur arsonists made. You had to leave a little air in the bulb. Fire is *oxidation*; like an animal it needs oxygen to live. He sealed the V-shaped hole with superglue. He made three of these special bulbs.

Caressing the smooth glass, smooth as the skin on a young man's ass . . .

His hands began to tremble again and the sweat poured from his face like water from a shower nozzle.

Sonny stood and paced frantically.

Why can't I calm down? Why why whywhy? His thoughts swirled. They were all *after* him. They wanted to kill him, stop him, tie him down, take his fire away from him! Alex, the fire marshal, that old faggot lawyer that Pellam kept hanging around. Pellam himself, the Antichrist.

Why wasn't life ever simple?

Sonny had to lie down on the cot and force himself to imagine what the last fire would be like. The big fire. That seemed to be the only thing now that relaxed him, gave him any pleasure.

He pictured it: A huge space, filled with ten, twenty thousand people. It would be the worst fire in the history of this fiery city. Worse than Triangle Shirtwaist on Washington Square, the worker girls trapped inside the sweatshop because the owners didn't want them to use the johns during working hours. Worse than the Crystal Palace. Worse than *The General Slocum* burning in the East River, killing over a thousand immigrant women and children on excursion; in its aftermath the entire German population of the city, too sorrowful to remain in their old neighborhood, relocated en masse to Yorkville on the Upper East Side.

His would outdo them all.

Sonny pictured the flames rolling past him like glowing surf, surrounding the masses, caressing their toes.

Flames rising to their heels. Then their ankles.

Oh, can you see the exquisite flames? Can you *feel* them?

With these questions in his thoughts he realized he hadn't calmed. He realized that he'd never be calm again.

The end was closer than he'd thought.

He crawled into the living room, pressed his head against one of the drums.

Knock, ping. Knock, ping.

He'd stayed the night.

Pellam had been operating under well-established protocol, which meant that after they'd wakened at ten last night, starving, thirsty, they went out for omelettes at the Empire Diner on Tenth Avenue and then he'd taken her back to her apartment, where they'd made love once more and lain in bed listening to the sounds of New York at night: sirens, shouts, pops of exhausts or guns, which seemed to grow more and more urgent as the night grew later.

He never even thought of leaving without saying good-bye.

It was Carol who broke the rules.

When he awoke – to Homer Simpson's loud Siamese wail – she was gone. A moment later the phone rang and through her tinny answering machine speaker he heard Carol's voice ask if he was still there and explain that she'd had to be at work early. She'd call him later at his apartment. He found the phone and snagged it but she'd already hung up.

Barefoot, in his jeans, Pellam wandered over the scabby

hardwood floors, mindful of splinters, toward the bathroom. Thinking that she'd sounded pretty brusque on the phone. But who could guess what that was about? The aftermath of an evening like last night's was wholly unpredictable. Maybe she'd already convinced herself that Pellam wasn't going to call her again. Maybe she was seared with Catholic guilt. Or maybe she'd just been sitting across her desk from a hulking eighteen-year-old murderer when she'd called.

Pellam tested the shower but the water was ice cold. Pass on that. He dressed and stepped out into a gassy, clear morning, scalding hot. Took a cab to his place on Twelfth Street. He climbed the steps of his apartment, watching two energetic youngsters, names razor-cut in their hair, streak past on skateboards.

He decided he wanted a bath and a cup of very hot, black coffee. Just sit in the tub and forget arson, pyros, Latino thugs, Irish gangsters, and lovers with enigmatic attitudes.

Climbing the dim stairs slowly. Thinking of the bath, thinking of soapy water. The mantra worked. He found he could forget it all – he could wipe all of Hell's Kitchen out of his mind. Well, almost all. Everything except for Ettie Washington.

He was thinking of all the flights of stairs Ettie had climbed over the years. She'd never lived in an elevator building, always walk-ups. She climbed stairs for seven decades. Carrying her baby sister Elizabeth. Helping Grandma Ledbetter up and down dim stairwells. Lugging food for her men until one left her and the other died drunk in the Hudson's sooty waters, then for her babies and children until they were taken from her or fled the city, and then for herself.

". . . That's a word for us here in the Kitchen. 'Anonymous.'

Lord. 'Ignored' is more like it. Nobody pays attention to us anymore. You got that Al Sharpton fellow. Now he'll go to Bensonhurst, he'll go to Crown Heights and raise some hell and people hear 'bout it. But nobody ever comes to the Kitchen. Even with all the Irish here the St Paddy's Day Parade doesn't even come over this way. That's fine with me. I like it nice and private. Keep the world out. What's the world ever done for me? Answer me that."

Ettie Washington had told the glossy eye of Pellam's Betacam that she dreamed of other cities. She dreamed of owning stylish hats and gold necklaces and silk dresses. She dreamed of being a cabaret singer. The rich wife of Billy Doyle, a highfalutin landlord.

But Ettie recognized these hopes as illusions only – to be examined from time to time with pleasure or sorrow or disdain then tucked away. She didn't expect her life to change. She was content here in the Kitchen, where most people cut their dreams to fit their lives. And it seemed so unfair that the woman should have to lose even this minuscule corner she'd been backed into.

Breathing deeply, he arrived at his own fourth-floor apartment.

A bath. Yessir. When you live in a camper most of your life, baths take on a great importance. Bubble baths particularly, though that was a secret he kept to himself.

A bath and coffee.

Heaven.

Pellam dug the keys out of his black jeans and walked to the door. His eyes narrowed. He looked at the lock. It was twisted, sideways.

He pushed against the door. It was open.

Broken into. He thought fleetingly that he ought to turn tail and use the downstairs neighbor's phone to call 911. But then his anger grabbed him. He kicked the door in. The empty rooms gaped. His hand went to the switch on the lamp closest to the door.

Oh, shit, he thought, no, don't! Not the light! But he clicked it on before he could stop himself.

＊◆＊

18

S tupid, he thought.

Pellam pulled the Colt from his waistband, dropping into a crouch.

Hitting the light switch had just announced to the burglar that Pellam had returned. Should've left it out.

He remained frozen in the doorway for a long moment, listening for footsteps, for cocking pistols. But he heard nothing.

Making his way slowly through the ransacked apartment, he opened closet doors and looked under the bed. Every conceivable hiding place. The burglar was gone.

He surveyed the damage, walking from room to room. The discount VCR and TV were still there. The Betacam and deck too, sitting out in plain view. Even the most low-tech thieves would have guessed the camera'd be worth a bundle.

And when he saw the camera he understood what had happened. He felt the shock and dismay like the blast of heat from the fire that destroyed Ettie's building. He dropped to his knees, ripping open the canvas bag where he kept the master videos of *West of Eighth*.

No . . .

He rummaged through the bag, hit *Eject* on the Ampex deck attached to the Betacam. And surveyed the damage. Two tapes were gone. The two most recent – the one in the camera and the one containing footage he'd shot last week and the week before.

The tapes . . . Who'd known about them? Well, practically everyone he'd talked to about Ettie's disappearance or who'd seen him with the camera. Ramirez, the elusive Alex. McKennah. Corcoran. Hell, even Ismail and the boy's mother, Carol and Louis Bailey knew. For that matter, Lomax and the entire fire marshal's department. Probably the whole West Side.

The Word on the street. Faster than the Internet.

Who? was one question. But why? was just as interesting. Had Pellam inadvertently taped the pyro himself? Or maybe the man who'd hired him? Or had there been some evidence he'd recorded that had escaped Lomax and the investigators?

He had no answers to these questions and as significant as they were to Ettie's case there was another implication to the missing tapes. In feature films, all the exposed footage was insured – not for the cost of the celluloid itself but for what it cost to shoot and process, which could run to thousands of dollars a foot. If a daily rough of a feature film is destroyed in a fire the muses may weep but at least the producers recoup their money. Pellam, however, hadn't been able to afford film completion insurance for *West of Eighth*. He couldn't recall what was on those twenty or so hours but the interviews might very well have been the heart of his film.

He sat for a moment in a squeaky chair, staring out the window. Then lazily he punched in 911, spoke to a dispatcher. But the tone of the woman's voice told him that a crime like this was low on the precinct's priorities. She asked if he wanted some detectives to come over.

Shouldn't they be volunteering to do that themselves? Pellam wondered. He said, "That's okay. Don't want to trouble anybody."

The woman missed the irony.

"I mean, they *will*," she explained.

"Tell you what," Pellam said, "if he comes back I'll let you know."

"You be sure and do that now. You have a good day."

"I'll try."

It was a dusty little office in the fifties, West Side, not far from where he'd sat beside Otis Balm and listened to the hundred-and-three-year-old man tell him about the Hell's Kitchen of long ago.

". . . Prohibition was the most fanciest the Kitchen ever got. I seen Owney Madden, the gangster, many times. He was from England. People don't know that. We'd follow him 'round the streets. You know why? Not for the gangster stuff. We was just hoping he'd say something so we could hear how English people talked. That was stupid of us 'cause he was also called Owney the Killer and a lot of people around him got shot. But we was young then and,

don't you know, it takes twenty, thirty years of getting by in the world for death to start meaning anything to you."

Pellam sized up the office, prepared his mental script and then pushed into the office. Inside, the bitter smell of paper filled the air. A fat fly buzzed repeatedly into the dusty window, trying to escape from the heat; the air conditioner was a twin of Louis Bailey's.

"I'm looking for a Flo Epstein," Pellam asked.

A woman with serpentine cheeks, hair pulled back in a sharp bun, walked up to the counter. "That's me." It was impossible to guess her age.

"How you doing?" Pellam asked.

"Fine, thank you."

John Pellam – wearing his one and only suit, a ten-year-old Armani, a relic from a former life – held out a battered wallet, which contained a special inspector badge, gold colored, sold at arcades on Forty-second Street for novelty purposes only, and let the woman look at it for as long as she liked. Which turned out not to be very long. She gazed at him eagerly and he could see she was a woman who enjoyed playing the part of witness. Celebrity, Pellam knew, is the most addictive of intoxicants.

"That Detective Lomax was here last time. I like him. He's kind of sober. Wait, I think I mean somber."

"Fire marshal," Pellam corrected. "They're not detectives."

Though they have full arrest powers and carry bigger guns and beat the crap out of you with rolls of U.S. coins.

"Right, right, right." Ms Epstein's forehead crinkled at the mistake.

"When we interrogate people together," Pellam said, "I play

good cop. He plays bad cop. Well, marshal. Now this is just a follow-up. You identified the suspect, didn't you?"

"You gotta be more buttoned up than that."

"How's that?"

"I've learned enough so I could be a D.A. myself." Ms Epstein recited, "What I told *Marshal* Lomax was, a black woman of approximately seventy years of age came to the premises here and asked for a tenant policy application. I confirmed that the mug shot they showed me was of her. That's all. I didn't quote identify any suspects. I've been through this a couple times."

"I can tell." Pellam nodded. "We sure appreciate intelligent witnesses like you. Now how long was the woman in here?"

"Three minutes."

"That's all?"

She shrugged. "It was three minutes. You having sex it's nothing, you having a baby, it's an eternity."

"Depending on the partner and the baby, I'd guess." Pellam jotted down meaningless scrawls. "She gave you a cash deposit."

"Right. We sent it all on to the company and they issued the policy."

"Did she say anything else?"

"No."

Pellam flipped closed his steno pad. "That's very helpful. I appreciate your time." The Polaroid square appeared quickly. "I just want to confirm that this is the woman who came in here."

"That's not the mug shot."

"No. This one was taken in the Women's Detention Center." Ms Epstein glanced at it and began to speak.

Pellam help up a hand. "Take your time. Be sure."

She studied the smooth black face, the prison department shift, the folded hands. The stiff salt and pepper hair. "That's her."

"You're positive."

"Absolutely." She hesitated. Then laughed. "I was going to say that I'd swear to it in court. But then I guess that's exactly what I'm *going* to do, isn't it?"

"Guess it is," Pellam confirmed. And kept his face an emotionless mask. The way all good law enforcers learn to do.

That evening – a hot, foggy dusk – found Pellam standing in an alley across from a brownstone, New York *Post* in hand.

He wasn't paying much attention to the paper. He was thinking: Geraniums?

The nondescript, buff-colored tenement was like a thousand others in the city. The flowers planted in front of it, fiery orange-red, would have fit fine with any other building.

But there?

He'd been standing in the alley for an hour when a door opened and the figure stepped outside, looked up and down the street then started down the stairs. He carried a large shoe box. Pellam tossed the paper aside and began walking as silently as he could along the hot asphalt. He finally caught up with the young man.

Without turning around, Ramirez said, "You been out there for fifty minutes and you got two guns aimed at your back right now. So don't do nothing, you know, stupid."

"Thanks for the advice, Hector."

"What the fuck you doing here, man? You crazy?"

"What's in the box?"

"It's a shoe box? What you think's in it? Shoes."

Pellam was walking abreast of Ramirez now. He had to move fast to keep up the pace.

"So, what you want?" the young man asked.

"I want to know why you lied to me."

"I no lie, man. I'm not like no white man. Not like you reporters. Telling white man's lies."

Pellam laughed. "What *is* that crap, the *Cubano* Lord's creed? You've gotta recite it to get jumped in your crew?"

"Don't give me no shit. Been a long day."

They came to the north-south avenue. Ramirez looked up and down and they turned north. After a minute he said, "I don't believe you. You too fucking much."

"What?"

"Hanging out in fronta our kickback, man. Nobody does that. Not even the cops."

"You plant the geraniums yourself?"

"Fuck you. You carrying?"

"A gun?" Pellam asked. "No."

"Man, you *are* a crazy fuck. Coming to my kickback without a gun. That how people get blown away. What you mean, I lie to you?"

"Tell me about your aunt, Hector. The one got burned out of the Four-fifty-eight building. She got a new place, I heard."

Ramirez grinned. "I tell you I look after my family."

"When did she move?"

"I dunno."

"*Before* the fire?"

"Around then. I don't know exactly."

"You forgot?"

"Yeah, I fucking forgot. Man, I'm busy, why you don't go have a fucking talk with Corcoran?"

"I already did."

Ramirez lifted an eyebrow, trying not to look too impressed.

Pellam continued, "You also forgot to tell me that she was one of – how many was it? – eight hundred eyewitnesses who saw Joe the Thug kill that guy from Corcoran's crew."

"Spear Driscoe and Bobby Frink."

"So are we all agreed that Corcoran didn't burn down the building because of your aunt? That's not a white man's lie now, is it?"

"Just go away, man. I'm busy."

"How well you get along with somebody named O'Neil?"

"I don't know nobody named O'Neil."

"No? He knows you."

Ramirez spat out, "What the fuck you talking to him for?" The young man had been playfully irritated a moment ago. Now he was mad.

"Who said I was talking to him?" Pellam touched his ear. "I hear things too. I heard maybe he had some guns. Maybe he was *selling* some guns."

Ramirez stopped walking, gripped Pellam's arm. "What you hear?"

Pellam pulled his arm away. "That you rousted him last week. 'Cause he's selling hardware to Corcoran."

Ramirez blinked. Then broke into a huge laugh. "Oh, man."

"True, or not true?"

"Both, man."

"What do you mean?"

"True and not true." He started walking again. "Look, I gonna explain this but you keep it to yourself. Otherwise I have to kill you."

"Tell me."

Ramirez said, "O'Neil, him and me, we do business. He supplies me. Gets me good stuff. Glocks, MAC-10s, Steyrs."

"You beat up your own supplier in public?"

"Fuck yes. Was his idea. He's a mick and I'm a spic. You know how long he'd last, Jimmy finds out he was selling to me? Some of Corcoran's boys, they were getting suspicious so we do some sparring out in public. O'Neil, he took a fall." Ramirez looked at Pellam closely. He roared with laughter.

"What's the joke?"

"I can see it in your face, man. You almost believe me." The young man added, "I can prove it. Yeah, there was guns in the building. I paid for 'em and O'Neil left 'em there for me to pick up only I didn't send nobody over there before the place burned. There was Glocks, Brownings and some pretty little Tauruses I had my heart set on, man. Twelve, thirteen of 'em. You talk to one of your reporter friends. See what the crime scene boys found there. If that's right then you *know* I no burn down nothing."

Pellam pulled a sheet of paper from his back pocket. "Three Glock, four Tauruses, and six Brownings."

"Man, you good."

They passed Forty-second Street, once the Tenderloin of New York and now about as dangerous – and interesting – as a suburban strip mall. Pellam asked, "Where're we going?"

"I'm doing a business deal. And I don't want you around."

"Your crew's in business?"

"Not a crew, man. It's a club."

"What kind of business?"

Ramirez lifted the top of the box, revealing a pair of new basketball shoes.

"I got a truckload of 'em."

"You buy 'em and then you sell 'em, that right?" Pellam asked skeptically.

"Yeah, I buy things and sell 'em. *That's* my business."

"What about the 'buy' part? You paid money and took delivery of a shipment of these? Invoice, bill of lading, all that?"

"Yeah, I *bought* 'em," Ramirez shot back. "Same way you fucking reporters pay people for your stories. You do that? You pay somebody to tell you things?"

"No, but—"

"'No, but.' Fuck. You take people's lives, write about 'em, and don't pay nobody for them." He mocked, "Oh, man, who'd do something terrible like that?"

A block later they segued around a Korean vegetable stand. Pellam said, "I need a favor."

"Yeah?"

"Somebody broke into my apartment last night. Can you find out who did it?"

"Why you ask me, you think I do that too?"

"If I thought you did it I wouldn't be asking you."

Ramirez considered. "I don't got real good contacts in the Village, you know."

"How'd you know I lived in the Village?"

"I said I got no real good contacts. I no say I don't have *any*."

"Ask around."

"Okay.

"Gracias."

"Nada."

They'd walked far north on Ninth Avenue, almost out of the Kitchen. Pellam leaned against a lamppost on the corner while Ramirez disappeared into a tiny bodega. When he came out he was carrying a thick envelope, which he slipped into the pocket of his tight jeans.

There was sudden motion from the alley nearby.

"Shit." Ramirez spun around, reaching into his jacket.

Pellam dropped into a crouch and stepped toward a parked car for cover.

"Who the fuck're you?" Ramirez said.

Pellam squinted into the gloomy opening of the alley. The intruder was Ismail.

"Yo, cuz," the boy said, glancing uncertainly at the Latino. The boy stepped forward uncertainly.

Ramirez glanced at him like he was a roach. "Man, you come up on people like that . . . I thinking I oughta cap you ass."

Ismail's cautious eyes swept the sidewalk.

To Pellam he said, "You know him?"

"Yeah. He's a friend of mine."

A faint grin seemed to cross the boy's face.

"A friend of yours?" Ramirez spat out. "Why you want a little *moyeto* like that for a friend?"

"He's okay."

"He okay?" Ramirez muttered. "He come sneaking up on me again, he gonna be one dead *okay* friend of yours."

"Hey, Ismail, how come you're not at the Outreach Center?"

"Dunno. Just hanging."

"Hear anything about your mother and sister?"

He shook his head, eyes slipping from Ramirez's scowl to Pellam's face. And for a moment Ismail seemed just like any other child. Shy, uneasy, torn between fear and yearning. It hurt Pellam to see this vulnerability. The street defiance was somehow easier to take. He thought about Carol Wyandotte's assessment. She was wrong. It *wasn't* too late for him. There had to be some hope.

Pellam crouched down. "Do me a favor. Go on back to the Outreach Center. Get some sleep. You eat anything?"

He shrugged.

"Did you?" Pellam persisted.

"I 'jacked some beer," he said proudly. "Me and a homie, we drank that."

But Pellam couldn't smell any liquor on the boy's breath. Childish bravado.

Pellam gave him five dollars. "Go to McDonald's."

"Yeah! Hey, you come by and see me, Pellam? I show you some good shit. We play basketball, I know all the moves!"

"Yeah, I'll come by."

The boy turned to leave.

Ramirez called out brusquely, "Hey, punk . . ."

Ismail stopped, looked back cautiously.

"You got big feet?"

The round, dark face stared up at him.

"I ask you a question. You got big feet?"

"Dunno." He looked down at his tattered sneakers.

"Here." Ramirez tossed the box of basketball shoes toward the boy. He caught it awkwardly. Looked inside.

His eyes went wide. "Shit. Be Jordan Air Pumps. Shit."

"They no fit now, not too good," Ramirez said, "but maybe, you don't sneak up on people, you live long enough to grow inta them. Now you do what he tell you." Nodding at Pellam. "Get the fuck outa here."

When he was gone Ramirez said to Pellam, "Let's go celebrate my deal." He tapped the pocket where the fat, white envelope rested. "You drink tequila?"

"Mescal I drink. Sauza I drink. Margaritas're disgusting."

Ramirez exhaled a derisive laugh, as he always seemed to do when somebody stated the obvious, and started off down the street, impatiently gesturing Pellam after him. Plans for the evening had apparently been made.

They split the worm.

Ramirez hacked the poor thing apart with an honest-to-God *West Side Story* switchblade as they sat in a smokey little Cuban-Chinese restaurant near Columbus Circle.

Pellam told him about location scouting in Mexico, where he'd spent hours with the off-duty gaffers and grips and stunt people, bragging about their psychedelic experiences ingesting fat white mescal worms. "I never felt anything though."

"No, man," Ramirez protested. "These guys, they fuck up you mind." And downed his portion of the worm.

After they finished two plates of tamales each they strolled outside. Ramirez stopped at a package store and bought another fifth of mescal.

Working their way downtown, Ramirez said, "Man, here it's Saturday night and I no got a woman. That sucks."

"That waitress at the bar. She was flirting with you."

"Which one?"

"The Hispanic one."

"Her?" He scoffed. Then he frowned. "Hey, Pellam, lemme give you some advice. No say 'Hispanic.'"

"No?"

"That's no good no more."

"Tell me what's politically correct. I'd like to hear it from somebody who says 'mick' and 'nigger'."

"That's different, man."

"Is it?"

"Yeah."

"How?"

"Just is," Ramirez announced. Then he continued. "Whatever country somebody come from that's what you say. Dominican. Puerto Rican. I'm *Cubano*. If you gotta use one word say 'Latino.'" Ramirez took a hit from the bottle. He began reciting, "*'Apostol de la independencia de Cuba guia de los pueblos . . . Americanos y paladin de la dignidad humana.*' You speak Spanish?"

"A little. Not enough to understand whatever the hell you just said."

"Those words, they on the statute of Jose Marti on Sixth Avenue. Central Park. You ever seen it?"

"No."

"Ah," he said, sneering. "How you can miss it? It thirty-feet high. His horse, it up on two legs and Marti is staring down Sixth Avenue. He look kind of funny, like he no trust nobody."

"Who was he? Marti?"

"You don't know?"

Art films aside, history in Hollywood is pretty much limited to very unhistorical Westerns and war movies.

"He fought the Spanish to get them out of Cuba. He was this poet. He got exiled when he was fifteen or sixteen and he travel all over the world to fight for Cuban independence. He live here in New York for a long time. He was a great man."

"You ever been back to Cuba?"

"Back? I never been there."

"Never? You're kidding."

"No, man. Why I go there? Havana got traffic jams and slums and dust, it got *las muchachas* and *las cerveza*. It got *hombres embalaos* on ganja. Crack too now probably. It just like New York. I want a vacation, I go to Nassau with a beautiful girl and gamble. Club Med."

"It's your home."

"Not *my* home, man," he said sternly. "Was my *grandfather*'s home. Not mine . . . There this guy at a warehouse I use sometimes, *Señor* . . ." Ramirez stretched the word out to work contempt into his voice. "Buñello. *Loco*, this *viejo*. Look at him – he want everybody call him 'Señor.' 'I have to live in *los Estados Unidos* for now. But I am *Cubano*,' he say. 'I was exiled.' Oh, man, I gonna punch him out he say that one more time. He say, 'We all going back someday. We all going to sit on sugar plantations and be rich again and have *los moyetos*, you know, blacks, do all the work for us.' *Puto*. Man, my father couldn't wait to get out."

"Your father, was he a revolutionary?"

"*Mi padre?* No. He come here in fifty-four. You know what they call us then? Latinos who come to America? They call us 'summer people in winter clothes.' He was a kid when he left. His family, they live in the Bronx. He was in a gang too."

"You mean a club."

"Back then crews, they was different. You move into a new neighborhood, you go one-on-one with the leader. You know, you got it up from the shoulders – you fought with your fists. Until you do that, you was nobody. So while the *fidelistos* were burning plantations and shooting *batistianos* my father, he was in this circle of punks and fighting this big *puto* on a Hundred Eighty-sixth Street. Got the crap beat out of him. But, after, they all went to drink *cervezas* and rum and he was jumped in. They give him a name. They call him, '*Manomuerto*.' That was the day he prove his heart. That's what they say. 'Proving your heart.' *Su corazón.*"

"Where's your father now?"

"Left six, seven year ago. Went to work one morning, sent my brother Piri home with half his pay envelope and say he call sometime. But he never call." Hector Ramirez laughed loud. "Who know? Maybe he in Havana."

A bunch of tiny worms were taking tie-dyed trips in Pellam's brain. He hadn't had that much really, five or six shots.

Okay, maybe more.

And, okay, maybe there *was* something psychedelic about the little critters.

As the two men plunged further into the dark heart of the Kitchen he realized Ramirez was talking to him.

"What?"

"Man, I asked you what the fuck you really doing here?"

"What am I doing? I'm drinking tequila with a criminal."

"Hey, you think I'm a criminal? I got a conviction?"

"I'm told you do."

He thought for a moment. "An' who told you?"

"Word on the street," Pellam muttered ominously.

"You no answering my question. What're you doing here?"

"My father," Pellam answered, surprising himself with his candor.

"*You* father. Where you father? He live here?"

"Not any more." Pellam turned his eyes north, where easily a million lights glimmered with different types of brightness. He took the bottle back. "I worked on this film a few years ago. *To Sleep in a Shallow Grave*."

"I never hear of it."

"It was about a woman who comes home and finds her father may not have been her father. I was just scouting locations but I rewrote part of the script too."

"Her mother, she a puta?"

"No, just had an affair. She was lonely."

Ramirez took the bottle, swallowed a mouthful, nodded at Pellam to keep going.

He said, "My mother lives upstate. Little town called Simmons. No, you never heard of it. I went to see her, this was two Christmases ago."

"You buy her a present?"

"Of course I did. Let me finish my story."

"Good you remembered her. Always do that, man."

"Let me finish. We drove out to see my father's grave like we always do when I'm there." Another sip. Then another. "We get out to the grave and she's crying."

They were deep into the Kitchen now and turned into the stinking cobblestoned alleyway that led to Ramirez's kickback.

"She's got a confession to make, she tells me. It turns out she doesn't think her husband was my father after all."

"Man, that was one big fucking surprise."

"Benjamin – her husband, the man I *thought* was my father – was away a lot. Traveled all the time. They had a fight about it, he went off on a trip. She took this lover. After a while he leaves. Ben comes home. They patch things up. She's pregnant, can't tell what day it happened, you know. But she's pretty sure it's not Ben's. She'd been brooding about it ever since he died. Telling me or not, I mean. Finally she finally broke down and did."

"Fuck up you mind, hearing that. So why you come here?"

"I wanted to find out about him. My real father. Didn't want to meet him. But I wanted to know who he was, what he did for a living, maybe find a picture of him."

"He still here?"

"Nope. Long gone." He explained how he'd found the man's last known address but he'd left that building years before and there were no other leads. Pellam had contacted the vital statistics departments in the five boroughs of New York City and all the nearby counties of New York, New Jersey and Connecticut. No response.

"Gone, huh? Just like my padre."

Pellam nodded.

"So why you stay?"

"I thought I'd do a movie about Hell's Kitchen. His neighborhood. He lived here for a while." Pellam held up the bottle. "Well, here's to your padre, the son of a bitch." He drank from it.

"Here's to *both* of ours. Wherever the fuck they are."

Pellam had just handed the bottle back when he felt, for the second time in several days, the chill of metal on his neck. This time, too, it was a gun muzzle.

Ramirez rated three thugs, Pellam only one.

"Fuck," the Latino spat out as two of them gripped his shoulders and the third frisked him carefully, taking his automatic pistol and his knife. Another grabbed the mescal bottle and flung it into the alley.

"Only spic faggots drink this shit."

Pellam heard the bottle crash.

Grinning, Ramirez nodded to the man who'd spoken, said to Pellam, "This is Sean McCray. I no know why he here. Most Saturday nights he got a date – at home with his dick."

Which earned Ramirez a fist. It slammed into his jaw. He staggered under the blow.

Pellam recognized McCray from the table in Corcoran's bar the other day. He'd been sitting near Jacko Drugh.

"I remember him," Pellam said.

Which, for some reason, earned Pellam a fist too, though he got slugged in the belly. He doubled over, gasping, breathless. His minder, a large man in a black leather coat like Drugh's, dragged him to the middle of the alley, dropped him in a pile, turned back to Ramirez.

The young Latino struggled, tried to kick one of them. But they just started beating him. When they stopped, Ramirez gasped, "Man, you stupid fucking micks." He seemed more exasperated than anything else by their behavior.

"Shut up."

McCray leaned close. "I had a little talk with O'Neil. He

told me you two were in business together. Which I can't say surprised me."

Another one of the men said, "Tell him what happened. To O'Neil."

"Oh, the swim?" offered Pellam's minder.

"Yeah."

McCray said, "O'Neil went for a fucking swim in the Hudson, next to the QE2. Ain't come up yet."

Ramirez shook his head. "Oh, that's brilliant. You cap the only gun dealer in the Kitchen . . . Jimmy buys from him too, you know. Now we all gonna go buy shit up in Harlem and East New York and the niggers gonna rob you blind. Oh, you soooo fucking smart. Jimmy don't know you did it, I bet. Man, you fuck this one up." He spit blood.

A moment's silence from the thugs. One of them eyed McCray uneasily.

"Shit," Ramirez spat out. "You know what happens if you kill me? Sanchez takes over and fucking wipes you out. We've got MAC-10s and Uzis. We got Desert Eagles."

"Oh, we're fucking scared."

"And when Corcoran find you started a war, if Sanchez don't nail your ass, Jimmy going to. Just get the fuck outa here."

"Man, you got a mouth on you, Ramirez."

"You fuck—"

McCray swung hard and caught Ramirez's jaw again with a glancing blow. Pellam struggled to get up and got a booted foot in the belly. He dropped to the ground, clutching his stomach, moaning.

The Irishmen laughed.

"Your girlfriend here, he's not feeling so good, Hector."

Pellam's guard gripped his collar firmly and the three around Ramirez wrestled him into an alcove.

"Why'n't you piss on him?" one of them asked.

"Shut up," McCray barked. "This ain't a game."

Pellam, retching, got up on his knees.

"He's gonna puke," his minder called, laughing.

But they lost interest in Pellam and concentrated on pounding on Ramirez. He fought hard but he was no match for the burly Irishmen and finally he dropped to his knees. McCray looked up and down the alley, nodded to his lieutenant, who pulled the hammer back on his pistol, aimed it down at the Latino. The other two stepped away. One squinted.

Ramirez sighed and stopped struggling. He gazed back at his killer, calm, shook his head. "Cristos . . . Okay, so go ahead and do it." He smiled at McCray.

No choice, Pellam thought, consoling himself. No choice at all. He gave up on the fake retching and rose into a crouch, knocked his minder's hand away then swept the Colt Peacemaker from his back waistband, cocking the single-action gun with his thumb. He fired toward the shooter's leg, which kicked out sideways under the impact of the large slug. The man dropped his gun, twisting away, screaming in pain, falling to the cobblestones.

Pellam's guard went for his own pistol but the barrel of the Peacemaker caught him in the nose with a loud crack. Pellam ripped the Glock from the screaming man's fingers as he backed away, hands up, "No, man, no, don't. Please!"

McCray had leapt for cover, sprinting for a Dumpster. The other Irishman, near Ramirez, started to turn but the Latino decked him with a solid fist in the chest. Three fast blows.

He cried out and dropped onto his back, gasping for breath and vomiting.

Pellam slipped behind a corner and fired another shot – toward but not at McCray – aiming for the brick at his feet, worried about bullets flying through the populated neighborhood. The shot drove the Irishman further behind the Dumpster.

The thug with the gunshot was screaming, "Oh, God, oh, shit. My leg, my leg!"

Everybody ignored him. Pellam's minder had vanished, running down an offshoot of the alley. McCray and the remaining Irishman were firing blindly at Ramirez, who was pinned down, looking for cover as best he could behind a pile of trash bags.

"Yo," Pellam called, ducking as a bullet from McCray snapped past him. He tossed the black automatic to Ramirez, who caught it one handed, pulled the slide and fired several covering shots. The man who'd been hit kept sobbing, hands over his face, crawling an inch at a time toward his comrades.

Ramirez gave a whoop and laughed loud. He was an excellent shot and the Irishmen could only peek out for a second or two and fire a careless shot before ducking back.

The gunfire lasted for no more than thirty seconds. Pellam didn't fire again. He was sure there'd be sirens filling the night, whipsawing lights. A hundred cops. But he heard nothing from the streets around them.

It was, of course, Hell's Kitchen. What was a little gunplay?

A hand reached out from behind the brick wall and grabbed the wounded man. He disappeared. A few minutes later the three Irishmen were stumbling out of the alley. A car started and squealed away.

Pellam stood, still struggling for breath. Ramirez too, laughing. He checked the clip in the gun and slipped it into his pocket, retrieved his own automatic.

"Son of a bitch," Ramirez said.

"Let's get—"

The gunshot was deafening. Pellam felt a hot, searing pain on his cheek.

Ramirez spun and fired from his hip, three times, four, hitting the man – Pellam's minder – who'd returned and fired from the shadows of the alley. The man flew backwards.

Hands shaking, Pellam watched the body twitch as he died.

Ramirez asked urgently, "Jesus, man, you okay?"

Pellam lifted his hand to his cheek. Touching a strip of exposed flesh. Looked at the blood on his fingers.

It stung like pure hell. But that was good. He remembered from his stuntman days that numbness was bad, pain was good. Whenever a gag went bad and a stuntman complained of numbness, the stunt coordinators got nervous in a big way.

In the distance, the first siren.

"Listen," Pellam said desperately, "I can't be found here."

"Man, it was self-defense."

"No, you don't understand. I can't be found with a gun."

Ramirez frowned then nodded knowingly. Then looked toward Ninth Avenue. "Here's what you do, man. Just go out to the street, walk slow. Like you out shopping. Cover up that." He pointed toward the wounded cheek. "Get some bandages or something. Stay on Eighth or Ninth, go north. Remember: Walk slow. You be invisible, you walk slow. Gimme your piece. We got a place to keep 'em."

Pellam handed over the Colt.

Ramirez said, "I thought you said you weren't carrying."

"White man's lie," Pellam whispered, and vanished down the alley.

19

"Louis," Pellam pushed into the office. "Got something you might want to look at."

It was late morning, close to ten, and Bailey the somewhat-sober lawyer had not yet been replaced by Bailey the somewhat-drunk apartment dweller. The lights were out in the office portion of the rooms and he shuffled in from the bedroom in a bathrobe, mismatched slippers on his feet.

Despite the agonizing groan, the air conditioner still wasn't doing anything but pushing hot dust around Bailey's office.

"What happened to your face?"

"Shaving," Pellam answered.

"Try a razor. They work better than machetes."

The lawyer then added, "I heard there was a shooting last night. Somebody from Jimmy Corcoran's gang was killed."

"That right?"

"Pellam—"

"I don't know anything about it, Louis."

"There were supposedly two men involved. One white, one Hispanic."

"'Latino,'" Pellam corrected. "You're not supposed to say Hispanic." He dropped the Polaroid onto the desk. "Take a look."

The lawyer's gaze remained on Pellam for a moment longer.

"Yesterday I showed that picture to Flo Epstein. At the insurance agency." He held up his hands. "No intimidation. Just snapshots."

Bailey examined the photo. "Wine? No? You sure?"

Pellam continued, "I took a picture of Ettie at the Detention Center. I showed it to the Epstein woman and asked if it was Ettie."

"And?"

"She said it was."

"Well." Bailey examined the picture. Squinted. Picked it up and laughed. "Say, this is very good. How'd you do it?"

"Morphing. Computer graphics at my post production lab."

The photo was the Polaroid that Pellam had taken of Ettie at WDC, body, hair, hands, dress. The face, however, was that of Ella Fitzgerald. Pellam had had the two images assembled by computer and then had taken a Polaroid of the result.

"Encouraging," the lawyer said. Though Pellam thought he wasn't as encouraged as he ought to be.

Pellam pulled open the door of the tiny refrigerator. Jugs of wine. No water, no soft drinks, no juice. He looked up. "What's eating you, Louis?"

"That poker game I told you about? With the fire marshal?"

"It didn't happen?"

"Oh, it did."

Pellam took the slip of paper Bailey offered with an unsteady hand.

Dear Louis;

   I did what we talked about and got a game together with Stan, Sobie, Fred and the Mouse, remember him? Been years. I lost you sixty bucks but Stan let me take a bottle of Dewar's, almost full, so I'll drop it off sometime after it's not so almost full any more.

   Here's what I found and I think you might not like it. Lomax found a passbook Washington didn't tell any one about. Grand total inside of over Ten Thousand. And guess what. She took out 2 Gs the day before the fire. Also they say your a prick because you didn't list the $ on her financial disclosure statement for the bail motion. But mostly they're happy cause it gooses they're case.

   Joey

Ten thousand?

Pellam was stunned. Where on earth had Ettie got that much money? She'd never mentioned any savings to him. When Bailey'd asked what she could contribute to the bail bondsman she said maybe eight, nine hundred, tops. He remembered the other day too. She'd said she couldn't have bought the insurance policy from Flo Epstein's agency because she didn't have the money.

He looked out the window, watching the bulldozer demolishing what was left of Ettie's building. A worker with a sledgehammer was pounding a star-point chisel into a scorched stone bulldog to break it apart.

He heard Ettie's voice:

". . . I'm trying and recall how many buildings were on this block. I'm not sure. They were all tenements like this one. But they're mostly gone now. This one was built by an immigrant in 1876. Heinrik Deuter. German man. You know those bulldogs out front? The ones on either side of the steps. He had a stone carver come and carve those because he had a bulldog when he was a boy in Germany. I met his great grandson a few years back. People say it's sad they pull down these old places to build new ones. Well, I say so what? A hundred years ago they tore down other buildings to build *these*, right? Things come and things go. Just like people in your life. And that's just the way it works."

Pellam said nothing for a long while. He picked up a large skeleton key from Bailey's desk, studied the brass intently then replaced it. "How'd the police find out about the account?"

"I have no idea."

"Did the teller identify her as the woman who took out the money?"

"I have a call in to somebody in the department to find that out. They've frozen the account."

"This is bad, isn't it?"

"Yep. It sure is."

The phone rang. It was an old-fashioned bell, the sound jarring. Bailey picked it up.

Pellam watched a car cruise slowly past. Again he heard the thump of bass notes from that hip-hop song. It must have been number one on the rap chart. "*. . . the Man got a message just for you, gonna smoke your brothers and your sisters too*."

It faded. When he looked back he saw that Louis Bailey was holding the phone absently. He tried to replace it. Needed to do it twice to seat the receiver in its cradle. "My God," he whispered. "My God."

"What, Louis? Is it Ettie?"

"There was a fire on the Upper West side a half hour ago." He took a deep breath. "The insurance agency. Two employees were killed. Flo Epstein was one of them. It was him, Pellam. Somebody recognized him. It was that young man from the gas station. He used that napalm of his. He burned them both to death. Jesus Lord . . ."

Pellam exhaled, stunned at the news. He was thinking: The pyro had followed him there, to the agency. He'd been to Pellam's apartment earlier and broken in, stolen the tapes. Then he'd followed him uptown. That's probably why he hadn't killed Pellam in his apartment. He was using him to find witnesses.

"*It was three minutes. You having sex it's nothing, you having a baby, it's an eternity.*"

And if you're burning to death . . .

Bailey said, "She'd signed an affidavit about identifying Ettie. That's admissible. What she told you about the ginned-up picture isn't. It's hearsay."

Pellam looked out Bailey's window at a square of earth near where Ettie's building used to stand, illuminated by sunlight shining ruddy and immaculate through a clear sky. It occurred to Pellam now that because the building was gone, sunlight would shine on places that hadn't been lit for more than a hundred years. This recaptured brilliance seemed to Pellam to alter both the present and the past, as if the ghosts of thousands of Hell's Kitchen residents long gone to bullets and disease and hard lives were once again at risk.

"You want to plead her, don't you?" Pellam asked the lawyer.

He nodded.

Pellam said, "You've wanted to all along, haven't you?"

Bailey steepled his fingers, his pale wrists jutting from dirty white cuffs. "A plea bargain is considered a win here in the Kitchen."

"What about the innocent ones?"

"This doesn't have a damn thing in the world to do with guilt or innocence. It's like Social Security or selling your blood for booze or food money. Pleading in exchange for a reduced sentence – it's just something that makes life a little easier in the Kitchen."

"If I hadn't been involved," Pellam said, "you would've gone ahead, right? And plead her?"

"A half hour after they arrested her," Bailey responded.

Pellam nodded. He said nothing as he walked outside and started down the sidewalk. The backhoe lifted a shovelful of rubble from the wreckage of Ettie's building – chunks of the hand-carved bulldog mostly – and dropped it unceremoniously into the Dumpster at the curb.

"Things come and things go. And that's just the way it works."

There was nothing to do but ask. Straight out.

Pellam watched Ettie walk stiffly into the visitors' room at the Women's Detention Center. Her dim smile faded and she asked, "What is it, John?" Her eyes narrowed at the streak on his face. "What happened . . ." But her voice faded as she studied his expression.

"The police found the bank account."

"The . . . ?"

"The one in Harlem. The savings account with ten thousand in it."

The old woman shook her head vehemently and touched her temple with her good hand, the ring finger of which had been broken long ago and had set badly. Her face shone with contrition for maybe a second. Then she spat out, "I didn't tell *anybody* about my savings. How the fuck'd they find it?" She was drawn and secretive now.

"You didn't tell anyone. You didn't tell the court or your bail bondsman. You didn't tell Louis. That doesn't look good."

"There's no reason for the world to know everything about a woman," she snapped. "Her man takes her things away, her children take things away, everybody takes and takes and takes! How'd they find out?"

"I don't know."

Bitterly she asked, "Well, so what I've got some money?"

"Ettie . . ."

"It's *my* damn business, not theirs."

"They say that you – or somebody – made a withdrawal just a day before the fire."

"What? I didn't take anything out." Her eyes were wide with alarm and anger.

"Two thousand."

She rose and limped in a frantic circle as if she were about to charge into the streets in search of the stolen cash. "Somebody robbed me? My money! Somebody told 'em 'bout my money! Some Judas did that."

The speech seemed too prepared, as if she'd planned an excuse if the money was found. More conspiracies, Pellam thought wearily. Under Ettie's shrunken frown Pellam turned away and gazed out the window. He wondered if she was accusing him. Was *he* the Judas? He asked finally, "Where's the passbook?"

"In my apartment. It got burnt up, I guess. How can somebody take my money just like that? What am I going to do?"

"The police froze the account."

"What?" Ettie cried.

"Nobody can take any more money out."

"I can't get my money?" she whispered. "I need that. I need every penny of my money."

Why? Pellam wondered. What for?

He asked, "You didn't use that money for bail. Don't look that way, Ettie. I'm just telling you what they're saying. That it's suspicious."

"They think I paid it to the firebug man?" She gave a sour laugh.

"Reckon they do," Pellam said after a moment.

"And you think that too."

"No. I don't."

Ettie walked to the window. "Somebody betrayed me. Somebody betrayed me good." The words were bitter and she couldn't hold Pellam's eye when she said this. Again Ettie remained still as stone. Then her head rose inches, just enough for her to gaze at the dimly lit windowsill. "Leave me alone now, please. I'd as soon not see anybody. No, don't say anything, John. Please, just leave."

When they got him this time, they frisked him carefully.

Oh, man, not now. I don't need this now.

Pellam had just walked into his apartment building lobby in the East Village, lost in his doubts about Ettie and her secret money, when six hands grabbed him from behind and slammed him against the wall.

Last time, with Ramirez, the Irishmen had been content to slug him once and forgo a search for wild west pistols. Now, they turned his pockets inside out and, satisfied that he was unarmed, spun him around.

Little Jacko Drugh was accompanied by a tall man vaguely resembling Jimmy Corcoran and a third one, a redhead. The lobby wasn't that big a space but it offered plenty of room for three guys to beat the crap out of him.

The look in Drugh's eye told him this wasn't his idea and Pellam had some sympathy for the young man.

Let's see. What scene would this be? Toward the end of Act Two in your standard Hollywood action/adventure script. The good gunfighter gets blindsided by the cattle baron's boys. The heroic reporter gets nailed by the oil company security guards. The commando gets set up and kidnapped by the enemy.

Score one for the bad guys – setting up the hero for his triumphant return. And audiences love it when their boy goes down hard.

"I'd invite you up," Pellam said, wincing at the vice grips on his arms, "but I don't really want to."

The taller of the thugs – probably Corcoran's brother – drew back a fist but Drugh shook his head. Said to Pellam, "Jimmy heard what happened last night. Seany McCray taking it on himself to wax Ramirez. Heard you were playing second for the spic . . . Anyway, like you maya heard, Jimmy don't want no excitement, too much attention in the Kitchen right now. So he ain't going to kill you and Ramirez, like he probably ought. But youse took out one of our boys so we gotta come and do something about it. There's gotta be some, you know, payback."

"Wait, why me?" Pellam asked. "What about Ramirez?"

"Well, what it is is Jimmy don't want to start nothing, no crew wars, so he figured everybody'd be happier we play Mike Tyson on you."

"Not everybody," Pellam muttered. "*I'm* not real crazy about the idea."

"Yeah, well, that's how it goes, doesn't it? Jacko don't make the rules."

And I just paid five C-notes to this guy. Damn.

"Look, you want me to apologize, I will. I'm sorry."

Redhead said, "Sorry don't count for shit." He stepped forward. Pellam turned to face him but Drugh held up an arm to stop his fellow gangster.

"Hold up. He's Jacko's. Isn't he now?" Five-foot-two Drugh turned to face Pellam.

Who relaxed considerably. He understood now. That's why Jacko'd volunteered. It'd be like O'Neil and Ramirez. A sham. Drugh'd pull punches, Pellam'd take a fall and it'd all be over with in three minutes. He knew how to fake-fight – from his stuntman days. Pellam shook free of the other two Irishmen and stepped forward. "Okay, you want some, you got it." He lifted his arms, making fists.

Drugh's first swing nearly knocked him out. The bony fist slammed viciously into Pellam's jaw. He blinked and flew back, his head slamming into the brass mailboxes. Drugh followed up with a left to the gut. Pellam went down on his knees, retching.

"Goddamn—"

"Shut the fuck up," Drugh muttered. He joined his hands together and brought them down hard on Pellam's neck. In two seconds Pellam was flat on the filthy tiles.

Drugh's coup de grace was a work-booted foot slamming into his kidney and gut. Jesus . . .

"You don't got no gun now, you asshole," Drugh recited, as if he'd been working on the line all day. He was a far worse actor than Pellam had suspected. "You've fucked with the wrong people."

Pellam rose to his knees, swung at Drugh, missing completely and took three hard blows to the belly.

The little man whispered in Pellam's ear: "How'm I doing?"

Pellam couldn't speak. He was close to vomiting.

Drugh whispered: "Hit me back. It's looking too fake."

Pellam crawled away from him, struggled to his feet. He spun around and swung hard. He connected, a weak glancing blow to the man's cheek.

Drugh blinked in surprise and screamed, "You fucking prick!" Redhead and the other one held Pellam while Drugh rained blows into his belly and face. Pellam simply gave up, he held his hands over his face and dropped to the floor again.

"Not so hot shit now," the redhead said. He was laughing.

"Way to go, Jacko."

Then Drugh had his gun in his hand and he pressed the muzzle against Pellam's face. Pellam, thinking how he'd never really trusted the trigger cogs in guns. They could be notoriously edgy. The little bantam leaned closer, whispered, "See, you get me that part in a movie, I can do my own fighting and everything. I don't need no stuntmen. An' I got my own gun too."

Pellam groaned.

"Shoot him in the foot or knee or something, Jacko."

"Yeah. Fuck up his hand. Boom, boom."

Drugh seemed to be debating "Naw, he's had enough. These fucking queers from Hollywood, they can't take shit."

Drugh leaned forward once again, whispered, "What it is, that kid Alex you wanted to know about? He's staying at the Eagleton Hotel on Ninth Avenue. Room 434."

Pellam mumbled something that Drugh took to be, "Thank you," though the phrase shared only one word with that expression of gratitude.

Drugh gave him a friendly kick in the ribs as a farewell and then vanished with the others. "Hey, Tommy," he said to Redhead, "you remember that scene in that movie I was telling you about? . . . What the fuck movie you think I mean? . . ."

The door swung shut. Pellam spit the loose tooth from his mouth. It rattled around on the tile floor for what seemed like minutes before it finally spun to silence.

20

It was just as a horde of bleary French tourists was checking into the tawdry hotel on the West Side that the elevator returned as summoned to the ground floor. And then it opened its doors.

"Mon dieu!"

The flaming liquid inside the car melted through its plastic container and spilled like a fiery tidal wave into the lobby.

"Jesus!" somebody screamed.

"Oh, shit . . ."

The flames appeared almost magically as the liquid ran along the floor and ignited the carpet, the chairs, the gold-flecked wallpaper, the fake rubber trees, the tables.

Alarms begin detonating with harsh baritone ringing – old-fashioned bells that make one think immediately of lifesaving systems vastly outdated. Screams filled the tattered halls. People began to flee.

More frightening than the flames was the smoke, which filled the hotel instantly as if it were pumped in under high pressure. The electricity simply stopped and, amid the palpable smoke, nighttime filled the lobby and corridors. Even the ruby exit signs grew invisible.

And sounding above all of the screams and ringing and alarms was a frantic pedal tone – the howl of fire.

The Eagleton Hotel was about to die.

The flames consumed the cheap carpet and turned it from green to black in seconds. The flames boiled plastic as easily as it puckered skin. The fire ran up the walls, melting plaster like butter. The flames spit out smoke thick as muddy water and suffocated a half-dozen foreign guests trapped in an alcove without an exit.

The flames kissed and the flames killed.

"Merde! Mon dieu! Allez, allez! Giselle, où es tu?"

In the downstairs banquet room, where three white-jacketed busboys cowered, there was a sudden flashover – the whole space grew so hot it ignited like one huge match head.

Upstairs a young man, fully clothed, leapt into a brimming bathtub, thinking cleverly that this would protect him. Sickened rescue workers would find what was left of his body, two hours from now, in water still heated to a slow boil.

One woman in a frenzy of panic flung open the door of her room and with the in-rush of oxygen an explosion engulfed her. The last scream she uttered wasn't a human sound at all but a burst of flame popping from her mouth.

One man fled from a searing wall of flames and hurtled through a fifth-floor window. He cartwheeled elegantly in silence to the roof of a yellow taxi below. The glass in the cab's six windows turned instantly opaque as if coated with winter frost.

Another man stepped onto a fire escape so heated by flames that the metal rods of the stairs melted through his running shoes in seconds. He climbed, screaming, on burnt, bloody feet to the roof.

In rooms on the higher floors some of the guests believed they were safe from the fire itself; they noticed only a faint haze of smoke around them. They calmly read the in-case-of-emergency cards and, as those reassuring words instructed, soaked washclothes and held them over their faces. Then they sat down calmly on the floor to wait for help and died peacefully in the sleep of carbon monoxide poisoning.

In the lobby, there was another flash-over. A sofa exploded in orange fire. So did the body of a tourist, lying on the carpet. He contracted into the pugilistic attitude – knees drawn up, fists clenched and arms bent at the elbows. In front of him a Pepsi machine melted and exploding soda cans shot through the lobby, the contents turning to steam before the aluminum hit the floor.

Sonny caught glimpses of these vignettes because he'd placed the jug of burning juice in the elevator on the sixth floor and then leisurely made his way down the fire escape. Lingering, watching. He told himself to flee, to be more cautious. But naturally he couldn't help himself. His hands were no longer shaking, he wasn't sweating.

The NYFD trucks began to roll up. Sonny slipped into an alley across the street and continued to watch, observing with pleasure that it was an "all-hands" blaze. This was quite a feather in his cap. There were ladders, engines and trucks from a number of companies. My God, it was a whole-battalion fire! He hadn't set one of those for months. He listened to his Radio Shack scanner and learned that it was a ten-forty-five, Code 1.

Fatalities already.

But he knew that.

The apparatus kept arriving. Dozens of Seagrave and Mack fire trucks and engines and ladders. Some red, some Day-Glo yellow-green. Intersection horns blaring harshly. Ambulances. Police cars, marked and unmarked. Men and women in heat-proof gear, with air tanks and masks, hurried into the con-flagration. More ambulances. More police. Lights and noise, cascades of water. Steam everywhere, like ghosts of the dead. Cars parked illegally were hacked open to make paths for the hoses.

Crowds filled the streets, looters sized up the risk.

The hotel became a storm of orange flame, towering up to the eighth-floor penthouse.

When the flames were largely under control the EMS medics started bringing out the bodies. Some were cyanotic – bluish-tinted due to lack of oxygen. Some were red as lobsters from the flames and heat. Some were charcoal colored and bore no resemblance whatsoever to the human beings they had once been.

More windows burst outward. Slivers of black glass rained to the street as rooster tails of water rose from the huge nozzles and converged on the weakening flames, turning to scalding steam.

Sonny watched it all from an alley nearby.

He watched it all until, finally, finally, he saw what he'd been waiting for.

His mother had told Sonny that his father used to enjoy hunting. Flushing birds with a boisterous lab named Bosco, Sonny's father had been a good hunter and he'd spent a lot of time perfecting his skill – though he probably shouldn't have, Sonny had concluded, because when he and Bosco were away his wife fucked anything that came to the door.

Sonny's mother's last lover, on the other hand, never hunted for much of anything – except a way out of his burning bedroom. Which he never did find, of course, thanks to Sonny and a very handy spool of wire.

Now, in the smokey chaos of the dying Eagleton hotel, Sonny saw the bird *he'd* flushed (using an all-hands blaze, rather than a cheerful black dog): Alex, the fag with the chipped tooth and a mole like a tiny leaf on his right shoulder blade.

Gasping for breath, staring at the building, the young man leaned against a lamppost. Probably thinking what people always thought at times like that: I could've been trapped in there. I could've died in there. I—

"True, you little faggot," Sonny whispered. "You might have." His head was close to the boy's ear.

Alex spun around. "You . . . I . . ."

"What does that mean?" Sonny asked him, frowning. "'You I . . .' Say, is that faggot talk?"

Skinny Alex turned to run but Sonny was on him like a mantis. He clocked him on the side of the head with a pistol, looked around and dragged him deeper into the deserted alley.

"Like, listen!"

Sonny slipped the pistol behind the young man's ear. Whispered, "Like, you're dead."

*   *   *

Pellam, breathless from running, paused, leaning against the chain-link fence of a construction site across the street from the Eagleton.

Oh, no. No . . .

The hotel was gone. You could see sky through some of the windows of the upper stories and gray brown smoke flowed from the dead heart of the building. He said to a passing EMS technician, a round man with a sweaty, soot-stained face, "I'm looking for a teenager. A blond kid. Skinny. He was in there. Name might be Alex."

The weary technician said, "Sorry, mister. I didn't treat anyone like that. But we got eight BBRs."

Pellam shook his head.

The tech explained. "'Burned beyond recognition.'"

Walking through the numb crowds, Pellam asked about the boy. Somebody thought he might have seen the young man climb down the fire escape but he couldn't be sure. Somebody else, a tourist, asked him to take his picture in front of the building and held out his Nikon. Pellam stared in silent disbelief and walked on.

Closer to the building he stepped away from the crowd and nearly ran into Fire Marshal Lomax. The marshal glanced at Pellam and didn't say a word. His eyes returned to four bodies lying on the ground, arms and legs drawn up in the pugilistic pose. They were loosely covered with sheets. His radio crackled and he spoke into his Handi-Talkie. "Battalion commander has advised fire is knocked down as of eighteen hundred hours."

"Say again, Marshal Two-five-eight."

Lomax repeated the message then added, "Appears to be suspicious origin. Get the crime scene buses down here."

"That's a roger, Marshal Two-five-eight."

He put the radio back in his belt. A rumpled man in general, he was now a mess. Shirt soot-stained, drenched in sweat, slacks torn. There was a gash on his forehead. He pulled on latex gloves, bent down and tossed the sheet off one of the victims, searched the horrible corpse; Pellam had to look away. Without glancing up, Lomax said in a calm voice, "Let me tell you a story, Mr Lucky."

"I—"

"Few years ago I was working in the Bronx. There was this club on Southern Boulevard, a social club. You know what a social club is, right? Just a place for people to hang out. Drink, dance. The name of the place was Happy Land. One night there was maybe a hundred people inside, having a good time. It was a Honduran neighborhood. They were good people. Working people. No drugs, no guns. Just people . . . having a good time."

Pellam said nothing. His eyes dipped to the macabre spectacle of the corpse. He tried to look away but couldn't.

"There was this guy," Lomax said in his eerie, dead voice, "who'd been going out with the coat-check girl and she'd dumped him. He got drunk and went out and bought a buck's worth of gas, came back and just poured it in the lobby, lit it and went home. Just like that: set a fire and went home. I don't know, maybe to watch TV. Maybe have some dinner. I don't know."

"I hope he got caught and went to jail," Pellam said.

"Oh, yeah, he did. But that's not my point. What I'm saying is there were eighty-seven people killed in that fire. The biggest arson murder in U.S. history. And I was on the ID team. See, it was a problem – because they were dancing."

"Dancing?"

"Right. Most of the women didn't have purses on them and the men'd left their jackets, with their wallets, hanging on the chairs. So we didn't know who was who. What we did was we laid all the bodies out and then we're thinking, Jesus, we can't have eighty-seven families walk up and down the street and look at this. So we took Polaroids of them. A couple shots of each body. And put it in this notebook for the families to look at. I was the one who handed the book to every mother or father or brother or sister whose kids were at Happy Land that night. I'm never going to forget that."

He covered up the body and looked up. "One guy did all that. One guy with a fucking dollar's worth of gasoline. I just wanted to tell you I'm putting a call to the D.A. to move Ettie Washington out of protective isolation."

Pellam began to speak. But Lomax, fatigue in every move, stood and walked to the second body. He said, "She killed a kid. Every prisoner in Detention knows that by now. I give her a day or two. At best."

He crouched down and pulled the sheet off.

————◆————

21

The shades were down in Bailey's office.

Maybe to stave off the heat, Pellam guessed. Then he realized that the blackout must've been at the request of the nervous man who sat forward on a rickety chair across from the lawyer. He was continually adjusting his position and looking around the room as if a hitman were sighting on his back from across the street.

Pellam paid no attention to the visitor. To the lawyer he said, "I found Alex but the pyro got to him first."

"The Eagleton fire?" Bailey asked, nodding knowingly.

"Yep."

"He's dead?"

Pellam shrugged. "Maybe he's dead. Maybe he just took off. I don't know. There were unidentified bodies."

"Oh, my God," offered the visitor. He looked like the sort who'd be wringing his hands if they weren't gripping the seat of the chair so desperately.

Pellam then told the lawyer what Lomax had said about protective custody.

"No!" Bailey whispered. "That's bad. She won't last an hour in general population."

"Goddamn blackmail," Pellam muttered. "Can you stop him from doing it?"

"I can delay it is all. But they'll release her. The D.A.'ll agree in an instant if they think it'll pressure her into giving up the arsonist." He jotted a note on a piece of sunbleached foolscap and turned his attention to the nervous man who sat before him. He was skinny, middle-aged and wore a clever toupee. His pants had a slight flare. A disco demon from the seventies. The lawyer introduced the men.

Newton Clarke rose slightly and shook Pellam's hand with a sopping palm, then deflated himself back to his cracked Naugahyde roost. He never held Pellam's eye for more than a second.

"Newton here has a few interesting things to tell us. Start over, why don't you? Some wine, Pellam? No? You're *such* an abstainer. Okay, Newton, talk to us. Tell us where you work."

"Pillsbury, Milbank & Hogue."

"Roger McKennah's law firm. The one his wife told me about."

"Right."

Newton's job, it seemed, was in the managing attorney's office.

Bailey explained, "They're the ones who handle scheduling, make calendar calls and so on, filings. You get the picture. They're not lawyers. Newton *could* be, right? With everything you know about the law." A glance at Pellam. "But he wants an *honest* profession."

Clarke smiled uneasily. His eyes flicked to the window as a passerby cast a hurried shadow on the dusty blinds.

Bailey swilled more wine. "Give us your take on Roger McKennah."

"Well, for one thing, he knows everything that goes on in the Kitchen."

"Like Santa Claus, is he? Making his list . . . Don't you worry, Newton, your mission here's safe. We'll give you bushy eyebrows and a fake nose when you leave."

Clarke forced his shoulders back and sat up straight. He offered a humorless laugh. "Jesus, Louis, his building's right across the street. We should've met someplace safe."

"Zurich, Grand Cayman?" Bailey asked with uncharacteristic acid. "Now what about McKennah?"

The man told his story. Newton indeed had a clerk's personality. Organized, precise, detailed. The kind of documentary interviewee, Pellam decided, who seemed perfect but whose testimony he could use only in small doses; for all his accuracy Clarke spoke without a bit of passion or color. We'll take robust lies over the pale truth any day, Pellam had come to believe.

"Should I—?"

"From the beginning," Bailey said. "The very beginning."

"Okay, okay. Well, Mr McKennah grew up in the Kitchen. He was poor, crude . . . When he was in his twenties he decided to remake himself. He dumped the girl he was engaged to because she was Jewish." Clarke glanced at Pellam's features to see how inappropriate this comment was. Then he continued. "He hired a speech and dress coach to help him improve his image and he started working his way through New York real estate. He bought his first building in Flatbush when he was twenty-three. Then a building in Prospect Park, then Astoria, then a couple in the Heights and the Slope. He was twenty-nine. He had nine buildings.

"Then he hocked all nine and came into Manhattan. One building on Twenty-fourth Street. Nobody was in that part of town then. It was a bum location. The city – the high-class commercial districts – went south to the Empire State Building and it stopped until you got to Wall Street. But he bought this building and what happened but New York Life bought it from *him*. Fast and with cash. He took that money and bought two more buildings, then three, then six. Then he *built* one. His first. Then he bought two more. And kept going. Now he's got sixty or seventy throughout the North-east."

Pellam was losing patience. He asked, "Was he ever connected with an arson?"

"That's my boy," Bailey said, nodding toward Pellam. "Good movie-maker. Gets right to the proverbial chase scene."

Clarke responded, "Well . . ."

But the words deflated as soon as they were spoken and Bailey prompted, "Come on, Newton. Pellam's a friend."

"Okay, okay . . . Well, nobody's sure. Couldn't prove anything. But recently there've been some accidents. Some union men – one of them went off the thirtieth floor of a building on Lexington. And a building inspector who hadn't been willing to pocket money got beaned by a stack of two-by-fours. None of this happened on a McKennah job site, of course, but they all were involved with Mr McKennah one way or another. Suppliers who tried to extort him – their trucks got hijacked. And yeah, a couple of places were fire-bombed – sellers who set ridiculously high prices. People who wouldn't *deal*. That was Mr McKennah's complaint. He doesn't mind negotiations. He doesn't even mind getting bested. But he hates it when people won't even sit down with him. That's the most important thing for Mr McKennah. You don't have to play fair but you have to *play*."

Pellam recalled the steely eyes of the brunette at the developer's party. Tough adversary, playing the game. "How'd you find out all of this?"

"Pellam's right to be suspicious, Newton." Bailey turned to him. "But we don't have to worry. Newton's sources are impeccable." More wine sloshed. "And so's his motive for helping us out here, isn't it? Pristine."

Pellam explained what Jolie had told him and asked, "Exactly how desperate is he?"

"His casinos have failed big. He's a step away from bankruptcy. And I mean complete bankruptcy. Apocalyptic bankruptcy."

"Now we come to the crux of it, right, Newton?"

The toupee was adjusted to quell an itching scalp. "Mr McKennah needs the Tower." He nodded toward the shaded window, on the other side of which the high-rise soared into the sky. "It's his last chance," added the flatlined voice.

McKennah, Clarke explained, had several tenants lined up for the Tower when it was completed but there was only one lease he really cared about. RAS Advertising and Public Relations was consolidating all of its many operations in one location – fifteen floors in the Tower under a ten-year lease, with generous cost-of-living increases annually. RAS would be paying annual rent of more than $24 million.

The ad agency employees, however, were upset about their move from midtown and were concerned that commuting through the streets of Hell's Kitchen would be dangerous. RAS would sign the lease only if McKennah, at his own expense, built a four-block-long tunnel connecting the building with the Long Island Railroad commuter line in Penn Station, which also had a subway stop.

The deal was signed and, like a piranha, McKennah's company began devouring underground rights to build the tunnel. The company negotiated easements to every building on the planned route of the tunnel – except one. A small plot of land on Thirty-seventh Street, directly behind the lot on which Ettie's building had sat.

"Odd coincidence," Bailey explained wryly. "The land was bought by someone just three days before McKennah's company approached the old owner."

"So, somebody had inside information that McKennah needed it. Who?"

"Jimmy Corcoran," Bailey said. "How 'bout that?"

"Corcoran?" Pellam remembered Jacko Drugh's telling him that Jimmy and his brother were planning some kind of big deal. And he recalled too what Jolie had said – the late-night meetings.

Corcoran doing a deal with Roger McKennah . . . Now, that was a bizarre thought.

Bailey continued. "And Jimmy's basically extorting McKennah. 'Cause without that parcel, no tunnel. No tunnel, no lease and hello bankruptcy court."

"Here's what the deal is," Clarke said, finally displaying some animation. "Corcoran owns the land Mr McKennah needs, right? Well, he's agreeing to lease it to Mr McKennah. Only

Corcoran insisted on taking a cut of the profits, not a flat fee. He gets one percent of the revenues generated by the property. That's brilliant for Corcoran because it looks like McKennah Tower's going to be making close to a hundred twenty million in annual rents."

"That psychotic punk is going to wind up with one point two million a year," Bailey said.

Clarke continued. "Mr McKennah's *never* given anybody a percent of the action before. *That's* how desperate he is."

Pellam considered this. He said, "Ettie's building – the one that burned – was right in between the Tower and Corcoran's property."

"Right," Bailey confirmed.

"So McKennah needs it to finish the tunnel. It's the last piece."

"So it seems," the lawyer said.

"What about this?" Pellam mused. "He cuts a deal with the owner – the St Augustus Foundation – so they let him build the tunnel. Only McKennah finds out he can't dig *under* the building. Maybe it's too old, maybe it's not stressed right. So he hires the pyro to burn the place down and make it look like Ettie did it. McKennah gets his tunnel and the Foundation can put up a new building."

Clarke shrugged. "All I can say is what I said before. I've never seen him this desperate."

Pellam asked, "What exactly happens if the Tower fails?"

"A dozen banks'll call Mr McKennah's loans. They're personally guaranteed," Clarke whispered, as if disclosing a social disease. "He'll go bankrupt. He owes a billion five more than he's got."

"Hate it when that happens," Pellam said.

Bailey asked Clarke, "You find anything at the office about granting underground rights to the property that burned?"

"Nothing, no. But McKennah always plays things close to his chest. The partners're always complaining that he never keeps them informed."

Bailey grimaced. "Never easy, is it? Well, all right, Newton, back you go to the salt mines."

Clarke hesitated then, eyes on the dusty, scuffed floor.

"What?" Pellam asked him.

But when he spoke it was to Bailey. He said, "He hurts people, Mr McKennah does. He screams at them and he fires them when they don't do exactly what he wants even if it turns out later he was wrong. He has temper tantrums. He gets even with people." Finally the eyes swung toward Pellam momentarily. "Just . . . be careful. He's a very vindictive man. A bully."

Cloaked as a warning, the man's words meant something else. They meant: Forget the name Newton Clarke.

He stood and left hurriedly, his disco boots making virtually no noise on the linoleum.

"So, we've got a motive," Pellam said.

"Greed. The Old Faithful of motives. One of the best." Bailey refilled his glass. He lifted the shade, looked out at the construction site.

Pellam said, "We've got to find out if McKennah has the underground rights to the land below Ettie's building. The head of the Foundation could tell you. Father . . . whatever his name is. Did he ever call you back?"

"No, he didn't."

"Let's try him again."

But Bailey was shaking his head. "I don't think we should trust him. But I can find out."

"Cleg?" Pellam asked. The skinny horseman, armed with his liquor bottles.

"No," Bailey said, reflecting. "I'll do this one myself. We should meet back here at, say, eight?"

"Sure."

Bailey looked up and found Pellam's eyes on him. "Thought I treated him a little harshly? Newton?"

Pellam shrugged. "I've finally nailed down your secret. How you clog up gears, Louis."

"Have you now?"

"You cultivate debts."

The lawyer sipped wine and chuckled, nodding. "I learned a long time ago about the power of debt. What's the one thing that makes a man powerful, a president, a king, a corporate executive? That people *owe* him – their lives, their jobs, their freedom. That's the secret. A man who knows how to milk debt is the man who can keep power the longest of anyone."

The dull ice cubes clinked on the surface of the lemon-colored wine.

"And what does Clarke owe you?"

"Newton? Oh, in crass terms, about thirty-thousand dollars. He used to be a broker. He came to me with a real estate investment partnership idea a few years ago and I plunked down a chunk of my life savings. I found out later it was all phoney. The U.S. Attorney and the SEC caught him and I lost the money."

"And this is how he's paying you off?"

"As far as I'm concerned, information is negotiable tender. Tough luck that none of his other creditors feel that way."

"How long till he pays you off?"

Bailey laughed. "Oh, he probably has. Ages ago. But he doesn't believe it, of course. And he never will. That's the marvelous thing about debts. Even after you repay them, they never really go away."

No one paid any attention to the young worker as he wheeled the 55-gallon drum of cleaning fluid up the ramp to the apartment building. It was seven-thirty, dusk, but Thirty-sixth Street was lit up like a carnival, workers scurrying to get McKennah Tower ready for the topping-off ceremony.

Wearing white overalls, Sonny rested the dolly carrying the drum on the floor and in front of the door. He glanced at the tarnished sign, *Louis Bailey, Esq*. He listened and heard nothing. Then he knocked several times and when there was no answer he easily picked the lock – a talent that he didn't possess when he entered Juvenile Detention but that he had with him when he left – and then wheeled the drum inside.

Sonny was a worried man now. The Eagleton fire had galvanized the police and fire department. He'd never seen so many cops and marshals on the West Side. They were practically stopping cars on the street and frisking drivers. They were getting close and he had to stop them. A rough drawing of him had made the dinner-time news.

Shaking hands, sweaty face.

And tears. He was so frustrated and frightened that once or twice on the way over here, wheeling the drum up Ninth Avenue from his apartment, he'd found himself crying.

Walking into the office and parking the drum beside the lawyer's desk. The young man then sat down in the swivel

chair. Fake leather, he thought disdainfully. Agent Scullery –
a bit shorter and a lot deader than she'd been when she looked
down at him like a squirrel – had had much better taste in interior
designs. Still, the office pleased him. There was plenty of paper.
He'd never burned a lawyer's office and he thought that it would
go up very fast because there was *sooo* much paper.

Sonny pulled a few books off the shelf, flipped them open.
Looked down at the gray blocks of type. He had no idea what
these particular words meant. Sonny used to read books all the
time (though he preferred his mother's reading to him). But that
was years ago and he realized now that they no longer interested
him. He wondered why that was. He couldn't remember when
he'd last read a book. Years ago. What was it?

The book drooped in his hand . . .

Yes, he remembered. It was a true story. About the Ringling
Brothers circus fire in Hartford in 1944. More than a hundred
and fifty people were killed when the big top burned in a matter
of minutes. The bandleader played *Stars and Stripes Forever* –
the traditional circus disaster march – to warn all the performers
and workers of the blaze but they hadn't been able to save that
many people. Sonny remembered particularly the story of Little
Miss 1565, who died in the crush of the audience trying to
escape. She was clearly recognizable but no one ever claimed
the body.

Why, Sonny thought when he finished the book, didn't he
feel the least bit bad about the girl?

He stopped brooding and returned to his task.

On the desk he noticed Pellam's name and phone number
written on a piece of yellow paper. The Midnight Cowboy Joe
Buck faggot Antichrist . . . Sonny's hands began to shake again

– the sweat was already peppering his forehead – and he felt the urge to cry once more.

Stop it stop it stopit stopstopstop itttttt!

He had to pause for a moment until he calmed. Get to work. Keep busy. He unscrewed the light bulb from the old lawyer's desk lamp and carefully opened his knapsack, taking out one of his special light bulbs, heavy and fat with the slick, milky juice. He rested it carefully on the desk and then turned to the oil drum and took his wrench from his overall pocket. He began to work the lid off.

———◆———

22

S parks flew high above his head, cascading off the top of McKennah Tower, an eighth of a mile into the air. He could see a dozen tiny suns of welders' arcs.

Thinking about Carol Wyandotte, remembering how he'd seen this same astonishing building on his way to her apartment, the night he'd stayed over.

He'd just returned from the Youth Outreach Center, looking for her. But she'd already left for the night. Her assistant said that Carol had been in court all day. One of the kids staying at the YOC there had pulled a knife on an undercover cop during a buy-and-bust operation and Carol had spent six hours with the A.D.A. trying to convince them that he'd just been scared, he hadn't really intended to murder the officer.

It hadn't been a good day for her and she'd been pretty upset, the assistant told him. She'd left no message for Pellam at the YOC. And there'd been none on his machine at home.

Pellam was returning to Louis Bailey's office, to meet the

lawyer as planned. He looked away from the crown of the
Tower and once again examined the billboard that he'd seen a
dozen times on his way to interview Ettie. An ad for McKennah
Tower. He noticed that beneath the slick picture of the building
were bullet-points of features. The 60-story structure would be
computer-controlled (a "smart" building), would have a ten-
thousand-square-foot public atrium, automated pneumatic waste
removal, custom landscaping, a five-thousand-seat Broadway
theater, a gourmet restaurant, boutiques, high-R-value insula-
tion, water-conserving toilets, self-programming elevators . . .

He was, however, less impressed with this than he was
with the facts that weren't quite so public, the facts Louis
Bailey had told him: the labyrinthine deals McKennah had
cut with City Hall, P&Z, the Board of Assessment, the Landmark Preservation Commission, the MTA, the Department of
Revenue, the unions, the Clinton Community Association, the
West Side Democratic Club – the deals in which every inch of
the building had been bought, sold or liened in exchange for
tax abatements and promises of contracts and public works
renovations and sidewalk improvements and employment
and oh yes hard cash pressed into very eager hands call
them contributions or call them what you will. The actual
construction of the monumental edifice was a dull anticlimax
to the deal-making that resulted in its building.

Maybe someday he'd do a documentary on a high-rise like
this.

Skyscraper would be the title.

Buy the companion book.

Pellam turned away from the Tower and walked into Louis
Bailey's building. He was surprised to find the door unlocked

and partway open – the rooms inside, he could see, were dark. Pellam squinted and saw Bailey's form hunched over the desk. The lawyer's head was resting on a law book and Pellam thought, Hell, passed out drunk. He smelled wine.

And something else. What? Cleanser? Something strong and chemical.

"Hey, Louis," Pellam called, "rise and shine. How 'bout a little light?"

He flipped up the wall switch.

The explosion was very soft, not much more than the pop of a plastic bag, but the sphere of liquid flame that leapt out of the lamp was huge.

Jesus!

The fiery liquid splashed over the desk and enveloped the lawyer, who jerked back in a hideous, writhing gesture. His face and chest were masses of white flame, and from his throat came an animal's desperate scream. He fell behind the desk and began to thrash, his heels making loud thuds on the floor as his hands tried manically to beat the flames away.

Looking for a blanket or towel to beat out the flames, Pellam ran into the bedroom. By the time he found an old quilt smoke had completely filled the office, thick vile smoke, burnt-meat smoke.

"Louis!" Pellam flung the blanket over the lawyer but it ignited immediately and just added to the growing mass of fire. Pellam grabbed the phone and hit 911. But the line went dead; the flames had melted the cord. Pellam dropped the set and ran into the hallway, hit the fire alarm on the wall and grabbed the old-fashioned canister extinguisher. He charged back into the office and turned the tank upside down, firing a hissing stream of water at the flames.

As he stood dousing the fire ghastly smoke encircled him, slipped into Pellam's lungs. He began choking and his vision filled with black pebbles. He kept blasting away with the extinguisher, covering the black mass of Bailey's quivering body with the gray water.

The desk and a bookcase were still on fire and Pellam turned the extinguisher toward them. The flames were shrinking. But the room continued to grow black with the thick smoke.

Pellam spit the black crud from his mouth, dropped the empty extinguisher and staggered back toward the door to find another one. Outside, a dozen people were fleeing the building. He tried to call out to them but he couldn't. He felt himself starting to suffocate. He fell to the floor. The air was a little better down here but it was still filled with smoke and the stench of broiling death.

His lungs began to give out. He turned, stumbled toward the door. A fireman appeared.

"In here," Pellam said. And passed out on the floor.

Pellam sucked hard on the mask, the dizziness from smoke replaced by the dizziness from pure oxygen.

A dozen emergency lights flashed around him. Fire trucks, ambulances, police cars. Piercing white light. And red and blue.

"You're okay," encouraged the EMS attendant, a young man with a faint blond moustache. Bulky medical equipment and supplies dangled from his belt and filled his pockets. "Breathe it in. Come on, big guy. Keep going."

The technician wrote on a clipboard then looked into Pellam's eyes with a thin flashlight and took his blood pressure.

"Looking good," the high voice confirmed.

The memory of the horrible fire returned. "He's dead, isn't he?"

"Him? 'Fraid so. Didn't stand a chance. But it's a blessing, believe me. I've had burn cases before. Better for him to've gone fast than deal with sepsis and skin grafts."

He looked over at the body lying on the ground nearby, a sheet draped over it.

The task of giving the bad news about Louis Bailey to Ettie was looming in his mind when a hand descended to Pellam's shoulder and a figure crouched beside him.

"How you feeling?" the man asked.

Pellam wiped smoke tears from his eyes. His vision was a blur. Finally the face came into focus. In a shocked whisper he said, "You're here. You're okay."

"Me?" Louis Bailey asked.

"That's not you. I thought it was you." Pellam nodded toward the body.

Bailey said. "It was *almost* me. But it's him – the pyro."

"The *arsonist*?"

The lawyer nodded. "The fire marshal said he was rigging a trap – to get us both, I'd imagine."

"I turned the light switch on and set it off," Pellam whispered. He coughed hard for a moment.

"The son of a bitch should've unplugged the lamp first," a voice growled. It was Lomax. He walked up to the two men. "Pyros eventually get careless. Like serial killers. After a while the lust takes over and they stop worrying about details." He nodded toward the bag. "He had all the windows in your office closed. There was no ventilation and an open drum of that napalm crap he makes. He passed out from the fumes. Then you got here, Mr Lucky, and turned on the light. Ka-boom."

"Who was he?" Pellam asked.

The fire marshal held up a badly scorched wallet in a plastic bag.

"Jonathan Stillipo, Jr. Oh, we heard about him. Goes by the nickname of Sonny. Did juvenile time for torching his mother's house in upstate New York – of course, it just happened that his mother's boyfriend was locked in the bedroom upstairs. Fits the classic pyro mold. Momma's boy, loner in school, sexual conflicts. Did vanity fires in college – you know, sets a fire then puts it out for the heroics. He's been burning for fun and profit ever since. He was on our list to talk to about the recent fires but he went underground a while ago and we didn't have any leads. We found this in his back pocket. You can still read some of it."

Pellam looked at a scorched map of the city. Circles around *X*s marked the sites of the recent fires: the subway on Eighth Avenue, the department store. Two of the *X*s weren't circled and Pellam assumed those were the targets to be. One was Bailey's building. And the other was the Javits Center.

"My God," Bailey whispered. The convention hall was New York's largest.

Lomax said, "There's a fashion exhibition scheduled for tomorrow. Twenty-two thousand people would've been inside. Would have been the worst arson in world history."

"Well, he's dead," Pellam said. He added, "I guess he won't be able to testify about who hired him."

Then he caught the glance that passed between Bailey and the fire marshal.

"What, Louis?" Pellam asked.

Lomax motioned to a uniformed policeman, who walked up and handed him a plastic bag.

"This was in his wallet too."

The bag contained a sheet of paper. The plastic made a crinkling sound that Pellam found disturbing. It reminded him of the flames he'd just doused. He thought of Sonny's shaking body. Of the smell.

Pellam took the offered bag and read.

Here's 2 thousand like we agreed. Try and don't hurt any body. I'll leave the door open – the one in the back. I'll give you the rest, after I get the insurance money.
—Ettie.

———◆◆◆———

23

Pellam stood uneasily, dropped the oxygen mask onto the sidewalk.

"It's a forgery," Pellam said quickly. "It's all—"

"I've already talked to her, Pellam," Louis Bailey explained. "I've been on the phone for ten minutes."

"With Ettie?"

"She confessed, John," Bailey said softly.

Pellam couldn't take his eyes off Sonny's body. Somehow the sheet – bedclothes of the merely sleeping – made the sight more horrible than the burned flesh itself.

Bailey continued. "She said she never thought anybody'd get hurt. She never wanted anybody to die. I believe her."

"She *confessed*?" Pellam whispered. He hawked hard and spit. Coughed for a moment, spit again. Struggled to catch his breath. "I want to see her, Louis."

"I don't think that's a good idea."

Pellam said, "They threatened her. Or blackmailed her." He

nodded toward Lomax, standing at the curb, talking to his huge assistant. The fire marshal had overheard Pellam but he said nothing. Why should he? He had his pyro. He had the woman who hired him. Lomax seemed almost embarrassed for Pellam at his desperate words.

Wearily the old lawyer said, "John, there was no coercion."

"The bank teller? When the money was withdrawn? Let's find him."

"The teller identified Ettie's picture."

"Did you try the Ella Fitzgerald trick?"

Bailey fell silent.

Pellam asked, "What did you find at City Hall?"

"About the tunnel?" Bailey shrugged. "Nothing. No recorded easements or leases for underground rights beneath Ettie's building."

"McKennah must've—"

"John, it's over with."

A blaring horn sounded across the street. Pellam wondered what it signified. The workers paid no attention. There were hundreds of them still on the job. Even at this hour.

"Let her do her time," Bailey continued. "She'll be safe. Medium-security prison. Protective seclusion."

Which meant: solitary confinement. At least that's what it meant at the Q – San Quentin – according to the California Department of Corrections. Solitary . . . the hardest time there is. People's souls die in solitary even if their bodies survive.

"She'll get out," Bailey continued, "and it'll all be over with."

"Will it?" he asked. "She's seventy-two. When will she be eligible for parole?"

"Eight years. Probably."

"Jesus."

"Pellam," the lawyer said. "Why don't you take some time off? Go on a vacation."

Well, he was certainly going to be doing that – though involuntarily. *West of Eighth* would never be made now.

"Have you told her daughter?"

Bailey cocked his head. "Whose daughter?"

"Ettie's . . . Why you looking at me that way?" Pelham asked.

"Ettie hasn't heard from Elizabeth for years. She has no idea where the girl is."

"No, she talked to her a few days ago. She's in Miami."

"Pellam . . ." Bailey rubbed his palms together slowly. "When Ettie's mother died in the eighties Elizabeth stole the old woman's jewelry and all of Ettie's savings. She vanished, took off with some guy from Brooklyn. They were *headed* for Miami but nobody knows where they ended up. Ettie hasn't heard from her since."

"Ettie told me—"

"That Elizabeth owned a bed and breakfast? Or that she was managing a chain of restaurants?"

Pellam watched hard-hatted workers carrying four-by-eight sheets of drywall on their backs walk around to the back of the Tower. The Sheetrock bent up and down like wings. He said to Bailey, "That she was a real estate broker."

"Oh. Ettie told that one too."

"It wasn't true?"

"I thought you knew. *That's* why her motive – the insurance money – troubled me so much. Ettie came to me last year and wanted to hire a private eye to find Elizabeth. She thought she was somewhere in the United States but didn't know where. I told her it could cost fifteen thousand, maybe more, for a search like that. She said she'd get the money. No matter what it took she was going to find her daughter."

"So Elizabeth isn't paying your bill?"

"My bill?" Bailey laughed gently. "I'm not charging Ettie for this. Of course not."

Pellam massaged his stinging eyes. He was remembering the day he met Bailey, in the bar. His uptown branch.

"You sure you want to get involved in this?"

He'd thought the lawyer was simply warning him how dangerous the Kitchen was. But apparently there'd been more to his message; Bailey knew Ettie better than Pellam had guessed.

Pellam wandered to the site of Ettie's building, looked over it. The land was nearly level. A battered pickup truck pulled to a stop at the curb and two men got out. They walked over to the small pile of rubble and pulled out a chunk of limestone cornice, a lion's head. They dusted it off and together carted it back to the truck. It was probably on its way to an architectural relics shop downtown, where it'd be priced at a thousand bucks. The men looked over the site, saw nothing else of interest and drove off.

Bailey called, "Let it go, Pellam. Go on home. Let it go."

The Eighth Avenue subway line offers no service for the time being, due to police action.

We are sorry for the inconvenience.

Riders are advised . . .

John Pellam considered waiting but like most passengers on the Metropolitan Transit Authority he knew that fate was the essential motorman of his journeys; he decided to walk downtown to a cross street where he could catch an Eastbound bus to his apartment.

He disembarked from the grimy subway car and climbed up the stairs of the station into the city.

West of Eighth Avenue, stores had closed and mesh gates covered windows.

Dusk was long past and the sky was filled with a false sunset – the radiance of city lights from river to river. This fiery canopy would last until dawn.

"Yo, honey, how, 'bout a date?"

West of Eighth, children had been put to bed. Men had eaten their hot meals and were sitting in their scruffy armchairs, still aching from the hard routine of their jobs at UPS or the Post Office or warehouses or restaurants. Or they were groggy from their hours upon hours in bars, where they'd squandered the day talking endlessly, arguing, laughing, wondering how love and purpose had eluded them so completely throughout their lives. Some of them were in those bars again now, having returned after an evening meal with a silent wife and noisy children.

In tiny apartments women washed plastic dishes and marshaled children and brooded about the cost of food and marveled with painful desire at the physiques and the clothing and the dilemmas of the people in TV shows.

It was a night like a hot stone but here the old buildings weren't wired for air conditioners. The hum of fans filled most apartments and some not even that.

"I'm sick. I'm tryin' to get a job. I am, man."

West of Eighth, clusters of people sat on doorsteps. Dots of cigarettes moved to and from lips. Lights from passing cars reflected amber in quart beer bottles, which rang against the concrete stoops with ever-changing tones as their contents emptied. Conversation was just loud enough to rise above the rush of traffic on the West Side Highway, thousands of cars fleeing the city, even at this late hour.

"Give me a quarter for some food. Got a cigarette. Have a good night anyway. God bless."

In the windows of tenements lights flickered, the emanations of TV, and often the hue was not blue but the pale gray of black-and-white sets. Many windows were dark. In some there was only glaring light from a bare bulb and a motionless head was framed in the window, looking out.

"You want rock, ice, meth, scag, sens, blow, you want you want you want? You want a lotto ticket, you got a quarter you got a dollar you want some pussy? Yo, I got AIDS, I homeless. Excuse me, sir. Gimme your motherfucking wallet . . ."

West of Eighth, young men loped down the street in their gangs. They were invincible. Here they'd live forever. Here bullets would pass through their lean bodies and leave their hearts intact. They glided along the sidewalk, carrying with them their own soundtrack.

It's a white man's world, now don't be blind.
You open you eyes and whatta you find?
The Man got a message just for you—
Gonna smoke your brothers and your sisters too.

It's a white man's world.
It's a white man's world . . .

One crew saw another across the street. Boom boxes were turned down. Glances exchanged. Then signs flew back and forth. Palms up, fingers spread. At some point bravado would become dissing. If that happened guns would appear and people would die.

West of Eighth, everyone was armed.

Tonight, though, faces turned away, the volume cranked up again and the crews moved in separate directions, surrounded by a tempest of music.

It's a white man's world. It's a white man's . . .

Lovers grappled in cars and beside the sunken roadbed of the old New York Central Railroad, near Eleventh Avenue, men dropped to their knees before other men.

It was midnight now. Young dancers hurried home from the topless clubs and peep shows. Broadway actors and actresses too, just as tired. Among the stoop-sitters, cigarettes were stubbed out, good nights were said, beer bottles were left on the sidewalk, soon to be scavenged.

Sirens wailed, glass broke, a voice called out in ornery madness.

Time to be off the streets.

It's a white man's world. It's a white man's world . . .

West of Eighth, men and women lay in their cheap beds,

listening to the song as it floated through the streets outside their window or thudded into their bedrooms from neighboring apartments. The music was everywhere but most didn't pay it any attention. They lay exhausted and hot, staring at their murky ceilings as they thought: My day begins again in so few hours. Let me get some sleep. Please, just cool me off, and let me get some sleep.

———◆◆◆———

24

"**Y**ou missin' a tooth, man. Don't you know how to fight?"

"It was three to one," Pellam told Hector Ramirez.

"So?"

Noon, the next day, Ramirez was sitting on the doorstep of the *Cubano* Lord's kickback, smoking.

"It's hot," Pellam said. "You got any beer?"

"Man, do I got beer. What kind you want?"

"Any kind. Long as it's cold."

Ramirez rose, motioned him toward the front door of their apartment. He nodded at his bruised face. "Who did it?"

"Some of Corcoran's boys. They heard about us the other night? With McCray? And drew straws to see who it'd be more fun to beat the crap out of, you or me. I won."

"Hey, I ice somebody for you, you want. Or do some knee-caps? I do that for you, man. I got no problem doing that."

"That's okay," Pellam said.

"It no problem."

"Maybe next time."

Ramirez shrugged as if Pellam were crazy. He pushed through the doorway. Pellam noticed a young Latino man standing in the shadows of the alcove, a gun in his belt.

He spoke in Spanish to Ramirez, who barked a phrase back. He looked at Pellam's face and laughed. Pellam wanted to believe it was in admiration.

Ramirez knocked on the door to a ground floor apartment and, when there was no answer, unlocked and pushed it open. He let Pellam precede him.

The apartment was large and comfortable, filled with new furniture. A couch was still in its plastic wrapping. In the kitchen were stacks of cases of food and bags of rice. One bedroom was filled with five sheet-covered mattresses. The other bedroom was packed with cartons of liquor and cigarettes. Pellam didn't bother to ask where the merchandise had come from.

"So, you want a Dos, Tecate?"

"Dos."

Ramirez took two beers from the fridge. Rested them against the counter, cracked the tops off with a single blow from his palm. Passed one to Pellam, who drank down nearly half.

The room was sweltering. There were two air conditioners in the front and back windows but they weren't running. Through the shaded windows blew hot, dusty air and the heat was like a liquid.

Ramirez found a shoe box sitting on a table in the kitchen. He took out a pair of athletic shoes and began lacing them up. They were similar to the pair he'd given to Ismail the other day. "Hey, man. Take one."

"What's the penalty for receiving stolen?" Pellam asked.

"Fuck, I *found* 'em." He bounced, looking down with approval.

"I'm not the running-shoe type."

"No, you the cowboy-boot type. Man, why you wear those fucking boots? They no hurt you feet? So, what you doing here, Pellam? Why you come visit me?"

"I'm leaving town," Pellam said. "Came to get my gun."

"I hear, that *moyeta*, she say she do it. Man, she your friend. That gotta be tough for you. But nobody oughta burn the old places here. That no good."

Ramirez was getting the shoelaces even, the tautness just right. He stood slowly, savoring the feel of the shoes. He bounced on his toes again then came down on his heels. He feinted right then left then leapt into a layup, his fingers knocking flakes of white paint off the ceiling.

Pellam noticed a hand-lettered sign on the wall next to a poster advertising a Corvette, on which a bikini-clad model reclined.

> *Your standing in the Crib of the Cubano Lords.*
> *Either you be a Friend or you be fucked.*

Ramirez followed his eyes. He said, "Yeah, yeah. You gonna say we spelled 'you're' wrong."

"No, I'm gonna say that's a hell of a poster."

"You play basketball?" Ramirez asked.

"A little."

Pellam's last games had been one-on-one against a man in a wheelchair and Pellam lost six, won two. It was a shame he wasn't going to have a chance to play with Ismail; he probably could've beaten the boy.

"I go down to the Village today, play half-court. Some big *moyetos* down there. Man, those niggers, they can *play* . . . You come with me."

"Thanks but I'm out of here," Pellam said.

"For good, you mean?"

Nodding. "Picking up my truck and heading back to the Coast. Need some work. Got some people I owe money to gonna be knocking on my door in about sixty days."

"You want me to talk to 'em? I can—"

Pellam wagged a finger. "Uh-uh."

Ramirez shrugged, lifted the corner of the linoleum in the kitchen and pulled up a floorboard. He lifted out Pellam's Colt and tossed it to him. "Man, you crazy, carry that old thing. I'll get you a nice Taurus. That a sweet piece. You like that. Bam, bam, bam. A man need a fifteen-shot clip nowadays."

"I don't have as much of a call for one as you do."

As he replaced the flooring Ramirez said, "I no watch TV much but I turn on you movie, Pellam, when it come on. When that gonna be?"

"I'll let you know," Pellam muttered.

The door pushed open and a young Latino man stepped inside, gazing suspiciously at Pellam. He walked over to Ramirez and whispered in his ear. The man nodded and his young associate left.

Pellam started toward the door. Ramirez said, "Hey, maybe you don't wanna go so fast. He got some news for you."

"Who is he?"

"My brother." He nodded after the young man who'd just left.

"News?"

"Yeah. You wanna know who broke into you apartment?"

"I know who broke in. The pyro. The kid who got burnt up. I figured I must've got him on tape when I was shooting the building the day after the fire."

Ramirez bounced again on his pristine shoes and shook his head. "You wrong, man. You dead wrong."

"Yo, cuz."

"Hey, Ismail."

Pellam stood in front of the Youth Outreach Center. The air was hot, dusty, filled with a glaring shaft of sunlight reflected off a nearby building.

"Wassup, homes?"

"Not much," Pellam answered. "Wassup with you?"

"Hangin', you know how it is. Whatchu got there?"

"A present."

"All *right*, cuz." The boy stared at the large shopping bag with huge eyes. Pellam handed it to him. The boy opened it up and pulled out the basketball. "Yo, you all right, Pellam! This be *fine!* Yo, homes, lookit!"

Two other young boys, a little older, came over and admired the ball. They passed it back and forth.

"How is it here?" Pellam nodded at the YOC storefront.

"Ain't so bad. They don't dis you so much. But what it is they make you sit an' listen to these hatters, like priests and counselors, don't know shit. They tell you stuff. Talking at you, wearing yo' ear off, axing you things they don't know 'bout." He offered an adult shrug. "But, fuck, that life, ain't it?"

Pellam couldn't argue with that.

"An', man, that Carol bitch," he whispered, looking around. "Don't go messing with her. She ax me why I be comin' in at three this morning. Give me all kindsa shit. I tell that bitch what she can do."

"Did you now?"

"Hell's yeah . . . Well, I tried. But there ain't no talking to that woman, cuz."

"Why *were* you out at three a.m.?"

"I was—"

"Just hangin'."

"That straight, Pellam." He said to his homies, "Let's get a game up." They disappeared toward an alley, happy as ten-year-old boys the world over.

Pellam pushed through the squeaking door.

Carol looked up at him from the desk. Her wan smile faded as soon as she saw his expression.

"Hi," she said.

"Howdy."

"Sorry I've been so hard to get a hold of," she said. "We've been busy as hell here." The words were leaden.

Silence. Motes of dust floated between them. Amoeba, caught in the brutal light.

"All right," she said at last. "I didn't call because I got scared. It's been a long time since I got involved with somebody. And my history with men hasn't been so great."

Pellam crossed his arms. He looked down at what Carol was working on, a stack of papers. Government forms. They seemed overwhelmingly dense and complicated.

Carol sat back in her chair. "This isn't about that, is it?"

"No."

"So?"

"I just heard a few things I was curious about."

"Such as?"

"The day of the fire you were asking about me."

The Word. On the street.

"Hey, a cute guy, wearing cowboy boots. Sure, I was asking."
She laughed but she couldn't bring the levity off. Her hands
rose to her pearl necklace then continued up to her glasses and
compulsively kneaded the taped joint on the frame.

Pellam said, "You found out where I lived. And you broke
into my apartment the morning I stayed over. While I was asleep
in your bed."

Carol was nodding. Not to agree or protest or to convey any
message at all. It was a reflex. She looked around. Set her pen
down. Her face was a grim mask as she considered something.
"Can we go upstairs? It's more private."

They walked to the elevator. Inside, Carol leaned against
the car wall, looking somber. She glanced down and brushed
absently at some dust that marred the stalwart Latin word for
truth on her sweatshirt.

Carol avoided Pellam's eyes as she made meaningless conversation. She told him in a breezy voice that an elevator
company was going to donate a new car to the YOC. It
would have a big "compliments of" plaque inside. As if the
kids would run out and buy elevators of their own. "Crazy
what people'll do for publicity." He gave no response and she
fell silent.

The doors opened and Carol led them down a deserted
corridor oppressive with dirty tiles and murky in the weak
fluorescent light. "Here." Carol pushed the door open and

Pellam stepped in – before he realized that it wasn't a lunch room or office, as he'd expected, but a dim storeroom.

Carol closed the door. She had purpose in her movements and her eyes had grown chill. In the back of the room she moved aside boxes. Bent down and rummaged for something.

"I'm so sorry, Pellam."

She paused. Took a deep breath. He couldn't see what she held in her hand.

His thoughts strayed to the Colt in his back waist-band. Ridiculous to think that she'd hurt him. But this *was* the Kitchen.

You're walking past a little garden at noon in front of a tenement, thinking, Hey, those're pretty flowers, and the next thing you know you're on the ground and there's a bullet in your leg or an ice pick in your back.

And her eyes . . . her cold, pale eyes.

"Oh, what a fucking mess." Carol's mouth tightened. Then suddenly she turned, her hand rising, holding something dark. Pellam reached back for his gun. But in her pudgy fingers were only the two videocassettes she'd stolen from his apartment.

"For the past week, I've actually thought about running away. Going someplace else and starting a new life. Not saying a word, just vanishing."

"Tell me."

"That man who mentioned me. About saving his son?"

Pellam nodded. He remembered about the young man nearly dying inside a building about to be torn down, how she'd rescued him.

She said, "I was afraid you might have me on tape. I can't afford any publicity."

He remembered her distrust of reporters.

"Why?"

"I'm not who you think I am."

A recurring motif in Hell's Kitchen.

"And who *are* you?" Pellam snapped.

Carol hung her arm around the riser of a shelf and lowered her head onto her biceps. "A few years ago I was released from prison after serving time for dealing. In Massachusetts. I was also convicted . . ." Her voice faltered. ". . . convicted of endangering the welfare of a minor. I sold to some fifteen-year-olds. One of them overdosed and nearly died. What can I tell you, Pellam? What happened to me was so boring, so TV-movie . . . I dropped out of school, I met the wrong men. Street dealing, basing, smack, fucking for dollars . . . Oh, brother, I did it all."

"What's this got to do with the tapes?" he asked in a cold voice.

She compulsively rearranged a stack of thin towels. "I knew you were making that movie about the Kitchen. And when I heard that man had mentioned me I thought you'd include me in the story. I thought somebody in Boston might hear about it and word would get back to the Outreach Center board. I couldn't risk any publicity. Look, Pellam, I've ruined my life . . . I'm so messed up from abortions I can't have kids . . . I'm a felon."

Carol laughed bitterly. "You know what I heard the other day? This bank robber was released from Attica and was having trouble getting work. He was furious that somebody referred to him as an ex-con. He said he was 'societally challenged.'"

Pellam wasn't smiling.

"Well, that's me. 'Societally challenged.' There's no way I

can get a job with a government social agency. No day care center in the world would give me the time of day. But the Youth Outreach Center board was so desperate for help they didn't have much of a screening process. I showed them my social work license and a massaged résumé. And they hired me. If they find out who I am they'll fire me in a second."

"For the good of the children . . . Why'd you lie to me?"

"I didn't *trust* you. I didn't know who you were. All I know about reporters is that they look for the dirt. That's all they fucking care about."

"Well, we'll never know what I would've done, will we? You never gave me the chance."

"Please don't be angry, Pellam. What I do here is so important to me. It's the only thing I have in my life. I can't lose it. I lied when I met you, yes. I wanted you to go away but I also wanted you to stay."

Pellam glanced down at the cassettes. "I'm not interested in today's Kitchen. It's an oral history of the old days. I wasn't even going to mention the YOC. If you'd asked I would have told you."

"No, don't leave like this. Give me a chance . . ."

But Pellam pushed open the door. Slowly, undramatic. He walked down the stairs then continued through the lobby of the YOC and stepped outside into a midtown filled with a searing sun and the cacophony of engines and horns and shouting voices. He thought Carol's might have been one of them but then decided he didn't care.

Walking east, toward the Fashion District on the way to the subway.

Crazy name for a neighborhood, Pellam was thinking. The least fashionable of any neighborhood in the city. Trucks double- and triple-parked. Tall, grimy buildings, dirty windows. Feisty workers in kidney belts and sleeveless T-shirts, pushing racks of next spring's clothing.

A woman stood at a phone kiosk, hanging up the receiver then tearing a slip of paper into a dozen shreds. Now *there's* a story, Pellam thought. Then he forgot the incident immediately.

He paused at a construction site on Thirty-ninth Street to let a dump truck back out, its urgent beep-beep-beep reverse warning jarring his nerves.

". . . Thirty-ninth Street – that was Battle Row, the headquarters of the Gophers. The worst place in the city. Grandpa Ledbetter said the police wouldn't even come west of Eighth a lot of the time. They wouldn't have any part of it over here. He had a boot with a streak across the toe where he got hit by a bullet from this shoot-out on Battle Row when he was a boy. That's what he said to us children. I never quite believed him. But maybe it was true – he kept that old boot till he died."

Two shrill whistles rose from the pit of the construction site. The sound brought more spectators to the viewing holes crudely cut in the plywood fence lining the sidewalk. He paused and looked through one. A huge explosion. The ground leapt under Pellam's boots and the mesh dynamite blanket shifted as the explosive shattered another fifty tons of rock into gravel.

Ettie's words wouldn't leave his mind, they looped endlessly.

"There was always construction going on here. Papa had an interesting job for a while. He called himself a building undertaker. He was in one of the crews that'd take the old demolished tenements out to Doorknob Grounds in Brooklyn. They dumped hundreds of old buildings in the water. Build up a shoal with the junk, and the fish'd love it there. He always came back with bluefish or halibut to last for days. I can't look at fish now for any money."

Three loud whistles. Apparently the all clear from the demolition crew. Hard-hatted workers appeared and a bulldozer moved forward. Pellam started back up the sidewalk. Something caught his eye and he glanced at yet another developer's billboard.

He stopped, feeling the shock thud within him like a replay of the explosion a moment before. He read the sign carefully, just to make sure. Then he started off at a slow walk but, despite the overwhelming August heat, by the time he was at the corner he was sprinting.

—•—•—

25

"It's a construction site."

Bailey asked, "What is?"

"The St Augustus Foundation. I remembered the number – Five hundred West Thirty-ninth Street. It's across the street from the church. But it's just a hole in the ground."

They were in Bailey's bedroom – his temporary office – because of the fire in the main room. It didn't seem much different from his office; the most noticeable difference was that the cooler for his wine rested beside the bed, not the desk. This room also sported a better used air conditioner than the office; if not cold, at least the air was less stifling. The burnt smell was overwhelming but Bailey didn't seem to mind.

"Maybe the Foundation moved," Bailey said.

"Gets better," Pellam said. "I asked at the church office. No one there's ever even *heard* of a St Augustus Foundation." He walked to the dusty window, which was momentarily darkened by the shadow of a crane that was lifting a large piece of sculpture into the open plaza in front of McKennah Tower.

The statue was wrapped in thick kraft paper and it appeared to be in the shape of a fish. The derrick moved very slowly and he guessed the piece of stone or bronze weighed many tons. Around it workmen cleaned the grounds and tacked up banners and bunting for the Tower's topping-off ceremony.

"But there *is* a St Augustus Foundation," Bailey said and shuffled through documents on the bed and found a stack of scorched photocopies bearing the seal of the Attorney General of the state. "It's been incorporated under the not-for-profit corporation law. It exists. It's got eight members on the board."

Pellam looked over the list. The men and women on the board all lived nearby. He touched one name – at an address on Thirty-seventh Street, a block away. James Kemper.

"Let's see what he has to say." Bailey picked up the phone. But Pellam touched his arm.

"Let's pay a surprise visit."

But there was no surprise, not to Pellam. Construction was scheduled to begin in two months on the vacant lot where the Mr Kemper supposedly lived.

"It's all fake," Bailey muttered as they returned to his office.

"When you called the director – that minister – who did you get?"

"Answering service."

"How do we find out who's behind it?" Pellam asked. "Without tipping our hand?"

From the movie business he knew the complexity of incestuous corporate entanglements.

"It's a not-for-profit foundation, which'll make tracing things a lot harder than with Business Corporation Law companies."

In Bailey's bedroom again Pellam happened to glance down at a paper, also scorched, sitting next to the corporate filings. It was the expert's report on the handwriting on the insurance application, comparing Ettie's to the sample.

He'd asked Ettie about letters she might have written lately, thinking someone might've stolen a sample of her handwriting. But he and Ettie both had forgotten about the waiver she'd signed for McKennah's company – giving permission for the Tower to exceed the Planning & Zoning height limit.

"It's McKennah," Pellam announced. Then, seeing Bailey's expression, he held up his hand. "I know, you don't think a top-of-the-line developer like him'd torch a tenement. And he wouldn't for the insurance. But he *would* if the whole success of the Tower depends on the tunnel to Penn Station. Newton Clarke – and McKennah's wife too – told us how desperate he was."

"But . . ." Bailey lifted his hands, dismayed. "Why are you bothering? Even if McKennah's behind the Foundation Ettie still confessed to the arson."

"That's not," Pellam said, "going to be a problem."

"But—"

"I'll deal with that. The big question is how do we prove a connection between McKennah and the Foundation."

The lawyer's face grew troubled. "Developers're geniuses at this sort of thing. And McKennah's top of the line. We'll have to trace offshore corporations, doing-business-as statements . . . It'll take some time."

"How long?"

"A couple of weeks."

"When's Ettie being sentenced?"

A pause. "Day after tomorrow."

"Then I guess we don't have a couple of weeks, do we?" Pellam's eyes were on the construction site across the street. The wrapped sculpture was seated as unceremoniously as a girder. Several passersby gazed at it intently, wondering what it might be. But the workers walked away without tearing off the paper.

Wearing the Armani again and crowned with a stolen hard hat cocked over his brow, John Pellam walked matter-of-factly through the lobby of McKennah Tower. This part of the structure was virtually completed and was already occupied by several tenants – including two of McKennah's development and operating companies and the real estate agency leasing future space in the building.

Pellam's saunter told everybody in the office that he belonged here and that no one better delay what was obviously an urgent mission.

And no one did.

Clipboard in hand, he passed a row of secretaries and walked boldly through a large oak door into an office that was so opulent it had to be that of Roger McKennah whom he'd seen leave five minutes earlier. He had several explanations prepared and rehearsed for the developer's minions but his acting skills weren't required; the room was unoccupied.

He strode to his desk, on which were two framed pictures – one of McKennah's wife and one of his two children; Jolie gazed out of the expensive frame with an artificial smile painted large on her face. The boy and girl in the adjoining frame weren't smiling at all.

Pellam started on the file cabinets. After fifteen minutes he'd worked his way through hundreds of letters, financial statements and legal documents but none of them mentioned the St Augustus Foundation or the buildings on Thirty-sixth Street.

The credenza behind the desk was locked. Pellam chose the direct approach – he looked for a letter opener to break the lock with. He'd just found one in the top right-hand drawer when a booming voice filled the room. "Nice suit." There seemed to be a bit of a brogue in it. Pellam froze. "But it's not exactly *you*. You ask me, you're more of a denim kind of guy."

Pellam stood slowly.

Roger McKennah stood in the doorway, beside his unsmiling bodyguard, whose hand rested inside his coat jacket. Pellam, who'd suspected metal detectors in the Tower entryway, had left the Colt in Bailey's office.

His eyes flicked from one man to the other.

"We've been looking for you," McKennah said. "And what happens but *you* come to see *me?*" He nodded to the assistant, who lifted something to a table. It was Pellam's Betacam. As of a few hours ago it had been hidden away in the bedroom closet of Pellam's sublet in the Village. He wondered if the rest of his tapes were now destroyed.

McKennah said, "Let's take a ride." He opened a side door into the dark garage where sat the Mercedes limo.

The assistant picked up the camera and gestured with his head toward the door.

Pellam started to speak but McKennah held up a long index

finger. "What could you possibly say? That you're looking for the truth? You're rubbing the places that feel good? You've got answers for everything, I'll bet. But I don't want to hear them. Just get in the car."

━━◆◆◆━━

26

They drove in silence for eight blocks.

The limo pulled up in front of a dilapidated old building somewhere in the Forties on the far West Side. The paint was scaling. It looked like dirty, white confetti. The wood trim was rotten and piled up against a side door were a dozen trash bags.

McKennah gestured toward it. "Artie."

The bodyguard opened the limo door, took Pellam's arm firmly, led him toward the side entrance. He shoved open a door and pushed Pellam forward. They waited as McKennah entered.

Down a long, dark corridor. The developer went first. Pellam followed, trailed by Artie, who carried the camera as if it were a machine gun.

Pellam looked around, squinting, waiting for his eyes to adjust to the darkness. He slipped his hand into his sleeve to grip the handle of the letter opener he'd copped from McKennah's office. It felt flimsy but Pellam knew from prison what kind of damage even the most delicate of weapons could do.

The corridor was lit by only one low-watt bare bulb. He coughed at the smell of mold and urine. A blur of motion at their feet. McKennah whispered, "Jesus," as the huge rat passed indifferently in front of them. Pellam ignored it. He gripped the letter opener again. Felt the point against his arm. Waited for reassurance. He felt none.

Then, the noise.

Pellam slowed at the sound of the faint high-pitched wail. It seemed to be a woman's scream. From a TV? No. It was a live, human voice. Pellam felt the hairs on his neck stir.

"Keep going," McKennah ordered and they continued to the end of the corridor. Then stopped.

The chill keening grew louder and louder.

He shoved the horrible noise out of his thoughts and concentrated on what he was about to do. His legs tensed. This was the moment. His right hand slipped to his left sleeve.

McKennah nodded to Artie once more.

The wailing rose in volume. Two people, maybe three, were howling in pain. The bodyguard pushed Pellam forward roughly. He set his teeth together and stepped forward, pulling the letter opener from his sleeve.

Artie pushed the door open, stepped inside.

He'd slash first at Artie – aiming for his eyes. Then try for the gun. He'd—

Pellam stopped just over the threshold, frozen, gripping the letter opener.

What *is* this?

He glanced back at the developer and his thug. McKennah

impatiently motioned him forward. And, following the tacit order, Pellam began to walk forward – but he did so very carefully; it was hard to maneuver through the sea of babies. Across the room was a pale, obese woman in a stained blue tank top and tan shorts, who sat rocking the loudest of the screamers – the infant they'd heard from the hall. Trying to feed the baby a Frito, the woman stared at them in angry shock. "Who the fuck'er you?"

McKennah nodded toward Pellam then said to his bodyguard, "Okay, give it to him."

The man handed Pellam his Betacam.

"Do it," McKennah urged. Pellam shook his head, not understanding.

Half of the babies were in cardboard boxes and the rest wandered or crawled about, playing with broken toys or blocks. On the floor sat plastic bottles of orange diet soda and Coke, some had tipped over and spilled. Two of the children struggled to open one, like young animals trying to crack open a coconut. Ammonia from dirty diapers wafted through the room.

"Who the fuck are you?" the woman repeated, shouting. "You want me to call the cops?"

Roger McKennah said petulantly, "Sure, why don't you?" To Pellam he said with irritation, "So go ahead. What're you waiting for?"

He asked, "Go ahead what?"

"Well, what do you think? Play Charles Kuralt. Start filming!" The developer's temper was staring to fray.

"Fuck you!" the fat woman shouted. "You get out of here."

One of the babies crawled rapidly over the filthy floor and began playing with Pellam's boot. He picked up the infant and dusted off his blackened hands and knees, set him on a blanket. "Why don't you take better care of these kids?"

"Fuck you too."

Okay. We'll do it your way. Pellam lifted the Betacam. Started the deck running. "Say, ma'am, you mind repeating that?"

"I'm calling the cops." But the woman remained seated, ignoring the intruders, and lost herself in an episode of *The Young and the Restless* on the small TV.

Pellam panned slowly around the room, having no idea what he would ever do with these shots; the squirming infants, the junk food and the raised middle finger of a fat woman hardly made the stuff of oral history.

Looking through the eyepiece, he asked McKennah, "You want to tell me what we're doing?"

"This's an unlicensed day care center. Most of the people in the Kitchen can't afford a licensed one so they drop their kids off at pigsties like this. It's a disgrace but there's nothing parents can do if they want to work."

The woman tossed a handful of corn chips at the feet of one baby who had just started sobbing. Pellam shot the scene.

With robust approval McKennah said, "Stone cold Pulitzer! Go, go, go!"

Twenty minutes later they were outside, deeply breathing fresher air. Pellam asked, "So, what the hell's going on?"

McKennah pointed at the building. "I'm trying to wipe those out of New York, places like that. They're a disgrace . . . Excuse me, do I see some cynicism? Wondering why Roger McKennah wants to do a good deed? Oh, I'm no Mother Teresa. But that kind of crap doesn't help anybody. It's in my *interest* to have good, cheap day care centers in this neighborhood."

"Day care?"

"And clean parks and pools. I want parents who can feel safe dropping their kids off and then coming to work in *my* office buildings. I want teenagers to play basketball on nice courts and swim in clean pools so they don't mug my tenants at night. Self-interest? Sure. Say what you want, I don't care. I read Ayn Rand in college and never got over her."

"Why did you bring me here?"

"Because I checked you out. You're doing a documentary on the neighborhood. And you were going to trash me like everybody else does."

"That's what you think?"

"I'm a tabloid-magnet and I'm fucking *sick* of it. I want to make sure you tell the whole story. Nobody has an inkling what I'm doing for the neighborhood."

"Which is what?"

"How 'bout the public park I'm renovating at *my* personal fucking expense on Forty-fifth Street. And the pool repairs for the Department of Parks and Recreation that I guarantee'll be finished by the time the schools're out next year. And the new day care center on Thirty-sixth and the—"

"Wait – on Thirty-sixth and Tenth? On the corner?"

Louis Bailey's building.

The supposed harem for McKennah's mistresses.

"Yeah, that's the place. I'm turning three floors there into the best day care center in the country. The parents show they're gainfully employed or looking for work and their kids stay for five bucks a day, everything included. Food, games, Montessori tutors, books . . ."

"And I suppose it was just a coincidence that the building next door burned down? It didn't have anything to do with the Tower?"

McKennah's temper flared again. "Listen, you may be a hotshot in Tinseltown but that's slander! I'll sue your goddamn ass! I have never in my life torched a building. You can check every one of my projects going back to day one. I'll go through the list building by building with you."

"What about the tunnel? You didn't torch the building to put it in?"

McKennah frowned. "You know about the tunnel?"

"And I know about your deal with Jimmy Corcoran."

The developer blinked in surprise. Then said, "Well, you sure as hell don't know *too* much about it. The tunnel doesn't *go* under the lot that burned. There's a Con Ed substation under there. It jogs west. Under the day care center building – which *I* happen to own."

Oh. Bailey's building.

"Sure, I leased subsurface rights from Corcoran. But I could care less about the other property. If you know so damn much about deeds and public records why the hell didn't you just look up the owner and go spy on *him*?"

Pellam explained about the St Augustus Foundation. "It's fake. I thought *you* were the ultimate owner. That's what I was looking for in your office. Some connection."

McKennah was no longer angry. He nodded, musing, "Using a not-for-profit to hide ownership. That's damn clever. There's no chance for pass-through profits so the Attorney General wouldn't pay much attention to it." He said this with admiration and seemed to file the idea away for future use.

"The board members of the Foundation are fake. But the lawyer I'm working with said it'd take weeks to trace who really runs the place."

McKennah's laugh was loud. "Find yourself a new lawyer."

"You can do better?"

"Hell, yes. I could do it in a couple hours. But why should I? What's in it for me?"

That's the most important thing for Mr McKennah. You don't have to play fair but you have to play.

"Let's do some horse-trading," Pellam said coyly.

"Keep talking."

"You've got leaks in your company, right?"

"I don't know, do I?"

"Well, I knew all about your Jimmy Corcoran deal, didn't I?"

McKennah said nothing for a moment, as he scrutinized Pellam. "You can give me a name?"

"You deliver," Pellam said, "I'll deliver."

They rose in silence to the velvet heaven of high-rise New York.

On the seventy-first floor of McKennah's flagship building on the Upper East Side the developer led him through a maze of offices and deposited him with a bushy-haired, well-dressed, nervous man. Elmore Pavone nodded an uneasy greeting, realizing he was about to receive yet another burden upon his sloping shoulders. But it was a burden being placed there by Roger McKennah himself and would therefore remain firmly affixed until he had solved whatever problem it represented.

The developer explained to Pavone about the arson and the St Augustus Foundation. The adjutant too seemed impressed with this illicit use of nonprofit corporations.

Pellam said, "I think it's Corcoran who's behind the Foundation."

McKennah and Pavone got a big laugh out of this.

The developer said, "This's way, way outa Corcoran's league. He's a putz. The phrase 'small-time' was invented for him."

Pellam cocked his eyebrow. "Yeah? I heard he negotiated you under the table."

"Oh, did you?"

"On the tunnel deal. Taking a cut of the action when he granted you the easement."

McKennah blinked in astonishment. "How the hell do you *know* all this stuff?"

Word on the street.

Pellam said, "Is it true or not?"

The developer smiled. "Yeah, Corcoran gets a cut of the profits. But the way the contract reads is that he gets one percent of the profit quote deriving from *his* property. That means he gets a piece of the action from any money I make from the tunnel, not the tower. The deal with the city is that I'm leasing the tunnel to the Transit Authority for a token rental – ten bucks a year. So Jimmy Corcoran's share is ten cents a year."

The developer added, "I'll always be one step ahead of punks like Jimmy Corcoran. I was in an Irish gang in the Kitchen too, you know. The difference is, I graduated."

"Not a great guy to have as an enemy," Pellam pointed out. "Corcoran."

McKennah laughed again. "You hear about the Gophers?"

Pellam nodded. The Hell's Kitchen gang that so fascinated Ettie's grandfather.

"You know who finally broke their back?"

"Enlighten me," Pellam said.

"Not the cops. Not the city. Lord knows the feds didn't do shit. It was *business* that broke 'em up. The New York Central Railroad. They hired Pinkerton and in six months the gang was history. If Corcoran hassles me, I'll tell you, that little shit is going down hard."

Pellam said, "Well, if it's not him then who's behind the Foundation?"

Pavone and McKennah conferred. Assuming the motive for torching the building was that it was landmarked, Pavone mused, the only reason you would clear a landmarked building was to put up something new. "To build something new, you'd have to file applications for construction permits and P&Z variances and an environmental impact statement."

McKennah nodded and explained to Pellam that builders often had to wait months before getting construction permits for major projects in the city. Planning and zoning variances, which necessitated public hearings and EPA and utility waivers were sometimes required too. These applications would have to be filed as soon as possible – to minimize the time the owner had to hold property that produced no income and yet on which steep taxes were levied.

There was some risk to the arsonist that the police or a fire marshal might find the applications. But in a city bureaucracy as unwieldy as New York's, arson investigators would probably be content with checking only the ownership of record, forgoing deeper scrutiny. Especially if they had a suspect in custody.

McKennah nodded to Pavone, who snatched up the phone and spoke in cryptic terms of art to an underling. He jotted some notes. In three minutes he hung up. "Got it. No P&Z but a White Plains construction company applied for a building permit for 458 W. Thirty-sixth Street – the site of the fire – two days ago. Morrone Brothers on Route 22."

McKennah nodded, seemed to recognize the name.

Pavone continued, "They're going to put up a seven-story parking garage on the lot that burned and the two lots next to it."

"Parking," Pellam whispered. All this death and horror for a parking lot?

"So John Doe sets up the St Augustus Foundation, buys the two vacant lots, torches the property on the third and builds his garage."

"I want John Doe," Pellam said. "How do we find him?"

"Who'd do Morrone's steel work?" the developer asked Pavone.

"Bronx Superstructures, Giannelli . . ."

"No, no," McKennah barked, "in *Westchester!* In Connecticut. Let's think tighter here, Elm. Come on. Whoever it is's got to keep some distance from the city."

"You're right, okay, okay. Probably it'd be Bedford Building and Foundation."

"No." McKennah shook his head vehemently. "They're doing the Metro North job. They don't have the capacity to do that *and* a garage. Come on! Think!"

"Then how about Hudson Steel? Yonkers."

"Yes!" McKennah snapped his fingers and picked up the phone, dialing from memory. A few seconds later he muttered into the receiver, "Roger McKennah here. Is he in?" In the time it took to drop another phone call like a red-hot drill bit the contractor was on the line.

"Hi, Tony . . . Yeah, yeah." McKennah's rolling eyes suggested how eagerly the man's tail was wagging. "Okay, okay, friend, I'm in kind of a hurry. Here's what it is. Don't fuck with me, okay? You gimme answers and you'll do our new dock in Greenwich. No bidding, no nothing . . . Yeah, pick yourself up off the floor . . . Yeah, lucky you. Now, I hear Morrone's the general on a garage in the city. West Thirty-sixth. St Augustus Foundation's the owner. What d'you mean it's supposed to be hush-hush? There's no *fucking* secrets from me, Tony. You're subbing the steel, right? . . . You meet anybody from St Augustus? . . . Well, check it out. And call me. And I mean in three minutes. And Tony, did I tell you, I'm budgeting one point three million for the dock job."

McKennah hung up. "He'll call back. So, that's *my* part of the deal. Now it's your turn. Who's the fucking spy who's leaking my secrets?"

Pellam said, "When I was over at the Tower a little while ago, taking that tour of your office?"

"Tour," the developer said wryly.

Pellam continued. "I noticed one of the secretaries in the rental office. Kay Haggerty? I saw her nameplate."

The flash in McKennah's eyes explained that voluptuous Miss Haggerty was more than a secretary.

"Kay?" McKennah asked. "What about her? She's a nice kid."

"She may be. But she's also your leak."

"Impossible. She's a hard worker. And I've . . ." He groped for a euphemism. "I trust her completely. Why d'you think she's be spying on me?"

"Because she's Jimmy Corcoran's girlfriend. I saw her last week in the 488 Bar and Grill. She was sitting on his lap."

The location scout turned filmmaker paced high in the midtown sky, looking out Roger McKennah's perfectly clean windows.

His Nokona boots silently pressed their narrow silhouettes into the lush blue carpet. It seemed to him that here, seventy stories above the streets, the air was rarified. He felt breathless but he supposed that wasn't altitude or corporate power but just the residue of smoke in his lungs from the fire at Bailey's.

Flanked by a billionaire and his ruthless associate, Pellam paced. Minutes passed like days then finally the telephone chirped.

The developer dramatically snagged the phone from its cradle the way he probably always did when others were present. He listened, then put his palm over the mouthpiece and looked at Pellam.

"Got 'em."

He jotted a note and hung up. Showed it to Pellam. "This name mean anything to you?"

Pellam stared at the paper for a long moment. "I'm afraid it does," he said.

27

"Yo, look, man. Her, she the bitch work at that place fo' kids."

"Man, don't be talking 'bout her that way. She okay. My brother, he all fucked up and he stay there a month. Was a cluckhead. Got hisself off rock, you know what I'm saying?"

"This nigger say she a bitch. All y'all think that be a okay place but all kinda shit go on there. Why you dissing me?"

"I ain't dissing you. I just saying she ain't no bitch. Got a minda her own. And look out for people is what I'm saying."

Carol Wyandotte sat on the pungent creosote-soaked pilings overlooking the murky Hudson and listened to the young men lope past on their way south. Where were they headed? It was impossible to tell. To jobs as forklift operators? To direct an independent film like John Singleton or young Spike Lee. To pull on throw-aways, take a box cutter and mug a tourist in Times Square.

When she heard the exchange she thought, as she'd said

recently to John Pellam, Oh, he doesn't mean "bitch" that way.

But apparently he did.

Anyway, who was she to say anything? Carol had been wrong before about the people whose lives she'd wedged her way into.

She sat on this pier under a torrid sun and looked at the ships cruising up and down the Hudson. Tugs, a few pleasure boats, a yacht. A ubiquitous Circle Line cruise ship, painted in the colors of the Italian flag, moved slowly past. The tourists on board were still excited and eager for scenery; but then their voyage had just begun. How enthusiastic would they be, hot and hungry, in three hours?

One thing was different about Carol Wyandotte today. She had pulled up the sleeves of her sweatshirt, revealing rather pudgy arms. She couldn't recall the last time she'd appeared bare-armed in public. Already a slight blush of sunburn covered her skin. She looked down and turned her right arm over, gazing at the terrible mass of scars. She rubbed her hand absently over this ruined part of her body then buried her eyes in the crook of her arm and let the tears soak the skin.

The car door slammed some distance away and by the time she counted, obsessively, to fifty she heard footsteps rustling through the grass. They hesitated then continued. When she reached seventy-eight in her count she heard the voice. It was, of course, John Pellam's. "Mind if I join you?"

"The property was willed to a charity years ago," Carol told him, hugging her knees to her chest. "And then got transferred to the Outreach Center. I was working in the main office then and saw those three lots on the books of the charity – the ones at 454, 456 and 458 Thirty-sixth. Then I noticed McKennah's surveying team working in the block where the Tower is now. I asked around and heard a rumor he was going to build. That neighborhood was a nightmare then. But I knew what was coming. I knew the value of those three lots'd skyrocket in a couple of years. Of course, none of the board of the charity would dare even set foot in the Kitchen; they had no clue what was going on. So I went to them and said we had to dump them fast because there'd been some reporters doing stories about teenage hookers and pushers and homeless squatting in the buildings."

"And they believed you?"

"Oh, you bet. All I had to say was that if the media got hold of the fact that the YOC owned them, the publicity'd be devastating. They were horrified at the thought of bad press. They all are – rabbis, priests, philanthropists, CEOs, doesn't matter. They're all cowards. So the board dumped the lots at a sacrifice." She laughed. "The broker called it a 'fire sale' price."

"You bought them yourself?"

She nodded. "With drug money my ex and I'd stashed away. I set up the phoney St Augustus Foundation. Learned how to do that when I was a legal secretary in Boston. I also knew I couldn't tear down the building because it was landmarked. So I just held it. Then I met Sonny."

"How?"

"He stayed at the YOC for a couple years after his time in Juvenile Detention for burning down his mother's house and killing his mother's boyfriend."

"And," Pellam continued, "you also knew Ettie."

"Sure," the woman confessed. "I was her landlord. I had copies of her rent checks and of her handwriting. I sent this black woman who looked sort of like her to get the insurance application. Paid her a few hundred dollars. I used my master key to get into Ettie's apartment while she was out shopping. I found her passbook."

Pellam looked over the flat, grassy land around them. "And you took the money out of her account?"

"The same woman who got the insurance application made the withdrawals. And the note they found on Sonny's body? About Ettie? He was just supposed to plant it at one of the fires so the police would find it. I forged that too."

"But why? You can't take any money out of the foundation."

She laughed. "Ah, Pellam. You're so Hollywood. You think every crook has to steal ten million bucks worth of gold, or a hundred million in bonds. Like in a Bruce Willis movie. Life's more modest than that. No, with the garage, the Foundation'd make a good profit and I'd hire myself as executive director. I could make seventy, eighty thousand a year without the Attorney General batting an eye. Add some petty cash, an expense account, and there'd still be enough money left to actually give some away to the poor folks in Hell's Kitchen."

She offered a grim smile. "Not contrite enough for you, am I?" The wolf eyes were like pale ice. "Pellam, you know the only times I've cried, I mean, *really* cried, in the past year? Five minutes ago, thinking about you. And the morning after we spent the night together. After I stole those tapes from your apartment I took the subway to work. I sat in the car and cried and cried.

I was almost hysterical. I thought what kind of life I might've had with somebody like you. But it was too late then."

A car drove past and they heard a powerful bass beat from the radio's speakers. *That* song again. *It's a white man's world* . . . Slowly the beat faded.

Pellam stared at the woman's horribly scarred arms. He found himself saying, "But you didn't cry for Ettie, did you?"

"Oh, that's the point, Pellam," Carol said bitterly. "Cry for Ettie Washington? All she could ever be is a *victim*. God gave her that role. Hell, half the people in this city are victims and the other half are perpetrators. That's never going to change, Pellam. Never, never, never. Haven't you caught on yet? It doesn't *matter* what happens to Ettie. If she didn't go to jail for this she'd go to jail for something else. Or she'd get evicted and move into the shelter. Or onto the street."

She wiped her eyes. "That boy who's following you around, Ismail? The one you think you can save? The one you think you have this *connection* with? The minute he realizes you're no good to him alive, he'd knife you in the back, steal your wallet and have the money spent by the time you died . . . Oh, you look so placid, staring at the grass there. But you're pretty horrified to hear me say things like that, aren't you? Well, I'm not a monster. I'm realistic. I see what's around me. Nothing's going to change. I thought it might, once. But, no. The only answer's to get out. Get as far away with money or with miles as you can."

"The tapes you stole? Why'd you give them back to me?"

"I thought by confessing to the smaller crime you wouldn't suspect me of the bigger one." She moved her hand within a millimeter of Pellam's. Didn't touch him. "I didn't want anybody to die. But it happened that way. It *always* happens that way, at least in places like Hell's Kitchen it does. Can't you just let it go?"

Pellam said nothing, moved his hand and touched the point of his Nokona, lifted off a dry, curled leaf.

"Please," she said.

Pellam was silent.

She said, "I've never had a home. All I've had are the wrong men and the wrong women." Her whisper was desperate. When she saw Pellam rise Carol too stood. "No, don't go! Please!"

Then she glanced toward the highway, where the three police cars were parked. She smiled faintly, almost relieved, it seemed – as if she'd finally received bad news long anticipated.

"I had to," Pellam said. He nodded at the cars.

Carol slowly turned back to him. "You know poetry? Yeats?"

"Some, I guess."

"'Easter 1916'?"

Pellam shook his head.

She said, "There's a line in it. 'Too long a sacrifice can make a stone of the heart.' It's my theme song." Carol laughed hollowly.

The Circle-Line was long out of sight, hooking past Battery Park.

Carol suddenly tensed and swayed closer, as if about to embrace and kiss him.

For an instant compassion stirred in John Pellam and it occurred to him that perhaps the harms Carol had endured were just as deep and numerous as those she had inflicted. But then he saw Ettie Washington, betrayed by Billy Doyle, and by so many others just like Carol Wyandotte. He stepped coldly away.

A horn brayed over the water, resonating from the Moran tug that pushed a barge as long as a football field through the roiling current. Pellam glanced at the sunlight shattered on the waves. The horn blared again. The pilot was signaling to a fellow sailor steaming upriver.

Carol whispered something Pellam didn't hear – a single word, it seemed – and her pale eyes turned to the skyline, remaining on this vista as she stepped backward so placidly that she tumbled into the gray-green water and was swept deep into the barge's undertow before he could take a single step toward her.

28

T he story was big.

The suicide of the youth center director who'd hired the mad pyromaniac . . . This was the classic stuff of the New York *Post* and Geraldo.

The Live at Five broadcast showed the Coast Guard cutters and the tiny blue police boats searching New York Harbor for Carol Wyandotte's body. The Associated Press got the most dramatic shot, which featured Ellis and Liberty Islands in the background as they lifted the woman's body from the water. Pellam saw the picture in the New York *Times*. Her eyes were closed. He remembered how pale they were, as pale as her skin after all those hours in the cold water.

Wolf eyes . . .

The charges against Ettie were dropped. That part of the story was almost non-news, except for a bite that brought the tabloids into play: Roger McKennah owned a piece of property right next to the building she'd lived in, the one that had burned. Everybody was eager to developer-bash, of course, but even the most zealous scoop-hog couldn't find any tie linking him and the arson. One network even ran a glowing story about McKennah's installing a high-tech day care facility in the neighborhood (the news account featuring a lurid videotape of an illegal day care center on Twelfth Avenue – dramatic footage that McKennah himself had somehow procured).

The bulk of the reporting devoted itself to the gala topping-off ceremony at McKennah Tower on Saturday. Good news: although former President Bush, Michael Jackson and Leonardo DiCaprio would be unable to attend, Ed Koch, David Dinkins, Rudolph Giuliani, Madonna, Geena Davis, Barbara Walters and David Letterman had RSVP'd in the affirmative.

At four-forty-five on Friday afternoon John Pellam pushed open one of the tall brass doors of the Criminal Courts Building and helped Ettie Washington outside then down the few stairs to the wide sidewalk.

They stood on Centre Street under a clear sky, the late afternoon unusually cool for August. It was the end of the civil servants' day and hundreds of government workers passed before them on their way home.

"You doing okay?" he asked the gaunt woman.

"Fine, John, just fine." Though she still limped and occasionally winced at the pain from her broken arm when she adjusted her makeshift sling. Pellam noticed that his signature was still the only one on her cast.

The woman had been released from the lockup without ceremony. She seemed even more frail than the last time Pellam had seen her. The guards were somewhat less antagonistic than on previous visits though Pellam put that down to lethargy, not contrition.

"Hey, wait a minute," the voice called from down the sidewalk.

They turned to see the rumpled man in windbreaker and jeans. He was trotting toward them. "Pellam. Mrs Washington."

"Lomax," Pellam said, his face an angry mask. Of all the batterings he'd taken in the last few days – bullet streaking across the cheek, the fire, the Irish Mafia – it was the fire marshal's skinny friend, the man with the roll of quarters, who'd inflicted the most painful damage.

Lomax paused. He'd stopped Pellam and Ettie as he'd planned but now that he had their attention he wasn't sure what to do. Finally he extended his hand to Ettie. She took it cautiously. He debated about doing the same with Pellam but sensed, correctly, that the gesture would be rejected.

"I don't guess anybody came by to apologize," Lomax said.

"The President and the First Lady just left," Pellam said.

"I thought Lois Koepel'd send flowers," the fire marshal tried.

"Maybe FTD was closed."

Ettie didn't participate in the uneasy banter.

"We made a mistake," he said. "I'm sorry for that. And I'm sorry you lost your home."

Ettie thanked him, still wary – as she probably had always been around cops and always would be. They talked for a few minutes about how shocking it was that a youth director had been behind the arson.

"Was a time when nobody would've cared what happened in

the Kitchen," Lomax said. "Life's changing. Slowly. But it's changing."

Ettie said nothing but Pellam knew what her response would be. He remembered, almost verbatim, one of her quotes.

> ". . . *That fancy building, that tower across the street, it's a nice one. But whoever's putting it up, I hope for his sake he doesn't expect too much. Nothing lasts in the Kitchen, don't you know? Nothing changes but nothing lasts either.*"

Lomax handed her a card, saying if there was ever any-thing he could do . . . Some help finding a new place. Public assistance.

But Louis Bailey had already found Ettie a new apartment. She told Lomax this.

"And I don't really need anything—" she began. But Pellam shook his head and touched her shoulder. Meaning: Let's not be too hasty here. Bailey was perhaps a bad lawyer but Pellam was confident he could toy with the city's gears well enough to negotiate a generous settlement.

Then Lomax was gone and Pellam and Ettie stepped to the curb. Several taxis, seeing a black woman and anticipating a Harlem- or Bronx-bound fare, sped past them.

This infuriated Pellam though Ettie took it in stride. She winced in pain and Pellam suggested, "Let's sit for a minute." He gestured toward a dark green bench.

"You know what this part of town used to be, John?"

"No idea."

"Five Points."

"Don't think I've ever heard of that."

"When the Gophers were ruling Hell's Kitchen this neighborhood was just as dangerous. Maybe worse. Grandpa Ledbetter told me. Did I ever tell you about his gangster scrapbook? He kept all kinds of clippings in it."

"I don't think you ever mentioned that, no." Pellam looked out over the parks and neoclassical courthouses. "The money you had saved up? In your savings account . . . it was so you could find your daughter, wasn't it?"

"Louis told you about her?"

Pellam nodded.

"I wasn't honest with you about that either, John. I'm sorry. But the fact is I said I'd let you interview me because I thought maybe she'd see me on TV down in Florida, or wherever she is. She'd see me and give me a call."

"You know, Ettie, that confession to Lomax was a nice try."

The woman looked in her purse and extracted a handkerchief. Pellam remembered that she washed them in perfumed water and let them dry on a thin string above the bathtub. She wiped her eye. "That was the one thing that hurt me so much – that you'd be thinking I lied to you. Or I tried to hurt you."

"Never thought that for a second."

"You should've," Ettie scolded. "That was the whole point. You should've gone home to California like you were supposed to. And stayed out of harm's way. You should've gone and you should've stayed gone."

"You thought that if you confessed then the killer'd give up, wouldn't try to hurt me again. It's the same thing Billy Doyle did: confessing so your brother wouldn't get killed."

"What he did gave me the idea," she explained. "See, I knew I wasn't the one who hired that psycho to burn down the building. But somebody did and they were still out there. And as long as you kept poking around that somebody was gonna try and hurt you."

Ettie gazed at the elaborate verdigris crown of the Woolworth building, sprouting gargoyles. Finally she said, "They took so much away from me, John. My Billy Doyle got taken away by his own nature. And some crazy man with a gun took my Frankie. And Elizabeth got taken off by some fancy man. Even my neighborhood – the developers and rich people're taking it. I didn't want 'em to take you too. I couldn't've stood that. I thought, Hell, I'll be out of jail in a few years. Then maybe you'll still want to talk to me, keep putting me on tape and listening to my stories. Oh, maybe you wouldn't and I'd've understood that. But I'd rather you were alive and well." She laughed a frail laugh. "That was the little bit I wanted to save for myself. See, sometimes you *can* fool 'em. Oh, yes, yes, sometimes you can. I'm tired. I think I'd like to be getting home now."

Pellam strode into the street, directly into the path of an empty cab, which squealed to a halt a foot from him. Pellam escorted Ettie forward, past three burly men hurrying a manacled prisoner toward the courts. The prisoner was the only one of the quartet who nodded respectfully at the elderly woman. Ettie nodded back. They climbed into the cab.

The Pakistani driver looked at Pellam, inquiring silently about their destination.

"Hell's Kitchen," Pellam answered.

He blinked.

Pellam repeated it but the cabby just shook his head.

"Thirty-fourth Street and Ninth Avenue," Pellam said.

His sunken eyes gazed at Pellam a moment longer, then he stabbed the meter and they clattered off madly through the busy streets.

29

The next evening, Pellam and Louis Bailey stood in the lawyer's newly painted office.

They were in identical poses. Leaning out an open window, squinting.

"The governor," Bailey said.

"No, I don't think so," Pellam responded. Though it had been almost twenty years since Pellam had been a resident of the Empire State and he had only a vague idea of what any governor, past or present, looked like.

"I'm sure."

"Ten bucks," Pellam bet. It was hardly a lock. But confidence, he had it on good authority, is everything.

"Uhm. Five."

They shook.

At the far end of the block the limo deposited its dignitary, whoever it might be, on the red carpet of McKennah Tower's main entrance and the tuxedoed gentleman and several body guards entered the building.

"The plate," Bailey said, "read, 'NY 1.'"

"It's probably a Mets pitcher."

"Then it sure as hell wouldn't say number one," Bailey countered sadly. The long black Lincoln vanished around the corner. Bailey closed the window.

Currently playing across the street was perhaps the only topping-off ceremony that had ever been held on ground level. Not being able to fit McKennah's six thousand invitees on the roof of the Tower, the ceremony was taking place in the building's theater, a lavish place intended for full-production Broadway musicals and plays. Tonight the placed rocked with MTV music, lasers, banks of video monitors, Dolby SurroundSound, computer graphics.

Pouring a very small glass of the jug wine, Pellam tuned in again to Louis Bailey. The man was ebullient and couldn't stop talking about the case, while in a dim corner of the freshly painted office Ismail, in his tricolor windbreaker, sat leafing through an old, limp comic. He was wearing his new Nikes.

"I've got to meet somebody," Pellam called to Ismail. "And you should be getting back to the Outreach Center."

"Yo, inaminute, cuz."

One of McKennah's personal secretaries had called earlier and asked if Pellam would like to attend the ceremony. He'd declined but agreed to stop by at nine; McKennah, it seemed, had a memento the developer thought Pellam might like. Pellam assumed it was something from historic Hell's Kitchen, maybe unearthed when the foundation for the Tower had been dug. Pellam, a die-hard Winnebago dweller, didn't have much interest in collectibles. But he supposed there was also the chance it was a nice check – for blowing the whistle on Corcoran's girlfriend or taking such stunning footage of the illegal daycare center.

He stood. "Let's go, Ismail."

The boy yawned. "I ain't tired."

"Time to go."

The boy stretched and walked to Bailey, slapped his palm. "Yo, homes."

"Holmes?" the perplexed lawyer asked. "Well, goodnight, Watson."

Ismail frowned then said, "Later."

"Yes, well. Later to you too, young man."

Pellam and Ismail stepped out into the darkness of Thirty-sixth Street. The crowds were inside the tower by now and the limos were parked elsewhere. The sense of emptiness was strong, Bailey's being the only remaining residential building between Ninth and Tenth Avenues. McKennah's choice to build his castle here hadn't magically turned this neighborhood into populated civilization.

Across the street the construction site itself was obscured by bunting and banners, which fluttered in the hot night breeze. It was dark, cordoned off. The only sound was the faint music from the theater.

"Empty, huh?" he asked.

"Whatcha say, cuz?"

"The street. Empty."

"Straight up." The boy yawned again.

They passed a large bulldozer, parked where Ettie's building had stood.

"What'll happen to the block now?" he mused.

Ismail shrugged. "Dunno. Who care?"

They walked toward the theater, where McKennah or his assistant was going to meet him. It was an attached building, not part of the Tower itself, and it rose eighty feet into the air above a sleek, glassy entranceway filled with marble and granite. A sort of Egyptian motif – colors were sand, maroon, green. The lobby was empty now; the festivities were underway.

As he passed the construction site surrounding the theater he peered at the landscaping. No grass had been planted yet but this evening the dirt was covered with AstroTurf and studded with redwood planters containing palms trees. Pellam paused.

"Whassup, Pellam?"

"You go on to the YOC, Ismail. I've got to meet somebody."

"Naw," he whined. "I'ma hang with *you*, cuz."

"Uh-uh, time for bed."

"Shit, Pellam."

"Watch the language. Now get going."

His round face grimaced. "Okay. Later, cuz."

They slapped palms and the boy walked slowly east. The too-big basketball shoes flopped loudly as he reluctantly headed toward the uptown street. He looked back, waved.

Pellam slipped through a gap in the fence and walked over the spongy fake grass.

What *is* that?

He looked more closely at what he'd seen from the sidewalk: The workers had anchored the potted plants to the handles on the exit doors, looping heavy rope through them. He supposed this was to keep the locals from walking off with the vegetation.

But the effect of what they'd done was to tie the fire doors shut.

And to tie them shut pretty damn tight – with coils and coils of thick rope. Of the twenty emergency doors only one wasn't tied closed. It was slightly ajar. From it came the mute sounds of applause and laughter and the solid thud of bass from the musicians. He walked to it and looked inside.

The doors didn't open onto the theater itself but into a fire stairwell that, Pellam guessed, led up to the theater and the loge and the balconies. The corridor was dark, except for the bulbs in the exit signs glowing eerily. The interior doors were chocked open and he caught glimpses of red velvet seats and walls and maroon carpet.

Then something on the wall of the corridor caught his eye. Stepped closer. He saw that it was a rumpled sheet of paper – a map of the west side of Manhattan. It looked familiar and a moment later Pellam understood why. It was similar to the one they'd found after the fire in Bailey's office. The one on which Sonny had marked all his fires.

Only on *this* map the last target wasn't the Javits Center; it was McKennah Tower.

Suddenly Pellam's eyes stung and he caught a whiff of astringent fumes. Like the cleanser in Bailey's office several days ago. He remembered smelling it just before the light bulb exploded.

But of course it wasn't cleanser at all. It was that homemade napalm. And here was its source, right in front of him: Four drums of the stuff. They lined the wall. The tops were off.

A noise behind him.

He turned abruptly.

The young blond man stood with his head cocked. A mad smile was on his face and his eyes danced in the reflected light from the Tower.

"Joe Buck," he whispered, "Pellam, Pellam. I'm Sonny. It's so nice to meet you at last."

The Colt had already cleared Pellam's belt and was half-cocked when Sonny swung the long wrench and connected with Pellam's forearm. The bone gave with a crack and the blow was so hard it laid open a large patch of skin. Blood flew. And Pellam, eyes rolling back in his head, collapsed back into the tunnel, gasping, hitting his head on the side of an oil drum, which rang, muted, like a bell on a foggy day.

Sonny set aside the wrench and slipped Pellam's gun into his waistband. Then, from his pockets, he took a pair of handcuffs.

And a cigarette lighter.

———•—••—•———

30

Pellam's first thought: There's no pain. Why doesn't it hurt? It's *loose*. My arm's loose . . .

Blood flowed from the gash on his arm.

Sonny, a caste mark in Pellam's blood on his forehead, bent down, fishing in his pocket. He emerged with a small silver key for the cuffs. His hands shook. His wispy hair floated around his head like water.

Why no pain? Pellam thought, staring at his shattered arm.

"If you're wondering who was in that lawyer's office," the crazy young man said matter-of-factly, "that was your friend Alex. The snitch-bitch. Wheeled him from my place in an oil drum – bent him nearly double. Now *that* was an unpleasant trip for him, I'll bet. And left him under the tanning lamp. Had to get all you faggot cowboys off my back." He opened one latch on the cuff.

Sonny nodded toward the theater. "This'll be the last one. Come on, front row seat." Sonny grabbed Pellam by the collar and pulled him to his feet. "We're going out together, Joe Buck, fucking Antichrist . . . You, me and about five thousand other good folk."

He kicked an oil drum over and the soapy liquid flowed through the corridor and into the theater itself. The second drum followed.

"This is my juice," he said matter of factly. "I invented it myself. See, you couldn't do this with gas alone. Gas is shitty. Low flashpoint, big flare, cool fire, and then it's over with. I knew this pyro one time . . ." Sonny began to unlatch the second ring of the cuff. His hands shook badly. He paused, inhaled deeply. While it nauseated Pellam the smell of the liquid seemed to calm Sonny down. He began working on the cuff again. He continued. "He used gasoline. Thought he was soooo cool. One time he had this job on the third floor of an old tenement. He takes two five-gallon cans up, douses the place and breaks a lightbulb so when the guy comes in and flicks on the light up he goes. Then he starts going through the guy's drawers, looking for jewelry or something. What he doesn't realize is that gas vapors're heavier than air and while he's fucking around upstairs the gas fumes are flowing down to the basement. Where there's . . . guess what? Ta-dah . . . A pilot light in the water heater. I think they found part of his skeleton."

Pellam choked. There was probably a hundred gallons of liquid flowing into the building. Pellam remembered what Lomax had told him about the Happy Land fire. A mere gallon of gas had turned the place into an inferno.

"Let's go, Midnight Cowboy." Sonny touched Pellam's shattered arm. The bone shifted and, at last, a searing jolt of pain shot up into Pellam's shoulder and neck and face. In pure reaction he lashed out with his left palm, catching Sonny in the jaw. It was a weak blow but it caught the young man by surprise and he stepped back a few feet.

"You shit." He shoved Pellam against the wall.

On his knees Pellam scooped up a handful of the napalm, splashing it into Sonny's face. It missed his eyes but splashed on his mouth and nose and he stumbled backwards, screaming in pain. He dropped the cigarette lighter, which Pellam grabbed. He started for the young man. But Sonny was madly pulling the Colt from his belt.

"Why did you do that?" he cried. He sounded incredulous. His cheek was bright red. His mouth was swollen. But his eyes were clear and brimmed with madness. He lifted the pistol, pulled the trigger.

Pellam turned and stumbled through the door.

Sonny wouldn't have realized that the gun was single action. You had to cock it before you could shoot. In the delay Pellam staggered outside and shouted for help.

There might've been a person at the end of the block, looking toward him. He wasn't sure. He tried to wave with his good arm but felt the gritty kiss of the ends of the broken bone in his other. Nearly fainted. Pellam shouted again but in his haze he couldn't tell if the person – if anyone was actually there – heard or noticed him.

Sonny spit the chemical from his mouth and followed. Glancing back, Pellam had an image of a white face, slits of blue eyes, the white hand holding the black pistol. White hair, dancing like smoke.

Oh, man, that hurts. He gripped his arm tighter and stepped into the middle of the street.

The twin eyes of a car flicked toward him. The vehicle approached and then paused. Choosing not to see him, the driver stared ahead with the uncomfortable distraction of someone late for a dinner party and sped on.

Pellam continued away from the theater, back toward the Tower itself.

A wave of pain flowed through him. Sweat flowed. Every jar of his boots multiplied the agony. He wanted to pause, just catch his breath.

Don't stop. Keep going.

A glance behind. Sonny was stumbling too but he was gaining on him. Pellam assumed he'd figured out how the gun worked. In a minute or so he'd be close enough to shoot. Pellam ran through an alley toward the back of the Tower, speeding over glints from bits of foil and bottles and syringes. Crack vials. The sparkle of ground glass smoothed into asphalt.

The blond man's feet sounded behind him.

Crack.

A bullet shattered the window of a deserted tenement.

Another shot.

Somebody might hear and call the police.

But no, of course not. Who'd pay any attention? This was just the soundtrack to an average night in Hell's Kitchen. Ignore it.

Keep walking, eyes down, people would be telling themselves.

Stay away from the window.

Come back to bed, lover . . .

It's a white man's world . . .

———•••••———

31

Pellam staggered out of the alley, turned into the middle of Thirty-fifth Street. He was now a block away from the theater and its festivities, and this street was even emptier than Thirty-sixth.

The only motion he could see was moths beating themselves to death on the heavy lenses of street lamps.

The sound of rock music was faint. At least, he thought, he'd led Sonny away from the people in the theater. The guests would smell the liquid and evacuate the building.

Pellam cocked his head and found himself in the middle of the street, on his knees. Looking back, he saw Sonny, lips blood red and puffed up from the chemical, getting closer, the handcuff dangling from his wrist. Pellam stood and struggled again down the street, which was in shadow, like the boarded-up tenements and the construction site and the alleys. He came to the fence that surrounded the base of the Tower and slipped through a gap in the chain-link gate.

Here, in the construction site, he'd be safe. It was very dark. Sonny'd never find him among the construction sheds, stacks of lumber and plywood, compressors, equipment, scaffoldings decorated with red, white and blue bunting. Plenty of shadows in which he could lie. Plenty of vehicles to hide under.

Places where he could stop running and lie down, stop the terrible pain.

He staggered to a small metal shed and climbed into the murky space beneath. Sonny approached. The chain link fence rattled once. Did the young man just test it and pass on? Or did he enter? No, no, he slipped inside too. His footsteps were nearby.

The steps passed very close.

"Hey, Joe Buck . . . Why're you running?" He sounded perplexed. "We're going together." The jingle of the handcuffs. "You and me."

Pellam opened his eyes and saw feet in tattered white shoes moving slowly over the gravel and dirt. One shoe was untied and the laces dangled gray and muddy. He thought of Hector Ramirez and the stolen Nikes.

Sonny padded over the gravel.

My blood, Pellam realized. He's following the trail of my blood to my hiding place. But why hasn't he found me yet? It was too dark, he supposed.

Metal grated on metal.

A resonating sound like a steel drum, a bell.

Then, a gushing sound as liquid began flowing on the ground. He clutched his arm more tightly. What was Sonny doing?

A second gush joined the first. Then another.

A pause. Then a gunshot sounded very nearby. Pellam jumped

in shock. There was a huge flash of light and Pellam realized that Sonny had opened drums of gas or diesel fuel in the construction site and set the liquid ablaze with the gun.

What had been dark now became dazzlingly bright.

"Ah, Pellam . . ."

There, clearly visible in the shocking, yellow light, was the trail of Pellam's blood, leading to his cave. Still, he remained where he was. No way, he thought, can I outrun him. In the fiery illumination he could now see Sonny prowling madly in the far end of the construction site, not far from the still-wrapped statue, looking for Pellam.

Pellam felt heat from all around him. The burning fuel was flowing into the scaffolding and piles of wood, setting everything aflame. And two, no, three of the wooden sheds. Then another. A truck caught fire. Tires burst and melted amid vibrant orange flames and turbulent black smoke. Wood snapped like bullets and there were explosions as fuel tanks – gas and propane – cracked apart, firing hissing buckshot through the night.

The whole site, a half block long, was suddenly awash with fire. More trucks ignited. The sheds, stacks of wood and rich, dark paneling – destined perhaps for Roger McKennah's penthouse – crackled and blazed. He saw timbers spontaneously sprout flames and the roiling hot wind passed the fire to pallets resting against the shed where he hid. Pellam scrabbled into a corner, away from the tempestuous inferno.

The noise of the fire was like a subway train.

At this moment – when the entire lot was enveloped in flames, when there was virtually nothing left untouched by the fire – a small half moon of red, white and blue bunting ignited. Unlike the massive tide of flame in the yard this scrap burned placidly. The hot, rising air carried it aloft.

And it was this shred of patriotic cloth, not the gallons of fiery gasoline or stacks of blazing wood, that finally ignited McKennah Tower itself.

The burning scrap wafted onto a stack of cardboard boxes in the open atrium. The cartons began to glow then burn brightly. In a few minutes the flames were in the lobby, rolling over artists' conceptions of offices, over the tall palm trees that had so astonished Ettie Washington when she watched them being delivered, over piles of linoleum and wallpaper, buckets of paint. More propane tanks, on parked forklifts and high-climbers, exploded, shooting shrapnel throughout the lobby and shattering the huge plate glass windows.

Fire everywhere.

The paper wrapping of the statue burned away but Pellam, stumbling toward the gate, still couldn't make out what it was.

Finally he could wait no longer. The flames were too close, the heat too much. He eased from his hiding space as the window of the shed popped out in a quiet burst and scattered scalding glass around him.

Only one exit remained – the way he entered, through the chain link. Sonny knew about that. But there was nowhere else to go; the plaza and atrium were completely engulfed.

As he staggered out from his hiding place and made his way to the fence he saw a rich glow in windows on the second floor of the Tower, then the third, then the sixth or eighth, then higher. The fire had been sucked quickly into the gullet of the building.

Huge sheets of Thermopane windows burst, glass shards and black pellets of plastic rained down.

He stumbled to the chain link and still could not see Sonny.
A stone of the heart . . .

He managed to squeeze through the opening in the gate but one side sprung out of his grip and struck his broken arm. For a moment he passed out completely and then found himself on his hands and knees. He inhaled deeply and crawled away from the site into the middle of Thirty-fifth Street. Behind him was a tide of yellow flame and tornadoes of orange flame and spouts of hissing blue flame. Windows exploded and walls collapsed. Heavy bulldozers and sheds and dump trucks settled down to die.

Then the hands got him.

Sonny's snake-like grip ratcheted the cuff around his good wrist. The young man began pulling him back into the job site.

"Come on, come on!" Sonny cried.

Pellam expected to feel the blow of a gunshot but Sonny'd tossed the Colt aside. He had something else in mind and was steering for a pit in the dirt near a contractor's shed. It was filled with flaming gasoline. He dragged Pellam toward it. He fell against his shattered arm and fainted again momentarily. When he came to he found that Sonny's manic strength had pulled him to the brink of the pit.

"Isn't it beautiful, isn't it lovely?" Sonny called, staring into the swirling fire and smoke at his feet.

He reached down – just as Pellam kicked out with a boot. Sonny slipped on the edge of the trough and fell up to his waist into the burning fuel. He began to scream and in his crazed state, jerking back and forth, thrashing, began to pull Pellam after him.

Blinded by the smoke, seared by the flames, Pellam had no leverage. He felt himself being tugged closer and closer to the inferno. A memory of Ettie's voice came to him.

> *"Sometimes my sister Elsbeth and me'd go where they led the lambs along Eleventh Avenue over to the slaughter-houses on Forty-second Street. They had a judas lamb. You know 'bout that? It'd lead the others to the slaughter. We used to yell at the judas and throw rocks to lead him off but it never worked. That's one lamb knew his business."*

And then he heard:

"Pellam, Pellam, Pellam . . ." A high voice, panicked.

A vague image through the smoke. It was a person. A thick coat of smoke enveloped him. He dropped to the ground. Sonny's thrashing body pulled him closer.

Pellam squinted, looking through the smoke.

Ismail, tears running down his cheeks, stood at the fence. "Here! He over here!" He was gesturing madly toward Pellam.

Then another figure. They both eased through the chain link.

"Get back!" Pellam shouted.

"Jesus," Hector Ramirez said and grabbed Pellam's wrist just before he slipped over the edge into the pool of flame.

Ramirez pulled a black gun from his waistband, pressed the muzzle against the links of the cuffs and fired five or six times.

Pellam hardly heard the shots. In fact, he hardly heard the roar of the flames or Ramirez's voice as he pulled him away from the fire. The only sound in his ears was Ismail's voice saying, "You be okay, you be okay, you be okay . . ."

32

T he roles were reversed.

Now it was Ettie Washington's turn to visit Pellam in the hospital. Unlike him, she'd had the foresight to bring a present. Not flowers or candy though. Something more appreciated. She now poured the smuggled wine into two plastic cups and offered him one.

"To your health," she said.

"Yours."

He swallowed his in one gulp. Ettie, as he remembered her doing when he gazed at her through the viewfinder of the Betacam, sipped hers judiciously. She was the epitome of a frugal homemaker, having learned those skills, Pellam recalled, young from Grandmother Ledbetter.

The private room in which Pellam now lay was below the one where Ettie'd been arrested and above the room where Juan Torres, the poor child, had died. Where would Sonny's body be? he wondered. The morgue was probably in the basement.

Or maybe he was in the city morgue. A routine autopsy then a final trip to Potters' Field would be his fate.

"People keep asking me what happened, John. Asking me – because I know you. The police, that fire marshal, reporters too. They want to know how you got away from that firebug fella. They think you know but you're aren't talking."

"Miracle," Pellam offered wryly.

But Pellam wasn't going to complicate the lives of his improbable friends by telling anyone how Ismail hadn't gone back to the YOC at all but had hung around waiting to spend more time with Pellam, had seen Sonny's attack, and had run up the street to summon Hector Ramirez.

"Well, that's between you and the doorpost," Ettie said, echoing a favorite expression of her grandfather's. "And that fire marshal said something else. Which I didn't exactly understand. He was saying that you might want to think about leaving the city before your name becomes Mr *Un*lucky. . . . So. That what you going to be doing, John? Leaving?"

"Not hardly. We've got a film to finish."

"That boy came by to see you. When you were asleep."

"Ismail?"

Ettie nodded. "Gone now. Has quite a mouth on him for a youngster. I put him in his place, though. Talking to grown-ups that way . . . He said he'll be back."

Pellam didn't doubt it.

I be your friend.

Well, I be yours, Ismail.

That's the marvelous thing about debts. Even after you repay them, they never go away.

Ettie had also brought him a *Post*, the huge headline ("Towering

Inferno") next to an equally huge photo of the flames consuming McKennah Tower.

There'd been no deaths. Fifty-eight people had been injured – mostly from smoke inhalation. The napalm in the theater had not ignited and the only injuries there were from crowds pushing their way out in panic. The most serious was a broken leg received when bodyguards shoved a woman aside to make sure their dignitary escaped before the commoners (the governor, as it turned out, costing Pellam a fiver, payable to Louis Bailey, the king of gears, both greased and clogged).

The Tower was totaled. Burnt to the ground. It was insured, of course, but the policy covered only the cost of the structure itself, not lost profits. Without the rents from the advertising agency the developer would miss his fourth quarter interest payments on his worldwide loans. McKennah and his companies were already preparing papers for the bankruptcy filing.

The sidebar in the paper read, "Welcome to the club, Rog."

Curiously, none of the pictures of the developer showed anything but a matter-of-fact businessman who seemed completely blasé about the prospect of losing several billion dollars. One shot showed him striding cheerfully into his lawyers' office accompanied by an attractive young woman identified only as his personal assistant. His eyes were on her; hers, on the camera.

The hospital room bristled around Pellam and grew dark for a moment. Pellam slipped a merciful Demerol into his mouth. He washed it down with wine.

When he looked at Ettie he noticed her face was stern. But her expression had nothing to do with mixing alcohol with medicine. She said, "John, you did so much for me. You almost got yourself killed. You should've just took off. You didn't owe me anything."

Should he say it or not? For the past several months Pellam had been debating. A dozen times he'd been on the verge. Finally, he said, "Oh, but I do, Ettie."

"You're looking pretty funny, John. What're you talking about?"

"I owe you a lot."

"No, you don't."

"Well, it's not exactly *my* debt. It's my father's."

"Your *father*? I don't even know your father."

"You *did*. You married him."

After a moment she whispered, "Billy Doyle?"

"He was my natural father," Pellam said.

Ettie sat completely motionless. It was the only time in all the months that he'd known her that he couldn't find a trace of any emotion in her face.

"But . . . how?" she finally asked.

Pellam told her what he'd told to Ramirez – about his mother's confession – her husband being away all the time, her lover, Pellam's suspect pedigree.

Ettie nodded. "Billy told me he'd had a girlfriend upstate. That'd be your mother . . . Oh, my. Oh, my." She thought back, her sumptuous memory unreeling. "He told me that he loved her but she wouldn't leave her husband. So he left *her* and came down here, to the Kitchen."

"She said she got one letter from him," Pellam said. "There was no return address but the postmark was from the general post office – on Eighth Avenue. That's why I came to the city – to find him. Or at least to find out about him. I wasn't sure whether I wanted to meet him or not. I did some digging in public records and found his wedding license application."

"To me?"

"To you. And your marriage certificate. It gave the address of the old tenement on Thirty-sixth."

"The one we lived in after we got married, sure. Got torn down a few years ago."

"I know. I asked around the neighborhood and found out that Billy was long gone and that you'd moved up the street. To the 458 building."

"And you came a-calling. With that camera of yours. Why didn't you say anything to me, John?"

"I was going to. But then I found out that he'd run out on you. I figured it was the last thing you'd want to do, spend any time talking to me."

She squinted and looked at his face. "That's why you remind me of James."

When Ettie had told him about her son a month ago, Pellam realized he'd have to spend some time getting used to the idea that he was no longer an only child. He had a sibling, a half-brother.

Ettie, she squeezed his arm. "That Billy Doyle . . . Let's see, my husband and your father. What's that make us, you and me, John?"

"Orphans," Pellam suggested.

"I was never one to chase after a man. When he left I never thought about going after him. Never looked for him. But I'm curious." A coy smile. "You ever get any clue where he might've gone off to?"

Pellam shook his head. "Nothing. I've tried all the recorders of deeds in the area. No trace."

"He talked about going back to Ireland. Maybe he did, who knows?" She added, "There are some of his old friends still around. I see 'em sometimes in some of the taverns. We could maybe talk to some of them if you want. They might've heard from him."

He'd have to think about that. He couldn't decide. He looked out the window and saw gray and brown and buff tenements next to squat warehouses next to shimmering high-rises next to the blackened bones of razed buildings.

West of Eighth . . .

It occurred to Pellam that Hell's Kitchen was in some ways just like his search for Billy Doyle: failure not wholly disappointing, hope not wholly desired.

The white apparition of the Southern nurse who'd tended Ettie last week floated into the room and told Ettie she probably ought to leave.

"He's lookin' a bit tuckered out," she said with that rasping Texas drawl of hers. Pellam thought she had freckles but his vision was still pretty blurry. She said. "Honey, don't you feel like restin' for a bit?"

"Not really," Pellam said. Or thought he did. Maybe not. His eyes closed and the glass drooped in his hand. He felt it being taken away, smelled a breath of floral perfume, and then surrendered to sleep.

AUTHOR'S NOTE

---•=•=•---

Readers interesed in oral histories of Manhattan and unable to find John Pellam's documentary, *West of Eighth*, at their local video stores might wish to read Jeff Kisseloff's *You Must Remember This*. This excellent oral history of Manhattan contains a section of Hell's Kitchen, which Pellam found immensely helpful in researching his own book (as did I in writing this one). Pellam also keeps Luc Sante's *Low Life* and Studs Terkel's *Talking to Myself* on his bookshelf in his Winnebago.

ABOUT THE AUTHOR

Jeffery Deaver is an internationally best-selling author of thir-
teen suspense novels. He's been nominated for four Edgar
Awards from the Mystery Writers of America and an Anthony
Award and is a two-time recipient of the Ellery Queen Reader's
Award for Best Short Story of the Year. His book *A Maiden's
Grave* was made into an HBO movie starring James Garner and
Marlee Matlin, and his novel *The Bone Collector* is a feature
release from Universal Pictures, starring Denzel Washington. His
latest books are *The Empty Chair* and *Speaking In Tongues*. He
lives in Virginia and California. Readers can visit his website at
www.jefferydeaver.com.